KISSING SARAH

"I need a bride," Benjamin said.

Sarah sighed and stood. "I know. You need someone who can put up with all your ... quirks and still thinks they're sweet."

"Do you?" he asked, standing too. They were so close, Sarah could smell his aftershave.

He towered over her, his gaze glowing in the gaslight. His hand came out and twisted a strand of hair around his finger. "Do you?" His voice was a mere whisper.

She forgot the question. She forgot her answer. She forgot everything except that he was so close to her they were breathing the same air. His breath held the scent of brandy and cigars, and it was so very pleasant.

Too pleasant. "Ben," she said.

"No." He placed his free hand lightly over her mouth. "Not a word, Sarah," he said. "Just this once, not a word." He gently pulled her forward. Toward him, closer and closer. His fingers caressed the outline of her mouth, following the full curve of her lips before covering her mouth with his own. . . .

Books by Rita Clay Estrada

BLISSFUL

TOO WICKED TO LOVE

Published by Kensington Publishing Corporation

TOO WICKED TO LOVE

Rita Clay Estrada

ZEBRA BOOKS
KENSINGTON PUBLISHING CORP.
http://www.kensingtonbooks.com

ZEBRA BOOKS are published by

Kensington Publishing Corp.
850 Third Avenue
New York, NY 10022

All Kensington titles, imprints and distributed lines are available at special quantity discounts for bulk purchases for
sales promotion, premiums, fund-raising, educational or in-
stitutional use.

Special book excerpts or customized printings can also be
created to fit specific needs. For details, write or phone the
office of the Kensington Special Sales Manager: Kensington
Publishing Corp., 850 Third Avenue, New York, NY 10022.
Attn. Special Sales Department. Phone: 1-800-221-2647.

First Printing: December 2001
10 9 8 7 6 5 4 3 2 1

Printed in the United States of America

First thanks go to my mama, Rita Gallagher! She's a whiz of a writer as well as being the one woman I want to be stranded on a desert island with! Mom, thanks for your help, counseling, support and writing skills with Blissful, as well as this one. I love you.

Steve Goodwin, you're a treasure with a wonderful sense of humor and a sharp mind. The rest is personal. Thank you so much for your input.

Chapter One

Standing naked in a Tombstone brothel, Benjamin Drake, second son of the duke of Glennock, clenched the grimy piece of paper that confirmed his world had just fallen apart. Instead of smiling at the naked woman in the crib, his heart thudded heavily as he stared at the telegram in his hand.

SIR *stop* DUKE OF GLENNOCK DIED SEPTEMBER 13 1889 *stop* CANNOT LOCATE YOUR BROTHER DUKE OF GLENNOCK *stop* PLEASE FIND AND INSTRUCT HIM TO ATTEND TO DETAILS OF ESTATE AS SOON AS POSSIBLE *stop* ESTATE IS HELD IN CHEQUE UNTIL HIS RETURN *stop* YOUR SERVANT MARTIN PRUETT, ESQ.

His father was dead.
The boisterous sounds of New Year's Eve celebrations in the Birdcage Saloon and gambling hall below melted away. The second-floor crib rooms

that circled the walkway above the main floor
receded into the hollow silence that encompassed
his heart. Instead of the din, Ben heard the sound
of his own blood rushing in his ears.

His father was dead.

His older brother, Anthony, was now the duke
of Glennock—an extremely wealthy duke of
Glennock.

His twin brother.

Still clutching the telegram in one hand, he felt
the notch carved into his ear just minutes after his
birth. It was done to tell the difference between
the twin who was to inherit everything and the
twin who would have to marry for money, join the
church or enlist in the military for his bread and
butter.

Less than four minutes between births had separated him and his brother, but it might as well have
been a year. It also divided him from his family in
a way that no one else could ever understand unless
they, too, had been placed in that degrading position.

His father had *chosen* to mark him, to scar him
so everyone would know just how lowly born his
second son was. What father in his right mind
would choose to mark his own son? Surely not one
who loved the child. Never one who cared a fig
about an innocent child . . . .

"Sir? Is there an answer?" The young messen-
ger's voice broke, ending on a high note. Ben
forced himself back into the gaudy saloon and
whorehouse. His blue eyes fastened on the lad
standing in front of him, narrowing on his clear,
unfurrowed features. His youthful face held none
of the guilt or shame that Ben had felt at that age.
But, then, this young man probably didn't have to

worry about being a part of his family or wonder about his status in life.

Ben walked over to the peg in the wall and pulled a coin from his vest. Handing it to the lad brought a big grin to the young man's face. "No," he said. "Nothing more."

"Thank you, sir!" And with a quick, longing look over his shoulder at the half-naked woman lounging in the crib, he was gone.

"Ben?" The soft, purring female voice detoured his thoughts.

Fairy, the beautiful queen of the cribs, was propped against the wall as she stretched out on the narrow lumpy mattress. Her red lace slip was pulled up to expose a slightly rounded stomach and a tuft of curling dark hair. She motioned seductively with a finger and a smile, the promise of tantilizing delights in her wide brown eyes. "Come here," she said softly.

He tried to force himself to return to the present but thoughts of making love weren't as thrilling as they had been moments before. His world had just crashed down around his ears. He reached for his pants. "Perhaps later, sweet."

She ran a finger around her navel. "If you're not in the mood right now, I bet I can get you there in no time."

"I think not." He didn't look up, instead buttoned his pants quickly, then reached for his shirt.

"Ben?" she said, her voice was soft and warm. "Are you all right?"

He looked up then, surprised at the sincerity instead of teasing in her tone. He flashed a smile. "I'm fine."

"Don't patronize me, Ben. We've become good

friends. Tell me what's the matter. You have to talk it over with someone. Why not me?"

She raised a brow and stared straight into his eyes. No teasing. No taunting. No beguiling him with cute, titillating sayings. Just pure honesty. For a moment, he forgot *what* she was and remembered *who* she was.

She was right. Whore or not, Fairy had been his constant companion since he'd arrived in town two weeks ago.

"Sorry, love," he said, his tone more soft now. "My father passed away and I just found out."

"Your father? I'm sorry," she said, and he had the feeling she meant it. "How awful for you."

He shrugged. "Not really. We weren't close. But it does put a crimp in my lifestyle, I'm afraid. With his death there will be no more allowance while I escort my brother around the country. I'll have to marry immediately instead of enjoying the delightful likes of you a while longer."

She frowned. "I can understand the father thing, Benjamin. But you don't inherit? I thought all you Englishmen were rich beyond belief and just trotting through the West as a lark before settling down."

"Not this Englishman." He tried to keep the bitterness out of his voice. "I'm a twin. My brother is older. He inherits."

Fairy's big brown eyes rounded. "Ohhh," she said, suddenly understanding. "You're the backup son. You only inherit if your brother dies."

"Right. And since I wouldn't wish that upon him, I must find another way to continue with my life." He looked grim. "I must find a wife."

"Marry wealthy."

"Yes."

"And your brother won't help you? Share the wealth?"

His brother would help, but Anthony was sort of funny about his title and inheritance. He would not be overly generous, only giving as much as guilt would allow. It was fair and Ben didn't blame him for it. It was another one of the quirks of the way Benjamin's father raised them. "He'll help but he won't support."

"So you'll marry? Regardless of love?"

He gave a short bark that was supposed to pass for a laugh. "What does love have to do with making a good match, my dear Fairy Princess?" he asked, surprised that the young woman could be in her chosen career and still be naive enough to believe in that commodity.

She got on her hands and knees, her face arched up to his in her earnestness to prove her point. "But if you don't marry for love, Ben, you will continue doing what some of these poor wretches do when they come here. And that would be awful!"

"And what do they do?"

"Most men don't come here to make love, like you do. They come for relief. They want it fast and over quick so they won't be embarrassed to go home and hide their dirty deeds. That way they can keep some of their own dignity. They can pretend they weren't involved and didn't really enjoy it." Her dark curls tumbled over creamy white shoulders and obscured the view of her cleavage. Although she was probably the most tempting woman he'd ever met, right now she looked so sad he almost wanted to comfort her.

"It's not that bad, is it?"

"Worse than bad." She shuddered. "I think it

is easier for a woman to pretend she loves her husband than for a man to believe he loves his wife. A woman feels obligation to serve and help because she's being taken care of, financially and emotionally. She'll deliver to the marriage whatever is needed to keep it together." She coughed to cover up the catch in her throat. "A man will just be unhappy until he strays. Then he'll find excuses that have nothing to do with his unhappiness." Tears formed in the corners of her eyes, glistening in the light of the gas lamp. "Don't marry for money. Marry for love and money, Ben. Believe me. You'll live happier longer."

"I'll keep that in mind," Ben promised, placing his arms through the sleeves of his shirt.

"Where's your brother?" Fairy asked.

"He's in Clear Creek, Texas, visiting a friend."

"Are you going there, too?"

"For a few days only." He remembered something that Anthony and Sam had said before they'd left. "I understand the town is trying to build a church, and since I'm not the religious kind, I won't be staying long enough for services." A memory of his pious father reminded him of his own religious upbringing. His father used to beat him black and blue, then force him to attend church as if he were closer to God for his beatings. The bastard.

"The town has enough money?"

"According to Anthony's friend, Sam, some guy just donated the land, and the citizens are raising the money now. It's one of those proper towns with proper people. Anthony seems to love the people and the town. It's where cotton is the king."

"Wealthy. Not like Tombstone," Fairy said softly.

"No. More like Bixby," Ben said, referring to

the nearest town where the mine managers and merchants lived; far away from the grime and grit of miners and shooters. "Only nicer, and off the beaten path."

"And you have to leave now?" she asked, slipping back into the role of seductress. "Can't you stay the night and we can . . . talk some more."

Ben hesitated only a moment. He and his brother had passed two months together in San Antonio before parting company for a while. Anthony was visiting a friend, Sam Bally, who owned a hotel in Clear Creek.

Ben had returned here to see how long the mines were going to stay open and to see if there was an easy way to earn a living.

Instead, he found the mines were closed and rumor had it that by tomorrow, the Birdcage would be closed too. No more mining business in Tombstone to keep the establishments open.

Remembering the train schedules, Ben figured he could catch the next train east tomorrow morning.

Meanwhle, the beautiful and ingenious Fairy was delightfully ready for lovemaking and patiently waiting for his attention. And he might never travel this way again.

Her mouth curved into an inviting smile, her eyes lighting with a warmth that intimated they would have a fine time together . . . one more time.

Hell, after Ben informed his brother of the news, he'd probably spend the rest of his miserable life trying to find a rich widow to marry.

He smiled and walked across the worn floor toward the beautiful young woman beckoning him.

If a loveless marriage was his fate for the rest of his life, he might as well make hay now. . . .

* * *

Sarah Hornsby propped a framed piece of intricate Irish lace on the loft bedroom dresser and stood back to study it. It seemed so dainty and fragile against the dark red-and-gray floral wallpaper of the bedroom.

"Perfect," she murmured before reaching for the hammer she'd learned to wield in the past six months. She carefully chose a nail from the small cup of nails she kept with her hammer. The head was just big enough to grab the frame and hold it safely against the wall.

Deep, loud guffaws bounced through her upstairs living quarters. She frowned, pursing her lips. For the past two weeks there had been far too much noise coming from the hotel that shared her east wall. Men playing poker into the wee hours of the morning, loud jokes, the occasional feminine squeal—she wasn't sure if it was delight or something else.

It wasn't seemly.

"They're at it, again," Lillie stated in a disgusted tone. She was the woman Sarah had befriended and hired to help her make organization out of chaos. Lillie had lived with her for the past four months, prefering to sleep downstairs near the stove.

"I gather so," Sarah said. She tucked a loosened strand of sandy blonde hair behind an ear and concentrated on the lace. She hated controversy. She hated all kinds of bad things. But recently she was being confronted with them despite her aversion to confrontation.

She'd left Blissful, Texas, six months ago, turning her back on the pain of her husband Thomas's death. It was time to get on with her life. She wanted to prove to herself and her family that she could succeed in life by starting her very own business.

She'd had an idea of what she wanted to do, but she'd never had the nerve when she was married. Thomas had laughed at most of her childish thoughts until she stopped sharing. For a while, she thought she'd dried up. But a month after he died, she realized that her creativity was bursting through the gray fog with fresh new ideas. Now, she was making a few of them come true.

She jumped at the sound of a loud crash.

"They're making hay while they can," Lillie said in resignation. "They'll head home for supper in a little while and be all self-righteous. They'll tell their wives just how to run the house and all the things those idiot women are doing wrong. Then they'll be back at the hotel tonight, raising more Cain."

"If they don't put a stop to it soon, I'm going to march over there and do it for them," Sarah muttered.

"You always say that." Lillie stored an extra quilt on the top of a dresser, piling it neatly on top of another to show off the beautiful colors. "But you never do." She stood back to examine her own newly emerging talent for merchandising.

"Don't say never, Lillie. I'm going to do it soon if they don't stop."

"Harumph," Lillie said.

Sarah wasn't sure if Lillie was giving an opinion of Sarah's declaration or Lillie's ability to merchandise. She ignored it.

Another loud guffaw. A crack and thud against the wall, shaking the hanging pictures.

A shout.

Her lips pursed even tighter.

She'd chosen this place because it was the only storefront in town with quarters above that would allow her to live and work in the same building. And she'd believed, mistakenly, that the hotel would be quiet. She'd honestly thought the other side, the saloon, and now on Sundays—church, would give her more problems.

Not a sound echoed from that side unless you could count the occasional evenings when the piano player got a little rambunctious. But that wasn't often. Maybe once a week or so. She could live with that.

Another loud, raucous burst of laughter.

Lillie gave her an "I told you so" look.

"That does it!" Sarah stated through gritted teeth. Moving the board that lay against the door, she reached for the large key hanging on the nail on the wall and, for the first time, slipped it in the door that connected her private quarters in the loft with the hotel next door. She didn't stop to think, didn't have the time to allow a chink in her invincible armor. If she had, she certainly wouldn't do anything that would displease another human being.

Never.

The door squeaked open and she stared down the maroon-painted hallway. The dark red carpet over the floorboards went all the way to the staircase at the end of the hall. Several doors on either side were closed. The closest door to the right was open just enough to let light spill out . . . along with gruff voices and a tinkling, affected giggle.

The irritating, high-pitched giggle was enough to get her feet moving in that direction. When Sarah reached the threshold there was a moment's hesitation, but she took a deep breath and stopped the flow of doubt.

Inside the hotel room might be a whole hoard of men who were rude, scratching and belching, like some men did. But outside and at the end of the hall was Lillie, the mistreated and man-beaten woman to whom she was trying to teach independence. Lillie, who gave brave lip service to reality but cowardice to the face of man.

She stiffened her spine and knocked boldly on the door. It inched open with every knock until it swung open all the way, gently bumping against the wall.

"It's about time. Liquor ran out about ten minutes ago!" a harsh voice announced.

"Maybe Sally's bringin' it up. I could use an ease on these old eyes," another voice stated.

"Well, hello, little sparrow," a deep voice with warm, suggestive overtones said.

The rich, husky sound shot down her spine, gathering heat as it went. A man. British, from the accent. And all male. That was something she didn't need in her life. Stepping in front of her, he filled her gaze with tall and wide and very trim maleness.

Sarah glanced at his face. In one sweeping look, she saw rich brown hair pulled into a club at the base of his neck, deep twinkling blue eyes, a strong chin and deep indentations on either side of full lips that ended in dimples.

Far too handsome for his own good. The glint in his eye that told her he knew it to be true. And from the cut of his clothing, just as wealthy.

Arrogant, too, if his stance was any indication. He stood, hands on hips, wearing black dress pants, white shirt, gray suspenders and dove-gray boots.

Exactly the kind of man she didn't want to be near. Sarah forced her bravery to return.

"Sirs," she stated in a much higher tone than she wanted. "I am the propietor next door and the noise you make in this room enters . . . " A loud squeal rang through the rooom. A female laugh. Suddenly the bed covers exploded and a disheveled young woman popped up. Two seconds later, an equally disheveled man did the same.

"Oh, my," the young lady said, clamping the sheet corner to her bosom as her laughter died away and she stared at Sarah.

Sarah felt her face flush bright red. ". . . my own place."

"She's a lady," one of the men muttered.

"Then what's she doing here?" another asked quizzically.

Sarah straightened her spine. She was here now, so she might as well make the best of it. "I'm appealing to you as gentlemen by asking you to please keep the noise down." Her face was red, her voice shaky and her breath short. But she had to get the words out. There was no one to fight for her. It was time she learned to do it herself. "It's most distressing to your wives and daughters"—she hesitated a moment for emphasis. Her heart was beating so hard and rapidly, she didn't know whether she heard a "harumph" or not— "who enter my shop to do business and hear the, uh, the, uh . . ." She got stuck on describing what was really going on in this room. The activity in the bed confirmed her worst fears. Now that she knew what was happening, she would never be able to face her customers with the same calmness as before.

Before she came up with the proper word, the

handsome gentleman in front of her spoke up.
"Joviality? Laughter? Or loudness?"

She looked at him, her eyes watching the movement of his mouth instead of the humor in his
eyes. She raised a brow. "Lewdness?"

"Loudness, miss," he corrected with a big grin.

Her face flamed as red as the jacket hanging on
the back of a chair. "Loudness that comes through
the walls to my own personal living space," she
corrected. It was hard to keep her dignity when
she felt as if she couldn't breathe. It was time for
a hasty retreat. "Please try to hold down the noise,"
she stated in a high-pitched voice, backing away in
a hurry and scurrying down the hall as quickly as
she could. It would have been wonderful if she
could have melted into the floor, not to be seen
again. But it wasn't to be.

She made it to her door despite the hoots, calls
and shouts, and with shaking hands, closed it
behind her. But not before seeing the tall man
standing by his doorway softly laughing as he
watched her scurry down the hall.

"I worry 'bout you," Lillie stated, her eyes as
round as saucers. "That 'tweren't brave. Just plain
stupid."

Secretly agreeing, she sighed in relief that the
ordeal was over. "Be that as it may, Lillie, they
needed to know they were interfering with other
people's peace."

Lillie's expression turned incredulous. "An' ya
think they really cared?"

"We won't know unless we try." Now that the
board holding the door was back in place, her
heart slowed down—a frantic steady beat instead
of attempting suicide by jumping out of her throat.
"They need to be enlightened about needs other

than their own. They're just people, like you and me, Lillie."

"My goodness, Mrs. Hornsby. You don't really believe that, do you?"

"Of course," she lied, walking across the room to get away from the door in case they decided to break it down and grab her for a game of toss. But there was another emotion that was blooming in place of the initial fear. Success. Success! Triumphant success at confrontation!

"They're men!"

"And that makes them human," she said, wishing she could remember what she was arguing about. But her face was still red and all she could do was pretend all was normal. That feeling wasn't going away. It was dancing in her blood like sarsaparilla bubbles.

"You *are* crazy!" Lillie was just a little sensitive when it came to men. Most of the time she told them off before they could get close enough to speak. Strike first was her philosophy.

"Probably." She couldn't deny it. "Let us go downstairs and pour a cup of tea. This morning Mrs. Petrie donated a wonderful portion of chocolate cake fresh from the oven."

"We probably kept her from gaining another hunert pounds," Lillie said in her dry, monotone voice. She was allowing Sarah to change the subject.

Mrs. Petrie, with her heart equally as big as her body, was a mainstay in Clear Creek. She led the women's choir, so strong a group that it shook the rafters in the saloon every Sunday. However, Mrs. Petrie could shake rafters by walking across the floor, too.

"Lillie," Sarah admonished, finally feeling her heartbeat slow down to double-time. Her feet touched the ground floor and she stopped for a moment, her eyes searching out the front window for a sign of any men coming in her direction. "It's not nice to speak unkindly."

"Might not be, but it sure is true." Lillie walked around her employer and filled the teapot from a pitcher of water that sat on the potbellied stove squatting in the middle rear of the store. From there, it radiated heat in the winter. Problem was, it did the same job in the high heat of summer. "But she can certainly cook," Lillie continued. "Every dessert in the world tastes like God's gift when she bakes it."

"I know." Sarah stared out over the display in the front window—the only main source of light from outside. There was a small window at the rear, and another small window in the loft, but that was it.

Her knees still shook from confronting the men in the hotel room. She'd never done anything like that in her life! Her own, dear departed husband, Thomas, had not got a cross word from her in the seven years they'd been together. How could she behave that way now? She'd more than stood up for herself; she'd insulted a room full of men with no morals! Women and whiskey and gambling, all in the same room! Certainly they would not let her get away with such a blatant confrontation!

"How right you are," she murmured, her gaze still glued to the boardwalk adjoining her storefront with the hotel next door.

"And there are bats in the belfry," Lillie stated with equal monotone. "And I'm not worried about them as much as I am about you."

"Hmmmm?" Sarah said, forcing her gaze toward Lillie.

"You never confronted anybody before, have you?" Lillie said as the kettle came to a boil. She poured the boiling water into the crisp white teapot. "Your bravery is all a ruse, to help show me how to stand on my own two feet. Just like my sense of humor."

"Don't be silly, Lillie," Sarah said in a more stern than ususal tone of voice. "Of course I've confronted people before! I've had to, just to get this far. Why, I even talked Mr. Forester into giving me a better price on this place. It was a hard negotiation, but it worked."

Lillie carefully placed the teapot on a tray, just like Sarah had taught her. Alongside it, she put two slices of Mrs. Petrie's cake. "Hadn't this place been empty for over a year?"

"Yes, but he was so stubborn about it. He thought that since I had already moved in, he should still get the price he had quoted to me five months ago."

"Silly man," Lillie said dryly. "He must have fallen out of the family tree."

Sarah looked shocked. "Are you calling him nuts?"

"Yes, ma'am," Lillie stated calmly as she set the tray down in front of Sarah and took a seat next to her.

Sarah's eyes brimmed with mirth, and when she couldn't hold it in anymore, she broke into laughter. Lillie grinned, obviously pleased with herself to gain a giggle from her employer. Sarah's laughter continued to tilt her mouth upward as she filled the two cups with tea.

The bell tinkled as the front door opened, allowing the chill of winter to rush into the room. The English gentleman from the hotel room walked in, holding a small bouquet of brightly colored Mexican paper flowers. His stance was confident and easy. His smile was just as it was when she had stood embarrassed in front of him earlier.

"Mrs. Hornsby?"

Her face flared red again. She had known they wouldn't let her get away with her confrontation. She had known she was living in a dream world. She had known . . . "Yes?"

He stepped inside the portal and closed the door behind him. The chill January air puffed around her, raising her skin to goose bumps.

Lillie stiffened, her hand clutching the teacup. Her eyes narrowed. It was Sarah's reaction, too, but she hid it far better than Lillie.

"Allow me to introduce myself and make my apologies," he said, in his lilting English tones, with traces of another accent.

"Yes." Carefully placing her teacup down, she stood and faced him much as she would a firing squad. She hated scenes. This one was no exception.

"My name is Anthony Drake, and I am here on an extended visit with my old friend, Sam Bally, who owns the hotel next door. When he found out how rude we'd been, he was outraged. And I certainly can't blame him." He smiled again. "You see, my guests and I didn't pay attention to the fact that someone was living next door. This storefront was empty the last time I visited. Instead of investigating, I assumed it was still so. It's my fault and I want to apologize from the bottom of my heart."

She nodded, his words soothing her ruffled feathers in spite of herself. "Apology accepted, Mr. Drake."

He took a few steps closer, his long strides reaching the coffee table. With boyish charm, he held out the bouquet of paper flowers to her as a peace offering. They were like sunshine on a rainy day. "I know it's not enough to make up for your distress, but will you accept these in the spirit in which they are given?" He bowed his head, although he was tall enough that even when he bowed, he could see her standing in front of him. "From your humble servant who wishes to make amends?"

She couldn't help the shy smile that peeped from her mouth. He was outrageous in his actions and his stance. "Of course, Mr. Drake."

"And will you allow me to share a cup of tea with you?" he asked, pointedly glancing at the tea and luscious cake on the table.

Lillie stood, her demeanor stiff and distant. "Take my seat, Mr. Drake. I have plenty to do."

"Are you sure you don't mind?" he asked her, not really paying attention to the woman.

"Not a bit. I've lost my appetite." She walked quickly to the back of the building.

Sarah was startled by her words and surprised at her actions. Usually, when men walked into the shop Lillie didn't leave her employer alone.

Anthony Drake took Lillie's place in the blink of an eye. He added two teaspoons of sugar to a cup and sipped at the tea as if he'd done it every day of his life. "Mmmmmm," he said. "The perfect amount of brewing. Just the right steep."

"Are you usually a tea drinker, Mr. Drake?"

"I used to be," he admitted. "My mother had my brother and I attending teatime at least twice a week. We learned our manners at her knee."

"In England?"

He nodded, leaning back to better watch her.

"Our home was at the border between England and Scotland, where the best sipping scotch whisky in the world is made."

Her smile peeped through again, despite her attempts at seriousness. "Of course, you would know."

"Of course, I would, ma'am." His tone dropped a little. "But don't tell my mother. She believes I haven't touched that wicked stuff."

"I'm amazed she hasn't caught you."

"No, ma'am. She caught my brother. But never me."

Sarah laughed. He was so charming and open, it was hard not to like him.

It was apparent that this man had spent many hours in drawing rooms filled with women. Sarah marveled at how perfectly at home Anthony was as he sat in the stiff, straight-backed chair. He even handled the chipped Meissen teacup as if it were the most natural thing in the world to be found in his hands. The fact that he was so . . . masculine was the only word that came to mind . . . didn't deter his manners in the least. In fact, he was even more appealing.

But it was his warm sexy smile that took Sarah's breath away. Simply from a disinterested point of view, of course. She tried to ignore it, but couldn't. In fact, she couldn't keep her eyes from his face. So improper. If Thomas were alive, he'd be very disapproving. She pushed that thought away instantly.

"I understand you're a widow." Anthony's voice was soft, sympathizing at her plight in life as if it were a handicap to her happiness.

So the town had been talking about her. There were a whole bunch of things she needed before sympathy—a carpenter, a plumber, a man to chop wood. . . . A handyman. None of the things a husband represented.

"Yes, I am." She couldn't help but inquire something personal about him. "And you, Mr. Drake? Are you married?"

"Alas, no." He didn't look the least sorry. "I've never been fortunate enough to find someone who'd put up with my shenanigans."

Despite the smile that softened his words, she realized what he was saying below the surface. He played around with a lot of different women rather than stay true to one. His charm had already told her that. Besides, that wasn't the smile of a married, or committed, man. That was the smile of a devil tempting the innocent. Well, since she was the one presently being tempted, perhaps the not-so-innocent but very naive and inexperienced would be a better description.

He took another sip of tea, his deep blue eyes darkening even more as he glanced around the decorated storefront. Filled with every sort of needlework for the home, it was like a patchwork quilt of colors, sizes and designs.

Then he looked directly into her eyes, keeping her pinned to her seat. "I'm so sorry about your loss," he said, changing the subject back to her. His gaze drifted down to the deep lavender dress she wore, hesitating at the swell of her breasts and showing appreciation of her form before drifting to her tiny waist.

She blushed. She was surprised that she didn't feel cheapened. Instead, he made her feel treasured and appreciated. Amazing. "So was I, Mr. Drake, but I've become used to it and have adapted well."

"You're very brave." Anthony raised a brow in disbelief about her comment on adapting well. She wondered if he could see the bruises on her arms from carrying the firewood inside. Her hand cupped her thumb where she'd hit it with a hammer earlier. There was no sense in discussing her big toe where she'd dropped the dresser corner on herself as she was moving it from one side of the room to another. Besides, the bruise was almost gone.

Anthony placed his cup back on the tea tray and leaned forward a little, hands on his knees. "I wonder if I could trouble you to take time out of your evening tomorrow to have dinner with me."

Sarah blinked. "I beg your pardon?"

He smiled apologetically. "It's my way of showing you that I'm not quite the villain I must have imitated standing in the doorway of my hotel room."

"I believe you just proved yourself by delivering flowers and sharing tea, Mr. Drake." She sounded so stiff! So formal! But she couldn't imagine anyone like this man asking her to dinner. She just wasn't the type to attract a man, especially a man like him—and certainly not for honorable purposes!

Obviously he read her mind, or at the least, her expression. "I want to show you I'm an honorable man, Mrs. Hornsby."

"There's no need for you to spend your hard-earned money to prove it to me. I believe you." She smiled to soften her words. "But I thank you for the thoughtful invitation."

"I won't be satisfied until you say yes."

"I'm sorry, Mr. Drake. I see no need."

Anthony leaned forward even more, his blue eyes entreating her. "Please. Just one hour. You have to eat and so do I. This seems like a wonderful way to spend that time. Tomorrow night.''

"Mr. Drake . . . "

"Anthony," he corrected.

Lillie loudly cleared her throat and Sarah got the message instantly. Be as strong as you were this afternoon. "Mr. Drake," she continued more firmly than she meant to sound. "Thank you, but no thank you."

Anthony continued as if she hadn't answered. "And please invite your friend, Lillie, or any other lady of your choosing to accompany you."

"I don't think—"

"And when you say yes, you'll be helping repair my reputation, too." His smile was endearing, melting her resistance like ice in the Texas summer sun. "I think it's the perfect solution."

She gave in to temptation. "Dinner only."

His smile widened. "Of course," he said. The look in his eyes said differently, but Sarah had been down this path before. Although this man was daring and bold, she was not a sweet young thing who didn't know the devil in city clothes. There was no mistaking that Anthony Drake was definitely a devil. But Sarah was not interested in any more than a hot meal she didn't have to cook or spend hard-earned money for. At least that's what she told herself. She ignored the "harumph" from the back of the building where Lillie lurked near the stove, banging the cover down with a resounding snap.

Anthony grinned, triumph gleaming in his blue eyes. "Wonderful. I shall pick you up at seven tomorrow evening." He stood, taking her hand in his and holding it far longer than seemed proper.

"Until then, I'll content myself with the memory of you and your warm, forgiving smile."

A soft gag from Lillie caught his ear and he gave a glance in that direction before turning the full force of his charm back to Sarah. "I'm looking forward to it," he murmured, his voice intimate. "It will be the highlight of my visit to Clear Creek."

That was enough of the compliments. She didn't want them and didn't know what to do with them when they were handed to her. Sarah stood, gently retrieved her hand and walked him toward the door. A gust of cold January wind blew against the large storefront window, rattling the pane. She felt a draft from the bottom of the door swirl up her skirt as she walked. It was going to be a cold night. One the old-timers who usually sat on the bench in front of the general store across the street from her called a "Texas chiller."

It was better to think of that than to imagine the heat of Anthony's gaze.

She stood for a second, her hand on the knob. "Thank you for the invitation, and I'll be ready at that time," she stated, sounding prim and proper even to her own ears.

"You won't regret it," Anthony stated. "I'll have Sam's cook do something special."

"That won't be necessary. Rafael does a good job at whatever he cooks."

"You know him?" Anthony frowned in disapproval. It was an immediate reminder of her husband, Thomas, who felt the lines of equality should be carefully drawn and never crossed. He drew the lines; she was to maintain them. Thomas's line was he and his wife on one side, and almost everyone else on the other side. Out of habit, she gave the explanation. "His wife, Serena, does some sewing for us. She's an excellent seamstress."

Anthony's brow cleared. "Of course," he said. Just as she'd thought, her explanation passed muster with him. Sarah felt an immense sense of disappointment. No matter what she told herself, she had secretly harbored hopes that he was bigger than that toward others. Although, why she would have reason to think so was beyond her. He was the same as most men she'd known, needing to be better than all the others. And if he thought that way toward men, it confirmed where women stood in his imaginary list of hierarchy, for women were usually considered slightly lower and far more ignorant than the lowest men.

"Good day, Mr. Drake."

"Good day, Mrs. Hornsby." He gave an audacious grin. "I'll see you tomorrow."

Although Sarah smiled, she was still disappointed. He was just like other men, but dressed in a nicer package. That was all. After being widowed for seven months, Sarah wasn't about to dive back into the pool of married women. There was nothing in marriage for her. Nothing at all. And the fact that she had gone into business for herself and was enjoying every moment of it was enough to keep her that way for the rest of her life. Nevertheless, Anthony Drake's boyish smile lingered in her mind.

"That blowhard," Lillie muttered as she reached for the tea service.

"Not a blowhard, Lillie," Sarah said with a disappointed sigh. "Just a man like all the others in the world."

"That says a whole bunch, right there," Lillie sniffed. "Too handsome for his own good and much too wealthy. Don't trust no one with those qualifications."

"Wealthy? How do you know?"

"I heard of him," Lillie muttered. She handed Sarah her piece of untouched cake, then walked toward the back balancing the tray. "He's the son of an earl or a duke or one of those royal foreign kind. And Sam, the hotel owner, he thinks high and mighty Mr. Drake is pretty important, too."

"And when were you going to tell me about this?" Sarah asked, walking behind Lillie as she bit into the cake. Delicious. She didn't want to let this conversation go until she knew what Lillie knew.

"I wasn't. That is, until you knocked on his door and gave him a what for." Lillie smiled in satisfaction. "That was a sight, it was."

Sarah grinned, too. "Bravely stupid is what you mean, don't you?"

"Well, yes," Lillie said before bursting into laughter. The sound was catching, and Sarah joined her. "What's done is done, and tomorrow's dinner is on him. Good food cooked by Rafael. We'll go and we'll enjoy it."

"You go and enjoy it," Lillie corrected.

"You won't go?"

"You don't need no chaperon in this day and age, missy. Especially when you're only goin' next door. You have a nice dinner and be bored out of your skull. I'm stayin' here and enjoyin' the peace and quiet and work on my readin'."

"Any chaperon," Sarah corrected automatically. Sarah was teaching Lillie to read. When Lillie had found her way to Sarah's doorstep just weeks after Sarah moved in, she had promised to work in exchange for tutoring. She knew her letters, but hadn't learned how to string them together to form

words. Sarah needed help and a purpose, and
teaching Lillie seemed to attain both goals. Two
months later, Lillie showed up bruised black and
blue, and quietly asking to sleep by the back door
under the stairs. She gave no explanation, and
Sarah asked for none. She'd been with Sarah every
day since.

"If you truly feel that way, I can have your dinner
sent over to you."

Lillie shrugged, but she looked pleased that
Sarah would think of that. "Don't worry, I'll be
fine."

Sarah felt the chill of a draft again, and this time
she got goose bumps. If anything, it was getting
colder. Apparently, Anthony had taken the heat
of her blushes with him. She glanced around, looking for the long-legged dolls she used to stop drafts
at the front and back doors. Spying one sitting on
the baker's shelf by the front door, she walked
toward it. Her gaze fell to the front window, where
others could look in and see the goods at the same
time she could people-watch the crowd. Today was
too cold for anyone to window shop.

But as she turned to reach for the doll, a tall,
broad-shouldered man stopped and stared at her
through the window. He was dressed in buckskins
and a tan cowboy hat. His glossy, sandy-brown hair
was pulled back in a club, and his blue eyes were
as piercing as the sharpest arrows and twice as
intense. He wore no coat, but carried a black
leather case. His strong chin held a day or two's
shadow, adding to his roughness.

He stared at her as if he'd never seen her before.
Never laughed at her. Never laughed with her.

Sarah's heartbeat quickened. *Anthony?* Her
mouth formed the name instead of stating it aloud.

But she knew the answer even as she mouthed the name. This was not Anthony.

He continued to stare, but his head moved slightly side to side, denying her assumption.

They stood for a long moment, silently staring at each other through the glass. Time stopped and no words came to mind.

For the first time Sarah could remember, she had nothing to do that was as important as falling into the deep blue eyes of the man who stood just outside her shop window. The man might have looked identical to Anthony, but she knew, deep down in the very fiber of her being, that it wasn't him.

But if it wasn't Anthony, who was it?

Chapter Two

His masculine face, shaded by the brim of his hat, made sharp planes of his cheekbones and carved mouth in the quickly fading twilight. He looked both solitary and strong. Perhaps Sarah's imagination was playing tricks on her and he was just another cowboy with the general build and good looks of Anthony. It was hard to tell in this light.

Even though her heartbeat quickened, her sense of propriety was firmly in place. She might have met someone who looked like him earlier this afternoon, but she didn't know who *this* man was. This was no way to converse with a stranger. Especially a male stranger. It was not proper.

Forcing herself to turn, she reached for the doll that she used to stop drafts, and grabbed it like a lifeline. She held the plump calico body and long legs stuffed with cotton as if it were a talisman. Taking a deep breath for courage, she turned back to the window. Her heart raced with anticipation she didn't understand.

The man was gone.

"Good," she muttered as she placed the doll at the bottom of the door. Its long legs stretched on either side of center, blocking the chilling draft that crept under the door.

"You're missin' someone," Lillie said, her narrowed eyes focusing on Sarah. Since moving in, she'd become extemely protective of Sarah's well-being.

"Not at all," Sarah declared firmly. "Not a whit."

She pulled the heavy front drapes together, stopping the draft from the show area at the bay-windowed glass. She headed for the back work table that sat in the center of the kitchen area and at the rear of the store. There weren't any more customers for today, and would be none tomorrow if this nasty weather continued.

"Drats," she muttered, wishing she could concentrate on the weather instead of the man in the deep-brimmed hat.

"Well, if you're not talkin' to me, you're talkin' to someone," Lillie stated matter-of-factly. "So I'd say it's someone you miss."

"I'm praying for better weather," Sarah fudged, praying God wasn't listening right now. That's where her thoughts should be. Good weather brought women out in droves. Pots of tea were constantly poured, and scones and biscuits with new-made jams and jellies were served as customers gathered to talk, buy ribbons, quilts or new knitted garments. They even shared patterns and new stitches with others. Even if they were only looking for needles or yarn to begin their own projects, they spent the afternoons with their neighbors.

Sarah loved days like that.

Bad weather was her enemy. No matter how badly quilts, hats or scarves might be needed to keep warm, bad weather had the opposite effect on sales. Even the town women stayed home with husbands and families.

This was one of those days, and it gave her too much time on her hands for her to daydream about things she had best not think about at all. She had to stay busy.

Sarah threw flour from the half barrel into her big wooden bowl, grabbed a dollop of lard and poured into the bowl a bit of buttermilk left over from the crock just outside the back door.

"Uhm," Lillie mused. "We are upset."

" 'We' are not at all upset," Sarah stated calmly, her tone cool, her brow unfurrowed. She hated it when others read her so accurately. Why couldn't she be queenly and mysterious, like other women she knew? Instead, she was ordinary and predictable.

With deft, strong hands, Sarah formed a well in the center of the flour, mixing it into dough as she blended buttermilk and soft lard with the flour a little at a time. She worked quickly, competently, as she concentrated on her task.

Lillie stoked the stove with another piece of wood. They would have leftover stew and fresh biscuits for dinner tonight.

Perhaps, when tonight's supper was over and everything was cleaned up, Sarah could talk Lillie into playing a game of checkers so she could work some of this anger . . . uh, energy . . . away.

* * *

The hotel bedroom had clothes strewn from one end to the other. Meanwhile, two identical men stood facing each other. The only difference was their mode of dress.

"What the hell do you mean, take the widow out to dinner?" Ben questioned angrily. He was tired, hungry and more than just a little irritated. He hadn't seen his brother in two weeks, probably wouldn't see him again in a monk's life, and he was being told what to do with his spare time. "It's *your* widow and *your* responsibility. I'm not paying for one of your women."

"It's just dinner," Anthony said as he reached for another piece of clothing to pack. "Besides, I'm leaving most of this clothing. It's tailored for a more casual lifestyle. Use whatever you want and throw the rest away or give it to the undertaker."

"Don't think I've got any good clothes left, do you?"

"No. I think you left your stuff in various whorehouses around the country." Anthony slipped his shaving equipment into a valise. "You remember how to dine, don't you, Brother? Or have you been on the frontier too long? If so, this hotel restaurant ought to be right up your alley. It's plain and simple, nothing to remind you of home."

"This isn't the time to be funny, Brother."

Anthony folded another shirt and stuffed it into the valise. "Why? Because our esteemed father died months ago? Don't tell me you miss him, Ben! He was a bastard and we both know it."

"He was a bastard to me. *You* were the apple of his eye. His heir," Ben corrected grimly.

"He was a bastard to both of us." Anthony's tone held a hard edge.

Ben feigned surprise. "Really? When did he last beat you, big brother?"

"He didn't, I grant you that. But he berated me constantly."

"Oh, I'm so sorry. Remind me to send you a portion of my inheritance," Ben crooned in mock consolation. "Or better still, why don't I give you all of it? After all, you'd do the same for me."

Anthony's smile never reached his blue eyes. "We both know you don't want the whole inheritance, you just want the money. If you had your way, you'd burn the wool factories to the ground. You want to be free to do whatever you want, wherever you want, not tend to an estate and factories in stuffy old England that bores you to death."

Ben finally let his frustration drop, and a grin emerged. "Nor do I want to marry the esteemed Miss Dabney, beautiful and wealthy shrew that she is."

"She may have some say-so in that. Maybe she doesn't want to marry me."

"You're dreaming again, Brother. Father set that plum of a marriage up for you the day she was born."

"Yes, and he set one up for you, too, but she died. It wasn't his fault. Nor was it mine. It was just your good luck."

"Thank you, Anthony, for those kind words of encouragement. I am still without a farthing or a bride. And I am *not* taking one of your little flights of fancy out for dinner."

Anthony finished packing the valise and turned to face his twin. His face was somber, but there was a hint of a twinkle in his eyes. When cleaned and dressed they looked so much alike, even their nanny had had a hard time telling them apart. But right now their clothing made it obvious who was who. One was angry, but the other was imperious. "She's a widow and I promised Sam that I would be nice to her because she complained about the noise, and, uh, other activities in this room. She lives in the building next door and, unfortunately, shares the wall with this room."

Ben's gaze sharpened as he remembered staring into the big brown eyes of a woman standing in the shop. "Right next door, in that frou-frou shop?"

Anthony nodded, his grin widening as he saw the interest in his brother's eyes. "Along with another woman. She might be the one for you, Benjie," he said, referring to his brother with his old nursery nickname. "Who knows?"

"Is she wealthy?"

His brother shrugged. "Enough to take care of herself, I'd guess. And she's pretty in a quiet way."

So that was the woman he'd seen in the window. She had had her hopes up when she'd seen him, probably thinking him to be his brother. Just what he didn't need. He refused to acknowledge his own reaction to the wide-eyed woman. "I've got to watch every penny I have if I'm ever going to have a ranch of my own, Tony. You'll have to extend your apologies, or get Sam to take her to dinner."

Anthony stared out the window that framed the grassland behind the hotel. It was a calm, pastoral view, one that also showed the widow Sarah at work on wash day, or gardening a small patch of ground on good days. Beyond were cattle and a few chickens wandering about. Even if it was dull in the long run, it had been a pleasant place for a rest in the road.

When he turned and looked at his brother, his eyes gleamed midnight blue. "What if I gave you this room and board for a month, and the promise of sending back some of our prime cattle to seed your own herd?''

"And pay for dinner with the widow tomorrow night?''

"Certainly."

"And cash," Ben stated, pushing his very wealthy brother to the limits and enjoying it. "I need to be reimbursed for having to come and get you. After all, I left the warm arms of sweet Fairy Princess to take a stage to El Paso, then catch a train. My horse is damn well worn out from being in that freight car for two days.''

Anthony grinned. His brother was always a bargainer. "You left the warm arms *after the brothel closed down.* The telegraphs *here* are still in working order, and Sam found out that when the Tombstone mines closed down, so did the saloons and brothels, Brother."

Ben grinned unrepentantly. "Alas, it's true, but Fairy was mine for the time being."

"Fairy belongs to anyone who has the money. My guess is her arms were warm from the last guy in the crib with her.''

Ben laughed outright, the deep booming sound genuine and catching. "Can't argue with that, either, big brother. But that's beside the point. Will you pay? Cash? Now?''

"Deal." Anthony laughed. They both knew he would do it anyway. "Who knows? If you play your cards right, you might find that rich widow you always wanted, right here in Clear Creek. It might be Sarah Hornsby, the widow woman sharing a table with you tomorrow night."

"I doubt it, big brother." Ben looked around the hotel room. Not fancy, but pleasant. Sam had done a nice job with his establishment. "But it's worth a month or so of looking before heading toward Oklahoma and seeing if I can find some free land. The American government is opening it up."

Anthony shrugged, his duty done now that he had taken care of the widow and settled his brother for a while. "Whatever you say. Meanwhile, I've got to catch that train. It leaves in half an hour."

It took a minute for Ben to realize he was losing his brother. Not just for a little while, but perhaps for a lifetime. Anthony had days of land to pass over and an ocean to travel before he reached their family estate and met his responsibilities. For the first time in their lives they would be separated by more than a couple hundred miles by train.

From the expression in his eyes, Anthony realized it at the same time. They looked at each other for a long moment, memories together connecting them as far back as either could remember. Ben clasped his brother's shoulder—a body as familiar as his own—and gave a hard squeeze. "You're going to be sorely missed, big brother."

Anthony gripped both shoulders and gave a bear hug. "So are you, Benjie. So are you," Anthony's voice was muffled against Ben's shoulder. "Damn, I hate this part. I hate it all the way down to my guts. You want to come along? There's no one there to hit either one of us, now."

Ben shook his head no, even before stating the answer they both knew. He'd never put his brother through that. "It's not my estate, Tony. This country is where I belong now." He pulled away and gave a lopsided grin. "Hell, in case you haven't noticed during our travels, the West is filled with

German farmers, Mexican ranchers and England's second sons."

"And rich widows." Anthony forced a grin.

Ben nodded. "And rich widows."

"I promise there will be a savings account waiting for you to draw from. It's small, but it's a start."

Ben kept his grin in place, but he could have kissed his brother. Independence, no matter how small, was precious. "Hold onto it for me. When I settle in one place, I'll need it for seed. Meanwhile, keep your own purse strings tight, Brother. If I remember correctly, the beautiful and bitchy Miss Dabney loves to spend."

Anthony reached for his valise. His eyes, usually filled with mirth, now resembled his brother's in seriousness, but without the walls others saw. "You know I've always loved her."

"I know," Ben said, equally soft.

"And you know she's always loved you." Anthony's voice held the sorrow that was heavy in his heart.

Ben sighed, wishing he hadn't brought up this topic and knowing they couldn't part without the obvious being said. "I know."

Anthony hesitated a long moment. Ben waited. He knew his brother well, and could have guessed what he was going to say.

"I know you understand when I say I'm glad you're not coming home yet, Ben. Not for a while. Not for a couple of years," Anthony said, showing for the first time his vulnerable Achilles heel. "Give me a chance to change her mind."

Ben gave his best reassuring smile, trying not to show how surprised he was at his brother's admission. Anthony hardly ever made himself vulnerable to anyone, including Ben. "Reality is much more potent than childish dreams, Brother. A couple of weeks after the wedding, and she'll see the error of her childish affections and thank her lucky stars she has you."

Anthony straightened his shoulders and gave a jaunty smile, one that often helped others separate brother from brother. "And take the widow out for me. Apologize and tell her how lucky she is to be with you instead of me."

"If she doesn't know that," Ben stated with a well-practiced Western drawl, "then she ain't deserving of my company."

Anthony laughed and slapped his brother on the shoulder. "Well spoken. Now walk me downstairs so you can order that bath you need so badly."

They moved toward the hallway. "Why? Did you catch a whiff of the ever-sweet Fairy?"

"No, more like old dogs and dust," Anthony said. He aimed his head toward Sarah's doorway. "The widow can probably smell you through the walls."

Ben glanced in that direction toward the door that looked solid enough to stop a herd of cattle. "She's well barricaded."

"On her side. I think she believes virtue really is virtue instead of a hindrance we men tend to think of it as. But if you charm her right, she might be able to introduce you to other God-fearing women in this town. Sam knows them all, but he's knee-deep in work until midnight every night."

"You're the brother with charm."

"I wish that were true."

"Well," Ben teased, "at least you've got as much charm as me, and a thousand times the money. That's quite an edge."

Anthony gave him a sidelong glance. "Just

remember to be nice to her. Sam says she carries
a lot of weight in this small town for such a tiny
thing. She's only been here six months and she's
got the congregation meeting in the saloon on
Sunday mornings until the church is built. And no
one, not even the preacher, is complaining.''

"I'll keep that in mind," Ben stated dryly. "Just
what I need, a dinner date with a virtuous widow.
Good thing for you that the price is right, Brother.''

Sarah lay in her bed and pretended to sleep. But
it was too hot in the loft area, where all the heat
rose, leaving the downstairs chilled. She should
have been tired, but she wasn't. No matter how
many sheep she counted, she wasn't sleepy—not
one bit.

She pushed the quilt down to twist around her
feet and lie with just the sheet covering her modest
flannel nightgown. Faintly, noise from the next
room came through the walls, drawing her attention. It was different from the usual clinks, clanks,
and grunts and groans heard around this time of
night.

Instead of bottles and glasses clinking, she heard
pacing. Instead of the usual women's squeals or
cursing men, she heard the old Mexican waiter's
lilting voice asking if he wanted anything else.
Instead of his answer bellowing beyond the walls,
she heard a softness in Anthony's voice that hadn't
been present the past few weeks—or even this afternoon.

The low tone drifted through her mind to touch
another, more distant memory. Her husband,
Thomas, had died seven months ago, leaving her
with more than enough to keep her comfortable

and able to begin this new life and venture. She
had paid for this comfort, however.

Thomas had also had a low voice. The angrier
he got, the lower his voice dropped. It took Sarah
a long time to realize that because he expected
her to listen to him, she had done exactly that.
Because he had expected her to be docile, she
became passive. And because he expected her to
be quiet, she turned silent. Even all the times when
he was wrong.

And when he died, he died unloved and unlov-
able.

The regrets and memories of their marriage were
so strong a taste, she had to remind herself those
days were gone. It didn't matter how afraid she
was of life now, there was a stronger piece of iron
keeping her backbone straight today. She could
stand the tug of past thoughts without buckling
under or hiding back in that passive pattern of
behavior. In fact, she was growing stronger every
day.

She had grown a lot since Thomas's death. She
had accomplished even more, overlaying bad memories and regrets and making it possible for her
finally to sleep.

The next evening, despite her own bolstering
talks to the contrary, Sarah's stomach clenched.
The closer the mantel clock came to chiming seven,
the more her stomach felt like a cold, heavy rock.
Why did she agree to this dinner? It wasn't as if
she couldn't afford it herself—and that's what she
should have done. She should have just said no.

But the decision was already made and she
wouldn't back down now. So, like many times in

the past, she pretended it was a solid decision and retained a calm facade on the outside.

She wore her dark lavender dress today, suitable mourning colors for a widow on the frontier, and yet one of the more becoming colors on her. Her sandy blonde hair, usually worn in a loose bun, was pulled neatly into a deep-gray snood, hanging heavily at her neck. It was the closest she could come to feeling filled with matronly dignity and decorum.

When she came downstairs, she saw Lillie's dark head bowed as she straightened up the front window and side areas where several quilts were kept on racks. She hummed under her breath, refolding material and blankets. Whatever was on her mind, apparently it made her feel better staying here rather than dining in the restaurant with Sarah and Anthony. Could it be she was looking forward to an evening alone? Probably as much as Sarah normally looked forward to dining in the hotel.

She told herself it was time for a change. It would be pleasant to converse with a man sitting across the table from her for a change, but it certainly wasn't a highlight. She wasn't interested in Anthony in a romantic way. He was not her type at all. He was too tall, too strong, too manipulative and far too charming in a studied way. He was definitely meant to be someone else's hero—someone who knew how to handle a sophisticated man who chatters and expects that chatter in return. That wasn't Sarah.

Besides, those days with a man at her table and in her bed were over and behind her. Truth to tell, those dreams died with her marriage to Thomas. Marriage and its "necessities" with a partner weren't for her.

But the thought of sitting down at a table and being served as if she were a fine lady—well, that was surely a real treat. It was as close to heaven as one got on earth. Just the anticipation of dining on food she hadn't planned for, paid for, prepared or cooked, was pure delight. Especially when she considered she hated to cook.

It was just one of the things poor Thomas had to contend with when he chose her to marry. He expected her to know the things that would make his house a home, but he never voiced those things until after they were married. She had been young and barely schooled in the things that were necessary to know to keep a home running smoothly. No matter what she prepared, it wasn't quite right. And six years of marriage didn't make it any more right than the day they were married. Obviously, his mother must have been a wonderful cook, for he requested all those Pennsylvania Dutch recipes that Sarah had never heard of before.

But she continued to cook his meals every day, although she never got joy from the task. The only thing she enjoyed in the kitchen, and made well, were homemade biscuits, and those she made best when she was at her angriest. No telling why. It didn't matter. The past years had proved her theory into fact.

As for the rest of the food and menu planning, well, she could make it passable and filling. But it certainly wasn't great.

Her cooking was the first thing that made her realize she wasn't cut out for marriage. Thomas had asked for her hand in marriage without ever tasting her cooking. He certainly got the short end of the stick when he made his choice of the three Dunne sisters. Every night of their marriage, he choked down a meal that was more likely tasting of hell than heaven.

And that wasn't all that was wrong with her.

She could knit, sew and crochet very well, but how many scarves, blankets, afghans and mittens did he need? She couldn't seem to do anything else that was "useful," according to Thomas. And, although he never mentioned that she was less than adequate in bed, too, they both knew it was true. Nor was she able to have children, since she never got in a family way in their six years together.

So it was just as well that she decided to remain alone the rest of her life, making herself and other unsuspecting men happier in the long run.

Sarah walked to the window and pulled the curtains closed for the day. It had been a busy afternoon, but the customer traffic had been steady, one at a time. Considering the chilly and damp weather, the coffers were nicely filled.

"Waiting for your new beau," Lillie stated knowingly, with a sidelong glance at her employer.

"Waiting for food I didn't cook and a nice glass of wine with my meal," Sarah said, mischievousness in her tone. "My idea of heaven."

"And a good man across the table," Lillie confirmed.

"As long as he stays on his side of the table and pays for dinner," Sarah said practically.

"Harumph," Lillie said, her tone telling Sarah exactly what she thought of Sarah's idea. "Men."

"Don't try to ramrod me into something that you wouldn't do yourself, Miss Lillie."

Lillie's face turned to stone. "I'm too old for such folly. Besides, the men my age aren't looking for a companion, they want a scapegoat."

"You're wrong, but it's not my place to argue.

You'll find out yourself someday," Sarah said gently, realizing how much of a shell still covered Lillie's hurt interior. What was silly was arguing about it. Sarah secretly felt the same way.

"I'm older than you are by at least ten years, Sarah, and I don't mind telling you I've seen a great deal more of the world of men than you have. You're a lady, and some man would be thrilled to have you for a wife. I'm just a working horse, and there are plenty of my kind around to fill the needs of men. I don't have to compete anymore, thank the Lord." Lillie spoke with such heartfelt relief, Sarah couldn't fault her. She was right. Who was Sarah to second guess another's motives?

"Lillie, I spoke out of turn," she began, but the bell above the door jangled and she turned quickly. Her eyes widened as she watched an unsmiling Anthony walk in the door and close it behind him.

Goodness! He was handsome.

Chapter Three

He looked like Anthony. He smiled like Anthony. But there was something different. . . .

"Miss Sarah Hornsby?" His voice had a lower, more somber timbre than before.

"Yes." She stood straighter, her head tilted just slightly. "And you are?"

His grin was the same, warm, engaging and so very open. But the moment the grin faded, so did the friendly openness. The eyes, still deep blue, were guarded. "You don't recognize me?"

"Anthony?"

His grin widened. "Yes and no." He took a step forward, then stopped. "Most people wouldn't notice the difference. What made you doubt?"

Sarah pressed her palms together and threaded her fingers. "Are you or are you not Anthony Drake?"

"I'm Benjamin Drake. His twin brother."

Sarah felt herself bristle. Was she supposed to

be so stupid that one man could pawn her off on another without the blink of an eye? "And what makes you believe you could come into my home and pass yourself off as your brother?" Her voice was low and calm. She was proud of herself.

"I wasn't planning on that, Miss Hornsby. I was about to explain. I promise." He sounded so sincere, so humble. But his stance was commanding. He wasn't a bit sorry about the mix-up. In fact, he still looked a little surprised that she'd suspected there was a difference.

"An explanation isn't necessary, Mr. Drake. I don't care to be the butt of someone's joke."

"Believe me, it isn't a joke. My brother left for England yesterday afternoon, half an hour after being told our father died and he was needed to take over the estate immediately."

Her hands relaxed their tight clamp. "I'm so sorry. I didn't know." She furrowed her brow. "But his father is your father. Why aren't . . . ?"

He finished the sentence for her. "Why aren't I with him?"

Sarah nodded.

"Although we're twins, my brother is the heir, not I. So he is needed at home. I'm just a second son. I'm not needed to carry on."

"That's barbaric."

"That's English law." His voice was soft, reminding her of last night and the voice she'd heard through the wall.

"I'm sorry," she apologized. "I didn't mean any disrespect to your father."

He shrugged, the expression that quickly crossed his face seemed bitter. "Why not? He deserves it."

Lillie walked toward the coatrack and reached

for Sarah's cape. "Well, you two can discuss this over dinner. I'm sure you'll have a lovely time."

"Oh, I'm not going, Lillie," Sarah stated, startled by her employee's actions. Her gaze darted around the room before landing back on Benjamin.

"You won't join me in Sam's chef's delights, Mrs. Hornsby? I was so looking forward to your company, especially after all the nice things Anthony said about you. You see, it's my first night out since I arrived yesterday, and I could use some company. I'm already missing my twin brother, whom I may not see for the next several years." He was laying it on just a little thick, but felt he had to move fast or the woman ten feet from him might disappear into thin air. She was a mere wisp that stood next to the stairs as if she were about to fly up them and disappear. He had to put her at ease or she'd do exactly as he thought. "Please don't let me spend this evening meal alone. I could sincerely use the company and the conversation to divert my thoughts."

"So could she," Lillie stated practically, settling the cape on Sarah's shoulders. "After all, it's only for dinner. Right?"

Ben felt the sharp gaze Lillie gave him and he nodded, taking a step forward. "Please, allow me to escort you to a meal fit for a Texan and company that will endeavor to keep you sufficiently occupied enough not to notice the clock ticking away." Good God, he sounded just like his brother! It wasn't his style at all, but it seemed to work.

"I hate to foist . . . " she began.

Ben took a couple steps more and held out his arm. "Don't even say it. I'm the one just arrived in town, Mrs. Hornsby. I don't know anyone but Sam, who is really my brother's friend. And you'll save me from a fate worse than death—that of dining alone and having no one but some lowly cowpoke at the bar to talk to."

"And that would be so terrible?"

"Yes. That's all I've spoken to in the past two weeks." He smiled a slow deep smile that finally glowed in his eyes. "I promise I'll be a gentleman. I won't bite or burp."

She laughed, blushing. "Well, perhaps this once," she finally managed, pulling the cape about her. "But I'll pay my own way, Mr. Drake."

"My brother has already made arrangements, paying for both of us, Mrs. Hornsby. It was his way of apologizing."

"To us both?"

He looked quizzical. "I beg your pardon?" His English accent was more pronounced than before.

"His apology is to me for being stood up and to you for being imposed upon, I gather." She said it with a dry wit in her tone, but the thought stung, just the same.

"Not at all. I came into town to let him know his new status, so dinner with you is actually my reward."

"Of course," she murmured, while not a bone in her body believed it.

"It's true," he said, and the more he protested, the thicker his accent became. "He arranged for what he thought might be your favorites at dinner because he was prime to share them with you. Besides, he truly wanted to be here, with both of us. But it was impossible due to the train schedules. . . ." His tone dwindled off. Then he smiled a smile that took her breath away. "Besides, *I'm* asking for the favor of your company this evening, not my brother. And I have another favor to ask later.''

He was either the world's smoothest con artist or the greatest actor—or he was telling the truth. Any of those, and he had still soothed her insecure feelings with his sincerity. Besides, she didn't know why, but she believed him.

"I'm not sure about the favor, Mr. Drake, but I do know that dinner with you sounds better and better," she teased, secretly astounded at her tone. She wasn't a flirt at all. She normally didn't speak to men unless it was in a schoolmarm tone—or at least, that's what she had been told. Other than her friend Kathleen's husband, Charlie, she wouldn't converse with a man for more than it was necessary. Kathleen's Charlie was different. He was kind, and sweet and very much in love with his wife and new family. And when he spoke, he was being polite, not trying to figure out how much money she had or how "loose" she was.

Benjamin held out his arm. "Shall we go?" he asked, every inch the courtly gentleman.

"Thank you," she replied, feeling every inch a queen—even if she was a short one. Her hand touched his arm and they walked toward the front door.

"Enjoy yourselves," Lillie said, right behind them. She was more than eager to close the door behind them. Poor Lillie, she needed time alone even as much as Sarah needed a dining experience again.

They walked silently down the twenty feet of covered boardwalk to the double doors of the hotel. Ben stopped, opened the door and stood back to allow her entrance. Sarah followed him, then walked to the dining room. A sweet-faced young man stood at the entrance, his willing arms waiting for her cape. After draping it over his arm, he led them to a table near the side window of the building. It was the farthest they could get from her own shop.

Ben pulled out her chair and allowed her to sit gracefully, then took a seat next to her instead of across from her. Sarah didn't want to admit that it felt confining to have him so close—she was already having a hard time hiding her shaking hands in her lap.

Benjamin, looking every inch of royalty, stared up at the waitress joining them. "I believe my brother, the duke of Glennock, arranged dinner for this evening. Please check with the owner to verify."

"Yes, sir. I know who you are, Your Sir," the young woman said, her eyes big as saucers. "The cook, he's fixin' it now, sir."

"And will it be long?"

Her dark head shook from side to side. "No, sir, Your Honor. But he said that ifen you want some wine, I was to bring it to you now." Her gaze darted between Sarah and Benjamin. "What's your likin', Your Sir?"

"Did my brother choose the wine, too?" he asked, a faint smile touching the corners of his mouth.

Her gaze again darted between Sarah and Ben. "No, sir. He said it wus up to you. He said you knowed what you wanted better'n he did."

"And what have you got?" Benjamin asked politely. But no matter how polite he was, Sarah knew he was also intimidating to any young matron . . . and one not so young. . . .

"He's got it writ down, Your Sir. I'll get it." She

curtsied and left as if the hounds were nipping at her heels, returning immediately with the list. Ben quickly scanned it and told the waitress his selection before she scurried away again.

"She's very sweet," Sarah said, for lack of anything else to say, and knowing she must break the silence between them. They had not spoken a word to each other since they'd left her shop.

"She needs an education. She keeps calling me 'Your Sir,' " he stated dryly, as if it were an everyday happening.

"Not too many ordinary people in America would know what to call you or how the titles range. Besides, she's intimidated by your English accent," Sarah said calmly, ignoring her pounding heart. She hated confrontation, but this man made it easier to come up with the words. "And if you find a father in either of our countries who thinks it is worthwhile to educate a female, please introduce me to him."

"Why? You want to shake his hand?" Ben asked, sitting back to better inspect her.

"No, I want to worship him."

His brows rose. "My, aren't we cynical."

Her brows rose. "My, aren't we naive." She glanced down, gathered her thoughts, then looked him straight in the eye again. "A man who has the foresight to give the women in his life credit for having a brain and being able to use it is practically a god." She had obviously shocked him, for the expression in his eyes was one of disbelief.

"I can't say that I believe that. After all, you don't seem to be the type to worship anything, let alone an old man."

"On the contrary. If my own father had had that outlook, I would have worshiped him. As I would have my husband or any other man with enough common sense to realize equality."

"I understand there are a group of women called Suffragettes marching in New York soon. Will you be among them?" His tone was dry and filled with disdain, letting her know just exactly what he thought of the conversation.

"The better question is, will you?"

"Me?" He pointed to his silk-shirted chest. "Why me? It's a woman's problem, if there is such a thing."

The young woman returned to their table with wine and filled plates. Strips of rare roast beef with baked potatoes and chopped squash were piled high as if work hands would be dining soon.

It certainly stopped the conversaton.

Sarah stared at the food as if it had appeared from thin air. "Oh, my goodness."

"Come now," Ben chided. "You want to vote like a man, you might as well eat like one."

That did it! *Like a man?* Sarah felt anger bubble up like a new spring bursting from below rocks. She placed her fork back to the side of her plate and stared at him with a cold demeanor. "If you insist on insulting me, Mr. Drake, you may consider yourself dining alone."

His face held a startled look, then became intrigued. "I meant no harm. I'm sorry if I offended you, Mrs. Hornsby. I said that without thinking."

"I gathered," she stated dryly, unwilling to stand down. He was too good-looking and probably used to having his own way with the female sex. "You are right to put voting and eating in the same sentence, sir. For they are both necessary to keep the world alive. However, women can vote like

women. Only men can vote like men. And in the
end, we shall see which is the wiser."

"You are absolutely right, Mrs. Hornsby." His
voice was low. "I humbly apologize."

She was not going to allow him to place her in
the same set of circumstances that he probably
placed all the other woman in his life. "I would
appreciate it if you remembered I do not care for
that narrow line of thought."

Ben looked as if she were the focus of a spyglass.
"Again, I apologize. Please stay and allow me to
be your companion for the meal."

The savory scents of the food in front of her
drifted up to tease her senses. Besides, as much as
she hated to admit it, she felt her blood flowing
quickly through her veins, her heartbeat racing
and her skin actually tingling! She felt *alive!* Was
this why men seemed to enjoy controversy so? It
made them feel this way?

She picked up her fork and smiled. "Thank you.
I think I will." With that, she picked away at her
plate.

Conversation was kept light. He asked questions
about the town and she answered, explaining distances from San Antonio and how the cotton crop
had done last year. Time flew, and her wineglass
was refilled twice before the dinner was finished.
She hated to admit just how nicely the time had
flown.

When she was finished and the waitress took her
plate away, it resembled a hungry lumberjack's—
wiped clean.

Before Sarah asked, hot tea was set in front of
her, coffee in front of Ben, as well as gooey, fresh-
made praline candies. They were a specialty of the
house as well as the dessert made by the Mexican

people. There were several variations of the candy, but this one was concocted of pecans, chewey caramel and brown sugar.

Sarah's stomach might have been full, but her mouth watered. "Next to my friend Kathleen's carrot cake, this is my favorite dessert."

"Did my brother know?" he asked, his deep-blue eyes trying to penetrate hers.

But Sarah didn't care. She had another problem.

"No," she murmured distractedly, wondering what the polite way of eating her dessert was. Pralines certainly couldn't be handled with a knife and fork, but was it proper while dining out to pick it up and eat it like she would do if she was buying from one of the street vendors?

Benjamin Drake, son of a duke and who should have known what to do, did. He picked it up and bit into it like a cookie.

Sarah smiled, following suit. It was absolutely delicious.

"What did he know about you?"

That startled her. "I haven't the foggiest notion what your brother knew about me. I'm afraid I was rather rude. I burst into his room and told him to quiet down. I didn't volunteer any information other than that I ran a shop and he was keeping me awake at night with his . . . uh, the noise."

"And that was the only time you two met?" His gaze twinkled at her as he imagined how his brother must have reacted. Anthony didn't like to be told anything, let alone how to behave.

"Oh, no," Sarah said. "I would not have made a dinner appointment with a man who did nothing but annoy me by keeping me awake all night." She couldn't help the blush that crept from her collar to her forehead. "We also spoke while having tea and cake together. Several of the women in our community bring desserts over to share with my customers. Your brother had an especially good piece of cake."

Ben took another bite of his praline, then motioned for more coffee.

"And then?"

"And then we spoke for half of an hour. Most of the time was spent with him apologizing for the noise from his room intruding upon my living quarters." She was satisfied she sounded prim and proper—not easy with a bit of sticky caramel praline in her mouth.

"I see," he said thoughtfully. "And on this bit of introduction between you, he informed me that you were the one lady in this town who could help me."

"Me?" She swallowed, immediately wishing she had chewed the bite caught in her throat a little more carefully. She reached for her tea and took a quick sip, burning her mouth from the heat. The food had been wonderful, the dessert even more so and the tea delightful enough to get up and dance into her stomach. She took a deep breath, hoping it would kill the pain of the blister instantly growing on her burned tongue. "Why? What on earth for?"

Ben waited for a moment, reluctant to continue.

"I'm waiting, Mr. Drake," Sarah reminded him softly.

"I'm a second son, just in case you didn't know." He spoke as if that explained everything.

"Yes. You're a twin. I gather that means you were born second?"

"Right."

"I see," she said, not seeing anything at all.

He grinned. "Then you understand my predicament." Something nudged her memory—a conversation she'd overheard between her father and a neighbor.

"He's not having the hand of my daughter," his friend had said.

"But his papa is so wealthy," her father had protested with a touch of envy.

"Yes, but you know how those Europeans are. They don't give the second son anything. He has to fend for himself. That young man is a second son."

"Ahhh," Papa had said, understanding his friend's reluctance. "I forgot about that silly custom."

So that was the way of it.

"Ahhh," Sarah said slowly, understanding dawning in her mind just as it had in her father's those many years ago. "But what has that to do with me?"

"Anthony stated you knew everyone in town . . . everyone female, that is. And that perhaps you could direct me to an elegible young lady looking for a husband."

She stared at him blankly. Was he asking what she thought he was asking? "You want to get married?"

"No, I want to have my own ranch, but I have no money."

Understanding was dawning. "So you'll settle for a wife, instead."

"Yes."

This *was* intriguing business. She leaned back and looked him over. "You're handsome and charming and presentable. Why not hunt for your own wife?" She didn't mention that she thought he was insane, too.

His grin showed deep dimples. "I thank you for the compliment. However, I'm not one to trip up the women walking on the boardwalk and ask them their marital status. I don't think they would be receptive to that. Do you?''

She tried not to smile. "No, but you could be invited into any house in the land and your host would be bragging about serving you the next day.''

"My thanks, again. I still have to meet the women in a respectable way.''

"Why marry? You're young, handsome and strong. Why not go after what you want? A ranch? This is ranch land. A farm? Cotton grows as tall as me.''

Ben sighed, staring down at his coffee. "Because I need money to begin either one of those. And money, according to your comments, is the only factor I do not have.'' He grinned. "Money and a wife.''

"And not in that order?''

He shrugged. "Any order will do.''

"And will any wife do also?''

Again he shrugged. "Probably.''

"Why not a wife from your own country?''

"Because they must marry wealthy for title and land, also. It's the way of things. Besides, what I really want to be is a rancher, not a sheep herder.''

"I'm sure you've met many eligible women in your travels.''

"A few,'' he hedged.

Sarah blushed. Apparently he kept the company of other types more often than not.

"Most of the women I meet are married, and I'm usually working with their husbands,'' he said blandly.

Thank goodness he'd explained. Her imagination was going crazy.

"... or they aren't the type to have a dowry

that would entice a man to shackle himself with marriage."

Her own hackles rose. She felt it on the back of her neck. "Shackle himself with marriage? Is that not what you're requesting my help to do?"

Ben must have realized his mistake. "Well, not really. I'm interested in marriage, therefore I won't be shackled."

His denial didn't fool her, but neither did it shock her. Many men felt that way. Thomas had not, but then, Thomas had needed an audience for all his expounding. Since then, she'd learned that there wasn't much difference between men when it came to that. "And what are your needs, Mr. Drake?"

"Needs?"

"Surely you're looking for something in a woman besides money."

"Of course. She must be kind and at least pleasant to the eye."

"What else?"

He thought for a moment. "She has to have something in her life that interests her. Something she enjoys doing from which she can derive pleasure."

So he wouldn't be bothered? So she would leave him alone? She thought of a dozen answers herself, but also recognized that her vision was warped. She would give him the benefit of the doubt on this one—until he answered. "Why?"

"Because people are happiest when they have something in their life they enjoy doing." He said it simply and quietly.

And that answer startled her more than anything he'd said that night. It was profound and interesting that he knew, and showed a depth of under-

standing people that she had not credited him with
. . . not at all.

"How true," was all she could murmur.

"Can you help?"

"Yes."

"Will you help?"

"Yes."

He smiled, and Sarah knew any woman would
be captivated immediately. He was gorgeous. The
twinkle in his blue eyes didn't hurt, either. Once
seen in Clear Creek, it was going to warm the cock-
les of many a woman's heart . . . single or married.

"What is the next step?"

"Well," Sarah said, her mind racing with alternatives. She was going to enjoy this. "I have to do
some planning. This is rather like a coming-out
party for a man, don't you think? It has to be
done properly to get all the right women to be
interested."

"How long will it take?"

"I have no idea, Mr. Drake."

"Please call me Ben so I may call you Sarah."

"Why don't we do this, Ben? Let's begin by you
escorting me to church this Sunday."

"That's three days away." He sounded like a
disappointed child.

"Yes, it is. It will give me time to put a bug in
everyone's ear about you. Gossip travels fast."

Ben flashed her that grin again. "Thank you for
your help. I'll make sure that Anthony sends you
a couple of trunks filled with ribbons and cloth."

"As a favor for marrying off his brother?"

"As a thank-you gift." His grin slipped. "The
family owns several woolen and ribbon concerns.
I believe he can well afford it."

Her heart, loaded with commercialism, beat

faster. She nodded. "In that case, I shall be most proud to receive it."

She was willing to admit she needed those crates even more than she was willing to admit. Her store's profitability depended upon how much her overhead was. Those trunks would help insure her store's future success.

They rose, and Ben helped Sarah replace her cape around her shoulders. Then, offering his arm to Sarah, he walked her to the entrance. He gave a nod to the young man at the desk in acknowledgment.

"Good night, Simon," Sarah said quietly.

The young man's Adam's apple bobbed. "Good night, Mrs. Hornsby. Lord Drake."

"It's Mister Drake or Lord Benjamin," Ben said just before closing the door behind them. They stood in front of the hotel while Ben adjusted his jacket around him. It was a bone-chilling cold.

"Is your title really a lord?" Sarah asked, looking up at his profile in the dim light. He was so very handsome. And, somehow, so sad.

"Not really. Because I'm a second son, my title is Lord Benjamin, not Lord Drake, who is my brother. But I believe it's too complicated for this land to bother with. So 'Mister' will do nicely."

"Are we too ignorant?"

"No, not devious enough to lay such a caste system on others."

They walked the short distance to Sarah's store, then stopped. She reached into her cloak pocket for the large key there, and he took it from her. Placing it in the lock and turning it to open, he stood back, not quite allowing the cold chill of night to enter the building.

"Thank you for your company tonight," he said. "It made a very bad evening turn into an event."

"You don't need my help," she said, pretending she wasn't touched by his sincerity.

"I'm serious. My brother left yesterday afternoon and it was very difficult for both of us. I've never been so far away from him before. I thank you for your diverting company. Maybe I'll get some sleep tonight."

Sarah wanted to give him a commiserating hug. She knew how hard it was to lose someone close and the gap inside that a loss left. It didn't matter that Thomas wasn't a twin—he'd left a yawning hole that she was still filling.

"I'm so sorry, Ben."

In the semidarkness he stared down at her, searching her features as if memorizing them. "Thank you. I didn't mean to burden you with my loss."

"You didn't."

"And I'll see you on Sunday morning."

"Come over early and you can have tea and biscuits with us before church. There are usually a few women that meet here before walking next door."

"I'll do that." His hands felt warm on her shoulders. "Meanwhile, sleep well." He bent forward and his warm lips brushed her forehead. Firm. Soft. Gentle. Kind. And, yet, heat sprang to her mind. "Thank you, again."

Before she could say a word, he was gone, his boots hollowly clicking against the boardwalk.

She was left with a full stomach, chaotic conversation in her head, no more conversation and a small space on her forehead that felt as if it wore a brand.

All in all, it was a most wonderful evening.

Chapter Four

Ben walked into the saloon and ordered a beer.
It wasn't the warm ale he was used to at home in
England, but it was good. Ice brought in by rail
from the upper United States kept the brew cooler
than home.

Several men played poker at a corner table. Two
more trudged downstairs, a satisfied gleam in their
eyes and a swagger to their step.

But his thoughts weren't on the temperature of
the ale or the cost of bedding upstairs. Instead, they
were on Sarah. Could she do it? Could she find a
wealthy woman willing to marry him and let him
have his way with her money? It was a big question.

That wouldn't be hard in England. He could
have his choice of many if he played the game
right. His father's name was worth a good dowry,
and perhaps a titled young lady. And he could
spend the rest of his life in the society he hated
so much.

He was in this country because he'd talked his brother into visiting, and had done what he knew he would do: he'd fallen in love with the West. It made him certain that he didn't want to go home and play the society game at all. He wanted to be loved enough for a woman to marry him of her own free will—not her father's or her brother's. A woman who owned her own money and who trusted him to care for both her and himself, making them both more secure in life.

A mother to his children.

A partner.

A life mate.

That wouldn't be easy. In fact, if Sarah could do it, he'd make damn sure she was in his will, for certainly he would have his dream: a working ranch, children and wealth.

American women were far different. And Western American women were even more so.

At first he'd been appalled at their directness. They could tell a man off and then plow the field and cook for a passel of children all in the same hour. It was amazing.

But after two years of the freedom of the West, he knew this was the type of woman for him. All he had to do was find one that was amenable to his way of doing things, and he'd be willing to settle down.

He specifically wanted to find a woman from the Southwest. These women weren't all simpering smiles and faints. They didn't shirk work or words. After the initial shock, it was nice to know exactly what was on a woman's mind and know she wouldn't swoon if a man forgot himself for a moment and said the wrong words.

Sarah's big brown eyes came to mind. She was

a Western woman and a lady. Everything she said and did reflected that. Her gaze was wise beyond her years, her fears were apparent for all to see, and, yet, she still spoke her mind while allowing her shaking hands to tell the toll it took to do so. She was genteel and intelligent and very sweet. If he had sized her correctly, she was far more knowing than she allowed others to see. And she liked him.

Well, at least a little.

Yes, she might be the very person to help him with his search.

Ben took the last drink of his beer and set a coin on the counter. "Good night, all," he said to no one in particular. The bartender, cleaning glasses at the end of the bar, nodded in acknowledgment. The barmaid's hungry eyes watched him leave.

Sarah sat in the darkened front of her store and stared at the curtains that held tempered winter winds at bay. Her cloak was still around her shoulders, her hands holding her gloves.

There was a smile upon her lips.

Nothing felt as good as a challenge she knew she was capable of winning.

In the five months since she'd moved to Clear Creek, she had met nearly every woman in town and even more living outside the city limits. She had intentionally made her store a meeting place for women of all ages and backgrounds, and it had worked in her favor.

Within three months, she'd realized that a church was needed—not only for services, but as a place where everyone could convene. Her store was not big enough for the whole town.

It wasn't hard to gather the women together to help her fight for the use of the saloon on Sundays. After all, it was the only big building that didn't have stock to steal, or tables of goods to work around, and it had plenty of chairs. It just made sense. Once they had a place to meet, it wasn't hard to get Pastor Strack to agree to lead the congregation.

With a place to meet and a preacher to preach, the next step was to insure that the women showed up, with their men, to donate money and labor for the new church and hall. Everyone thought it was an excellent idea, even the bar owner, who was paid two dollars rent every Sunday, got his floor swept for free and his spitoons cleaned out once a week—the men did so every Sunday before church sermon time.

And several of the women were looking for a husband. Out of those, at least half were widows with dowries and inheritances.

"Sarah? What are you doing?" Lillie's groggy voice called from the back of the store, where a sheet-draped screen separated her bed from the kitchen and shop. "Are you all right?"

"I'm fine," Sarah replied, standing to take off her cloak and hang it on the coatrack at the door. "It was a lovely evening and I was just relaxing from the heavy meal."

"How did Mr. Drake behave?" Lillie asked.

The heat of Ben's soft kiss was still on the center of her forehead. She touched it and it rekindled again.

She must be lonely to be thrilled by such a chaste kiss.

Sarah heard the rustle of bedclothes and the

squeak of old springs. "He behaved fine, and don't get up. I didn't mean to disturb you."

"You didn't. I just blew out the lamp not two minutes before you opened the door. Water is still hot if you'd care for a cup of tea. I certainly would."

"Thank you," Sarah said, spreading her skirt to ease the wrinkles of sitting, and walked toward the back where the kitchen area was, cleaned and ready for tomorrow.

Lillie struck a match and lit the lantern on the table, then got down cups. Sarah reached for the tea tin. They worked well together after just a few months. It was easier living with a woman, that was certain. No worry about appearances, no wondering the split of labor, no waiting on someone even when you were tired.

She didn't remind herself of the other differences that Ben had brought to mind. After all, those things were important to men, not to women.

Lillie placed two cups of tea on the table just as Sarah sat down. "Now, tell me what you had," Lillie said, her eyes glowing with the anticipation of the story.

Sarah obliged, giving descriptions of everything as she went.

"That sounds wonderful," Lillie said, just a little enviously. "But why did he do it? Was it really because of his brother?"

"He had an ulterior motive," Sarah said dryly, a small smile flashing in the dim light.

Lillie leaned forward. "Was he a cutter?" she asked, using the expression cowboys used for the chase of a calf, cutting him off from the herd, circling him and tying him up for branding before letting him go and finding another.

"Not at all." She took a deep breath. If she

couldn't tell Lillie about her plan, who could she tell? "He wants me to help him find a wife."

The other woman stared at her blankly. "A wife?"

Sarah nodded. "A wife. He needs a wife with money."

"Now, don't that beat it." Lillie shook her head but her eyes stayed on Sarah, waiting for her to admit to a joke. "And isn't that what we all want, now."

Sarah chuckled. "I think it probably is, but that's not quite the reason he has in mind."

"Would you like to wager on that?"

"I mean that he wants a wealthy wife so he can buy his own ranch, have children and settle down."

"I see," Lillie said slowly, letting the information sink in. "And does he know who he wants?"

"Not at all. What he wants is to be introduced to the eligible women in town and that will allow him to take his pick."

"Just like in the East. He wants a matchmaker to do all the work for him." She frowned. "But why? He's nobility, for heaven's sake. Why wouldn't he go home and find the best woman to suit him and marry her? Why here?"

Sarah frowned. "He didn't say. But I think he wants to remain here instead of returning to England, where his brother has inherited the title."

"He hardly has an accent," her friend said.

"Unless he gets intense and excited."

Lillie's brows rose. "Really? What would he get intense and excited about?"

Sarah felt the blush begin and was so glad it was dark. "He was talking about his life with a wife."

"And did you remind him you were a widow?"

"No, because I'm not in the market for a husband and he is not in the market for my kind. He's looking for someone more . . . more . . . ''

"Simple? Adoring? Busty? Dumb?"

"Young." Sarah sighed the word, feeling every inch ten years her own senior.

"Ahhh," Lillie said knowingly.

"Compatible," Sarah said, trying to portray another image instead of the one she inadvertently gave.

"Ohhh," Lillie said. "Of course,"

Sarah took a gulp of her tea and tried to rearrange her thoughts to the problem at hand. "So who do you think might fit this bill?"

"Hmmm," Lillie said. "What about Trudi Gross-mann?"

"I don't think so. Too demanding."

"Faith Browning?"

"Noooo," Sarah said. "She's always in a snit about something. She pouts more than anyone I know."

"Pansy Haude."

"Too short."

"Short?" Lillie said, taken by surprise.

"Well, he's rather tall and she's barely five feet tall. Don't you think that might be awkward?"

"For whom?" Lillie asked dryly.

"For Ben," Sarah said in what she thought was a very logical tone of voice. "After all, there has to be compatibility of stature as well as personality. He'd spend the rest of his life looking down at the top of her head."

"Oh, yes, that would be a problem, wouldn't it?"

Sarah drank down the last of her tea and stood. "Well, think about it and we'll talk more in the morning."

Lillie took both cups and put them on the

wooden counter next to the basin of washing water.
"Fine. I'll think hard and come up with three or
four more choices, and you can tell me why they
won't work."

"That's not true," Sarah said, yawning. "But
you'll have to see for yourself." She headed toward
the stairs. "Good night, Lillie. Thank you for the
tea."

"Good night, Sarah. Thank you for the conversation." Lillie's answer was in the same tone, mimick-
ing Sarah.

She decided to ignore it. It was late and she was
exhausted.

But the next morning, when the sun shone in
the upstairs rear window, Sarah was wide awake
and ready to discuss the issue of a bride once more.
The thought both intrigued and interested her.

Lillie was already in the kitchen, brewing coffee
and baking eggs and buns. The smells wafted
upstairs, setting Sarah's stomach growling. She
washed and dressed quickly, anxious to talk to her
friend about some thoughts she had.

"Good morning," Sarah said brightly, throwing
back the heavy curtains at the front window and
letting the light into the room. It would not be
time to open for another two hours, but at least the
sun could help warm the place for their customers.

"Mornin'," Lillie stated in a tone that cut off
any conversation. It was obvious from the one word
spoken that Lillie wasn't in as good a mood as
Sarah was.

She was undaunted. "It's a beautiful day, isn't
it?"

"Cold," Lillie stated as she pulled the buns and
baked eggs from the oven and set them on the
closed burners.

"Not inside."

Lillie gave a grunt as she took two buns, placed them on a plate and sliced them in half.

"It's nice and toasty." Sarah glanced at the front and realized Lillie had already set the fire in the front fireplace. "Thanks to you."

Lillie gave another grunt and placed a baked egg inside each bun, then put the plates on the table.

Sarah gave up. She poured two coffees, added cream and sat down at the table. Lillie sat across from her, sipped her coffee and fiddled with her bun.

Eating in silence, they sat across from each other and Sarah waited. And waited. And waited.

Finally, Lillie stared out the far window and spoke. "You want him to be your husband, don't you?"

The words completely surprised her. "No."

"You say that, but do you mean it?"

"Of course. I have no reason to lie, Lillie. I don't ever want to marry again."

Lillie looked directly at her. "Why?" she asked bluntly.

"Why . . . because."

But she wasn't about to leave it at that. "Why?"

"Because I was married and it wasn't right for me. Thomas fell out of love with me, and I don't think I was ever in love with him. Even though we both would have stuck it out for the rest of our lives, I vowed I would never lose myself again. Marriage seems to do that to a woman."

"I know."

"Is that what you think, Lillie? That I'm looking for another husband?"

"Well," Lillie hedged. Then her courage came forth and she stared at Sarah a moment. "Yes."

"Well, I'm not," Sarah stated. "And I'm not even sure I'm going to accept his offer. But I can tell you this. The idea intrigues me because I know there are plenty of women in this town who would love to marry and settle down and have children by a man who is wanting the same things. There is honor in being a rancher's wife, and they covet that honor. Why shouldn't I help them?"

"Why, indeed?" Lillie muttered. "Perhaps because another marriage is what you want for yourself?"

Sarah legs tensed, not allowing her to sit anymore. If she weren't a lady, she would be pacing the floor and ranting by now. "Please understand, Lillie. I am a widow. I *like* being a widow. I *enjoy* being my own boss and deciding my own future. Please do not pattern your likes and dislikes over me. We are not the same in that way."

Lillie's hands clenched her teacup. "If you say so, Mrs. Hornsby." Her tone was calm and distant. But her gaze blazed with heat as she stared up at her boss. "And I'll remember to keep my place and not get in your way."

That last sentence pierced Sarah's heart. She'd found Lillie, bloody and shivering, at her back door, hiding from her husband and scared as a mewling kitten. When she'd brought Lillie inside, and then offered her a job, Lillie had said those same words—the words of a beaten woman.

At that time, Sarah had dismissed those words with a loving hug and made sure the sheriff intervened with the man who called himself Lillie's husband. After a month or so, he'd cursed Sarah and Lillie and then disappeared from the area.

Four months of working and living with Sarah, and she had come into her own. Lillie had become more than assured—she had swung to the other end of the pendulum. She was now angry with almost everyone, especially with men, and usually not afraid to show it. Angry with everyone but Sarah, whom she worshiped. Until now.

But Sarah's own pride, recent and still rocky, was in need of bolstering. "Please, suit yourself," she said quietly. "I can't tell you what to do or how to do it. It is your life, just as mine is mine." Sarah stood, and, without speaking another word, walked into the store area.

Her arms shook, her knees quaked, her fingers were numb, but she was *not* going to allow Lillie to deter her from what she considered an adventure!

Without giving their confrontation another thought—well, perhaps more than another thought—she sat down with a piece of paper and began a list of prospective brides.

It began with Chloe Givson, a widow who might be a little older than Benjamin, but had more money than the mayor of Houston. Her father was part landowner in both the stockyards in Ft. Worth and in several small ranches in lands north and west. She'd returned to her mother's home here in Clear Creek to set up residence when her mother died. Although slightly bucktoothed, she was sweet and charming—and spoiled. But the right husband and a firm hand would bring her 'round.

Faith Strovinski was the second candidate. She was also a year or two older than Ben, and her widowed papa was still active and constantly smiling. That had to say something about his daughter, who took care of his clothing and food by handling the servants. She wasn't plain and she seemed to have an easy disposition. And her father's pig farms were prosperous.

Then there was the town sweetheart, Christine Garret. She was blonde-haired, blue-eyed and sweet. Well, most of the time. Sarah had seen her throw a few snits aimed toward her parents. Granted, she was spoiled, but she was also wealthy enough to give Ben what he wanted: a ranch and children. He could teach her anything else, including helping her control her temper.

Then there was sweet and gentle Kay Mayne. Her one flaw was crooked teeth, consequently, she rarely smiled with her mouth open. She wasn't as wealthy as the others but she did have money. Given time, she might even have spunk.

There were three or four others, but Sarah didn't bother to put them on her list. They were not the prime marriage partners these were.

Now that she had gotten her main list, she had to think of a way to introduce Ben to her chosen candidates.

Sarah grinned. First she had to introduce herself and let them know about Ben. The saleslady in her bloomed, and her grin turned into a Cheshire cat smile.

She walked directly to the coatrack and took down her cloak, gloves and hat, carefully putting them on and checking herself in the mirror at the doorway before turning back to the room. In a voice more loud than ususal, she called to Lillie, "I'm going calling but I'll be back by this afternoon. Please mind the store."

And with a quick hand, she turned the CLOSED sign to OPEN, and left the store, walking purposefully down the boardwalk to the first candidate's— ah, young lady's—home. Ten o'clock was not too early to call on Chloe Givson. She should be up and dressed by this time and ready to meet any callers.

The two-story house was at the end of the main street area, its yellow and gray gingerbread woodwork a piece of art that all admired. The fenced front, side and backyards were neatly kept and clipped by two goats and a cow.

A small stand of tall pine trees clumped together in the side yard, giving slight shade to the roof in summer. Chloe was even wealthy enough to have had a concrete sidewalk poured all the way up to her front door from the the packed dirt street. The roadway didn't become brick until where the town boardwalks began.

When Sarah knocked at the door, she was ready to interview the young woman as if she were a candidate for the office of president . . . all without Chloe knowing of course. She had to be subtle and kind and not scare the woman off.

The door opened and Chloe looked startled before she smiled through the screen. "Why, Mrs. Hornsby, how nice to see you."

She was surprised but didn't lose her manners. Sarah took that as a good omen. "I'm sorry to drop in uninvited, but I received some news," she lied, "and I thought I'd ask your opinion."

The screen door opened and she was ushered inside.

"Why I'd be delighted to help if I can." Without looking at the middle-aged woman behind her, Chloe spoke over her shoulder. "Constancia, please bring some tea for my guest," she said to the older Mexican woman. "We'll have it in the parlor."

Sarah followed, anticipation flowing through her veins like the rushing water of Peach Creek that ran through town. She felt effervescent from the headiness of her mission. This was fun!

"What seems to be your problem, Mrs. Hornsby?" Chloe said, bringing her back to the lie at hand. "Is it something with the church committee?"

"Oh, no. The committee doesn't meet until tomorrow. Now that Mr. Heine has donated the land, we can set about designing the church we'll put on it," Sarah said, making sure she pronounced the "e" at the end of the name like an "a."

"That's wonderful. You've done such great work for this town," Chloe said primly. Sarah wondered if she ever completely relaxed. "I don't know how you've managed to have your fingers in so many pies and do such a splendid job." Chloe leaned forward. "So, what is the problem?"

"Well," Sarah said slowly. Her mind was a blank. Now that she was here, she had to say something! "I was wondering. I'm sending for some delicious carrot cake to sell in my store. A friend of mine makes it and has won awards at the fairs, it's so good." Sarah brightened. Chloe looked interested, so maybe this was believable after all. "And I thought I would ask if you wanted me to order some for you, too."

Chloe's brows rose. "Me?"

Sarah nodded.

"Why me?"

"I'm not sure," Sarah said with a smile. She felt so silly. This was the worst excuse she'd ever come up with. She wished she'd thought this through a little more before rushing out the door and barging into this parlor. "Your name just popped into my head. I know that you do a lot of entertaining, and I thought that if you served it occasionally, others might want to buy it at my store and I would be creating a clientele for my friend, who now has two babies at home and can't get out much anymore."

Sarah wanted to groan. She should have kept her mouth closed and not given so much information. What was the matter with her? Hadn't the past taught her anything? Suddenly she went from ten years of silence to seven months of nonstop talking.

Chloe looked a little confused. "Your friend?"

"Yes, Kathleen."

"I see," Chloe said, showing that she really didn't.

"So I wondered if you might want some," Sarah repeated.

"Certainly, I think," Chloe said, totally confused. "I mean, if it's no trouble."

Chloe's maid walked into the room, one slow step after another as she carefully balanced a full tea tray. Both women pretended not to watch as she reached the low table and placed the tray carefully in the center.

Chloe gave herself away as she heaved a sigh of relief and relaxed her shoulders. "Very good, Constancia. That will be all."

Sarah heaved a sigh, too. This was apparently a new task that Chloe had taught her, and Constancia had done well. That's what Sarah loved most— seeing women accomplish something they'd never done before.

Chloe poured tea in silence, gave them each a cup, and then offered a saucer of cookies. But her smile was as bright as Sarah's had been earlier, pleased with her maid's achievement.

"Chloe?" Sarah said casually after sipping her tea and pronouncing it perfect. "Have you ever thought of marrying again?"

Chapter Five

Sarah brushed her hair a hundred strokes, then climbed into bed. She made sure her coverlet was evenly folded at the top and her feet were covered, then lay back and closed her eyes.

Tinny piano sounds pretended to be music at the saloon next door, and Sarah's active mind wondered what everyone was doing.

Was Ben there? Was he being lured by loose young women to go up those steep steps to the rooms that circled the balcony? Laughter burst through the wall every now and then mixed with occasional raised voices, but all was muffled. She had to listen hard to hear anything.

It was all right, she told herself. She had other things to think about tonight. She had arranged the first meeting between Benjamin and Chloe today. She had honestly done it!

Then Sarah sat straight up in bed, her eyes round and open wide. She had been so smug and self-congratulatory, she'd forgotten the most important element of that meeting: she'd forgotten to inform Benjamin of the plans! He had to be ready for church by ten o'clock in the morning, looking handsome, rested and respectable in front of his soon-to-be intended.

She rose quickly and relit the gas lamp at the side wall. With deft quickness she penned a note to Benjamin, telling him of her plans for tomorrow morning. Sanding it lightly, she blew on the sand and then folded the note in two, slipped it into an envelope and addressed the envelope to him.

Rather than find out where he was or cause people at the front desk to wonder why she needed to correspond with him, Sarah slipped her robe over her nightgown and pulled her long hair from underneath the collar.

Hoping the sound would not echo through the house and wake Lillie, she carefully lifted the wood piece barring the door and set it against the wall. Then, taking the key from the nail, she unlocked the door that separated her from the hotel. The door creaked open and, with a backward glance at the stairs to see if Lillie was standing there watching, Sarah slipped through the door and into the dimly lit hallway, closing it with a snap behind her.

She moved to Ben's hotel room door as quickly as possible, then slipped her envelope under the door. She didn't want to find out he wasn't there. Or worse yet, that he was entertaining one of the barmaids. She didn't need to know that information.

With a swish of her robe, she turned to run back down the twenty or so feet it took to be back in the privacy of her own room.

"Wait!"

The word stopped her in her tracks and she looked over her shoulder.

Ben stood at the door, his collarless shirt unbuttoned at the strong column of his throat, his dark dress pants and suspenders even more black against the whiteness of his shirt. His skin was tanned to a light copper, his eyes a midnight blue under the hallway gas lamp. "What is this?" he whispered, holding her envelope in his hands.

Instead of fleeing to her room, Sarah turned and walked toward him, one slow, hesitant step at a time. "It's your command performance tomorrow morning."

His brow furrowed. "Command performance for what?"

She stopped two feet in front of him and stared up. Until now she hadn't realized how tall he was. Barefoot, she had no advantage of height to balance against his masculinity. "Church," she said primly. "You're meeting your intended tomorrow."

"Intended?" His frown cleared, replaced with a smile. "Don't I have any say in this?"

"Not if you want a bride and I want trunks full of fabric and ribbons."

He gave a low laugh, and, still speaking softly, said, "Anything to accommodate your wishes, ma'am."

Before she could answer, men's voices echoed up the staircase. She glanced over her shoulder, readied to turn and run back home before being caught standing in the hotel hallway in night-clothes. It would be a scandal and ruin everything!

She turned to run, but Ben grabbed her arm and pushed her inside his room. She plunged into a chair facing the fireplace just inside the door. It was just in time, for the men that turned the corner must have known Ben.

"Hey, there, are you lookin' for somebody special," one of the males asked. " 'Cause she sure ain't with us, if that's what you're thinkin'."

"But she might be servin' the last brew in the saloon," the other man jested.

"No, I just stepped outside to catch a breath of night air. I did too much cigar smoking in my room tonight and the window won't raise far enough to let me air it out."

Sarah grinned. Ben was a quick thinker, if nothing else.

"Well, here, we'll help you pry that thing open," one of the men said.

Panic. Sarah's gaze darted around the room, looking for a hiding place. The only place she saw that would hide her was under the bed, and she dove for it.

"No, that's all right. I have the handyman coming up in a few moments," Ben said.

"Are you sure? It ain't no trouble at all."

"No, I can manage. But that's kind of you."

"No trouble. No trouble at all."

"Thanks," she heard Ben say, and flattened her body to the floor, praying to all the saints she knew the names of to protect her from being found out. She was only trying to do a favor for a friend. Certainly she would get a little something from it, but that was all right as long as everyone was happy, wasn't it?

She continued to fervently pray. Please, God, don't let them find her under the bed. They would see what they thought was evidence that she was a fallen woman and draw all the wrong conclusions. Her reputation would be ruined and she would never be able to hold her head high in this town again. Not only that, but all the good work she'd done for some of the less fortunate women would be for naught. Her church plans . . .

Ben's voice boomed through the room. "And while you try to pry open that window, Tom, why don't you scoot that material under the bed again? I know it looks like a woman's robe, but I wouldn't have a woman in my room. No, siree. Not me. Any woman who came in here would be loose and wicked and wild! And that's not my kind of woman. Why, I'm looking for a God-fearing, no-nonsense type of woman who would warm my bread . . . and my bed with equal fervor."

Sarah froze. Her gown was showing? She was afraid to pull it in in case Tom noticed it disappear by itself. She was afraid to move. . . .

She scrunched her eyes shut, as if blocking her view would keep her from being seen. Her legs quaked. Her arms were stiff from being used as a pillow for her head. Her nose twitched. She wanted to sneeze from all the dust motes floating under the bed, but she couldn't.

Benjamin's voice came closer. "No, sir, it would be awful to find a woman under my bed."

The top of the bed creaked and Sarah held her breath.

"Why, whoever it was would be here without my invitation. I swear!" Ben's voice was soft, a tinge of laughter twisting through each word.

Very slowly, Sarah twisted her head to look in the direction of his voice. Ben's smiling face was just in front of hers. His blue eyes twinkled with mirth.

Mirth.

Mirth?

Mirth!

"Why, you . . . " she began.

Ben pretended shock. "Are you about to curse me, Mrs. Hornsby?"

"I'm about to kill you, Mr. Drake," she gritted as she slid toward him to get out from under the dusty bed.

"Oh," he said softly, his warm breath touching her cheek. "I'm getting scared, Mrs. Hornsby."

She scooted closer. "You well should be."

"You ought to be wondering what Tom's gonna say when you get out from under here."

Sarah froze.

". . . and you ought to apologize for slipping under my bed instead of meeting trouble head-on and chin high."

Sarah barely heard him. Instead, her gaze darted around the floor perimeter, looking for another pair of boots. There were none. He was teasing her. If there were another man here, she was pretty sure Ben wouldn't be joking with her. He'd be all manners and haughtiness. Anger welled up. He was teasing her about a matter that could ruin her reputation.

Instead, with great restraint, she held her temper in check and smiled. "I'm sorry, Mr. Drake. I assure you that if I could have reached your arms, I would have fainted in them. However, I wasn't sure that approach would be best, so I thought I'd wait until you fell asleep and then I'd seduce you."

Ben's gaze widened, the blue of his eyes deepening to a dark, inky hue. His mouth formed an "O" and he stared at her as if she were a new species.

"Now, if you'll move, Mr. Drake, I'll slip out from under your bed and stand up tall enough to apologize to Tom and explain to him what a stellar gentleman you are."

"Really," he drawled, not moving.

"Oh, yes," she said, scooting as close to him as she could. The minute he moved, she would be out of there and in her own bedroom. The very minute. . . .

"And will you tell him that you tried to compromise my standing in the very community in which I'm trying hard to establish myself?"

"Of course," she readily agreed. Inside she seethed. Outside she smiled. "And I'll apologize to you."

His gaze narrowed. "Apologize now."

"Let me up."

"Apologize now or I'll kiss you."

"You kiss me and I'll claw your eyes out."

His dimples showed. "That could be fun."

"Don't tempt me, Mr. Drake. I'm doing you a favor by saving your reputation so you can find a wealthy wife in this town. Make no mistake. This isn't London or New York. One sniff of compromising situations and we're both outcasts."

"I'm wondering if it would be worth it, Mrs. Hornsby. You have a lovely mouth and such sweet skin . . ." He reached out and caught a strand. "And your hair is like spun caramel," he said, sounding as if he were far away. "Soft as silk."

"If you could ask my husband, he would tell you I'm not worth it." A slight bitterness crept into her tone and she hoped he hadn't noticed it. She hadn't meant to say that. She hadn't wanted to give anything of her past away.

"Your husband must have had no manners in bed, or perhaps he was an oaf."

"My husband was a good man," she defended.

"But I'm not here to discuss him. I came here to do you a favor, and this is how you treat me. I'll remember this," she said, full of bluster and bravado. But her breath was shallow and her nostrils were filled with Ben's scent, a scent that danced on her tongue, and seemed to taste of male. It was far too pleasant.

"You're right, of course," he said, unable to take his eyes off her. "Please accept my apologies for teasing. I couldn't help myself."

Her chin tilted defiantly. "More crimes are committed by men in the name of that phrase than any other. Please let me out."

He gave a long look as if memorizing her face. Then he slipped out and the bedspread fell back down as he stood. "Please, be my guest."

As she slipped from under his bed, his hand was there, waiting to pull her up. But her shaking body wasn't about to accept his help. She never wanted to be that close to him again! "I can do it myself, thank you."

"Don't be silly. We're alone and there's no one here to see whether or not you're strong or weak." He ignored her protest, his hands spanning her waist easily to lift her up to her feet.

As she turned, she was in his arms. She felt breathless and dizzy. Instead of succumbing, she gave his face a resounding slap.

Ben blinked, flinched, then dropped his hands. "I apologize for taking liberties I shouldn't have, Mrs. Hornsby." His voice was calm, even-toned.

"Don't . . . talk . . . to . . . me."

Without looking at his face, she walked around him and out of the room. When she reached her door, Sarah opened it quietly and then slipped through. Twisting the key in the lock with a brutal strength she didn't know she possessed, she forced herself to take a deep breath.

Her knees were quaking, her limbs as tired as if she'd pushed a wagon a mile.

"Are you all right?" Lillie's voice echoed in her ear and she jumped, then turned. Lillie sat on her bed, her white gown glowing in the moonlight streaming in from the small upstairs window. The woman's hair was twisted in a fat braid that hung over her shoulder almost to her waist.

Her face flamed at being caught in a compromising position. Especially by someone she had preached to about the "male" problems and "female" duties that weren't and shouldn't be considered that. "What are you doing here?"

"I heard you leave and got worried when you didn't return right away. I was deciding what to do. I was thinkin' about going after you, but I wasn't sure." The woman shrugged. "So I just waited."

"I'm sorry. I got caught talking to Mr. Drake in the hall. I want him to show up at church tomorrow and meet someone. It was imperative I speak with him quietly."

Lillie gave a sigh and placed both hands on her knees and stood up. "I see." She began heading down the stairs.

But Sarah couldn't leave it alone. Not after the talk they'd had earlier that evening. "You doubt me."

She didn't halt. "Nope. I was just worried. That's all."

"It was all innocent."

"I know."

"So you believe me?" Sarah's body sagged with relief.

"Yup. Besides, your gown and robe are still tied

very neatly, not thrown together. And your night-gown collar is still outside your robe."

"What does that mean?"

Lillie reached the bottom stair and headed for the rear of the room. "It means you didn't dress in a hurry, and that means you weren't undressed and runnin' in here."

"I don't understand."

"You dressed carefully to go see him. You stayed dressed, I can tell, because after a woman mates with a man, they ususally throw on their clothes and leave. You're still neat."

Logic. Good, sensible logic. Sarah sighed in relief. "Good night, Lillie."

" 'Night." Her reply was distant. A few seconds later, Sarah heard the squeak of the cot.

Sarah sat on her own bed and relived the evening. Each step, each thought, each inneuendo in their conversation. She weighed his responses to everything she'd said. Did he think she was pretty? Did it matter? He wouldn't think *she* was after him and loose, would he? Was he always so teasing and fun?

A thousand questions plummeted in her mind . . . all without answers.

She still didn't have the most important answer to the original question. Would he be in church tomorrow? After slapping him, she was sure he would do as requested. He might not forgive her, though.

Sarah spent the rest of the night staring at the ceiling and thinking.

Ben got ready for bed with a smile on his face. Every time he thought of Sarah diving under his bed, he wanted to laugh. It might not have been nice to tease her, but it was definitely fun. He hadn't even minded the slap. For the first time, he forgot his problems and enjoyed life again.

He'd never tell her but he even enjoyed her slap. It meant she wasn't the little wanton she'd innocently acted.

With a smile still on his mouth, Ben turned off the lamp and climbed under the covers. His last thought was that the scent of her still lingered in the air around his bed. Clover and violets. Wonderful. He was sound asleep in the blink of an eye.

Sarah watched Ben walking toward her and prayed he wouldn't speak about the incident last night to pay her back for the slap. She wished he didn't look so handsome in an unbuttoned overcoat of fine black wool with an equally fine-quality suit underneath. The suit was gray, and a crisp white shirt that was obviously hand tailored in London or New York fit like a second skin over his chest. His Hessian boots shone in the mid-morning sunshine. The handsomest catch of the town—this or any other in Texas.

But Sarah still wanted the ground to open up and swallow her whole as he walked right up to her. "Good morning, Mrs. Hornsby. How are you this fine day?"

She had to brazen this through, she told herself. "I'm fine, Mr. Drake. Just fine. If you wait just a few more moments, I'm sure the chairs will be set up for church. Meanwhile, let me introduce you to our pastor."

He fell in step with her. "Trying to pawn me off so soon?" he asked in a low voice. "I'm crushed."

"You're a scoundrel, Mr. Drake, and if we hadn't made a deal and I wasn't an honorable woman, we wouldn't be talking at all," she said in a whisper.

Before he could answer, she called out, "Pastor Strack! I'd like you to meet a new member of our community," she said as they approached an older man who was as tall as he was stooped. But his face was alight with curiosity and calm. "Mr. Drake is from Great Britain and is visiting us for a while."

Pastor Strack held out an arthritic hand, his face beaming with good thoughts. "So pleased you could join us, Herr Drake. Ve need more men to hear da vord of Gott."

"I agree, Pastor," Ben said smoothly.

Sarah faded away, stepping back so she could turn to walk swiftly in any direction except the one in front of her.

"It's this lady who persuaded me to come. I thought I would wait until I was more established in town before attending, but Mrs. Hornsby said no."

She stopped, smiling weakly. "I don't believe Mr. Drake is the type of person to come to our service if he didn't want to." *No*, she thought. *He only came to harass me.*

"Don't be so modest, Mrs. Hornsby. It was your kind ways to a stranger that made me want to meet the rest of this lovely town."

Her grin hardened. "To say nothing about your brother's recommendation."

"Brosser? You haf a brosser here, too? How fortunate for you," the pastor chimed in.

"Yes, but he was called back to England on business. I only got to visit with him a day or so."

As the pastor continued talking, Sarah took

another step back, then, when no one was looking, turned and almost ran toward the saloon.

She threw herself into the small crowd of appointed men and women whose chore it was to clean up the saloon this Sunday. She began by sweeping the last of the cigarette butts out the door, across the boardwalk and down to the muddy street. Then she helped line up chairs to face the front bar where the pastor preached from. Hymnals were stacked neatly by the door for each member to receive as they walked in.

A glance at the watch pinned to the bodice of her dress told her it was time to get everyone inside and begin church.

"Should I add a few more pieces of wood to the fire, Mrs. Hornsby?" one of the men asked politely, pointing toward the potbellied stove in the center of the room.

"Please. I think there's some in the rear of the building, Jed."

"I brought some." Ben's voice cut through the calm, making her jump. She glared at him. He stood with an armload of chopped wood. "The pastor showed me where it was and I thought I'd bring it now, in case we needed it." His tone was light and his gaze was filled with laughter again. Was she nothing more than a perpetual cause for his amusement?

"How kind of you!" Jed's wife said, an older, softly rounded woman with a smile for everyone. "Please place it there near the stove," she said.

Sarah dropped the last chair in place with a resounding thud and walked to the door, ready to distribute the hymnals. Where in the world was Chloe? She had promised to be here, and once she was introduced to Ben, Sarah's job would be complete. She'd get her merchandise and Ben would have a wife. Finished. Done. Over.

As if on cue, Chloe came down the street driving her spanking new horse-drawn, two-seater carriage. She was impervious to the wind that whipped around the buildings and scattered leftover leaves twirling through the cobblestone street. Dressed in her finest, Chloe wore a bright green felt hat, with a plume to match, covering all but the bunch of chestnut curls on each side of her face, and a matching double cape covering her dress. She looked as if there were nothing she wanted to do more on this sunny winter day than drive her carriage into the country for the sheer fun of it.

Reaching the saloon, Chloe pulled up smartly and sat, looking at the men as if they should have been at the edge of the boardwalk awaiting her arrival. Several accomodated and jumped up to tie off her horses.

It was quite an entrance, even for the town's richest woman. Even Sarah was impressed. She glanced in Ben's direction. He ignored the commotion, too busy leaning against the bar smiling at Jed's wife as she explained how to make one of her famous potato dishes. He didn't even look up to see what the flurry of activity was about.

Sarah gave a sigh. She might as well greet Chloe and get this over with as soon as possible.

Both women reached the door from different directions at the same time.

Chloe's expression was calm and very cool, but her mouth barely moved and her voice was hardly above a whisper when she spoke. "Did he see me drive up?"

"I don't know. He's talking to Jed's wife."

"I thought you said he was eager?"

"I said he was eligible and looking. He's not uncivil," Sarah corrected. "Why don't I take you over and introduce you?"

"Bring him here. I'll not go to him."

Sarah sighed again. Her father used to call this "jockeying for position," and Chloe was in position to do so. "Very well. Why don't you take a seat by the fire?"

Still, Chloe's mouth hardly moved. "I'll wait here."

"Then you'd better step aside. There are a whole line of parishioners behind you who want to enter and get warm." Before Chloe could answer, Sarah turned and walked to stand in front of Ben.

She waited patiently for Jed's wife to finish her recipe, then crooked Ben's arm in hers. "I hope you don't mind, Opal, but I promised an introduction to someone. I'll bring Mr. Drake right back."

"Oh, honey, I've bored him enough for one day. But I must say, Mr. Drake is a good listener for all his fancy ways!" She laughed. "You two go and enjoy." The older woman walked over to her husband and began a conversation.

Sarah's eyes drifted around the room to insure everything else was in place. Suddenly beside her, Ben said softly, "You heard the lady. We're supposed to enjoy ourselves."

"I don't know why everyone is whispering. This is a saloon, not a church. At least, not yet," Sarah said in defense of . . . she wasn't sure what. "Chloe is here. Please come over and let me introduce you two."

"Chloe, the woman I'm supposed to marry?" Ben asked.

Sarah looked up at him and wished she hadn't. His gaze was darting around the room, assessing each and every female entering and seated. Then his gaze lit on Chloe and he stopped. "Is that her by the stove?"

"The one in green. Yes."

"Very nice. Very nice, indeed," he said, his English accent more pronounced than usual. And certainly more appreciative. He covered her hand with his. "Shall we go before the pastor begins the church service?"

Sarah gave a sharp nod. If that was the way it was going to be, she'd just introduce them and good riddance. She led him to Chloe's side.

"Chloe, I'd like you to meet Mr. Benjamin Drake from England. He's here on a visit. Benjamin, Chloe is one of our leading citizens in Clear Creek. She's helped me establish my local Ladies Needlework Club."

Ben dropped Sarah's hand and took Chloe's extended gloved hand. "I'm enchanted, ma'am." His smile was positively lethal. "Intelligence and beauty together is a fetching combination. May I sit?"

Chloe looked as if she'd be more than delighted to have him in the *same seat* with her! "Please," she said, moving aside her coat that flowed over the seat next to her.

"Excuse me," Sarah said to no one in particular. "I have to distribute the hymnals."

"Sorry," Ben said. "I didn't mean to hold you up."

Chloe gave a blushing smile before turning back to Ben. Neither one seemed to care.

Shortly after, Parson Strack began the services with a hymn. Mrs. Karlson, who declared to everyone she met that she was almost a hundred years old, played the piano in fine style. She was bone thin, and her long fingers always found the right keys and slammed them properly.

Sarah forced herself to pay particular attention to each word, devoting all her attention to everything except the couple on the other side of the room. But just before the last verse was sung, she peeked in their direction. Ben and Chloe were sharing a hymnal, both singing while stealing glances at each other.

Good, she told herself. In no time those two would be married and she would have her store filled with merchandise from England. It was exactly what she wanted.

After the service, the same couples who helped clean and set up began putting the chairs and tables back in place. When they were through and the hymnals were once more stored under the far end of the bar counter, it looked less like a church and more like the saloon it was. When two of the four ladies of the evening strolled out from the cribs to look over the balcony, the transformation was complete.

Sarah, the last one to leave, looked up at the young ladies. The youngest one had to be sixteen or so, and the oldest was perhaps twenty-four or twenty-five. Sarah was older than any of them.

"Good day, ladies," she said softly.

"Bye, Sarah," they called in unison.

She closed the door behind her and walked swiftly toward her store. But her eye was caught by Chloe's carriage still standing in front of the saloon. Ben was still talking, his foot propped on the wheel hub as he leaned toward her. He must have said something funny, because Chloe's laugh trilled in the chilly air.

Sarah moved on quickly, dropping her head so

that her bonnet spoiled the scene. Just in case, she averted her eyes so she wouldn't have to speak to either one of them. She walked past them, hoping to get by swiftly and close the door to her own home quickly.

"Mrs. Hornsby?" Benjamin's voice was soft.

She ignored it, pretending she didn't hear his sexy voice.

"Mrs. Hornsby," he said in a much louder voice, and one that she couldn't ignore unless she wanted either of them to be snubbed. That wouldn't do.

Pasting a surprised look on her face, she turned to face them. "My, are you two still here?"

"Yes," Chloe said with a laugh. "I've just asked Mr. Drake to dinner this afternoon and wondered if you would join us?"

"Oh, thank you, but I must really get some work done today."

"And here I thought you wouldn't do any more than necessary since it's Sunday," Ben's teasing voice raced along her spine.

She ignored him, speaking directly to Chloe. "Please accept my apologies. Have a wonderful time." With a nod, she walked to her door and opened it quickly, closing it even quicker behind her.

Safety. Her heart began slowing. Safety.

But from what? Herself? Chloe? Ben?

She didn't know and refused to delve into it. It was Sunday and she had a new book that was waiting to be read. And she refused to label the feelings that assailed her as jealousy. They didn't deserve that and neither did she.

Later that night, after a light supper in Lillie's company, Sarah turned down the light and crawled into bed. It was time to count her blessings.

She loved her life and the way the days passed. Even today. And for whatever reason she had been jealous of Chloe's new-blooming romance, she didn't want one for herself. She was proud of making it on her own and being a competent force in her new hometown. A man would only get in the way of the new life she'd set for herself.

Her feelings this morning after church were just a momentary lapse into old thoughts and ways. It wasn't the new her at all.

With that realization came a sense of peace. She closed her eyes and began drifting into a pleasant sleep.

Tap, tap, tap.

Her eyes opened.

Tap, tap, tap.

The door between her bedroom and the hotel was being tapped on.

Sarah stood and put her ear against the door.

"Sarah," Ben's voice whispered.

"What do you want?" she whispered back.

"Open the door."

He was less than two inches away from her with only a slab of wood separating them. Her skin flushed with the thought. "No. Go to bed."

"Please."

"No. Go to bed."

"I just want to thank you."

"You just did," she whispered back.

His chuckle rumbled through the wood and she felt the vibration of it on cheek. "You're a tough lady," he said. "I can't even thank you properly."

"Good night, Lord Benjamin," she stated purposefully, her voice far more in charge than her thoughts.

"Good night ... Sarah," he said. His footfalls echoed down the hall to his own room. Then she felt, or heard, the click of his closing door.

Suddenly she felt the chill in the air and scrambled back into bed, shivering under the covers.

He liked Chloe, that much was apparent.

She had succeeded.

How wonderful.

Why didn't she feel more elated?

Chapter Six

When Sarah opened the store the next morning, business was brisk. Two women dropped by to sell their crafts, one with several beautiful quilts, and the other with fine knitting. Both were perfect for Sarah's shop.

She also received a letter from a shop in Dallas, asking her if she wanted to ship some of her stock to a store there. The weather was chillier in north Texas and needed the warmer crafts even more. It thrilled Sarah to know she could find another outlet to sell the women's work.

Many of her customers were more talkative than usual and sat with their tea until way past noon. The weather, a little warmer than the past week, made it possible for many to get out and enjoy the sunshine and company.

Sarah pulled a shawl out of the window display for a customer and Lillie joined her. For just a second, they stopped and glanced out the window.

Even the brick-paved streets were crowded with wagons, horses and drays. Several men sat on a bench outside the sheriff's office, leisurely talking and smoking.

"Look at 'em. Swappin' lies, again," Lillie said. But this time there was a note of teasing in her voice—unusual for Lillie. She wasn't frowning at every man who crossed her path anymore. Perhaps she was getting over her past with a mean husband and realizing that not all men were created the same any more than all women were.

"Oh, no," Sarah teased. "Everything they say is absolute truth. Just ask them and they'll tell you."

Both chuckled before turning back to the room full of customers. The very large presence of Mrs. Petrie, smiling sweetly, stood behind them. She smiled at their surprise. "I overheard your comment about those old coots across the street. Well said, Lillie."

Lillie smiled. "Thank you. I get strokes of genius at times."

"Speaking of men." Mrs. Petrie's voice dropped to a loud whisper. "Tell me about the duke's brother."

Sarah should have known. The town had a communication system that was better than any Indian drum or telegraphic system. It was called gossip, and Mrs. Petrie was the best gossip and the best dessert maker. One was easier than the other to deal with, but Sarah was never sure which was best.

"I don't know much, Mrs. Petrie," Sarah said.

"But, dear, you had dinner with him at the hotel and I understand you introduced him to Chloe Givson at church on Sunday. Everyone says he speaks very highly of you, and no decent man would say he knew you well enough to talk about you, unless he did."

Lillie coughed. Sarah realized she couldn't afford to snub a patron like Mrs. Petrie. She had a good heart and helped Sarah with jobs for many of the women who worked in town. Besides, her only sin was that she was a talker. Everyone knew it and went to her for all sorts of information. Might as well get it right now.

"His name is Lord Benjamin Drake, but he prefers to be Ben Drake, and he's visiting Clear Creek for a while. He's single and seems to be taken with our town and our ladies."

"Is it true he's a twin?" Mrs. Petrie asked.

Sarah felt as if the woman was sealing her in a corner. Taking Mrs. Petrie's arm, she walked her over to the stuffed horsehair sofa, where the woman could perch without breaking furniture. "Yes, it is. I met his brother and, although he's the duke now, I must say that I enjoy Lord Benjamin's manners. Lillie and I both enjoy his company."

"And are *you* interested?"

"I'm interested in all my friends."

Mrs. Petrie's eyes narrowed as she stared at Sarah. "Don't prevaricate with me, Mrs. Sarah Hornsby. We are both aware of what I'm speaking."

Sarah's face reddened. "I'm not interested in anything more than friendship. And I think he would make an excellent addition to our community and my hopes are that he meets a woman who will make it worth his while to remain in Clear Creek. I promised I would introduce him to others. He was amenable and said he would enjoy that."

"And?"

"End of story. That is it, Mrs. Petrie. Anything else would be a lie."

"I see." The woman sat down but still didn't allow Sarah to go. Her hand held Sarah's. "You're sure there's no interest, Sarah?" she asked softly.

Sarah looked into the older woman's gaze. "Not the kind you're thinking, Mrs. Petrie. I hope he finds a place in our community, and no matter whom he finds interesting, that we remain friends."

Mrs. Petrie nodded her head. "All right, if you say so."

Sarah laughed. She was not about to lose her reputation in this town. Unlike her sheltered and ineffective married life in Blissful, the townspeople here thought she was strong, sensible and intelligent. Nothing was worth losing her hard-won reputation for, including—and especially—a man.

Lillie walked up alongside of them, her smile too sweet to be real. "Excuse me, Mrs. Petrie, but Mrs. Hamilton is waiting to try on that shawl, Sarah."

Sarah nodded, her hand clenching the material she'd taken from the display window. "Thank you, Lillie." She hadn't realized just how much Mrs. Petrie's questions bothered her until she looked at Lillie and saw concern on her face.

It wasn't fair that anyone could harm her hard-won reputation. Nor was it reasonable that she refuse to accept payment and return trunks full of goodies in exchange for helping Ben out with introductions to eligible young women.

By lunch hour, Sarah felt as if she'd run around the block several times. As the last customer filed out the door, she twisted the sign hanging there announcing she'd open again at two o'clock.

Her feet, encased in tie-up boots, hurt and burned like fire. Both she and Lillie sat down, propped their feet up on the small chest she used as a table and grinned at each other.

"It's a banner day, Lillie."

"I know. It must be the new man in town. I thought I'd never get Mrs. Petrie to stop talking about Ben."

"Neither did I," Lillie stated dryly. "She began pumping me first. When I walked over to you, it was to get away from her."

"I didn't know."

"Don't feel too bad, though. She left the most delicious cake behind. Want some after lunch?"

"Why not?"

Just as Lillie rose, the bell above the door tinkled.

Ben strode in and brought the clean smell of sunshine and chilled air. "Don't move, you two. I brought lunch for you."

"Lunch?" Lillie asked.

"Of course," he said, placing two large gingham napkins on the table. From his coat jacket, he produced a jar of liquid. "Apple cider," he said with a smile. "Cold, but very good."

"You sampled?"

He flashed a grin. "Of course."

"And what's the occasion?"

"Why, a thank-you, of course. My mama wouldn't let it be any other way. Mrs. Givson and I are attending the Literary Dinner to support the new library being built."

"Not until we get more money from the townspeople," Lillie stated.

"Did you have something to do with the Literary Dinner, too?"

She nodded, a grin on her face.

"And are you happy about it?"

"Of course. It gives people a chance to meet and

talk and exchange ideas. Mr. Carnage is helping us."

Ben leaned over and opened the napkins. Slices of thick dark bread wrapped around chunks of cooked sausage. "Try this."

Sarah and Lillie looked at each other and grinned. They were tired, and being served was wonderful.

Sarah picked one up and took a dainty bite, wanting to down it immediately but restraining herself. "Delicious," she said before taking another, not-so-dainty bite. Lillie did the same thing. "Very good," Sarah said again.

Ben had gone to their kitchen area and grabbed two small glasses, filling them with the apple cider. Sarah washed down the last bite of sandwich with the chilly drink and sat back, her stockinged feet demurely on the ground and hidden by the table.

"That was very kind of you," she finally said.

Ben bowed his head. "It was my pleasure, Mrs. Hornsby. I have to stay on your good side. This entire town knows you and wants to protect you from the big bad gentleman who just rode into town."

She almost giggled at the image he portrayed. It was positively ego-soothing to be known as competent and a valuable member of the community she chose to live in. "That's wonderful news, and I'd appreciate it if you remembered that yourself. I don't need my name bandied about by the men here." She sounded so prim and proper. Lillie's held-in smile confirmed how stuffily she was reacting. But she didn't care. "I hope you understand," she said.

"Completely," he murmured with a straight face. "I won't curse or swear in your presence, gamble on your doorstep or walk down hallways in my drawers imprinted with your name, or call you sweetie . . . in public."

Sarah felt a blush tinge her skin from the tips of her toes to her rosy-red cheeks.

Lillie burst out laughing. "I should say not! Why, that would ruin everything!"

Slash dimples appeared in Ben's cheeks. "I thought so, too. So I will be very careful." He pretended concern. "Bringing lunch isn't on that list of do-nots, is it?"

"Of course not," she snapped, hiding behind irritation her memories of his teasing behavior in his room. She reached for the gingham napkins, folding them.

"Are you all right, Mrs. Hornsby?"

"I'm fine."

"And I'm leavin'," Lillie said, standing. She picked up the remains of the impromptu picnic. "I'll bring a cup of hot tea for all of us in a few minutes."

"Thank you, Lillie," Ben said with a smile.

"Trying to win Lillie over?" Sarah asked, her eyebrow cocked.

"Of course. That's what I do with all the women," he answered, acting surprised.

"To what purpose?"

"I haven't a clue, ma'am," he said in his imitation of a Texas drawl. It sounded authentic. He leaned forward as if telling a secret. "But you just never know when you might need the help and support of a good woman."

"But wouldn't you receive that from a wife?" she asked stiffly.

"Perhaps. But since I don't have one, I see no reason to make an enemy out of any woman."

"In other words, you don't mind spreading your charm around."

His grin was devilish. "If you want to call it that, I can spread it around."

Sarah stood, staring down at him self-righteously. "I'd call it bull chips, Mr. Drake." She pressed the wrinkles out of the front of her gingham dress. "If you'll excuse me. I have work to do."

"Of course," he said, but there was still a hint of mischief in his eyes. "I will see you at the Literary Dinner at the jail this week. Please save a dance on your card for me."

"I know you will be very busy sharing your . . . kindnesses with others, including Chloe Givson," she said stiffly.

"I always have time for you, Mrs. Hornsby," Ben said smoothly. "After all, you're the one person who can help me find the bride of my dreams. And I'm the one who can help you succeed in yours. I found out that you have a waiting list of women who are anxious for supplies to begin working on sewing projects."

"Is there something funny about that?" she said, finally staring up at him with daggers she should have delivered long ago.

"None at all. But it makes me realize how important a boatload of material can be for you."

Sarah's heart hammered. "I thought we discussed ten trunks full. Are you saying you would now like to be so generous as to donate a boatload full of supplies?"

Ben shrugged. "We didn't discuss any particular number. It depends upon how well my bride is endowed."

Sarah blushed again. "I beg your pardon?"

He grinned. "Your mind is traveling in the wrong

direction, Sarah," he said softly. "I meant . . . with funds."

"You're a tease, directing me to the wrong place." She handed him the folded napkins and the jar. "I think lunchtime is over."

"I do too. And the only reason I tease you is that you react so beautifully. I would not have done it if Lillie was with us."

"Then I'll make sure she is from now on."

He shrugged. "Whatever you say. But I have a feeling you enjoy our banter as much as I do."

"Have a good day, Mr. Drake."

"You, too, Mrs. Hornsby."

He glanced over her shoulder in Lillie's direction. Then, before Sarah realized what he was going to do, he bent forward and kissed the tip of her nose.

"See you at the Literary Dinner," he said before walking out the door. It shut behind him with a whoosh of chilled, clean air billowing around the large room.

She stood unmoving. All her senses were centered on the tip of her nose. It felt hot, then cold, then hot again. Her cheeks were red, as if she'd been out in the cold air. Her mouth was formed in an "O," as if puckering for the kiss she wished she'd had.

"No," she said softly.

"No, what?" Lillie said, setting the tray filled with tea cups and pot on the table. "And where did our luncheon guest go?"

"He had other things to do." Sarah sounded short and gave a smile to soften her words.

"He has eyes for you."

Sarah rubbed her nose with the palm of her hand and gave a sigh. "He's a tease."

"He has eyes for you."

"He's a rake."

"I won't say it again."

"Good." She sounded satisfied. "I'm not answering such a terrible thought."

"Better drink your tea. We have a busy afternoon scheduled." Lillie picked up her cup and began sipping. "You'll need it to keep warm."

Sarah ignored Lillie's cute comments. Her mind was already filled with thoughts of her own.

Meanwhile, her nose burned in the exact same place Ben had kissed.

Lillie closed the door after the last customer around supper time. Sarah and Lillie worked another half an hour cleaning up the area, restocking the sewn items bought that day with others stored in several trunks by the stairs. Sarah sat on the floor and went through stock in the lower drawers of their parlor furniture.

"Our inventory is getting low," Lillie said as she pulled out a thick pair of mitts for the stove. "This is the last pair from Genna."

Genna lived on a farm about three miles from town. Her husband had died of a stroke the year before and she took care of her ailing mother and two children. She worked in cotton fields during growing season and sewed through the winter. Her handiwork was sought after, but now she sold only to Sarah, who made sure she got the right price for everything she did. She didn't have to haggle with the customers or worry about having to sell something at half price because she was low on funds. Sarah paid Genna money she could count on every month all year long.

"I'll be making rounds tomorrow, so I'll go out to her place and pick up what she has. She'll need more supplies."

The front bell tinkled and they both looked up. Sarah's heart skipped a beat, anticipating Ben standing in the doorway, his devilish grin forecasting a wicked sense of humor at her expense.

Instead of a devil of a man, a strikingly beautiful young woman dressed in black boots, cape and bonnet stood at the door. A small valise was held tightly in her gloved hand. "Mrs. Hornsby?" she asked.

Sarah rocked back on her heels and smiled. "I'm Mrs. Hornsby." She should get used to this by now. Homeless and underprivileged women were the main reason she ran her business. "How can I help you?"

The young woman closed her eyes and took a deep breath, then stared at Sarah. "I'm Sister Merci from Bixby, Arizona Territory, and I need a place to stay. The young man at the hotel said to check with you. He said there weren't any rooms left at the hotel for the next two weeks."

Sarah's glance went to the young woman's hands. They were held in front of her, clothed in black gloves. And they were shaking like an Aspen leaf in the wind.

Sarah stood and walked over to the young girl. The closer she got, the younger Sister Merci seemed to be. Her hands closed over the black gloves. "Come sit and warm up," she said quietly, leading her to a chair.

"I'm sorry," Sister Merci said. "I'm not usually so cold, but it seems the wind went straight through me today. I must have caught a chill in the hotel and haven't stopped shaking since then."

"When did you eat last?"

The young woman's brow furrowed in thought. "I ate on the train this morning. I had toast and tea."

"I'll get something," Lillie muttered, then hurried off to the rear of the room.

Sarah walked the young woman to a chair. She was strong and beautiful, but her eyes seemed old and tired; the depth of them seemed to be full of dread.

Merci must have read Sarah's thoughts. Her chin tilted in courage. "I'm not a charity case, Mrs. Hornsby. At least not by your standards. I have some money. But I need a place to stay and young Simon almost swallowed his Adam's apple trying to tell me that you could help anyone who needed help."

"You came to the right place," Sarah said. "Are you on a journey?"

"No. I . . . I heard about Clear Creek and wanted to see it for myself. I was told that the church wasn't built yet, and thought I might be able to help with the building."

"How?" Lillie asked bluntly as she returned from the kitchen area with a glass of chilled milk and a fat wedge of chocolate cake. She placed it in front of Sister Merci. "Do you have money of your own you want to donate?"

"No, I . . . well, I have some money of my own, but just enough to get along for the next few months if I'm frugal." Her face brightened. "But I can help solicit donations. I'm very good at that. I can get some people to donate when they'd never thought of it before."

Sarah knew that method. With someone as beautiful as Sister Merci, men would reach into their pockets for change in a heartbeat and never think of it as more than a donation and a flirtation.

"But I need a place to stay this evening." She looked up at the two women, a fork full of cake on the way to her mouth, her eyes full of bravado. "Is there a chance that you ladies would know where I can get lodging for the night?"

Sarah and Lillie looked at each other. Sarah could practically read the other woman's mind.

She should sleep upstairs with you. There isn't enough time to make a pallet down here.

Should we find room with another woman in town or keep her here?

Let's keep her here tonight, but she will have to sleep upstairs on your floor on a pallet. We don't have another bed that we can get before tomorrow.

Sarah looked back at the young woman. "You can spend the night here if you don't mind sharing the bed with me. Tomorrow we can figure out something else."

Sister Merci's eyes brightened. "Are you sure? I wouldn't mind making a pallet on the floor. I promise I won't take up much room."

Sarah laughed. "You couldn't take up room if you tried. You're just not big enough. So not another word. We're about to have some stew. Take off your cloak and hat and we'll get dinner served."

Sister Merci stood up and shed her cape. Her bonnet and gloves were off quickly and hung on the coatrack by the door. She smoothed the front of her drab gray dress, then adjusted the collar on her high neck, insuring it was still in place. Midnight-black hair was pulled tightly back into a braided bun. "Let me help," she said. "Although my cooking isn't good, I'm fairly useful in the kitchen. I can clean and serve with the best."

Lillie, ever practical, handed her an apron from the cabinet drawer. "Suit yourself. Bread's on the counter and needs cutting." She glanced at Sarah. "We were too busy today for Sarah to make her famous biscuits. We'll just have to make do."

Sister Merci added a festive element to their evening. She chattered about how good things smelled, what beautiful work she saw in the sewing area and how to set a table. By the time they sat down, everyone was at ease and joking.

"So, where were you born?" Lillie asked as they finally dug into the stew.

The young woman hesitated only a moment. "I was born in Indiana, but I haven't been back since I was a child. My dad decided he needed to find opportunity farther west, and so west is where we headed. My dad, his brother, my two brothers and baby sister."

"What happened to your mom?"

"She died giving birth to my little sister. I was eleven when she was born, and took over the raising of her."

"Where is she now?" Sarah asked.

Sister Merci carefully placed her napkin in her lap and smoothed the fabric. "She died when she was seven," she finally said, her voice slightly thick. "About five years ago. It was a wagon accident."

"I'm so sorry," Sarah said, covering the young woman's hands with her own. It was easy to see that Merci was still upset over the loss of such a young child she thought of as an almost-daughter.

Sarah gave Lillie a no-nonsense look that said not to ask anymore questions. Lillie shrugged and kept her mouth closed.

"Who wants tea and more cake?"

"I do," Sarah said. "And so does our guest if she feels up to it."

Merci laughed, attempting to dispel the pall that had entered the room. "I do, too. The cake's delicious."

"It's Mrs. Petrie, our saint of all desserts. She bakes something every day and usually donates half of whatever she makes to us for our customers, and we're always grateful."

"She has a large family?"

"No, she has no one except her husband, who isn't any bigger than a minute." Lillie chuckled. "He can't eat sweets. But she can. And she proves it every hour of the day."

"It sounds to me like the two do just fine," Sister Merci said with a slight grin. "Does she eat her entire half?"

"Every bite, in one sitting."

The young woman's eyes widened. "My goodness!"

Lillie nodded sagely. "It's a talent."

After cleaning up from dinner, they finished stocking the front room. Sarah made a list of the women she was visiting tomorrow and the supplies she needed to take to them in exchange for the work they did. By the time they crawled into bed, they were all exhausted. It had been a busy day.

It wasn't until the lights were out that Sarah realized a difference in the evening. Since Sister Merci had arrived, Sarah hadn't thought of Ben once.

Progress.

The next day was as busy as the last one. Sarah left early in the morning to make rounds in the buggy. She visited five women and received finished goods from four.

The fifth one, Elsa, was a wisp of a woman who barely contained her blonde hair into a rigid bun. Stray hair flew everywhere, looking like a living, moving halo around her face. She was mother of three and the wife of a German who'd come to America only a few years before. Her husband barely spoke English and his wife was his interpreter. He was stoic and always frowning while she was normally sweet and smiling. But not this time. She was in tears as she told Sarah her husband would not let her sew anymore. "He says he will not take charity from anyone."

"Charity? Doesn't he realize how hard you work to earn that money?"

"He says my work doesn't count and that if I want to knit, I should only knit for the family. He says I should obey him, for that is the most important thing he needs from me."

Sarah felt her anger rise. Why were some men so stubborn? "You are very talented, Elsa. If you want to sell your sewing through our store, you should be able to. That money can be used to help benefit your children, and *that* is the most important thing you can do."

"Ya, I know," she sighed. "But I cannot show him where he is wrong, Sarah. He will only get more angry." Elsa looked beaten, tears forming in her blue eyes. "He will have to find out for himself how silly he is being. I cannot put our children at the mercy of his anger."

How could she tell the woman she shouldn't be at his mercy, either? It wasn't her place to preach to others about their situations in life, especially when she'd been there herself. If Thomas hadn't died, she might never have spoken up for herself.

"If you change your mind, let me know. If you want to work a little at a time, I can certainly use your help in making scarves for next winter. That way you won't be under pressure to do a lot at a time. If you begin now, you can have many done by then."

"I cannot, Sarah. But I will continue to try to convince him otherwise. I promise."

"Good luck, Elsa," Sarah said as she clucked the horses into heading home.

Women like Elsa were the reason she kept the store going on a shoestring. They needed the feeling of equality that selling their goods for money gave them. They needed to stand tall and straight and take bad treatment from no man. Unfortunately, that didn't happen often enough. Here, in the West, some of the women without family around to help support them emotionally were victims of the whims of any man.

"If we only had the vote, we could make laws," she said softly. But no one heard her and no one offered to tell her how to go about setting up such a radical change.

When Sarah returned home late that afternoon, Lillie and Sister Merci were ready, helping to unload the wagon and get Sarah a cup of tea while she perched her feet on the footstool and discussed the day.

Sister Merci was now being called Merci by Lillie, who said the whole name was just too much to get out every time she wanted to speak to her.

"This is beautiful," Merci said as she unwrapped a quilt in reds, yellows and browns. Giant sunflowers were quilted to a sand-colored background on material of earth brown. "How do they do that?"

"With more patience and talent than I have," Sar.. .aid. "That's why I sell it and they create it."

"Oh, my," Lillie said, walking around to view it. "It's beautiful. Must be from the Ingram ranch."

"It is." She explained to Merci. "The Ingram ranch is the most rundown, oldest, most drab place you'd ever want to see. Several poor families live there. The only color there is the green of the cotton field before harvest."

"And someone there can make this?"

"Sometimes, quilts are like art. They're the only color in their lives."

"I know that feeling," Merci said softly.

Sarah could tell Merci was speaking from the depth of her own heart. It was time to change the subject. "By the way, Merci. Tomorrow is our Literary Dinner. Please come with us."

Merci froze in place for one long moment. Then she smiled. "Oh, I couldn't impose . . ."

"You wouldn't be imposing," Sarah said, laughing. "It's a dinner to raise money for the new library. They *want* people to show up. Besides, it is the perfect place to meet the people of this fine town and decide whether you would like to settle here."

"Well, that sounds wonderful, but I have no clothing. . . ."

"Wear what you have. Many won't know the difference. This is a farming community, Merci. We don't have high society here, with the exception of four or five women who have nothing better to do than look like they just strolled across the water from a London drawing room."

Merci didn't look as if she quite believed Sarah. "Well, if you're sure."

"We're sure," Lillie stated without hesitation. "I have three dresses and none of them are fancy. I'm wearing the one I wear to church on Sunday."

Merci grinned. "In that case, how can I go wrong?"

It was settled. Sarah was looking forward to introducing Merci to their townsfolk. She would also have the opportunity to see how Ben was doing with his bride-to-be.

"It looks like it will be a wonderful night for all," she said as they got ready for bed.

Sarah didn't ask if Lillie had spoken to Merci about finding another place to stay. She had spied the extra cot at the rear of the kitchen. Besides, it didn't seem important. . . .

Chapter Seven

The town's Literary Dinner was held in the new jail on a cold, starry night that made Sarah's blood pump with excitement. The jail was lit with gaslights and candles that shimmered through the street. Along with the music that spilled from the doorway and into the town, it made a festive atmosphere.

It wasn't the location that made it exciting, for the town jail, although new, held all the ordinary things one expected. It also had a large entry office, two file rooms, and the upstairs held jail cells without doors. The metal ironworks were not in place yet, but the manufacturer promised they would arrive from Houston sometime in the next week.

It was the night. Friends and almost friends would get together and they were the same people who had rallied around Sarah when she had arranged for the church to be built. She was so proud to be a part of this community, to feel the

bond that she felt when she was active in the community—a part of something that affected everyone. It was heady, especially on a night like this.

Sarah had bought the expensive five-dollar tick-
ets for the three of them, although Lillie hadn't
decided about attending until Merci agreed. Lillie
was still a little frightened about being in the company of what she called "town swells." Sarah recognized her reaction and knew that Lillie was
probably secretly afraid of how they might treat
her. So defensive about her circumstances of being
married to the town drunk and allowing him to
humiliate her all those years, she was ready for a
fight at the same time she was just as ready to run.

Merci seemed to be encased in ice. Her quiet
manner was nothing like the girl had been for the
past few days. She was so calm, Sarah wanted to
check her pulse just to make sure she was alive.
Occasionally, Sarah thought she might be in a
trance.

Sarah herself was just the opposite. She was so
nervous, she walked around the shop rearranging
the merchandise in several different ways before
Lillie intervened.

That night, dressed in her best—the same deep
purple dress she had worn for her wedding seven
years ago, she stood at the mirror and wondered
what she was doing. Would it finally happen?
Would the townspeople see though her no-nonsense attitude and realize there was nothing but
quivering jelly beneath?

She reminded herself she was not asking people
for favors this time. This was just a town dinner.
She was not seeking a husband nor was she the
belle of the ball. If anyone would attract attention

or speculation, it would be beautiful Merci. So why was she worried?

"Enough of this nonsense." She hadn't realized she'd spoken aloud until she heard Merci's voice.

"What did you say?"

Sarah gave a laugh. "I was just telling myself that no one will care how I look and to stop worrying about my hair."

Merci finished tying her shoe and stood, calmly eying her benefactor. "Your hair is beautiful, Sarah. But if you like, I can sweep it to one side for you. I am kind of good with hair."

One more glance in the mirror and Sarah snapped at the chance. "I'd love it," she said, and sat on the edge of the bed.

In less than ten minutes, Merci had taken her ordinary knot and turned it into a knot with curls draped over one shoulder. Wisps of hair fell by her temples, softening her features. Sarah sat stunned. She had never looked this pretty!

"There," Merci said, her voice laced with satisfaction. "That is so much better."

"My God," Sarah said in a whisper. "Is that me?"

"Yes. Don't you like it?"

"I love it." Sarah smiled, then laughed. "I love it! Thank you so much, Merci. You are so talented! You have such a way with hair! My goodness, you should go into the business! You'd be the wealthiest woman in all of Clear Creek!"

Merci blushed all the way to the roots of her dark hair. "You really think so?"

"Think so? I know so! Why, women would flock to have you do their hair. If you can do this for me in less than ten minutes, I wonder what you could do given more time."

"It's just a knack."

"A knack is a talent that needs to be used, Merci. Don't sell yourself short. There are always others who will do that for you," Sarah warned.

"I didn't know a genteel lady like yourself would know that."

"It's human nature that some will tear down others. It's the only way they can compensate for their own shortcomings." Sarah looked calmly at her new friend. "You know that."

Merci nodded. "But do you think it's that good?" The younger woman looked undecided and yet so hopeful.

"I'm certain." Sarah stood and went to the rail. "Lillie, please come up and see what Merci has done."

When Lillie got to the top of the stairs, Sarah stood in front of the mirror. Lillie stopped and stared.

"Well," Sarah said, "what do you think?"

"My goodness, you look like a fairy princess!" Lillie exclaimed, her eyes as wide as teacups.

"Merci did it."

"Merci?" Lillie's gaze switched to the young woman, who wore a pained expression on her face. "Merci can do hair like that?"

Sarah nodded, almost giddy with happiness. She'd known that everyone had a talent and all they had to do was to find it. This just proved that theory. Merci was a wizard at something besides drumming up money.

"Can, uh . . . " Lillie touched her slick, pulled-back hair. It was in the same style as Merci's, only on Merci it looked fashionable and French. But on Lillie, it wasn't flattering at all. "Could you do something with mine?"

Merci smiled. "Of course." She patted the side of the bed in front of the tall mirror. "Sit down."

Within fifteen minutes, Lillie had a softened bun, but this time there were small bangs across her forehead, accenting her wide brow and bringing out her eyes.

"I look . . . nice," she said, a little awe in her tone.

"Is it all right?"

"It's better'n all right," Lillie said, still staring at herself in the mirror. "It's wonderful." She turned, impulsively giving Merci a hug that took the young lady by surprise.

Then, suddenly, Merci was hugging back. Whatever walls Merci had built were breaking down, and so were Lillie's.

They joined in laughter until all of them were crying with the effort. It felt so good!

Sarah straightened her bodice. "Well, ladies. I believe we're all ready to face the citizens of Clear Creek."

Donning cloaks and picking up their contribution of Sarah's best biscuits, scalloped potatoes and a green bean-and-onions-in-vinegar casserole for the dinner, they walked out the door and down the boardwalk to the building across the street and at the end of the paved brick.

Once inside the warm jail, one of the men acting as host escorted them into the party, taking their dishes and giving them to one of the women at the serving table.

"His Royalness, Mr. Drake, is over there, mooning over Mrs. Givens," Lillie whispered to Sarah as she gave a slight nod in Ben's direction.

Merci stood behind them quietly, ignoring their

conversation and looking over the room before staring somewhere around the corner.

Sarah followed Lillie's gaze across the room. Chloe Givens, dressed in a new blue satin gown, was glowing as her arm was wound around Ben's, her gaze adoring. Ben's head was cocked, listening intently to Horst Heine, the benefactor of the church land. He was dressed in a formal black suit that fit him so well, Sarah knew it had to be hand tailored in London.

Horst spoke stiffly in stilted English, obviously searching for words every few seconds. But Ben was attentive, and listened patiently to whatever he was saying. Chloe looked bored.

If Sarah judged by looks alone, they made the ideal couple, well on their way to the altar. Sarah didn't want to think about what that meant, nor did she want to remember the good things about being a couple. She had work to do, and a man in her life would only take her away from her mission.

But the joke was on her. She was protesting against something that wasn't available. There was no man in her life. There were no suitors waiting in the wings for her to find a break in the work she did. There was no one.

"Good. They're still together." Her words sounded a little hollow.

She forced herself to focus on something else to occupy her thoughts, instead of wondering about the private life of two people so obviously in love.

"There's Mayor Cookson," Sarah whispered, finally focusing on another person. He was a tall, obese man with a handlebar moustache he was very proud of. His clothing seemed to barely cover his huge stomach. He stood talking to several others in a small circle, sipping his drink between pontificating.

"That little wife of his sleeps in her own room with the door locked," Lillie stated.

Merci followed their gaze.

"It's a good thing. He'd break every bone in her tiny body."

"Both of you. Stop that," Sarah whispered.

"I used to live next door to their maid. She told me that and more." Lillie rolled her eyes.

"Lillie!"

"Don't blame Lillie, blame the maid who spoke first," Merci said under her breath.

Sarah turned to admonish Merci and instead found the new pastor and his wife. "So good to see you," she said, introducing Lillie and Merci to the pastor and his wife, Ina. The rotund woman's happy smile and twinkling eyes made her seem as if she was always on the verge of a belly laugh, or at least knew a happy secret.

"We were invited guests of the mayor's and thought we could come here and see who wasn't attending church," Ina teased. "If they had the money to attend this affair for the library, then perhaps we could persuade them to help us pay for the community's new church."

"Ina," the pastor said, admonishing his wife with a gentle smile. "We haf to save souls. We don't haf dem come out of guilt."

"Anything that gets them to join the church and lighten the load with a donation should be allowed by God, don't you think?"

"I don't sink so."

"Doesn't giving and receiving make most people feel better?" asked Lillie.

"Of course, but . . . " the pastor began.

"No buts, dear," Ina said, a determined twinkle in her eye. "You know what you have to do and I know what we need to get it accomplished."

Sarah laughed. "She's right, you know. A few of these charming citizens need to help contribute to the building of our church and community hall. After all, the entire town will benefit from it. If nothing else, we won't have to have meetings in the new jail or the saloon anymore."

Lillie nodded solemnly. "It wouldn't hurt none for them to pay for the privilege of staying in bed on a Sunday morning, either."

Ina's sharp eyes began looking around, ready to launch at anyone she knew hadn't attended church in the past month. The pastor moved off to wrangle a few glasses of warm punch for the ladies. But when he turned his back on his wife, she spotted who she was looking for.

"Excuse me, ladies, but I see Mr. and Mrs. Hermann. They haven't been to church in a month of Sundays! Perhaps I need to reintroduce myself." She patted Sarah's hand and was off.

When the pastor returned, he distributed the drinks and then took off after his wife, insuring she wouldn't try to mix her business with his pleasure.

"They're so sweet," Sarah told Merci.

"And funny. I didn't know pastors could be so funny."

"They're just people," Lillie said, suddenly very sure of herself. If the pastor and his wife accepted her presence here, then she was happy. The battered ex-wife of the town drunk was redeemed in the face of society. Every once in a while she would touch her bangs and smile.

They spoke to other citizens of Clear Creek, introducing Lillie and Merci to each and every one.

With each introduction the two women seemed to bloom a little more.

The dining lines began and the crowd slowed down their perpetual circle of talking. Sarah shooed both women in front of her as they took their place in line.

A deep voice behind her spoke in slow English. "It is good to see you again, Mrs. Hornsby."

She turned and looked up at Horst Heine. He was a handsome gentleman, but so reserved it was hard to tell what was on his mind. "Good evening, Mr. Heine."

"Horst, please," he said with a smile. "I am honored to be standing in the rear of you. You have done so many good works for our town."

She ignored his misinterpretation of standing. "Not at all. You're the one who donated the land."

"Ya, but that was easy."

"Are you here alone?" she asked, searching for any conversation.

"Ya," he said. "You look very fine this evening."

"Thank you." She smiled.

"Ya, and your hair is very nice. I like the twisted way you wear it."

Was he flirting? She didn't quite know what to do. "You're too kind."

They filled their plates from two tables laden with food and found a table in the rear of the room. As they sat down, Sarah realized that Horst was right behind her, joining them. When she looked up, he smiled. "You smell goot, too."

"Thank you."

With patience, she introduced Lillie and Merci to their table company. Suddenly, his eyes narrowed and he stared at Merci.

"Did we not meet before?" he asked.

Merci sat stiffly, one hand in her lap, one holding her fork so tightly her knuckles were white. "Perhaps. Are you from Indiana?"

Sarah was surprised. Merci had said she'd only lived there as a child. Why would Horst remember her from there?

"No," he said, dismissing the subject. He speared his sausage. "More west, maybe."

"No. I don't think so." Merci pecked at her warm potato salad as if it were the most important food in her life.

Horst studied his sausage, chewed another bite. When he was done, he turned back to Sarah. "When will we build the church?"

"As soon as we get enough money," Sarah said.

Merci spoke up. "I want to add my thanks to you for your donation, Mr. Heine. But if you have enough money to donate the land, then why don't you help with the building too? Perhaps donate the lumber?" she asked challengingly.

Sarah started to protest, but Lillie touched her hand and gained her attention. She barely shook her head, but Sarah got the message.

"I sink donating the land was enough, ya?"

"Not if we don't have enough to build the building. Why, I bet you have lumber on your property that would be perfect to build the church. If your lumber mill would donate that, we could get volunteers and begin construction immediately."

Horst stared at her a long moment. "You smell goot."

Her challenging gaze never wavered. "Thank you."

"Like mine mother."

"That's a very nice compliment." She stared back. "Would you?"

"Will you do the work? Set this up with the lumber mill?"

Merci's gaze glanced at Sarah, then back to Horst. "Yes."

"I will sink about it."

Merci gave him a long, daring look. "Please don't take too long. I'm also thinking of approaching someone else. But it is your name I think would be best on a plaque at the front of the church."

He stared off into space as he swallowed his slice of sausage. With a nod as if he had discussed the problem in his mind and come up with a decision, he said, "Ya. Ask me again on Wednesday."

"Wednesday?"

"Ya. Please come Wednesday to my office. We will talk then."

Sarah's brows raised in question. He might have donated land for the church but he didn't have to put the young lady in a compromising position.

Merci didn't blink an eye. "Very well. I'll be there Wednesday afternoon, just before closing. Please insure there are other workers there."

Horst nodded, his attention once more on his sausage. "Goot."

Sarah started to object, but Merci gave a warning look and shook her head to dissuade her.

They cleaned up the table and began circulating again, Sarah introducing the women to many of the couples in the community.

Merci danced with the deputy, a nice-looking young man who was obviously smitten with the beauty upon sight.

Lillie got deep in conversation about quilting patterns with one of the women in the monthly sewing circle.

Sarah, bored, wished she had what Mr. Lebowitz

called chutzpah. If she had whatever that was, she would be walking home and curling up in bed with her new novel right now. She had ordered it from St. Louis last month and it finally came in by train two days ago. However, the business had been so busy lately and she'd been so tired that the book was still wrapped and waiting for her.

"Wonderful party."

She turned. Ben stood at her shoulder, his smile warm and sexy.

Her breath caught in her throat but she refused to let him know just how much his presence affected her. She didn't understand it herself, yet. "It is. And you seem to be having a wonderful time."

"The citizens of Clear Creek are more than kind. I've met many I would like to know better when circumstances permit."

"Knowing this town," Sarah said dryly, "I would imagine you'll be asked to dinner for the next month without a break."

"Is that because of the townspeople, or because of my scintillating personality?"

"Both. And your title doesn't hurt, either."

"I don't use it. Besides, my brother and I are twins. Not one and the same." His voice held an edge to it.

Sarah wasn't surprised. It must have been very hard to live in a household where one was never good enough to do more than shore up a lineage in case of death. She had a feeling that he had suffered from that position far more than he let on.

"And how is Mrs. Givson?" she asked, changing the subject.

"She's a very nice lady, as you said."

Sarah smiled even though she didn't feel like it. Benjamin was all wrong with Chloe. But if they didn't know it, why should she tell them and risk losing her trunks? "I'm glad you two are managing."

"What an odd word to use, Sarah." He gazed down at her as if reading her face. Or her thoughts. "Don't you believe in love?"

Her heart sank. So that was it. He was deeply in love with Chloe and wanted everyone to know just how it felt to be in love.

"I believe in it. I just never experienced what the silliness of love is like." She looked up at him. "And I don't want to know. I want to be able to go about my life without interference."

"And a man will interfere?"

She sighed. Why were men so blind? "Yes."

"I'm beginning to get the picture, Sarah," he said quietly. "Always be friends but never lovers." He smiled wistfully. "In that case, will you dance with me?"

"I'm in mourning."

"I didn't ask you to forget your husband. I asked you to dance." Without paying attention to her refusal, he took her hand and led her to the dance floor. "You can remember him as we go around the floor."

One hand over hers, the other hand on her waist, Ben slowly waltzed her around the room with other couples. Sarah's heart pounded in rhythm to the music, her gaze on his handsome face. Their steps fit perfectly. His eyes held hers, his gaze velvet-blue and seeking. Saying. Speaking things she didn't want to hear, couldn't look away from. She was mesmerized by everything about him, including his mere presence.

As the musicians wound down their song, the rest of the dancers slowed also. But Sarah barely noticed when that happened. One minute they were dancing, the next they were on the far side of the room swaying to music that wasn't playing. Ben's hand was still on her waist, his palm heated against her dress.

She looked around in surprise, seeing the dance floor empty. "Mr. Drake," she admonished, trying to sound stern and knowing she sounded breathless instead. "That's no way to act in mixed company."

His hand dropped quickly and he stepped back. "Speaking of which, where is Lillie the Outspoken?"

Sarah laughed. "She would like that title. She's with some members of the sewing group," she said, glad to get back on even footing again. "And we have a new member of the household. I'd like you to meet her. She's from Bixby, Arizona Territory, and her name is Sister Merci."

"Bixby?" Ben said, his interest piqued. "I just came from that area, but I never met a nun."

Sarah looked around, trying to find her houseguest. "She's not a nun, Ben. I believe she's part of the new Protestant group who does good works for others through the church. She's very pretty, beautiful really."

"Prettier than you?" Ben teased.

Sarah felt herself flush. "Stop flirting, Ben. We both know I'm not pretty, and I'm not your type," she admonished with a smile she hoped covered up her flustered state.

"And we both know the first isn't true, and it's not my type that you're worried about. It's the other way around. I'm not your type, Sarah."

"What do you think my type is?"

"Someone who won't make any demands or frighten you by making demands that you're not ready for. Who will stay away from you until you make the first move."

"That's poppycock," she stated.

"Is it?" His blue eyes delved into her. "Then why don't you let any male close to you?"

"I'm a recent widow, Mr. Drake," she stated stiffly. "I have another five months of mourning to go before I can even think of someone in my life."

"Not someone. Some man." Ben gave her a disbelieving look. "And we both know that only those in high society of New York, Paris or London pay attention to that folderol." He stood directly in front of her. "No one west of the Mississippi would wait for a year to begin life again unless they didn't want to get involved or were living in a cave. Survival makes us all cling together."

She couldn't think. His nearness was more disconcerting than she could have ever believed. Her breath was shallow. If she looked straight ahead, he filled her vision from broad shoulders to trim thighs encased in well-fitted pants.

She stepped back, fighting for breath.

"Is something the matter?" Ben's voice sounded far away.

"No. I . . . "

His hand wrapped around her arm and he led her around the makeshift dance floor where a rousing square dance was being played. They stepped out the door and down the boardwalk a few feet. There were several others outside, smoking and talking, but no one payed too much attention to the two who stopped at the dark railing.

"I'm sorry," Sarah finally murmured, leaning her hip against the rail and staring up at the moon. Its light poured down on the rooftops and spilled onto the partially cobblestoned street. Just enough light shone to turn horses and carriages into silhouettes . . . and to shadow the vulnerable expression in her eyes. "I have been so busy."

"Hiding behind busyness, Sarah? I thought you were more honest than that," Ben chided softly.

"I am honest," she defended herself. "I have been busy and I am not interested in flirting with you. You're supposed to be interested in finding a wife. Don't you think that's something you should pursue instead of trifling with every woman who walks in front of you?"

"There you go, tilting at windmills again," Ben said with a deep sigh. His hand held hers, his thumb rubbing the center of her palm in a mesmerizing motion that filled her with yearnings she hadn't felt since she was a young girl first noticing boys.

"I don't know what you mean." She sounded stiff but couldn't help it. She would *not* allow him to know his effect on her. She would show him just how impervious she was to his charm.

"No, I would guess that you don't." Ben seemed tired of flirting. He raised an eyebrow in question.

"You don't need to be outside, Mr. Drake. I'm sure Chloe will be wondering where you are."

"Chloe be damned," he muttered, his mouth twisting wryly.

"Is something wrong between you? Did you two have an argument?"

"No," Ben said. "Nothing is wrong and we didn't have an argument."

"Then why aren't you with her?"

"Because she's talking to some other women and

I felt out of place discussing patterns and babies
and the proper way to heat tea.''

Sarah smiled. Suddenly she felt lighter of heart.
"Poor you. All this sacrifice to gain a wife.''

"It's not too bad . . . if you like the wife-to-be.''
He stared out at the darkness across the street, his
face somber.

Her hand shook slightly. "And do you?''

That question brought his intense gaze back to
her. He hesitated just a moment before flashing a
smile. "Could we discuss this another time? I'm
standing in the moonlight with a beautiful if obsti-
nate woman and I would like to enjoy the moment.
After all, I'm only a man. . . .''

Sarah's eyes rounded. "Oh.''

Ben chuckled. "Look at the moon,'' he said
softly, pulling her closer to the warmth of his body
and allowing her to share his heat. "It's as round
and full as your mouth.''

The scent of him filled her lungs, tingling her
nerves all the way down to her toes. "Don't make
fun of me,'' Sarah said. "I may be more naive than
you, but I'm not a child.''

His head bent closer, his broad shoulders
blocking out the people standing behind him. "I
was hoping you'd say that.'' His voice was a mere
whisper, the sound rasping down her spine like
gentle fingers.

Her mouth opened slightly, her eyes half closed
from his nearness. What was it about him that made
her react so very differently to him? She didn't
react that way with any other man. Ever. Not even
Thomas.

Thomas.

She placed her hand on his chest. "Don't.
Please.'' It was more like begging than a plea.

"Don't stop me," he said, his voice the same rough whisper. He placed a finger under her chin and bent his head toward her mouth. Their warm breath mingled.

"Sarah?" Lillie's voice sounded hesitant. Not at all like she usually was.

Ben stiffened but didn't move. Sarah stared up at him, her own voice stilled in her throat. "Answer her," he said softly.

Sarah cleared her throat. Then cleared it again. "I'm here, Lillie."

Ben raised his head slightly and Sarah took a deep breath, only then realizing she had been holding it.

Lillie walked around Ben's big back and stopped as she reached Sarah's shoulder. She looked back and forth at Ben and Sarah, her eyes taking in the somber expressions on both their faces. "Is everything all right?"

"Everything's fine," Ben said with a smile that didn't reach his eyes. "Sarah was feeling a little light-headed from dancing and I thought I'd better get her some air. She's doing much better now."

"Sarah?"

"Fine. I'm fine," Sarah repeated, slowly returning to the present. "Are you ready to go?"

"Yes. So is Merci. She's waiting by the door with your cape. And my tired old bones can't stay up any longer." She looked at Ben as she spoke. "Do you want Mr. Drake to take you home later?"

"Yes," Ben said.

"No," Sarah overrode, pulling back to put more space between them. "I'm leaving now, with you." For the first time she realized just how cold it was outside. She was without cloak or hat, and chilled to the bone. She began shaking. "Thank you for your company, Mr. Drake. I appreciate it. I'll speak to you another time."

"Fine, Mrs. Hornsby," he said, his low voice speaking to her back as she turned away.

Leaning against the post, he picked a small cheroot from his waist pocket, struck a match and lit it in the darkness. His eyes watched every nuance as she walked away from him and toward the door where a tall, thin woman stood in the shadows holding a cape. Sarah slipped the fabric over her shoulders and the three women walked down the steps and across the cobblestones. Their capes flowed around them but their bare heads all moved distinctly.

He frowned. There was something vaguely familiar about the tall woman's profile. He narrowed his gaze and searched his memory.

Nothing came to mind.

". . . and then Chloe walked off in a huff and Ben just stood there, smoking his cigar and frowning!" Mrs. Emerson's voice raised at the end of the story. She had the attention of all five of the women in the shop.

"Does that mean she won't have him back?" one young girl asked wistfully.

"I would imagine that *he* won't have *her* back, dear," Mrs. Emerson pronounced with authority. "Any woman who throws a temper tantrum in public like that for whatever reason doesn't deserve to have an elegant man like Mr. Drake in her life."

"Yes, but she's so rich," the young girl said. "I heard she's got a cattle ranch in Montana!"

"I heard she throws temper tantrums all the

time," said one of the town matrons with an authoritarian nod.

"She should have waited until they were married," Mrs. Emerson put in her two cents' worth.

"Why? So he could be miserable the rest of his born days?"

"At least he'd be miserable rich."

Sarah came into the store area carrying a load of newly crocheted ecru napkins. "At least he wouldn't be the object of gossip.

"And he has some money of his own, as well as a title. That ought to have pleased her to no end. The least she could have done is been private about whatever bothered her."

"Now, Sarah," Mrs. Emerson said. "You know you might very well be the object of their argument."

Sarah's brows raised. She ignored her rapid heartbeat thumping against her breastbone. "I'm not. But thank you for the farfetched compliment."

"Didn't he meet Mrs. Givens because of you?"

She spread the napkins across the dresser top to display them properly. She didn't look at any of the ladies in the room. It was easier not to. "Yes, he did. We are friends. We are *not* anything else you can imagine."

There was a long drawn-out silence as the women looked at each other . . . and imagined.

"Well," Mrs. Emerson said as she stood and walked to the dresser to view the napkins. "All I know is that I can't wait to see who's going to snatch His Lordship Drake up next. This is the best gossip since '84, when old James Nunn had that affair with the wicked Myrtle and the town watched as his wife took the shotgun to the hotel window, blasting glass all over the place."

Two of the women giggled, while one of the young girls grew a shocked look and her eyes got as big as eyeglass lenses. "Really?" she whispered.

"Oh, yes," Mrs. Emerson confirmed as she chose four of the napkins and turned to face her audience. "She sprayed so much glass it cut him on the shoulders and neck when he was clear across the room. And that hussy had cuts all over her legs and, uh, bosom. And that's not all. He was unable to sit down for months, he had so much glass in his bare, well, you know."

Even Sarah's mouth popped open at that rendition of the story.

"I know," Mrs. Emerson said wisely, enjoying her audience's rapt attention. "I was walking out of the general store at the time, buying some needle and thread, don't you know. And I saw the whole thing. They had to carry him down the stairs with a sheet draped over his bare body to get him to the doctor's office. He screamed all the way, but he still couldn't scream as loudly as that Myrtle! Why, she sounded like an Irish banshee, the sheriff said. He oughta know. He's from the Emerald Isle, you know, and swears he's heard them before."

"My word," Mrs. Hillsmore said. "I'd heard that story, but I never really believed it."

"It's true," Mrs. Emerson stated. "I saw it with my own two eyes."

"No, Frances, I mean about the banshee wails."

"Oh, well, that's true too," she said. "Anyway. It will be interesting to see who Lord Benjamin is with next."

"What makes you think he'll be with anyone?"

Sarah asked; her curiosity at what the other woman had been saying was at a peak.

One of the older women looked at Sarah over her wire eyeglass rims. "Do you honestly believe that a man as handsome as he is will stay single very long?"

"Why not?" she asked, stubbornly persisting it was a possibility.

"Because his kind has to have someone to care for his social life and take care of him. And he needs children to carry on."

The other women nodded sagely in agreement.

"Perhaps," Sarah said, smoothing a piece of fabric hung over a chair. It was busywork to keep her from looking at the women she refused to agree with.

And she was sure the women knew it.

Chapter Eight

All the women in the household had plans.

Lillie left at dawn in the wagon, heading for San Antonio to pick up some lace and deliver different cottons to a few of their women in the area. She would also keep her eye out for new items that seemed to be needed.

Also early that morning, Merci donned her worn black coat and hat, then took the large casserole dish off the table counter, placing it inside a fabric bag. "I will be back in two days' time. Three at the most," she promised, as if Sarah needed to be reassured that she would return.

In truth, it was Merci who needed that reassurance. In the nine days she'd been with Sarah, Sarah had learned just how vulnerable she was. She didn't have the heart to ask Merci to go or to find another place for her at this time. Instead, she'd found another bed and set it up just a few feet from Lillie's, placing a large dresser between them for

privacy. It seemed to have satisfied all the women
and made Merci work all the harder for the shop.
. This day Merci was going to visit one of the
women who sewed quilts for them several miles
out of town. Sarah had received a small shipment
of fabrics and wanted them put together.

The older seamstress, July Hastings, had a small
house nine miles from town, just steps from Peach
Creek. Merci had offered to ride to her home and
deliver the goods needed to make the new quilts.
She would spend the two nights and visit another
ranch on the way, then return.

Sarah was sure Merci was looking forward to it.
It might even be that she was looking for another
place to settle and wanted to see if she and the older
woman were compatible enough to live together.
Sarah didn't think so, but she wasn't sure of anything. Right now, even her own feelings weren't
making sense to her.

Lillie had traveled in the opposite direction. Old
Mr. Anchors had gone with her, to visit his sister
in San Antonio.

For the first time since Lillie had come to live
with her four months earlier, Sarah was alone for
more than an afternoon.

It was exciting.

She thought of a hundred different things she
wanted to do in the evening.

She would sew.

She would bake biscuits.

She would change the display in the window.

She would clean out her small dresser.

She would find the screen she wanted to separate
Lillie's bed from the kitchen, so the older woman
could feel as if she had her own room ... and
some privacy.

She would dine at the hotel.

She would wash her hair and let it hang loose to dry all evening long.

Sarah smiled.

Shortly after Merci left, Sarah opened the shop and began a busy day's work. The chilly weather had broken and it was warm and beautiful outside. In fact, it was so nice that Sarah opened the rear door and let the breeze flow through the long length of the room to air out the scent of dyes.

Business was brisk for the lookers and gossipers. Sarah constantly filled the coffee and teapots. It was part of her service. If she didn't, half the women wouldn't stay around to buy. Instead, they would probably sew it themselves.

By the time the day was over, Sarah was tired of smiling. She hadn't realized just how much of a help Lillie had become. Aside from helper and friend, she was also a part of Sarah's business, knowing as much as Sarah did.

After closing the door and window curtains, Sarah took the last of the tea and sat down with it, enjoying the sudden quiet.

Suddenly, she was lonely. Used to sharing little tidbits with Lillie, she had no one to talk to. She glanced at the kitchen area and decided this was the night to dine in the hotel.

Energy flowed through her body, revitalizing her as she lifted her skirt and bounded up the stairs. In a minute she was stripped down to her chemise.

With Ben's comments about mourning still ringing in her ears, it took no time at all to choose an outfit. A grosgrain skirt—considered the cutting edge of style when she bought it—and a smart military-style jacket over a plain white blouse was her choice. It was one of her favorites. She hadn't worn it since the first year of her marriage, but, then, the West didn't have much use for such a frivolous outfit. Gingham and cottons were the dress of choice here. She checked the mirror and was surprised at what she saw. She looked as if she were Thomas's wife again. She belonged to someone. It was an unusual but comforting feeling. One she was familiar with amid the sea of other unlabeled emotions she'd been through lately.

She took the matching hat out of one of the hatboxes stacked neatly in the corner of the loft and tilted it at just the right angle.

It was a strange feeling, and one she wasn't yet willing to delve into.

Half an hour later and wishing that Merci had been home to help her with her hair, Sarah walked into the dining room of the hotel. With a gracious nod of her head, she accepted the same table she'd dined at with Ben.

Two other women sat quietly dining across the room from her. She felt their eyes, and knew if they were visiting from the East, they would think it scandalous for a woman to dine alone. But this was the West, and things were done differently, thank goodness!

Her gaze was calm and strong as she returned their look. They had the graciousness to look down and turn away quickly. Shortly after, the waitress took her order. "And please add a cup of tea to my order of chicken and dumplings."

As the young waitress returned to the kitchen, Sarah wished she'd waited to come here instead of dining alone. When the food came, Sarah ate quickly, suddenly wanting to go back to her own quiet place and relax without scrutiny. It wasn't as much fun without the company of others.

Placing her money carefully on the side of the table, she grabbed her reticule and quickly walked out of the dining area. As she passed the front desk, she smiled at young Thomas behind the hotel desk.

He grinned back and came around the desk to open the door for Sarah. Instead of making way for her to step out, however, Thomas's hand hesitated. "Is Sister Merci staying with you, Mrs. Hornsby?"

"Yes, she is," Sarah said, surprised he'd heard of her already.

His face reddened. "I saw her at the Literary Dinner," he confessed. "She's so beautiful."

"Yes, and I'll tell her you said so. She'll be flattered."

"No . . . I . . . " Thomas began, blushing even more. Suddenly, a shadow filled the door and blocked out the light from the gas lamp just outside the hotel boardwalk.

They both looked up.

Benjamin Drake stood in the doorway, a black coat wrapped around him, a matching black scarf around the collar. The hat was beaver, and the darkness of it blended with his hair, making him look taller and more imposing than he already was.

"Ben, let me get in from the chilled night air. If you insist on dining here, at least allow me entrance first."

Until then, Sarah didn't notice the black, glove-clad arm wrapped around his. Chloe.

Sarah stepped back and they all stood in the suddenly crowded entry.

Chloe's eyes widened and she tightened her grip

on Ben's arm. "Why, hello, Sarah. What are you doing here?" Her gaze darted to the stairs, then back at Sarah again.

Sarah smiled tightly. "Since I'm alone this evening, I decided to treat myself to dinner."

"Really? Where is Lillie?" Ben asked, his gaze narrowing. "Is she all right?"

"She's fine. She's picking up supplies in San Antonio."

His gaze narrowed even more. "Alone?"

"No," Sarah said patiently, wishing she was anywhere but here. This was uncomfortable.

"I hear you've adopted another waif," Chloe said, her tone just the slightest bit patronizing. Sarah bet she wouldn't have been acting quite this way if they had been alone. It was all for Ben. "A nun or something?"

"Sister Merci isn't a nun, just a woman trying to help others."

"I see. And how does she help others?"

"In many ways."

"Explain," Ben said gently.

"She's visiting some of our seamstresses right now." Sarah shrugged. "She helps."

"That's important."

She smiled. He understood. "Yes."

"So you're all by yourself tonight." Chloe's voice sounded just the tiniest bit shrill. "Such a shame you've already eaten, or you could've dined with us."

"Thank you, but I have plans for tonight," Sarah said, suddenly relaxed. She was going to do what she wanted, and wash her hair.

"With anyone in particular?"

"No." She smiled again to lessen the shortness of her answer. "Have a good night."

"We will. And we hope you do, too," Chloe said, willing to be generous since Sarah wasn't encroaching on her.

As Sarah walked back to the store she felt Ben's eyes on her back. It warmed her through and through.

Half an hour later the stoked stove warmed the room as it boiled water and Sarah prepared for the shampoo. Since she had all the time and no one around, she'd taken her bath and donned a new nightgown. It was a treat, for she'd taken one of her favorite gowns on display. The moment she saw the pale peach flannel with its long, puffed sleeves and scooped beribboned neck, she fell in love with it.

She washed her hair with the shampoo she'd bought during her first trip to Houston when she was seeking a place to settle and call home. Shopping in the large town of Houston had been an experience. The shops had everything, including soaps and shampoos from France. She'd chosen one that smelled of lavender and tea roses, and just the scent of it made her relax and smile.

The shampoo frothed and bubbled as she rubbed it into her long hair. She luxuriated in the feeling and flow of the water and slick soap as it ran through her fingers. Her thoughts and worries disappeared as she concentrated on the task at hand.

After rinsing with warmed water, Sarah wrapped a bath sheet around her head and poured the tea she'd brewed into her best china cup.

The tinny music of the old piano played gently through the wall as the player began an old Irish ballad. Taking off the towel and beginning to brush her hair, Sarah halted in the task as she wondered who was playing. The music sounded more melancholy than most tunes played in the saloon.

She remembered the four women who stayed upstairs most of the time, unseen by most of the townsfolk. They were young and tired, with the bright light of anticipating life gone from their eyes. It was such a shame to see women so young feel so sad that it washed over her like a wave, enveloping her to feel the same for a little while.

Her hair crackled as she brushed it in front of the fire, the motion mesmerizing her with the peacefulness of the action. She kept in time with the music. Her hair draped over her shoulder to fall just inches short of the well-worn wooden floor. She continued to brush it dry, her thoughts drifting in and out of the story of her life, not making ripples, just indecisive thoughts.

She smiled to herself and switched her hair to the other shoulder to brush.

For everything that brought her to this point, and everything that she had suffered to get where she was, she was so very glad she was here. Now.

The music changed from an old Irish ballad to a toe-tapping version of a waltz, the sound vibrating through the floor to faintly tickle the soles of her bare feet. She wiggled her toes in tune to the beat.

The evening went quickly, and by the time her hair was dry, her eyelids were drooping. She hadn't been this relaxed since she was an innocent child.

With slow movements, she stoked the fire and rinsed out her teacup. She lit a candle, then extinguished the gas lamp in the front area and walked up the stairs to her bedroom. At the top of the stairs, she stopped and stared at the area.

It was plain but clean, and ... feminine. She looked at the Battenburg lace-and-cotton duvet and matching pillow covers that were carefully piled against the headboard of her iron bed. Yes. Definitely feminine.

She placed the candle on the table next to her bed and pulled the duvet down, ready to crawl onto the soft feather mattress. One knee in the middle of the bed. And then she jumped at the soft sound of a knock on the door that led to the upper hotel hallway.

Ben.

Just the same, Sarah tiptoed to the door and put her head against it. "Who's there?"

"Guess." Ben's voice was low and sweet.

She took a deep breath as if breathing wasn't a habit. "It's late."

"You're up."

"That doesn't mean I have to open the door."

"Then I'll sing to you all night from the hallway," he said, still speaking softly. "You'll be awake all night until you'll hate every word I sing."

"I don't hate anything."

He gave a low chuckle. "You haven't heard me sing."

Her heart smiled at his self-deprecating humor. "Are you saying it will be a first?"

He chuckled. "It will be if you open the door."

"What do you have to say that can't wait until tomorrow morning?"

"If you don't open the door, you'll never know, will you?"

She smiled. He was adorable. It was a good thing she wasn't going to open the door. "Good night, Ben. I'll see you in the morning. I'm making biscuits for breakfast. See you then?"

"I'll take you home, Irene," he began singing in a low tenor. Sarah grinned, but she backed away from the door. As if he knew, his voice got a little louder with each step she took. "And I'll never leave your side again. . . ."

She crawled into bed and pulled up the duvet to her chin.

"Daisy, Daisy, give me your answer, do. I'm half crazy all for the love of you."

Sarah was still smiling.

"I can't afford a carriage . . ."

She began to giggle like a young girl.

"But you'll look sweet upon the seat of a bicycle built for two!"

Her laughter couldn't be contained.

"Daisy, Daisy," Ben began again, and this time it was a little louder.

Sarah bounded back out of bed. "Shhhhh," she said loudly. "If you keep it up, someone will hear you."

"That's the point."

"They'll wonder what you're doing at my door."

"Then open it up and let me in."

"Come back tomorrow."

"Daisy, Daisy," he began. This time he was singing at the top of his lungs.

Quickly, Sarah moved the board away from the door, grabbed the key from the hook on the wall and slipped it into the hole. Equally as fast, she opened the door. Ben stood leaning against the side wall, his collar gone, his suit jacket open, the strong column of his throat tight with song.

He had the biggest grin on his face—one that showed the depth of his dimples and the mischievous glint in his blue eyes.

She didn't waste any time. Grabbing his sleeve, she pulled him into her room and closed the door behind him.

"Thank you." He grinned. "You kept me from a fate worse than death. You saved me from myself."

Sarah pushed him over to the slipper chair and sat him down. Then, with arms crossed, she stared down at him. "Now, tell me what is going on that can't wait until tomorrow to discuss?"

Ben heaved a sigh and looked so sad, Sarah almost believed him. Almost. . . .

"Chloe isn't the one for me."

Sarah didn't move. She couldn't. Her mind was disappointed but her heart was tripping over itself in happiness. "You're serious, aren't you?"

"I mean it. She's not the one for me. Please start looking for someone else."

"Someone else? *Who* someone else?" she asked, her mind in a turmoil.

Ben shrugged and gave a sheepish grin. "I don't know. Someone. Anyone."

Visions of ribbons and lace daintily floating across the great Atlantic Ocean suddenly sank beneath foamy waves of depression. But not enough depression to stop her heart from its frantic beating.

She tried to gather her thoughts. "And where do you suggest I find another heiress?"

"Widow. I asked for a widow." Ben took in her nightgown and smiled his appreciation. "Pretty gown."

"No, you asked for a widow that you could get along with. Marry," she said, her mind still on the problem. "And I gave you over to the best choice I had."

"Then find me the best choice *for me*." He saw her toes peeping from beneath the small ruffle at the bottom of her gown. "Nice toes."

"Thank you," she said absently. "I have a few

thoughts on the next one, but first I have to know what went wrong with this one.'' She sat on the side of her bed and faced him. ''What went wrong? You two seemed so perfect for each other at the Literary Dinner.''

''She organizes every move I make and then gives me a grade on it. I pass table manners, but I don't pass attention to detail because I didn't notice when her peas were gone from her plate.''

''So?''

''So I decided that if she didn't like my boots and told me how to tie my cravat, I didn't need to further offend her by telling her she was a country bumpkin with no charm or reason for being.''

Sarah's eyes widened. Odd, but he was right. That had been Sarah's first impression of Chloe. It had also been her last. Once Ben had seemed settled with her, Sarah had begun to count on the marriage as if it were fact.

''You're sure?'' she asked before her last drop of hope for the trunks sank to her toes . . . the very toes Ben liked. She looked down at the offending appendages. She straightened her legs out to get a better glimpse.

''I told you they were nice,'' he said with a smile in his voice. ''Worthy of sucking.''

Her gaze darted up, eyes wide and startled. ''What?''

His smile was slow in coming from his voice to his face. ''You heard me.''

''That is sick.''

''If you say so.''

''Is that what you expect from your bride-to-be?''

Ben shrugged. ''Not unless she likes it too.''

''I see.'' Sarah said, concentrating all her thoughts on her toes. The image of Ben doing just that sent heat through her body. The heat of a blush stained her all the way from her cheeks to her waist. "That's disgusting."

Ben laughed. It was a low, mellow sound that ran down her spine like warm lotion. "That's more revealing than you can possibly imagine."

"Really," she drawled, full of bravado on the outside while she quaked on the inside. "And you know women who would love to have that done?"

"Of course." His smile was an indication that he was remembering something she didn't want to know about. It was none of her business. "Who?"

"Several."

"Who?"

His grin turned to a chuckle. "Well, the most recent, uh, episode, was in Tombstone. A charming young lady of the evening I spent a few weeks with before visiting here."

"You're drunk."

"No, uh, well, perhaps." His expression was sheepish. "Just a little."

"It's time to go back to your room."

"But what about my problem?"

"You don't have a problem."

"I need a bride."

Sarah sighed and stood. "I know. You need someone who can put up with all your . . . quirks and still thinks they're sweet."

"Do you?" he asked, standing too. They were so close, Sarah could smell his aftershave.

He towered over her, his gaze glowing in the candlelight. His hand came out and twisted a long strand of hair around his finger, then around his wrist. "Do you?" His voice was a mere whisper.

She forgot the question. She forgot his answer. She forgot everything except that he was so close to her they were breathing the same air. His breath held the scent of brandy and cigars and it was so very pleasant.

Too pleasant. "Ben," she said.

"No." He placed his free hand lightly over her mouth. "Not a word, Sarah," he said. "Just this once, not a damn word." His hand tightened in her hair, his fingers twisting the strands around as he gently pulled her forward. Toward him, closer and closer. His fingers caressed the outline of her mouth, following the full curve of her lips.

"Damn," he whispered just before covering her mouth with his own. It was gentle, fragile as a butterfly before he pulled away and stared at her mouth again. "Damn," he said, but this time she barely heard him. His mouth covered hers again, then again, each time at a different angle with a lighter touch and a softer sigh.

She craved for him to stay. Not to pull away. She loved it when he returned to her mouth again and again with a tenderness that made her want so much that her heart and head filled with it. Every nerve was tuned to him and, although her body never moved to touch his, her skin and bones and muscles and thoughts were fluid and jelled.

"So wonderful," he said just seconds before taking her lips with his own, this time running his tongue around her parted mouth. "Open your mouth, Sarah. Open it and let me in," he said.

She did what he asked, and she was glad she did. With firm gentleness, he took her mouth and shared the most wondrous feeling she'd ever experienced.

She felt as if she was on fire in places so wonderful, so thrilled. Heat filled every corner and nook and cranny in her, made her swell, made her fluid,

teasing and tempting and promising something—
something she couldn't put her finger on or call
a name. The heat filled her, making her restless.
A small sound mewed in her throat and escaped
into his.

Reacting instantly, Ben pulled back, unwinding
his fingers from her long hair. "Oh, my God, I'm
so sorry. I . . . I . . . Damn!" he said.

"Shhhh," she said, reassuring him.

Ben ran a hand through his hair. "Listen,
Sarah," he said, his tone filled with regret he didn't
have to put into words for her to understand. "I
didn't mean for that to happen. But I saw your lips
and they were so . . . it was just so . . . damn!"

Suddenly, she realized what he was saying. He was
embarrassed he'd stooped to kiss her. But not half
as embarrassed as she felt at acting wanton. . . .

"Please leave," she said, standing as tall as she
could in her bare feet. "I think it's best."

"Yes, of course." He stepped back and bumped
into the slipper chair. He stepped aside and walked
to the door. "Thank you, Sarah," he said. "It was
a wonderful gift."

"Just go," she replied, every inch of her dignity
at the fore.

He opened the door and stood looking over his
shoulder at her for what seemed like an eternity.

An instant.

"I'll see you tomorrow," he said.

She couldn't talk. Couldn't speak.

Instead, she nodded.

"Sleep well, Mrs. Hornsby."

The door slowly closed and she was once more
left alone in her shop. In her home.

But not quite so alone in her heart. . . .

Chapter Nine

After the initial euphoria wore off, Sarah was scared.

She had spent the entire night regretting opening the door to Benjamin Drake. She relived his kiss over and over, finally acknowledging that her toes—the very toes that had begun the sensuous conversation about sex—had actually curled when Ben kissed her! Curled!

As embarrassed as she was for her reaction, she would be forever thankful for that kiss. It proved that she was human after all. A feminine being. Something she had never thought herself to be.

She wanted to hate Ben, and she wanted to kiss him again for creating such a reaction and making her feel as if she wasn't a wooden character moving like a carved wooden Indian through life.

She didn't know how she would cope with the embarrassment of seeing him again, but secretly, she was excited at the thought.

She also didn't know what it meant.

Staring at her bare toes peeping from under the coverlet, Sarah knew with certainty that just the thought of Ben's mouth . . .

She changed that thought immediately.

But what made her sit up straight in the center of her bed was the knock on the door between her and the hotel.

"Open up."

It was Ben's voice, and her heart skipped beats as she waited for him to leave. She would not answer.

"Sarah! Open up."

Sarah eased off the bed, quickly stripped off her new gown and slipped into her clothing.

"Sarah, please."

She began brushing her hair back, then braided it into a crown on her head.

"Sarah! Please!"

She slipped black hairpins into her braid.

With quick movements, she glanced in the mirror, checked her dress from the front and rear, touched her crown of braid and started down the steps. She still had to brush her teeth and wash her face in the kitchen area.

There was another series of knocks. Then there was silence. Sarah tried not to listen as she put the kettle on and began making a ring of flour. She added milk, then lard, her hands busy with the task, her mind concentrating on what she was doing. In less than fifteen minutes she had placed a bowl of dough on the center of the kitchen table, covered it with a towel and begun finishing her own toilette. The dough wouldn't be ready for another fifteen or twenty minutes or so, and that gave her plenty of time to get the rest of the chores done.

By the time the biscuits were baked, Sarah had

filled pots with butter, jams and jellies and set them on a tray. Coffee and tea were ready for her customers. The pendulum clock on the wall by the stairs said the doors would open in half an hour. Good, that would give her time to straighten up and sweep the front area.

She donned her apron and reached for the broom. Opening the front door, she swept the threshold first. *Keep busy. Keep busy.* Her mind focused on the words instead of any of the random thoughts that might intrude.

She hadn't thought ahead far enough or she would have known not to open the door before she was ready to open the store.

Ben strode down the boardwalk and stood in front of her before Sarah could move. "Inside, please."

Sarah held the broom in front of her as if it were a thousand-pound block Ben couldn't get through. "No."

"Fine, then we can have our conversation right here, where everyone can hear, Mrs. Hornsby," he said. He was smiling, but it certainly didn't reach his eyes. His blue gaze was frosted with anger. "I want to discuss last night."

Two women, dressed for shopping, walked past. They might not have heard Ben's words, but they certainly understood the no-nonsense tone. Their eyes widened as they looked at Sarah curiously.

She smiled sweetly and stepped back. "Please come in. I have fifteen minutes before the store officially opens." Her tone was not loud, but loud enough to have the other women hear.

Ben followed her in and closed the door behind her. The chilly air swirled around them, but it didn't matter. They were both so hot with anger they had their own heat.

Blood pounded in her veins, but she knew she had to keep a cool head. "What could you possibly say that you would embarrass me in front of the town?" she asked coolly.

"All I wanted to do was apologize for last night. But when I tried to tell you this morning, you refused to answer the door, to speak to me through it or even to acknowledge me on the other side of the door."

She raised an intimidating brow. "And you believe I have no rights in this matter?"

It must not have been as intimidating as she thought, for he never hesitated in his answer. "You're bloody right I think that! You can't leave what happened last night without giving me time or explanation about the next step."

"Now, just a moment," she began, but he refused to stop.

"Or, knowing you, there won't be a next step. You'd rather not face me at all than discuss our way out of this mess, logically and intelligently."

"Now just a moment," she said in a calm voice, admiring herself for keeping her anger in check.

Still he didn't stop. "But you! You'd rather act as if I committed a sin and a crime instead of—"

She took a deep breath. *"Just a minute!"*

Ben looked at her, his anger still apparent, but at least she had his attention. She spoke again. "Just because you knock on my door, doesn't mean I have to answer. I may not have the right to vote but I *do* have the right to decide whom I allow in my home and speak to."

"You were embarrassed to talk to me."

"I was not."

"Yes, you were."

Sarah was going to bluff this through if it was the last thing she did. She stood tall and stared him straight in the eyes. "Mr. Drake, I said whatever needed saying last night. I have nothing more to discuss with you about that incident. It was something that happened late at night when we were both vulnerable. However, you are not my idea of a marriage partner—or any other kind of partner. I like my life just the way it is!"

The tension eased around his mouth and eyes. "Really?"

"You can be relieved, Benjamin. It's fine with me." Sarah's tone sounded bored with the entire conversation. But her heart was pounding like a blacksmith feverishly working on his anvil. "I want to find a suitable wife for you so you can order my laces and fabrics, and for both of us to live happier lives. Is that so hard to believe?"

The doubt in his eyes didn't match his words. "No, not at all. I'm just happy you feel the same way."

"I do." She glanced over at the clock, realizing that there was no time left to gather her thoughts. Three women were ready to cross the street, and she'd bet they were heading toward her shop.

Sarah squinted her eyes. One of them was just the woman she wanted to see.

"Don't leave yet," she said, fluffing the curtains she'd pulled back earlier. Quickly slipping her arms out of her apron, she hung it on the coatrack under her cape. "Stay still." She turned around. "No, pretend you're looking at something."

"What?"

"The quilt, look at the quilt!" Sarah felt the top of her head and made sure her braid was still in place, then quickly straightened the tea table that held the drinks and biscuits she'd put there just minutes before.

Just as Ben was about to question her sanity, the bell rang, announcing the customers. Sarah turned and smiled. "Why, good morning, ladies. How has your day begun?"

The three women walked in and smiled, but the secretive glances toward Ben showed their main interest. And when they looked back at Sarah, she knew they were wondering about the relationship between them.

"By the way, have any of you met Lord Benjamin? I mean, Mr. Drake?" she asked. "He's new to our community and has decided this might be the town to settle in and make his home."

All three women glowed with the news. Mrs. Owens was old enough to be his mother, but the other two ladies were both young and single. That had to stand for something. Besides, one of them was on her list of eligible women for Benjamin. Smiling sweetly, she made the introductions. Ben seemed as pleased as she was.

Or was it relief?

While the women spoke to Ben, Sarah reached for her biscuits and spread a few with Martha Good-man's homemade mayhaw jam, then cut them in fourths.

Keep busy. Keep busy.

"Mrs. Hornsby?" Ben's voice drew her attention back to the room.

She looked up to see Ben standing beside one of her younger customers, Judith Russell, his smile as bright as a shiny new penny. "Mrs. Hornsby, would you care to join us for luncheon at the hotel today?"

She smiled back, pretending regret. "No, thank you. As much as I would enjoy it, both Lillie and Sister Merci are away on business, so I'm doing triple duty these days."

"We're so sorry," Judith said, and Sarah was sure she was honest. The young woman was a little in awe of Sarah, if her behavior at church was any indication. "Please, if you feel you can get away, join us."

Sarah took the hand offered. "I will, but meantime, have some tea and biscuits," she said before excusing herself and joining the new customers walking in the door.

The morning was busier than ever, the day even more so. Sarah gave a few stray thoughts to Ben and his date, and said a few small prayers that he would find Judith attractive enough to marry and keep his part of the bargain by ordering her trunks full of fabrics and ribbons.

Fabric from England! Her mind reeled with the thought. That a small town in the middle of Texas could have such a wondrous thing as English cloth and ribbons for sale, was near a miracle in her mind. Why, hers could be the one place other women traveled to from all over the state to shop!

The fact that Ben could make all this possible if he just married and settled down long enough to order the goods, was enough to keep her hunting for a woman who would fit his criteria.

Late that night, after reading most of the evening, Sarah went to bed, tired but content. Lillie and Merci would be home in the next day or so, and they would have more stock to display and sell. It was exciting to think about what the goods would be and how they would display. It was the part that Sarah liked best.

She gave a short prayer that it would all work out for the best . . . the best being what she needed most, of course.

Ben walked home, his horse trailing behind him as he stared up at a full moon so bright, it lit up the rocks in the road and made them look like markers pointing the way back into the downtown area of Clear Creek.

Judith was a sweetheart of a young lady. At nineteen, she was almost too young for Ben. He felt even more jaded than his thirty-two years, but that came with the territory of his history. Meanwhile, here he was, looking for a bride to put up with him and settle their fortune on him in trust and marriage. It wasn't an easy decision for either of them. He'd met Judith's parents tonight, and they'd enjoyed a cigar out on the porch of the Russells' small ranch home just three miles outside of town.

After asking the ususal questions about Ben's family and past, Mr. Russell got right to the point. "I'm lookin' for someone to take care of my sweetie right and proper," Judith's father had said. "In return, I've got a growing business with the cotton gin and my own fields. Someday, whoever marries her and gives me grandchildren will have all that, too."

"That's a nice legacy," Ben said, sending smoke up in the air.

"Has to be the right man," her father had said meaningfully. "Someone who will take care of her properly and treat her like the lady she is."

"I can imagine how you feel," Ben had said.

Then he got directly to the point. "Are you in the market for a wife, Mr. Drake?"

"Eventually, sir," Ben had said slowly.

"Well, you couldn't do much better than someone like my Judith."

"I bet not, sir," Ben had said. Suddenly, he realized that the feeling of being smothered with wet rags was back. Just like with Chloe, he was stepping into a situation he didn't want.

"Well, I'm not favorable to anyone fooling with my daughter who's not honest and upright."

"I wouldn't be, either. However, I just met your daughter today, and at this point, I don't have any plans other than to enjoy this town and the people I've met."

The father had grown quiet then, and they'd both relaxed and enjoyed the rest of their cigars while the women cleaned up from dinner. But all Ben could think of was getting back to the hotel and talking to Sarah.

Now that he was on his way, he realized he couldn't talk to her. She wouldn't answer the door. She wouldn't talk to him until the store opened and there were people—women—surrounding her.

The thought of the kiss last night had haunted him all night and the next day. He'd never known such gentle caring touches—the sweetness filled his heart. And when he'd looked down to take his focus off his own instant reaction, her toes were curled in delight, too.

He grinned at the darkness. Imagine that.

And her eyes . . . those big brown eyes had grown as wide as tonight's moon. So bright and soft, like the Navasota Lake from which Peach Creek poured, he could have dived into them and swam around.

Ben reached the edge of town and stopped. His horse nudged his shoulder gently, but Ben ignored him. It was almost ten o'clock at night and the shops were closed, all locked doors and drawn curtains. The saloon doors were closed, but several horses were tied to the hitching rail in front. The lights within proved there were still people playing poker—or just plain playing.

The hotel was dim and several of the front rooms were dark, but Ben knew that young Thomas was on duty tonight, standing behind the desk, his head buried in whatever newest book he'd just gotten in the mail. He read dime westerns or classics. It didn't matter. He just had to read. Tom's ambition was to be a writer of pulp fiction. Everything he did was aimed in that direction.

Ben wished he'd been that focused as a kid. He might have been in a different place now, instead of searching for a bride to get what he wanted.

He looked at Sarah's shop, then past it to glance down the street at the jail.

Even though he was staying at the hotel, which should have put space between him and the rest of the citizens, he was becoming embroiled in the town's goings on. He liked the people and the camaraderie. He was even beginning to think of this small town on the outskirts of Houston as a home. That was more than he'd ever thought of any other place, other than his real home in England.

Odd. That wasn't his real home anymore. His last connection to it had died, and nothing in the manor house belonged to him other than a toy rocking horse and a few misplaced memories of dreams that were never fulfilled.

A light above the grocer's store dimmed.

All lights but one at the end of the street in the Heine household were out, in a room one of the men at the Literary Dinner had said was the front parlor but was used as an office. Mr. Heine must have decided to work late tonight. From everything he'd heard from Chloe about the man, Mr. Heine had no fun or secret or delicious personal life. Odd that such a handsome man would donate so much to the town. He had asked Ben to breakfast tomorrow. Ben didn't know what it was about, but he was interested in getting to know the man. He didn't think anyone in town was close to him.

From Ben's viewpoint, that was lonely. He ought to know; until coming to this town and meeting Sarah, and through her, others, he'd felt very alone, too.

Ben gave a cluck and a tug on the rein, and started walking down the street again. Three doors from the hotel was an alley that led to the stable. He aimed toward it, but his eyes were fixed on looking up at the window above Sarah's shop. There wasn't a floor there, her room was a loft at the rear. But there was a dim light still glowing through the darkness. She was awake.

He continued walking. He wondered what she was doing, what she was thinking. Did she ever think of him? Did she ever wonder, let her mind wander to the what ifs of their relationship? Like, what if they got together for a while? What if they made love? Would it work for a time? Would it be as good as he thought it would be? Or would they wish they'd both never taken that step into intimacy? Somehow he doubted it. In fact, his dreams were filled with visions of a naked Sarah.

But now wasn't the time to take chances with his

life. He had given himself two more months to find a wife. He didn't have the luxury to fool around with the very woman who could help him the most.

Leading his horse into the stable, Ben heard the young lad of about seven or eight who slept on a tattered bale of hay away from the doorway. Rubbing his eyes, the boy ran forward to grab the reins.

"He doesn't need a rubdown," Ben said. "He hasn't been ridden this evening."

The little guy looked relieved. "Thanks, mister."

Ben gave the boy a quarter and left slowly, making sure the barn door was closed a little tighter to keep out the chilling night air. It looked like things were bad enough for the lad, he didn't need to catch a cold, too.

In the hotel, he gave a nod to Thomas, and headed up the stairs, almost reluctant to go there. No one waited. No one cared. He was feeling sorry for himself and had a double case of wanderlust.

Without giving it another thought, Ben turned around and headed down the stairs.

"Did you forget something, sir?"

"Yes. A drink in the bar," Ben stated, and headed out the door and into the darkness of the boardwalk. A gaslight across the street dimly lit his way past Sarah's shop and into the saloon.

The piano player was winding up a fast little ditty that had two of the girls dancing with men who didn't have a clue how to dance. Worn boots stomped against the wooden floor as if they were hammering nails. The girls wore brave smiles as they endured the clumsy attempts.

He strolled over to a table in the corner under the stairs and sat down, back against the wall. There were a couple of men he recognized from the Literary Dinner. A few made eye contact, then nodded, but all stayed away. His brother, the duke, had made an impression on most people in town and they stood a little in awe of the title and the thought of growing up wealthy in England. They had no idea just how awful life could be under those circumstances.

Laughter echoed down the stairs, then a pair of long, lovely legs floated down, only to stop in the middle of the case and pose provocatively. Several groups of men slowed down in their conversation to watch the dramatic entrance, then turned back.

A glass and a bottle of expensive scotch was set on his table along with a wink and a nod from the bartender. He knew Ben would pay fair and square when he left.

Ben poured himself a glass, sipped and waited. Just a month ago, he'd spent two weeks in a Tombstone brothel much like this. He'd been with the bright and beautiful Fairy Princess, who had been a prostitute since the age of twelve. He'd never asked why and she'd never volunteered. They both had enjoyed each other's company and let it go at that. Perhaps he'd been reluctant, but he'd known better than to promise anything more than what they had shared. And she hadn't asked for more, either.

He downed another gulp and wished he felt better about life. But his emotions were unsettled and his thoughts scattered.

"Lord Benjamin?"

He looked up, surprised he hadn't heard anyone walk up to him. Too many thoughts and not enough paying attention. "Yes?" he asked the young saloon girl in front of him.

"Mr. Roberts"— she nodded her head in the direction of several men playing poker in the opposite corner of the room—"he wants ta know if you wanna play cards."

His brow rose. "Poker?"

She nodded, smiling.

Ben stood. "Why not," he said softly. But he wasn't in the mood for a woman. He wanted to win at something. Just one damn time. Something that didn't have anything to do with lineage, females or marriage.

Chapter Ten

Sarah sat in bed reading one of the new books she'd ordered from a bookstore in eastern Missouri. It was the story of a young girl from England who didn't marry by nineteen, so she would probably always be a spinster and never marry. Instead, she became a nanny for a wealthy duke.

The more Sarah read, the more she understood how Anthony and Benjamin must have lived. The confining rules and regulations as well as the wealth and station were unbelievably restricting compared to America in general and Texas in particular.

She completed a chapter and put the book down for a moment to absorb the scene. "Amazing!" she whispered to the empty room.

She was so deep in her thoughts she didn't notice the piano playing louder than usual. Or the raucous laugh. Or the argument that was building just on the other side of the wooden wall between her loft and the upstairs portion of the saloon. Occasionally, noise had come from that area, but not often enough to alarm her.

Instead, she continued to think about the book and lives it portrayed. Could this story have any basis in truth? Deep down, she knew it did, but wasn't sure just how much.

Was Anthony really told who to marry? And if so, why wasn't Benjamin?

Or was he?

A thousand questions flew through her thoughts, and none had answers except one: If he didn't have a wife, it wasn't because he couldn't find one. It was that he hadn't found *the Right One.*

Was there really such a thing?

Her eyelids drooped and she thought about turning off her lamp and falling asleep.

The argument between two or three men and a high-pitched yelling woman rose to a different octave. She continued to ignore it, thankful that Lillie wasn't downstairs trying to sleep.

For the first time since she'd moved from Blissful, Sarah had to admit she was lonely. She was glad both Lillie and Sister Merci would be back tomorrow. She had realized just how much she'd insulated herself against loneliness by the people she'd surrounded herself with. The few times she'd been alone, she'd treasured it instead of thinking of solitude as undesirable.

The voices got even louder, with the main shouting just on the other side of the wall.

Sarah didn't care. She placed a dried sprig of lavender in the book as a marker and blew out the oil lamp. With a yawn, she climbed back into bed and pulled the covers up to her chin. The fire had turned to embers in the big potbellied stove

downstairs and the chill in the air was beginning
to permeate even the upstairs.

She closed her eyes and instantly drifted into
sleep. Visions of ladies in ball gowns of satin and
silks, and men in top hats and spit-polished Hessian
boots danced through her dreams. She was the
heroine, flirting with Ben as if she were as sophisticated as he was—when he wasn't trying to pretend
he was a Texas cowboy in the middle of cotton
country. She was succeeding very well, saying all
the witty and sophisticated things she knew she
could, if she had the nerve.

Until the explosion.

The boom made Sarah's heart jump into her
throat. She bolted up in bed and stared straight
ahead at the wall that used to be solid wood
between her room and the saloon. The boom she
heard wasn't half as loud as the noise that rang in
her ears and flowed through her body.

In the darkness of her loft bedroom, a bright
swinging light blinded her from the view of the
shattered wall. Shouts buffeted back and forth
while several men shoved and pushed each other
through a large hole in her wall. They looked like
a huge hive pushing here, rolling there, none willing to let go of the others.

A woman in a thin chemise was silhouetted in
the gaping hole, her ear-splitting screams aimed
directly at Sarah's ears.

Sarah couldn't move.

Shadows and light swung back and forth, playing
on the walls, moving like a child's bogeyman, growing large, then small and grotesque with each
swing.

A menacing shadow appeared by the screaming
woman for only an instant—or forever. Sarah

wasn't sure which. Then, with sure-step delibera-
tion, the shadow moved toward the ball of grunts
and groans crawling its way toward her bed.

"Enough, you godforsaken idiots!" the large
shadow shouted with authority. "Can't you see
you're not in the saloon?"

The shadow picked a pea-coat collar and jerked
one piece of the ball apart. Then another. Yanking
them to their feet, the large shadow held each one
an arm's length apart.

"Now look what you idiots did." Ben's angry
voice, thick with his English accent, filled the room
and bounced off the walls. "You've disturbed the
very woman who could tell your wives, mothers,
sisters and daughters all your bad habits in detail."

Sarah sighed with relief. Benjamin. Whatever the
problem, he would help her. With shaking hands,
she struck a match and lit her bedside lamp, then
stared at the middle of the room and the chaotic
scene in front of her. Heavy breathing and a high-
pitched keening sound were the only noise in both
buildings.

Two of the young saloon girls stood by the hole in
the broken wall, scanty clothing barely concealing
their attributes. Their eyes were wide, their expressions as startled as Sarah felt. She recognized them
from Sundays, when she cleaned up the saloon
after services. They were sweet and tired, and Sarah
had felt each of them had wanted to join in, but
were afraid of what the crowd might do. Instead,
they cracked their doors and listened to the sermon
and occasionally joined in the hymns. One of the
girls, the youngest one, with beautiful blonde hair,
stood holding her strap up. Even in the dim lamp-
light, one side of her face and neck was beet red.

Behind the women, winding all the way down the

stairs, were men holding glasses filled with amber liquid or still-splayed cards, all staring through the broken wall toward the tableau in the middle of her bedroom.

Sweat, lamp oil, wet wool, stale cigar and cigarette smoke, along with the faint stench of liquor, all mingled in the space to gag Sarah.

She took a deep breath and calmed herself down. "Good evening, gentlemen and ladies."

Stifled laughter quickly muffled at her calling the women ladies. Obviously they felt the term gentlemen was perfectly all right.

She held her head high and her hands clasped in front of her to keep everyone from seeing them shaking. "Since this is not my birthday, I trust there is a good reason for this surprise party?"

"Uh, sorry, ma'am, but Sammy, here, thought he orta not wait his turn."

"His turn for what?" she asked calmly. "Surely he didn't want to buy a quilt in my shop."

More laughter.

"It doesn't matter, Mrs. Hornsby," Ben said quickly, and she felt her skin blush with the belated thought of what he was trying to cover. Of course. His turn with one of the girls. "What is important is that they apologize immediately, get out of here and promise to return tomorrow to repair the wall and make any other recompense you deem necessary."

"Wha . . . ?" one of the men held by the scruff of his collar said.

"But I din't do it by myself, Your Honor, Ben!"

"Well, neither did I, you goddamned son of a—"

Ben shook them both. "Enough!"

There was a commotion at the stairs and every-

Take A Trip Into A Timeless World of Passion and Adventure with Kensington Choice Historical Romances! —Absolutely FREE!

Let your spirits fly away and enjoy the passion and adventure of another time. With Kensington Choice Historical Romances you'll be transported to a world where proud men and spirited women share the mysteries of love and let the power of passion catapult them into adventures that take place in distant lands of another age. Kensington Choice Historical Romances are the finest novels of their kind, written by today's bestselling romance authors.

4 BOOKS WORTH UP TO $24.96— Absolutely FREE!

Take **4 FREE** Books!

We created our convenient Home Subscription Service so you'll be sure to have the hottest new romances delivered each month right to your doorstep — usually before they are available in book stores. Just to show you how convenient Zebra Home Subscription Service is, we would like to send you 4 Kensington Choice Historical Romances as a FREE gift. You receive a gift worth up to $24.96 — absolutely FREE. There's no extra charge for shipping and handling. There's no obligation to buy anything - ever!

Save Up To 32% On Home Delivery!

Accept your FREE gift and each month we'll deliver 4 brand new titles as soon as they are published. They'll be yours to examine FREE for 10 days. Then if you decide to keep the books, you'll pay the preferred subscriber's price of just $4.20 per title. That's $16.80 for all 4 books for a savings of up to 32% off the publisher's price! Just add $1.50 to offset the cost of shipping and handling. Remember, you are under no obligation to buy any of these books at any time! If you are not delighted with them, simply return them and owe nothing. But if you enjoy Kensington Choice Historical Romances as much as we think you will, pay the special preferred subscriber rate of only $16.80 each month and save over $8.00 off the bookstore price!

We have 4 FREE BOOKS for you as your introduction to
KENSINGTON CHOICE!

**To get your FREE BOOKS,
worth up to $24.96, mail the card below
or call TOLL-FREE 1-888-345-BOOK
Visit our website at www.kensingtonbooks.com.**

Take 4 Kensington Choice Historical Romances *FREE!*

KN070A

YES! Please send me my 4 FREE KENSINGTON CHOICE HISTORICAL ROMANCES (without obligation to purchase other books). Unless you hear from me after I receive my 4 FREE BOOKS, you may send me 4 new novels – as soon as they are published – to preview each month FREE for 10 days. If I am not satisfied, I may return them and owe nothing. Otherwise, I will pay the money-saving preferred subscriber's price of just $4.20 each... a total of $16.80 plus $1.50 for shipping and handling. That's a savings of over $8.00 each month. I may return any shipment within 10 days and owe nothing, and I may cancel any time I wish. In any case the 4 FREE books will be mine to keep.

Name _____

Address _____ Apt No _____

City _____ State _____ Zip _____

Telephone ( ) _____ Signature _____

(If under 18, parent or guardian must sign)

Terms, offer, and prices subject to change. Orders subject to acceptance by Zebra Home Subscription Service, Inc. Offer valid in the U.S. only.

one but Ben turned around to see what was happening.

The women stepped aside as the sheriff passed through the crowd and eased through the girls.

"Hello, Lord Benjamin." His tone was easy, his manner calm.

"Hello, Sheriff," Ben said, equally calm. "Glad you're here. I was just telling these men that they need to apologize to Mrs. Hornsby and to promise to return tomorrow morning to repair the damage and whatever else she needs done."

"Excellent idea." The sheriff turned toward Sarah. "Evening, ma'am. Sorry to barge in like this," he said, tipping his hat. They could have been at the Literary Dinner or the hotel dining room.

"It's quite all right with me that you're here, Sheriff. You bring a little sanity to the situation."

Ben smiled. "And I don't, Mrs. Hornsby?"

"On the contrary. Yours was the third face I saw, Mr. Drake. And I am thankful for that."

The sheriff turned toward the broken door. "Treat? Put those cards down and get over here right now," he shouted. "It's time to act like a deputy."

"Aw, Sheriff, I got a winning hand!" Treat's voice came from the stairway.

"And Mrs. Hornsby has more hands in her room than she wanted," he said, exasperation lacing his tone. "You should have taken charge of this situation the moment it started. That's what a deputy does."

Sarah watched everyone moving, shifting and changing places. All of this was going on in and around her very personal, private bedroom where only a handful of people had ever set foot. A handful plus Benjamin Drake. But that didn't need to be said.

"Get 'em out of here, Treat," the sheriff stated, once his deputy made it into the room to stand by the older man's side. "Lock 'em up until I decide what to do with 'em tomorrow. Mrs. Hornsby may want to press charges."

Treat pulled his gun reluctantly. "I don't think they meant to harm Mrs. Hornsby, Sheriff. They're usually pretty good about their drinkin'."

"Can I say somthin'?" One of the intruders ran his hands down the front of his jacket, pretending Ben was not holding his collar from the rear, making him look like an imitation of a marionette. The obvious drunk stood a little straighter and looked at Sarah. He formed each word slowly and carefully, as if impressing her with the fact that he wasn't drinking. Even Sarah knew that was a lie. "I'm sorry I busted your wall an' all, ma'am. I dint mean ta do it. Honest."

"As long as it's fixed, I'm sure there's no harm done."

"Thank you, ma'am," he said, slowly and distinctly. "An' may I say that you look lovely by gaslight? Your gown is most becoming and very"— he took his hands and placed them on his chest as if he were holding two breasts—"pretty."

The man was startled out of his manners when Ben shook his collar. "Don't you dare insult the woman by discussing something so personal after breaking into her room!" Ben growled. "And don't bother apologizing again, you bag of no good nuts and bolts! Stay away from the lady. You're not even fit to look in her direction!"

"Okay, okay," Sammy said, his voice slurring slightly in his attempt to make Ben stop shaking him. "Sorry," he mumbled. "So sorry. Dint mean anythin'. Honest."

"I understand," Sarah said, refusing to reach for a cover. It was too late now, for the whole saloon had peered at her in her new nightgown. The exact same gown Ben thought was beautiful. It could have been worse. She could have been wearing something terribly tatty. Then she would have been embarrassed and shamed at the same time.

"Sorry, too, ma'am," the other gentleman said. He was a small, wiry man, and his gaze toward his opponent was filled with hate.

"Apology accepted," she said softly. "Now, if everyone would just leave so I can . . . " She could say go to bed, but not in mixed company. Her mouth refused to work.

Ben smiled. "So Mrs. Hornsby can relax from all this excitement."

She smiled in return. "Thank you."

Ben reluctantly let go of the collars of both men, then wiped his hands against his thighs as if cleaning them from scum. Slowly, people filed out, including the deputy and sheriff with both the culprits.

It took several minutes for everyone to pile downstairs and into the few rooms upstairs. Finally, only Ben and the piano player stood in the hole in the wall, surveying the damage.

"Whaddaya think, Ben? A couple of boards oughtta do the trick for the evening, don't ya think?"

Ben leaned down at the other side of the open door. "I don't know, Eb. That's a pretty big hole."

Her mind was scattered, unable to put together any organization. She hunted around for her bathrobe, not having used it in weeks because she so seldom needed it. She lived upstairs by herself and dressed immediately after getting up and before going down the stairs. The last time she used it was when she'd dived under Ben's bed. . . .

No wonder she wasn't embarrassed to have them in her room! She'd already had her fair share of degrading moments with men!

Ben noticed her frantic efforts and strode to her, placing his own coat around her shoulders as if it were a cape. "Will that do for the moment?"

"Yes, thank you," she said, equally softly.

With as much dignity as she could muster, Sarah stepped around the broken wall and looked at the splintered wood. It was a mess. Her heart dropped. She wouldn't have privacy, her most treasured possession, for at least a few days, she thought.

"The entire wall will have to be replaced."

Ben looked down at her, his blue-eyed gaze appreciative. "Yes."

"But not tonight."

"No."

"What do I do?"

"Get a room in the hotel?" Eb said, standing on the other side of her.

"No." She was firm. "I'll not leave my possessions available to the world without protecting them."

"Take my room, and I'll take yours," Ben said. "It's the only way to protect the belongings."

"No, I can't do that," she stated instantly, even before her mind could figure out an answer.

"Why not?" Ben said. His smile was as endearing as he was. "It's perfectly sensible. No one will come in here knowing I'm on the other side of the, uh, what's left of the wall," he said, looking down at the offending piece of wood. "And I'll make sure your personal effects aren't touched."

"I can't," she said again, her thoughts swirling with images of walking around Ben's room, feeling his clothing, smelling him on every piece in the room.

Sleeping in his bed.

A rush of heat filled her cheeks.

Ben's hand came up to cup her chin, and he looked into her eyes. Finally, he smiled, and slowly, she smiled back. Without looking at the other man, he spoke to him. "Eb, can you stay here while I walk Mrs. Hornsby to her room for the night?"

" 'Course I can, Mr. Drake. I'm as honest as the day is long."

With firmness, Ben walked her to the door on the other side of the room, took the key from the hook on the wall and opened the door to the hotel hallway. He replaced the key and stood aside. "After you, Mrs. Hornsby."

Sarah hesitated only a fraction of a moment before walking regally through the doorway and down the hall.

Ben stood at the doorway and watched her walk all the way to his door. The soft sway of her hips beneath his coat was enough to stir any man.

Especially this man.

She stood in front of his door as if she were waiting for her own execution. With a heavy sigh, Ben closed the door to Sarah's bedroom and walked down the hall, unlocked the door and let it swing open.

The maid had been there and the room was as neat as a pin. "If you need anything at all, you know where I'll be."

Standing in the middle of the room and looking

all around, Sarah looked lost and forlorn. Ben placed his hands on her shoulders and gently turned her toward him. "You'll be fine here."

She nodded, but her gaze was focused somewhere over his shoulder.

"And I'll be fine there. I won't let anything happen to your things."

Her gaze shifted up to his face, tears forming to sheen her brown-eyed gaze. Now that the excitement had died down and everyone had left, she began shaking. "I thought I was safe," she said in a small voice, surprising herself with her words.

"No one is completely safe, my Sarah."

"I was." She blinked as two big tears rolled down her cheeks. "I had a store that made money so I could live. Friends who thought I was good. Workers who thought I was smart. A committee that I arranged to build a church that would serve the whole town."

Ben was beginning to see where she was going. This was the first time she'd showed those little vulnerable spots she held so tightly inside. "All this to keep you safe," he guessed.

She nodded as more tears fled down her cheeks. "But it doesn't work."

"No. Not always." He smoothed her shoulders. The largeness of his coat highlighted her small frame. She was so much more tiny than she appeared when she was dressed up in her Victorian armor, both physical and emotional. "Not ever."

"What do I do, Ben?" she asked.

"Sleep here and feel safe again. I'll handle your room until tomorrow morning. Tomorrow, I'll get E.Z. to help the men who broke the wall. They'll have it fixed by tomorrow afternoon."

"E.Z.? Is he here?"

"Yes, and he's bringing supplies from Houston this next week."

"He's from Blissful, you know."

Ben soothed her neck. "Yes, I know. He'll help me get things squared away tomorrow."

"You're sure?"

"I promise," he said. Then, going on gut instinct, Ben brought her small frame against his and held her there. Her head leaned on his chest, just shy of his shoulder. The top of her head touched his chin. She fit perfectly.

Ben let out a sigh, and so did Sarah. Her arm circled his waist and used him as a solid anchor. Her small hand rested on his chest at heart level. He was sure she felt his heartbeat, and just the thought of it made it beat faster.

"I'm scared," she finally admitted.

"You didn't look like it," he said, his mouth touching the softness of her hair. She smelled like flowers. Spring flowers. And woman. Feminine, sensuous, vulnerable, delicious woman. More woman than he'd ever handled in his whole life.

Damn.

"Are you sure I didn't act like an idiot?"

"You were like a queen, Sarah." His voice was low and vibrated in her ear, soothing her as well as making her very aware of his presence. "You were calm and regal and didn't look a bit surprised that all those disreputable people stood in the center of your bedroom in the middle of the night."

"Really?" she asked, raising her head from his chest and looking up at him, wanting to believe so badly.

And he wanted to ease her wounds.

"Really," he said. "You were the calm while the storm raged around you. Everyone admired the

way you conducted yourself in front of a bunch
of oafs.'' He wasn't lying. She was regal. She was
beautiful. And he was jealous that he couldn't tell
the others how much he admired her.

Her hand cupped his jaw, the softness of her
palm rasping against his evening beard. She smiled
and the whole room seemed to glow with it.
''Thank you for flattering me into calm,'' she said
in a soft whisper.

''It wasn't flattery,'' Ben admitted, watching her
mouth as it moved over her tongue in soft words.

''Then for indulging me in my hour of weakness.''

''You're welcome,'' he said, and before he thought
of anything else to say, his mouth came down on
hers and fitted over her own sweet lips. It was a
perfect fit—one that he'd felt before and had
yearned for ever since.

His hand came up and touched her side just
under her arm where the swell of her breast began.
Her mouth stilled, but she didn't move. Ben
slipped his hand around, cupping one soft breast
in his palm and feeling the weight of it. She was
soft, so soft. As he felt her with the heat of his
hand, her breast hardened and her nipple peaked
directly in the center of his palm.

Her breath caught in her throat.

But still she didn't move his hand.

His tongue danced across her lips, then softly
pressed against her slightly parted mouth, edging
inside.

Her hand clenched his shirt. Still, she didn't move.

Ben stiffened with want. With need. With desire
so strong he could hardly keep standing. His arm
tightened, holding her even closer.

Sarah moaned into his mouth, her hands clenching his shirt.

"Uh, um," a discreet cough came from behind the partially closed door.

Sarah stiffened and drew back. Ben wasn't willing to let go just yet. He'd waited too long to hold her like this. "Just a minute," he said in a voice loud enough to be heard out in the hallway. In a softer voice, he said, "I didn't mean to scare you, Sarah."

Her eyes opened, wide and bright. But there were no more tears waiting to be shed. Instead, she stared up at him as if seeing him for the very first time.

"I know, Ben."

"This isn't the end of it. You know that."

"Please, before someone finds us." Her voice was so soft, he had to bend to hear the words. He'd made her beg for the one thing that meant the most to her . . . her reputation.

"Good night, Sarah Hornsby. I'll see you in the morning." He kissed the tip of her nose and let go of her waist and breast reluctantly.

"Good night, Mr. Drake." She cleared her throat before speaking in a louder voice. "Thank you for your help. Sweet dreams."

"You're welcome. Sleep well."

Ben strode from the room, closed the door with a definite click, then almost ran down Eb as he walked toward the end of the hall and Sarah's bedroom.

Eb followed behind, but there was a definate glint of surprise in his eyes.

Ben didn't care. He had enough to worry about.

How in the hell could he fall for the one woman he couldn't afford to alienate? Especially if he was ever going to find a wealthy wife in rural Texas, which was exactly where he wanted to be?

He didn't have any answers.

Chapter Eleven

Sarah's sleep was interrupted by the sound of a saw in the backyard. It was bad enough that she hadn't closed her eyes until after three in the morning, but to be awakened at—she looked at the small clock ticking on the wall—six o'clock.

She sat up and stretched, wondering why she wasn't smelling Lillie's coffee. Her gaze widened as she realized where she was. Ben's hotel room. His very male scent clung to the covers, echoed from the clothing hung in the armoire, and wafted around her.

Benjamin. The man who, in the midst of her frustration and vulnerability, had held her in his arms in the center of this room as if she were the most precious piece of porcelain.

Benjamin, who had infiltrated her dreams, during the day, the evening, and in her sleep. Benjamin.

"Damn him!" she muttered aloud, and was star-

tled by her own voice and choice of words. The
words rolled off her tongue and felt so very good!
So dangerous! "Damn him!" she said again in a
soft voice, but with just a little more strength.

The roof didn't cave in, the earth didn't move.
Nothing happened because she'd expressed anger.

She grinned, then laughed.

She felt wonderful!

Stepping onto the warm floor and scooting to
the window, Sarah peered down at the rear grounds
where the noise was coming from. The day was
beautiful, with sunshine spilling everywhere and
making her squint her eyes against it.

Ben, Sammy and Eb stood with another man
who had witnessed the fight. All four were wrapped
in coats and discussing the merits of whatever
pieces of wood they were trying to cut. Their warm
breath created clouds of smoke as they spoke. Ben
was winning if the charades were any indication.
If Sarah was right, it looked as if the repairs would
be completed in no time.

She turned to realize she had no clothing in the
room. It was all in her room. She would have to
return to her room, get her clothing, then come
back here to change.

She looked around, not quite sure what she was
looking for until she spotted Ben's thick velvet robe
hanging on the back of the door.

She took it off the hook and slipped it on, feeling
the heaviness of it as if it were armor, protecting
her. It smelled like Benjamin, too. The warmth of
her own body echoed through the flannel and
returned it doubly.

She smoothed the rich fabric on the sleeve, lost
in the thought of Benjamin wearing the robe.

A no-nonsense knock on the hotel room door

echoed through the room, and Sarah's face flamed as she thought she'd gotten caught reveling in her most intimate dreams about the man in who's room she was sleeping.

"Mrs. Hornsby? I have your breakfast," a female voice called out. Sarah recognized the waitress from the hotel dining room.

She opened the door. The waitress stood holding a tray with cups and plates, a napkin draped over the food. "I didn't order any—" she began.

But the waitress's smile stopped her words. "The Lord of Drake ordered it sent up as soon as we got the sign from him."

"Lord Benjamin," Sarah corrected softly.

"Yes, ma'am."

The older woman put the tray on the small table near the window. She swept off the napkin that covered a plate piled with eggs, ham, grits and toast. A small silver pot was filled with hot tea that smelled slightly of jasmine. "Mmmm, my favorite," she said, bending over to get the full effect of the smells.

"That's what Mr. Sir Drake said," the waitress said, smiling knowingly.

"Lord Benjamin," Sarah corrected.

"Yes, ma'am."

Sarah tried to ignore that look. It was one she became familiar with when she was growing up. It hinted that someone thought they knew a secret about her.

Sarah forced herself to smile in return. "Thank you for your service. I'll be sure to let Sam know how attentive you were." She hoped the reference to the owner of the hotel would ease the situation. The girl might not be so quick to judge Sarah's presence in Ben's room.

The knowing smile disappeared quickly at the reminder of her boss. "Yes, ma'am," she said, leaving the room almost as quickly as she lost her smile.

Sarah enjoyed every bite of her breakfast. It was delicious, making her feel pampered and indulged by Ben's thoughtfulness. And she didn't cook it herself. Another luxury. She wasn't too worried about the waitress. Sooner or later the story about Sarah's bedroom would leak out and people would understand why she was in the hotel.

Once she ate, Sarah darted glances down the hallway and then toward her own door. Within seconds, she scurried down the hall and made it safely inside her own place, surrounded by her own things. She let out a sigh of relief.

Someone had propped wood planks against the largest of the gaping holes. There were two more holes in the splintered wall, the left one smaller than the right.

A deep, booming voice came from down the saloon stairs. Ben was talking to someone who grunted a lot in answer. ". . . and then cut each one about two inches longer than the tear . . . "

Grabbing a dress from the hook on the wall, and her shoes, along with her undergarments, Sarah ran back to Sam's room. She quickly slipped her nightgown over her head and dropped it to the bed. Turning, she caught sight of herself in the mirror attached to the closet door and was startled by the image. In all these years, she'd only seen herself completely naked once or twice, and then it was for only a second or two. Thomas had thought it was unseemly. But Ben had told her how lovely she looked over and over. Was it true, or were they just words to spout?

Standing straight, Sarah looked at herself dispassionately. Her long braid was almost completely undone, leaving soft tendrils to curl around her face and neck. She hadn't realized that her hair was so light on the ends and so dark at the roots. She had firm breasts with light-colored nipples, not at all like her sisters, who had dark ones that formed small, protuding bullets aiming straight ahead. She had a small waist; that was supposed to be nice. And round hips. Although women weren't supposed to have muscles, her legs were well-formed and firm from all the times she marched up and down steps. Her arms were also firm, with muscles from lifting and lugging furniture and piece goods all day. Her neck was slim but strong. She saw nothing to rave about, but it wasn't that bad, either. Her skin was clear, her eyes were direct. Her hair was her crowning glory, but no one ever saw it down except her. In public she kept it up and carefully tucked inside her crown or bonnet.

She brushed her hand over her stomach. She almost wished she had stretch marks and breast sags with large nipples that proved she'd had a babe and was a full-blown mother. But that wasn't to be, and she refused to allow the usual sadness to cover her that came from that thought. This wasn't the time.

But one thing was true. Naked or not, she'd bet she was an ordinary-looking woman.

She reached for her chemise just as the door opened and Ben strode into the room. With a jerk, the door slammed behind him and he turned to throw down his jacket on the chair. The look on his face verified that he'd forgotten Sarah was there.

She stood stock-still, unable to move or to breathe. To hide. Even the scream that threatened to force its way from her belly to her throat died.

So she stood, poised like a sprinter being handed a baton.

Ben turned, his eyes still dark blue with anger. His eyes widened, then slowly dropped down the length of her body and then back up. Each nuance was like a physical touch, skimming here, resting there, all admiring, suggesting and wondering what it would be like . . . .

Although unable to break the spell that bound them into this tableau, her mind scurried forward. She swore she could hear his heartbeat. It thudded rich and deep and heavy in double-time, just like it had last night under her hand. The very sound was sensuous, like beating drums in the dark of night. Anticipation raced through her, but she wasn't sure what that anticipation was for.

His heart skipped a beat. Or was it hers?

A door slammed down the hall and the sound thudded softly into the room, shattering the absolute quiet where only heartbeats were heard. The sound broke the spell.

Sarah quickly completed the reach for her chemise and held it in front of her. "Please leave." Her voice sounded low, calm, and husky. Her tone had nothing to do with the slivers of raw embarrassment racing through her body. There was nothing she could do about the blush that stained her cheeks and swirled down her neck and breasts only to curl into a tight ball in the pit of her stomach. Even her husband had never seen her naked!

"I," he began, then cleared his throat. "Certainly. But I have to comment that I've never seen a more beautiful woman," he said. "You're glorious, Sarah, and don't allow anyone to tell you different." His voice was low and soothing, as if talking to a bolting mare.

Her laugh was tight and short. "Please spare the false compliments. My ego may be damaged, but not shattered. Now, please leave. I'll be done quickly."

He didn't move. Instead, he continued to stare at whatever flesh he could see around the bunched-up chemise. "Sarah, I don't know where you've been or who you've been with, but your body is exquisite and you have nothing to hide. I apologize for my forwardness if it offends you, but I don't apologize for my error in timing. Apparently we both forgot where we were, and the gods in heaven above gave me a treat to remember for the rest of my life."

The man was not just handsome and charming; his wonderful voice held the tone of truth. He was worthy of a title. True or not, the words flowed over her like soothing balm.

Knowing the chemise covered her front from shoulder to hip, she held up her head and stared back at him. "You think this a treat?"

"Of course," he said, his boyish smile touching her heart. "And it's my reward for being such a nice guy."

"And what is my reward?"

"Why, being admired for the truth of you. You're beautiful, and you obviously don't believe it. I'm here to tell you that it's true."

Suddenly, she felt brave again. Feminine and brave, a wonderful combination to the balm he'd offered before. "Ah," she said, "a man with a mission."

His grin widened. "But, of course."

"With your mission completed here, now, please leave."

"Your looks and demeanor are worthy of a princess," he said softly, his brow raising in question. "Would the princess dare to give her loyal subject a kiss?"

Just the thought of such a daring move made her feel weightless and in danger. "Please. Leave." Her voice sounded far more certain than she was. Her traitorous body wanted to run to him, press against him. Follow him.

She blushed again. "Now."

His blue eyes, now softened with conversation and teasing, positively twinkled. "Yes, ma'am. If you insist. But this sight will remain alive and well in my mind far beyond this moment. It will cry out to me in every dream. Every waking hour. And probably every other moment of my life no matter where I am or what I'm doing." His gaze narrowed. "Remember that as you walk this earth in search of mortal things. You had a chance at heaven and turned it down."

"You're heaven?" she asked, meaning her words to sound disbelieving. It didn't do any such things to her ears.

"As far as you and I are concerned, yes, ma'am."

Sarah straightened up. She looked him straight in the eye. "Get out."

Ben sighed, almost resigned to her order. "Yes, ma'am." He made it to the door, then turned. "But this isn't over, Sarah. There is something very real and special between us, and I mean to get to the bottom of it."

"My, you're busy," Sarah said softly. "You're looking for a wife *and* someone to satisfy you all at once. So much for commitment to your vows."

"When my vows are taken, I'll be committed to them, Sarah. But I'm not married yet, and just because you're a widow doesn't mean you're dead yet, either. That makes both of us up for grabs.''

The door closed behind him. He did it quietly but it could have been a slam.

For the next ten minutes Sarah was certain she had not taken one breath of air. Her muscles, so tight and rigid while Ben was in the room, were now like a bowl of homemade jelly—all wiggly and without shape.

She felt as if she'd just been touched by the heat of dragon's breath and lived to tell the tale.

As quickly as she could, Sarah dressed and redid her hair into the tightest bun she'd ever created. Knowing she'd have a headache in an hour or so from the tension of her wrapped hair was punishment for wanting Ben to stride over to her and take her in his arms. Kiss her like he'd kissed her in her very own bedroom. Hold her like he'd held her last night in his bedroom . . . make love to her in a different way than Thomas had . . . in the way that Ben had begun. Soft, firm, sensuous, knowing, and believing she was the embodiment of beauty.

In other words, lying to her.

She wanted that lie. She wanted to feel that just for once, she was the most desirable, most beautiful woman on earth. And that she was perfect and just for him. That she belonged to someone as wonderful and handsome and masculine as he was.

''No,'' she said as she stared into the mirror. That was Cinderella stuff. Fairy tales. Life had taught her that reality was far different than what was real. Life, especially for women, was tough. She'd made it this far, and she wasn't about to take the chance of shooting herself in the foot by cleaning a gun that didn't need it!

With thoughts and resolve channeled in another

direction, Sarah grabbed her nightclothes and walked out the door to her own bedroom—the safe haven she'd made for herself.

After depositing the nightclothes on the hooks near her bed, she studied the damage done to her wall last night. Cleaned up, with boards resting against the broken wall, it still looked like a mess.

"Damn wall!" she muttered, feeling better for having sworn at the cause of her misery. Then she hastened to alter that thought, knowing full well God was probably listening and knew her part in the hotel room fiasco that had just played out. A glance at her watch confirmed that church would start in three hours. Wonderful. She marched downstairs to the kitchen and began stoking the fire.

The sound of sawing in the backyard was only a minor intrusion into her world. They could finish that up this morning and still be in time for church services at ten-thirty. Good. She had also laid plans for another woman to introduce to Ben. Pansy Haude was coming in from her farm several miles outside of town. She was staying with friends in town and was on a shopping expedition, according to customer friends.

She would ignore—yes, ignore—what had happened in the hotel room this morning. She would pretend it never happened. As bad as it was, it was not the end of the world, she firmly told herself. And they would never speak of it again—Ben would certainly agree with that. He still wanted a wealthy wife. She still wanted trunks full of ribbons and cloth. Nothing had changed except that he'd seen her naked. He hadn't touched her, kissed her—this time—or compromised her in any way that others knew about.

Her imagination created images of those thoughts and she felt her body warm in places that had never warmed before.

"No more!" she muttered, slamming the empty pail on the table. It was time to work.

Muffled voices came down the stairs, then invisible hands began fitting wood into the holes in the wall. She walked slowly toward the stairs, listening to the words. Ben's muffled voice mingled along with Eb, Sammy and the piano player from last night.

"Fit it in here."

"I gotcha," Eb grunted.

"No, wait, that ain't the way to do it," Sammy whined.

"Yeah, it is, so just do what we tell you, Sammy. You don't know shit about building. Fact is, you don't know shit anyway."

"Watch your language. For all you know, Sarah, Mrs. Hornsby might be able to hear you."

"She up?" someone asked, his tone breathless as if lifting something.

"She's up."

"You sweet on her?" another one asked. "She's one to be sweet on, but kinda cold, don't you think?"

"I'm respectful. Something you don't know about," Ben stated harshly.

"Oh, 'scuse me, Yur Highness. I didn't know she got to you. She musta warmed up some."

A crack and thud echoed downstairs and Sarah knew someone had been hit. "Try ruining someone else's reputation, but not hers. If she had said the word last night, you'd be in jail today. But she didn't. So try your sarcasm on someone else," Ben stated. Immediately, the hammering began.

Not another word was said.

Shaking, Sarah sat down hard on the kitchen chair. Ben had been challenged on her honor and had stuck up for her. No one, not even her own husband, had done that. It didn't matter that she'd never given him cause to defend her, it was enough that Thomas never did defend her, just hound her about appearances as if she didn't know the difference. And Ben, without lectures, just leaped at the chance to defend her.

She held her hands in her lap to keep them from shaking. The awful truth washed over her like a chilling cold blanket. It had been lurking in the corners of her mind for at least a week. She might as well face it because she'd have to live with it for the rest of her life.

She was in love with Benjamin Drake.

All the signs were there. All the feelings that she'd tried so hard never to feel again were spilling out like an enormous waterfall. She was so in love that just the sound of his voice caused quakes in her stomach and tremors in her hands. And thoughts to form that should never see the light of morning.

She raised her hands to her cheeks and felt the heat of her own skin.

She was in love. . . . It was so hard to understand! When did it happen? How? She'd promised herself she would never again have a man in her life. Men controlled women. They controlled their life, their words, their thoughts, their actions. The status of widowhood enabled her to live with grace and control without the pressure of a man who expected her to act a certain way, do a certain thing or be a certain type of person.

Certainly, Ben was different than her dictatorial

father or Thomas. But he was still a man. That
alone was enough reason to stay away from him.

She finally had a goal, a job, a reason to get up
in the morning and complete her day. Hard as it
was to believe, she was *useful!* It was the headiest
feeling in the world, and she didn't want to lose
it just so she could rest her head against one of
the most masculine, sexy chests in the world.

No matter how much she thought she loved him,
Benjamin wasn't worth losing everything that made
her feel good and useful about herself.

"Oh, dear God," she muttered aloud. Although
her thoughts seemed crystal clear to her, her mind
wasn't paying as much attention to those clear
thoughts. Her mind was paying attention to a
quickly beating heart and even more chaotic
thoughts.

"Mrs. Hornsby?" Sammy's voice echoed down
the stairs.

As if the world could see her, Sarah stood and
brushed her hands down the front of her dress.
"Yes, Mr. Sammy?"

"Ain't you gonna be up here soon?"

"Do you need me?"

"No, ma'am, but the girls, they was wondering.
They wanted to step out of their rooms and get
some food downstairs of the saloon before the
church people got there, but they dint want to
offend you."

"They would never offend me, Mr. Sammy.
Please tell them to feel free to move about any way
they wish. After all, there is, well, *most* of the wall
to secure our privacy."

"Not for long, ma'am. We gotta take the whole
thing down to finish the job. It'll be down until
after church, ma'am."

"That's fine." Sarah sighed, wishing she was anywhere but in her own kitchen. Wishing she could hide somewhere, walk a beach, march between cattle, sit and have tea with Kathleen and listen to her no-nonsense approach to life.

The one thing she did *not* want was to be in Ben's arms. No. Not at all.

"They said to tell you they'd be dressin' so's not to offend, ma'am."

"Tell them I appreciate the effort."

"Yes, ma'am. An', uh, Harmony, here, was wonderin' if she might borrow this here dress an' shawl you got. . . ."

"Fine." Sarah sighed again.

The buzz of voices continued for a few minutes, then nothing but hammers, grunts and groans filtered through the rooms.

Sarah had to go to church. It was almost time and she had no choice, because she'd already made arrangements for Ben to meet another woman.

That meant that if Ben liked this one, they would marry and settle outside of town, where she could see him every Sunday for the rest of her miserable, lonely life.

And the price for that pain was trunks of ribbons, lace and cloth. She wanted to cry, but couldn't.

By the time Sarah opened the front door and stepped onto the boardwalk, townspeople were standing around the storefront, walking or buggying to converge on the building that held church services.

The doors to the saloon were wide open, the windows up, and several men pushed brooms or mops, while a few of the women were cleaning windows with vinegar and newspaper. Streaks of yellow were soaking the paper.

"Goodness, the place is a mess!" one of the women muttered.

"It's the cigars," another one said. "They just don't think about the smell and smoke."

Sarah grinned. "And that's why Hiram smokes outside?" she asked, talking about the older woman's husband.

"Of course. At his own request, I might add." The older woman smiled fondly out the door at a short, bald, heavy-set man standing with several others as they discussed the size of crops or fish, Sarah wasn't sure which. "He's such a good man," the wife said with contentment lacing her voice.

"How long have you been married?"

"Thirty-three years." The woman's head bobbed with the words. "And been happy alla time."

"You been obedient," the other woman muttered between breaths. "That's all."

"That's not so and you know it," the older woman argued, and Sarah walked off, checking to make sure the hymnals were out. Her mind was occupied with the next step toward obtaining her fabric, she almost convinced herself.

"Sarah?"

As if she'd conjured him, Ben was at her side, looking devastatingly handsome and very out of reach. He was born of nobility and looked every inch his lineage. If not a man to live with as man and wife, he was at least a worthy man to love.

He looked puzzled. "Sarah?" he asked softly. "Is something wrong?"

She realized she hadn't answered and quickly said, "Yes. I mean, no. Nothing is wrong. Is something wrong?"

He smiled. "You're not really here, are you? Are you worried about the repairs? If so, let me put your mind at ease. I've got the men working on it right now, following my explicit instructions. I don't think they can mess up the job." His expression turned grim. "At least, I don't believe so. Not yet, anyway."

"I'm sure they'll do a very fine job," she said primly, reining in her feelings and making sure that she looked a little bit pious as she stood in the saloon-transforming-into-a-church. "And I have someone for you to meet."

"Really?" he asked, his gaze still pinning her to the floor. "Who?"

"Her name is Pansy Haude. She's a sweet little young lady, although her stature is small. But her sense of humor and wealth more than make up for that small problem."

"And the wealth is?" Ben asked, his voice low, his head bent over hers to hear every word. She could smell his aftershave of pine, and his maleness, and she took a deep breath, knowing that soon she wouldn't have the opportunity. A lump formed in her throat and she swallowed quickly to ease the pain.

"Her father's a pig farmer and his wealthy wife makes the best cheese in three counties."

Pastor Strack walked in, his wife, Ina, and an entourage of townspeople behind him as if he were leading a parade.

Several people behind, Sarah saw Pansy in a bright pink beaver bonnet with dark gray trim. Very stylish. Her matching gray cape swirled as she walked toward Sarah, a smile forming on her rosebud mouth. If she hadn't known better, Sarah would have sworn the girl had smeared her lips with berry juice.

"Sarah!" she called, walking directly to her. She

seemed to ignore Benjamin standing at her side. Her diminutive stature was perfectly balanced by her full, feminine figure. She looked like a perfect Dresden doll.

Sarah's heart sank as she realized Ben's response to the feminine figure in front of them. He was enchanted with her. What man wouldn't be?

Chapter Twelve

Sarah's bedroom wall wasn't repaired until more than two hours after church services. One of the carpenters in town came to take a look, then add his advice to the growing list of curious people before him. The problems were discussed and directed again and again.

Directly after the services, each man with an opinion and owning a hammer wandered upstairs to stare at the mess, shake his head and leave, dropping one or two pieces of advice as if every other man had been wrong before him. Sarah thought that, just perhaps, each man had wandered up there to see what there was to see on both sides of the landing.

Sarah, cleaning the downstairs thoroughly while she waited to get her privacy back, had plenty of time to think.

The pastor had announced from the pulpit that Horst Heine had offered to donate to the church the needed lumber. And his sawmill would cut the lumber free of charge. All they needed were the men to volunteer their time to building the church.

Horst also made the surprise announcement that Lord Benjamin had agreed to oversee the church building, having extensive building experience in his own home country. Lord Benjamin and Horst would be the only two people in charge of the project.

A list was made up, and the building process would begin next Saturday. Ben announced that since he didn't have a family or a business to worry about at this time, he'd get together with Mr. Heine's builder before then. According to the consensus of opinion, it would only take a month's steady work to complete the exterior. Another month to finish the interior.

Sarah listened as the men all conversed as if it were an open meeting. The women's heads bobbed back and forth between the talkers giving their two-cents' worth. It was funny to think that these same men accused the women of talking too much, but they never saw themselves in the same light. According to them, they were discussing something "important."

Just like the work done on her wall.

Another carpenter was the last one to inspect the damage. "If I were you," he said, "I'd tear down the whole wall to the stud, then rebuild. It's the only way."

With that, he walked off, obviously feeling better for his input, and having no idea they'd already planned on doing just that.

Nothing had changed or been resolved.

Sarah had to grin at the thought of it.

In between all this commotion and inspection, Harmony, the girl who had borrowed Sarah's dress and shawl, had not taken it off all afternoon. Except for the length, the dress fit pretty well. Harmony walked the balcony of the saloon with it on, to be seen by every man in the place. She might not have had more business than the others, but, then, she certainly wasn't hanging onto the dress to get more business.

Back in her shop, Sarah searched the downstairs and found a roll of mauve grosgrain that matched the color of the tiny flowers in the fabric. It would do nicely to lower the hem. On one of her walks past the open shop door, Sarah gave it to Harmony. "Stitch this on with tiny stitches and it will do well for an extra dress," she said quietly, giving the girl a needle and thread to match. "The fabric is just right for your coloring."

She might as well have given the girl the moon and stars. "Do you mean it? What a wonderful gift! Thank you! I won't disappoint you!" she said, practically gushing the words. "I'm pretty good with a needle, and this will do well for Sundays. Thank you. Thank you so much," she said several times before Sarah was able to get away.

Why on earth had she thought this business would be easy? Or in the right location? She was between a hotel and a saloon and whorehouse, and had accepted it as normal!

"This is insane," she said aloud to an empty room. It was the first time she'd been alone in her home since last night. The men were upstairs on the saloon side, putting the last boards in place.

Sarah shoved more wood in the stove and began the process of baking her biscuits. Instead of waiting until tomorrow, she would do them now. It would keep her hands busy and calm her heart.

First, she made the small well of flour in the bowl on the table, then she began mixing the buttermilk and lard in by hand.

It relaxed her, letting her shoulders slump slightly.

She added cold water from the pail at the door. All thoughts went back to . . . Ben.

He and Pansy had talked before church and talked after church. They seemed to have hit it off. Good for him, she thought, breaking off a piece of dough and turning it into a ball before setting it aside to make another one.

The rthymn of doing something familiar and repetitive worked its magic on her again, restoring a semblance of order to her chaotic world.

By the end of the preparation, she was more relaxed. She popped a dozen biscuits in the oven and shut the iron door with a snap.

"Mrs. Hornsby, ma'am?" The male voice from upstairs intruded and she tightened up again.

"I'm downstairs, Sammy."

"I think we got it done, now, ma'am."

"Wonderful."

"I'm gonna use the door through the hotel and I'll close it when I leave."

"Please let me know and I'll lock it."

"Yes, ma'am. I'll be ready in just one minute."

Sarah decided to go upstairs and be ready to lock the door. She took the stairs one heavy foot at a time, suddenly feeling tired.

Sammy stood at the door, ready to shut it behind him. Harmony stood in the hotel hallway, watching both of them. They looked so young to Sarah, and much too naive to have been involved in a whorehouse brawl.

"You call if you need anything else done, Mrs. Hornsby, an' I'll be here in a flash."

"I will, Sammy."

"An' if you need anything else done, you call me and I'll do it straightaway. It's the least I can do since you dint even press charges agin me for bustin' this up."

"It's not a problem, Sammy. If I'd put you in jail, you wouldn't have been able to fix it, would you?"

"No, ma'am." He nodded his agreement vigorously. "So you call me whenever you need somethin' done."

"I'll remember that," Sarah said. "And Harmony, have a nice Sunday," she said, placing her hand on the door to close it.

"Yes, ma'am. And thank you for helping me," she said, looking down at her dress. "You're a woman with a big heart."

"Thank you," she said. "We'll talk again later." She felt as if she were almost slamming the door in their faces, but fact was, she was exhausted.

She closed the door, then slumped against it. She needed a nap. Being a woman in love was hard work. Being in love with a man who was catnip to ladies was even harder. Not being able to tell the man or act upon all her pent-up emotions was the hardest of all.

After finishing the biscuits, wrapping them in a large cotton cloth and setting them aside, Sarah aimed straight for the bed. She slipped off her slippers and undid the buttons on her dress until it slipped off her shoulders. The upper floor was warm and cozy with the scent of fresh-baked biscuits drifting through the room.

Without another thought, Sarah slipped between the sheet and comforter and rested her head against the goose-down pillow. Within seconds, she was sound asleep.

Benjamin stood, hands on hips, as he watched Sammy and Eb clean up and put away the tools they'd used to fix Sarah's wall. It took fifteen minutes for the two men to get the mess and tools back to where they belonged.

Once or twice, Ben looked up at the upstairs window. He never saw Sarah, however, her oven flue filled the cold, crisp afternoon air with the smell of fresh biscuits and warmth. He yearned to be inside. Instead, he was insuring two grown men would do their job properly—just like he used to do at home for his father.

When would he do it for himself?

Once more he looked up at Sarah's window. Nothing.

A glance at his pocket watch told him he had a long afternoon ahead of him. What he wanted most was to see Sarah. Talk to her. He remembered last night's kiss, and how his body reacted instantly to this morning's sight of her naked and beautiful, standing in the middle of his room. He wanted her in his arms. Now.

Instead, he stomped into the rear of the hotel, ordered a private bath to be prepared, then stormed into his room, not stopping until he hit dead center. He threw his coat on the bed and turned around. It all looked the same as it did before, but he knew the room was different now.

It smelled like Sarah: sweet, female and sensuous.

Angry at himself for reasons he didn't want to explore, Ben deliberately lit a cigar and puffed on it, filling the room with the smell. Squinting through the smoke, he pulled out his pocket watch and checked the time. It was almost three o'clock. He was due at Pansy's house at six that evening. She was a sweet woman; her parents were hoping for a good match in marriage.

He wasn't it.

"Hell, maybe I am and I'm just too stupid in the ways of women to know it." But he knew who had the wisdom to know.

Sarah.

Without even thinking about it, Ben doused his cigar and strode out of his room and down the hall to Sarah's. He prayed she was upstairs and willing to talk. He needed her thoughts and answers. He needed her commonsense approach. He needed . . . He doused that thought. The funny thing was that he'd never asked a woman an opinion before, let alone an opinion that had to do with a life-altering situation.

He tapped gently. "Sarah, are you there?"

No answer.

He tapped again, but this time he realized the door was more loose than it should be. He touched the knob, then turned it. It turned freely and opened like magic.

"Sarah?" Still no answer.

Ben stuck his head in the door, now worried. If she wasn't here, where was she?

She was in bed. Asleep. Beautifully, wonderfully, sexily, asleep. Dreams couldn't be better than this.

Without thinking it through, Ben stepped in and closed the door behind him. He walked to the small slipper chair near the bedside and sat down, his eyes glued to the woman in the bed.

Sarah's usual braid crown had come undone and lay across her throat. One hand was above the cover, dainty fingers splayed. The other hand was under the soft pillow, her thin wrist visible between pillow and comforter.

The chair squeaked, and her mouth formed a perfect little "O." Her lashes fluttered and he stiffened, hoping no more sounds would wake her.

He wanted to watch her, stare at her like he wasn't allowed to when she was awake. He wanted to absorb her into his body with his eyes so he would never have to let her go.

Sarah stirred and turned on her side. Still, he sat and watched, as if protecting her thoughts and dreams just by being ready to slay dragons.

He was amazed at her tiny size. She was such a powerful woman in the town. It was her spirit that was enormous. It was so big, she had most of the townspeople doing her bidding. Even the wealthiest man in town was donating above and beyond the call of duty by giving both the land and the lumber to her pet project, the church.

And then there were the women who depended on her, both for the supplies and pay when she bought their work, and for the ones who bought their goods from her store to use themselves or to be sold in larger towns. He knew she wasn't wealthy because she counted her pennies too closely, but she was making more than enough to earn her keep and continue the circle rolling.

In fact, most men in England could take a lesson or two from Sarah on how to create loyal employees—and how to squeeze a profit instead of squeezing the people who worked for them.

She sighed and he moved closer, sitting on the bed. "One kiss," he whispered. "Just one, my sweet."

He was lying.

He didn't care.

Ben's mouth touched hers, his breath as soft as his lips. Sarah sighed. If this was part of her dream, she didn't want to wake up. Her arms came up and circled his neck, keeping him exactly where she wanted him. Exactly where he wanted to be.

His mouth, still soft, continued to brush against hers, making her follow every movement of his head. She puckered, seeking more, and he allowed her to, only easing a small part of her desire.

"More," she whispered when he pulled away. "I want more."

"More what?" he asked, a teasing note in his own whisper.

"More kisses."

His chuckle was low and sweet. "I'm at your service, sweet," he said, then began giving the lady what she asked for.

She felt his body stretch out to the length of the bed beside her, the heaviness fill the free space next to her. Her heart beat faster, but her muscles were limp and relaxed. His hand cupped the back of her neck as his mouth moved down from hers to explore the slope of her chin, jawline and then to the curve of her throat. His tongue dipped into the small hollow at the base, and she held her breath. She wanted to tell him not to stop, but she was afraid. Afraid of being the biggest disappointment of his life. Afraid of being laughed at. Afraid . . .

"No." She whispered so softly she didn't think he heard, but she didn't have the strength to say it louder.

Ben's head came up and he looked into her eyes, now wide open. "Why?"

"Because," she began, but found no words that would explain what she was trying to say. Her mind refused to focus on reasons and whys and wherefores. And she would not let Thomas come into the bed she was sharing with Ben. Never having felt this way before, she had topsy-turvy emotions and curiosity combined, and that was enough to overcome.

"That's not reason enough to halt this ecstasy, Sarah." He waited a moment, watching her moist mouth. She licked her lips, and it was all he could do to restrain himself. His mouth covered hers again. Tempting. Teasing.

He was right. If she couldn't come up with a reason, then there wasn't one to use. She loved it. She was light-headed with the very touch of him. She took his hand from the side of her face and pushed on it lightly.

"Don't make me stop yet," he said, his face buried in her cleavage, his tongue dancing on her skin making heat and chills. "Tell me what you like. What you want."

"Don't stop," she managed, putting his hand under her chemise and over her breast. She was shocked at her own audacity, but not enough to stop.

"Wonderful, sweet Sarah." His voice was a warm whisper against her skin. "I love it when a woman knows what she wants and goes after it."

Unable to speak, she shook her head instead. It didn't mean no, it meant she wasn't sure that she

knew what to say. She prayed he'd continue with
the wonderful feelings he made her feel.

Two or three times in her life she had felt tingles
like this, but much more tame. Thomas had never
liked her to mention them, and she had been afraid
to pursue the matter.

But it had always felt as if something was building.
Something was about to happen. She didn't know
what the feelings were, just as wonderful as they
were scary. When Thomas refused to talk about
them other than to warn her not to pay attention,
she did what was best. She stayed silent.

"Feel me beside you," Ben said.

Would he continue to speak? To say things she
might have to respond to? That meant she couldn't
retreat into her own little world while he had his
way. She would be alert every moment of their
lovemaking. . . .

"Touch me, Sarah. Feel me."

She didn't know where to go or what to do.
"How? Where?"

His chuckle was low and sexy. "Never mind,
sweet. Just do to me what I do to you this time.
We'll figure it out as we go."

His placed a kiss on her chin, then lowered his
head to her breast and laved the nipple with his
tongue.

It took her breath away. With infinite slowness,
he covered her nipple with his mouth and gently
sucked, running his tongue over and over the nipple and making her nerves tense so much she
thought she would break into tiny pieces.

While sucking, his hand wandered down the flat
of her stomach and under her chemise, smoothing
her thighs as he ran his hand up the insides before
stopping to cup the apex of her thighs.

Breath caught in her throat, and she stiffened.

"Part them, sweet Sarah. Let me feel you. Feel your moisture and your utter sweetness." His mouth drifted from breast to mouth again. His warm breath stirred the words on her tongue, making her unable to speak.

He gave a gentle tug against one leg and she moved it in the direction he wanted. His body tensed, then relaxed as he slipped his palm down and up the inside of her thighs, feeling the soft sweet skin and knowing he was close to heaven. The touch was like music to Sarah. She moved her legs, unable to keep them still while he touched her. He made her feel so good. So very good. She opened her legs just a little more to allow him freer access.

Ben groaned in satisfaction as his fingers found and touched the inner part of her that gave such pleasure to both of them.

Her gasp told him what he wanted to know, and he felt powerful in the knowledge. She had not been touched there before . . . at least not softly, playfully. The thought made him even harder, and he forced himself to slow down. He didn't want to lose her now to thoughts of fear.

His mouth took a dusky nipple and she gasped again. Her hands touched his sides, rubbing her palms up and down from arm to hip, sensitizing him to her every nuance. She scraped his nipple and he had to take a deep breath to hold onto his own control.

"Benjamin," she half sighed, her voice barely a whisper.

"Yes, I know," he soothed. "It's all right. You're supposed to feel this way, sweet Sarah."

One hand touched his cheek, catching his attention. He looked into her eyes and saw the doubt there. "Are you sure a woman should feel this?"

His smile was slow and just as sweet as the expression on her face. "I'm sure, sweet Sarah. I'm real sure," he said, a slow drawl that made her smile.

"Then don't stop, Ben. Please don't stop."

His low chuckle filled her, not relaxing her but at least taking some of the tension away. Then he kissed her full mouth, filling her with the warmth of his breath. His body slipped over to cover her, touching her with delicious heat from head to toe.

"That's it, Sarah," he said, fitting inside her like a sword into a perfectly fitted scabbard. She gasped and stiffened. He couldn't move for a moment, couldn't speak. Being inside her felt so unbelievably right, he couldn't afford to lose himself in her yet. Over and over again, he told himself that he had to take her with him to paradise. He *had* to.

Sarah groaned, then, with tiny movements at first, began to rock against him. The tiny movements became more bold. Her breath touched his cheek as he held his own breath in wonder. Her muscles contracted, then expanded, and then ached so bad, she had to hold tight to Ben's waist to keep from crying out in frustration. Her head turned from side to side.

Suddenly, Sarah's eyes opened wide, staring up at him in awe. "Ben?" she whispered. Her hands clenched, then her eyes closed as the most brilliant light seemed to burst into the room, filling her head with wonder. "Ben." She sighed, riding the crest of the wave that had taken her to that magical place.

Ben's chuckle echoed in her head, then his own body stiffened above hers and a moan echoed through the room. Slowly, very slowly, his body lowered to hers, covering her like a heated blanket. Sarah let out her breath, tears forming in her eyes with the wonder of what he had just taught her.

She had met many men and never thought of them once after the introduction. But one man had stuck in her mind from the first glimpse of him through the store window. Benjamin was meant to teach her the ways of love. She knew it as well as she knew her own name. But was he to teach her love . . . or lovemaking?

The first was so very complicated. The second he had just succeeded in doing.

Chapter Thirteen

"Ben?" Sarah whispered, staring down at the man beside her.

Late afternoon light filtered through the small upstairs window, emphasizing the strong planes of his face in repose. His eyes were closed, his mouth tilted ever so slightly, as if thinking about smiling. He was the handsomest man she'd ever seen. What was he doing in her plain-Jane bed with her plain-Jane self? He deserved someone so much more beautiful. More young. More adventurous, while still being a grand lady.

She was none of those things. He'd given her the gift of a lifetime. And she felt treasured and undeserving at the same time. Benjamin had shown her what it was like to be with a man who cared.

The chiseled mouth finally tilted into a smile. Ben's hand reached for her, touching her neck then drifting down the curve of her throat. "Let me see if I can do that again."

Sarah pushed aside her dark thoughts. She would have plenty of time to remember later. Now was the time to enjoy and make the memories that she would carry into old age, warming her body on many lonely winter nights to come.

She smiled. "You know what you're doing, Ben. I bet you can do it anytime you wish."

His hand trailed down to her breast, gently stroking her nipple. "Ah, my sweet. The trick is to make *you* feel like that every time we make love."

A click filtered through the air, but Sarah ignored it. The old building had too many creaks and groans to investigate each and every one. She was too engrossed in what Ben was doing. His mouth touched her breast and she sighed in delight, anticipating his every move and now knowing where it was going and what would be happening.

By the time she heard her name called, it was too late.

"Sarah? Where are you?"

She froze. Her hand in midair on its way to Ben's bare chest. It couldn't be. Not now. Not now!

"Sarah?" Sister Merci's step touched the stairs, traveling quickly up the steps.

"Sarah?" she said once more, unable to stop her tongue from completing the name even after touching the landing and then seeing them in bed.

Sarah grabbed the covers, holding them up to her neck, wishing she could disappear. It was a useless gesture because it was obvious she was naked and in bed with a man. From the expression on Merci's face, the young woman jumped to the right conclusions immediately.

"Sarah!"

Ben gave a low growl and turned over, sitting so

that he shielded Sarah from view. "Who in the bloody hell . . . !"

Merci stood like a statue in action, her hands out, her feet looking as if she was taking a step. Her dark hair was disheveled from the wind, and her long gray dress was even more gray with dust. She stared at the two of them as if unable to grasp the situation. Then, suddenly, her eyes widened even more as she gaped at Ben. "Benjamin!"

Sarah placed a hand on Ben's back and peeped around his shoulder, an abject apology on her mind. But the words never made it to her lips. Merci's face was white, her hands clenched into fists.

Ben's back muscles stiffened. "Fairy?" he said, disbelieving even as he said it. "What the hell are you doing here?"

Merci flushed deep red as the blood flowed back to her face. She stood her ground, looking down at him imperiously. "*I* should be asking that question."

Ben's voice was a growl. "But you're not, damn it! I am. What the hell are you doing here?"

"It's Sister Merci . . . and that's none of your business."

"You've got that wrong, Fairy. It's none of your business why I'm here. But it's certainly my business as to why you're here."

"No, it's not!" She stood tall and straight, looking like a wrathful goddess. "I was wrong about you, Mr. Drake. You've just proved you're no better than any other man, skipping from one bed to another. But this time your velvet tongue has taken you too far. You've invaded the wrong woman's bed. Sarah Hornsby deserves much better than you. Much better."

"You wouldn't know one way or the other," Ben stated. "And how in the hell did you find your way here? Looking for a little excitement?" He sneered. "You lost your way. The whorehouse is upstairs in the next building, not this one."

"You . . . !"

"Stop it!" Sarah stated emphatically, her whole body shaking. Getting caught was one reason to shake, but their conversation was a very big other. Confrontation and denigration, the likes of which they were doing, hurt her even when it had nothing to do with her.

She grabbed the sheet and wrapped it around. Then she got to her knees and stared at both angry people. "I gather you know each other," she stated, emotionally pulling away by letting her own anger and exasperation lace her voice. She almost forgot what they were all doing in her bedroom and why she should feel so guilty for being caught in the arms of a man.

"It was a lifetime ago," Merci finally admitted, her angry eyes locked with Ben's.

"Where was that lifetime?" Sarah asked.

"Tombstone," they both said.

"Tombstone?"

Merci's face flushed even deeper red. "We, uh, met through some mutual friends."

Sarah glanced at Ben's profile. His expression was carved in stone. "Nicely put, even if it is a lie."

Sarah knew they didn't meet in church or they would have said so immediately. "Where in Tombstone?"

The silence was so thick it fogged the room.

"I'm sorry. I didn't hear that answer."

"In the Birdcage Saloon. . . ."

It was one of the most famous places in the West.

Sarah's heart dropped as she finished where they'd left off. ". . . and whorehouse."

"Yes."

"You were a customer there." It was a statement she hoped he'd refute. But he didn't.

Ben never took his eyes off Merci . . . Fairy. "And Merci was just one of the girls," he drawled.

Merci's chin tilted in defiance. Her eyes were bright and hard as rock candy. "Yes. *Was* is the operative word, Lord Benjamin."

One thought tumbled over another and another, leaving Sarah confused and frightened. She tried to collect herself. It was time to take the situation in hand. "Would you please wait downstairs, Merci?" she asked with all the dignity she could muster under the circumstances.

"Yes," Merci finally answered, then turned and skittered down the stairs.

"Why not put the kettle on for some tea?" she called after the girl, not realizing how silly it sounded until after it was said. This wasn't a party; it was the most embarrassing moment of her life.

The door slammed, the sound echoing through the loft, and to the beat of Sarah's heart. Merci— Fairy—had run outside. She would tell. She was going to someone to reveal what she'd seen, and soon the whole town would know that Sarah Hornsby's wanton behavior was no better than the girls' above the saloon. Panic set in, sending her mind spinning. She tried to grasp the chaos, but her thoughts refused to be tamed. Instead, they ran amok, creating even more havoc than she could fathom.

She said the first thing that came into her mind. "She's going to tell the whole town."

"No, she's not." Ben's words brushed her fears off.

But they didn't stop them from growing. "Yes, she is. Soon the whole town will know I've acted like a ... "

Ben turned and gave her a hard stare. "Like a what? A woman? A living, breathing female?"

"No."

"Then what? A lonely woman? Don't you think there're plenty in this town to go around?"

"In this town? No." She didn't even stop to think of what he might be implying. "No. A wanton. A harlot."

"That's a bloody damn lie!" he stated, dropping his pants in mid-reach. He turned to confront her on the middle of the bed, his hands resting on her shoulders. "Listen to yourself. Would you accuse a woman of being a wanton or a harlot if rumors got around she might have slept with a man?"

"No, but ... "

"Then I resent your saying so."

Her eyes were wide as she stared into his, wishing with all her heart he was right. But he wasn't. She knew it, and so did he. He was speaking of the way things should be, not the way they were in real life. "Other people would, Benjamin. We both know that."

His fingers tightened on her shoulders. His gaze hardened, then slowly he released his hold. "She won't tell."

"Why? What makes you say so?"

"Because she would be telling on herself. That wasn't what she came here for. She came here to get away, not relive Tombstone."

"Maybe," Sarah said. But she wasn't convinced, and wouldn't be until she spoke to Merci. All she could hope was that the young woman returned before discussing with anyone else what she'd seen.

Still holding the sheet in place, she turned and confronted Ben. "Tell me."

He stood and reached for his pants, slipping into them quickly and efficiently. "There's nothing to tell."

"I need to know exactly what's going on here before we go down and talk to her when she returns. After all, we'll be asking her to keep our secret."

Ben's brows raised. "What secret?"

"Nothing much," Sarah said. "It's just the small one where we were found in bed. Together."

"Ah," Ben muttered, reaching for his shirt. "*That* secret." He smiled humorlessly at her discomfort.

The door slammed again, the bell above it tinkling merrily, as if there were good news. And there was. Merci was back.

Sarah let out a sigh of relief.

Ben grinned smugly, then pretended nothing unusual had happened. "You're speaking of the secret where you seduced me, pulling off my clothing and leading me into temptation like a newborn lamb."

"Wrong analogy, Ben Drake," Sarah whispered back. She quickly slipped her dress over her head. "It's the one where you snuck into my bedroom and caught me while I was sleeping and unaware."

"Are you saying you didn't know I was making love to you?"

"Of course I did," she hissed, so angry and frustrated that arguing seemed to be the only release she had. "I just didn't think we would get caught!"

"Oh, I see," Ben said. "I'm good enough to take

to bed, but not good enough to let the world know I'm worthy of *your* bed.''

"Don't put words in my mouth, or they might wind up looking an awful lot like your foot!" she hissed, keeping her voice down while trying to shout out her frustration. "Please explain to me what is going on so I know what to do next!"

Tucking in his shirt, Ben turned to face her. His hands came down to rest on her shoulders. His face was stern. Earnest. She knew without a doubt that no matter how bad things looked just now, she trusted him to help her do the right thing to save her reputation.

"Listen carefully." He gave a sigh, gathered his thoughts and then spoke, slowly and distinctly. "Fairy is, was, a whore in the Birdcage Saloon. I spent time with her for a while and we became friends as well as lovers. She was, is, sweet and kind and very intelligent. We parted friends when I received the news of my father's death and came here to find Anthony."

Sarah tried to ignore the hurt at the thought of his relationship with someone as pretty and kind as Merci. It was one thing to know he was experienced, but quite another to know who he was experienced with.

She didn't even want to think of him comparing her older body with such a young and beautiful, and no doubt talented, woman. She had the rest of her life to worry about that. Right now, she had her reputation to keep. "But she found her way here. Was it to find you?"

He looked disgusted. "I have no idea what brought her here, but I will certainly find out."

"And then what?" Sarah asked. "The town

believes her to be an honorable woman. I vouched for her myself with friends and neighbors. Will you marry her?"

"I will not apologize for my actions before I came here, Sarah. My actions with Fairy, then and now, have nothing to do with marriage."

"Are you sure?"

"I'm positive. And Fairy's apologies are up to her. As far as I'm concerned, she's in the past, and this new woman, this Sister Merci, can have whatever she can get."

"A new start?"

Ben nodded. "If that's what she wants. I won't tell anyone." His face turned grim. "And she won't say anything, either, if she knows what's good for her."

Sarah nodded, her heart feeling so very heavy with guilt. Who was she to condemn Merci when she'd been doing the very things Merci used to get paid to do? The only difference was the exchange of money. . . .

That wasn't true. The difference was much bigger than that. Sarah loved Ben.

Did Merci love him, too? Was that the reason for her shocked reaction and running away from them? Was he the reason she was here? Had she been following him? Waiting to see him alone? Had she used Sarah to find Ben? It was a horrible thought, but Sarah couldn't shy away from it now. She rolled on her stockings and slipped her small feet into a pair of dainty ballet shoes she had been given as a gift, then, with all the dignity she could muster, walked down the stairs to the kitchen to confront her fate.

Ben's heavier step was right behind hers.

* * *

Merci stood at the kitchen table filling a gauze square with tea, tying it, then placing it inside the blue ceramic pot. The kettle boiled and she grabbed it, poured hot water into the pot. She didn't look up or acknowledge that Sarah and Ben had joined her until her task was completed.

Ben watched her through narrowed eyes. He didn't know what her game was, but he was going to find out if it killed him . . . if he didn't kill her first.

Fairy looked up and glared at him. Her chin tilted defiantly, much like Sarah's did when he knew he was about to see her stubborn streak come out. It was amazing what a difference in attitude and clothing made. He knew the body under her gown as well as he knew his own. God knew, he'd explored it more. But with that drab gray, high-necked gown, no one would have guessed what she could do with her . . .

Merci looked at Sarah, her gaze as pleading as it was angry earlier. "Whatever you're thinking, it's not true."

Sarah sat down at the table. "Tell me."

"Ben told me about this place and it sounded so good. So . . . decent. After my sister died, I knew I had to change my life. I started saving my money, little by little. When the Birdcage closed down, I packed my bag and came here to start again."

"Why?" Ben asked.

She darted him a disgusted look, then continued talking to Sarah. "I want what everyone wants, Sarah. I want a home and family and a decent place to raise children. I want someone to love and to love me. I may not have been a saint in the past, but I did whatever I needed to do in order to survive."

Sarah looked confused. "But why, Merci? Why here and why me?"

"I didn't know you knew Ben, Sarah. I didn't even know Ben was still here! I thought he was coming to tell his brother and they would both leave for England!"

"I didn't tell you that!" Ben declared.

"No, I know. But we talked about Clear Creek, and you told me a lot about it. It sounded so . . . so right. It was the perfect place to begin again, and this time do it right." She sounded so forlorn, so desperate.

"What went wrong?" Sarah asked softly, her hand reaching out to Merci's. "Where did this all start?"

Merci held Sarah's hand tight, and sat down. "My father sold me to a house in Nevada when I turned thirteen. It wasn't something new," she said bitterly when she saw the expression on Sarah's face. "My father'd been using me since I was six. I didn't know what else to do. He told me that as long as I sent home money, he'd leave my little sister alone. So I did what I was told. I sent home every dime I could."

"Where was your mother?"

"She died giving birth to Emily. My dad had beaten her the night before, and she was in pretty bad shape. I was put in charge of the infant." Merci smiled sadly. "She was the sweetest thing you've ever seen, Sarah. All pink and fuzzy and so beautiful." Merci closed her eyes for a moment, but two tears managed to squeeze their way to freedom after all.

Ben's stomach churned with her story. It was an

old one, and Merci wasn't the first woman to go through hell before she was old enough to walk. But to think he'd been with her all that time and had never taken the time to find out what made her choose the path she was on . . . well, that made him pretty mean-hearted.

"And Emily?" Sarah asked softly, her voice thick with emotion.

"Emily died two years ago. My dad said she lost her balance and fell down the well." Her expression changed to one of pure hate. "But I knew better. I knew *him*."

"You can't prove it, though," Ben interjected.

"I don't have to. Besides, it's all over now. He's dead, too."

"How did he die?"

The look she gave Ben chilled his blood down to the bone. "He just did," she finally said.

But Ben knew. Fairy had killed him. He didn't blame her.

"Merci. Fairy . . . " Sarah began.

"Merci. It's my real name, Sarah. I didn't lie to you."

Ben got the implication. "Instead, you lied to me."

Merci shook her head. "No. That was my name doing what I did when I met you. No one uses their real name in that profession, Ben." She raised a brow. "Or did you honestly believe all the women would have done what they did for nothing? Just to enjoy the company and be with a man?"

"Obviously I was mistaken." His voice was dry. His thoughts were shamed. Hell, until this moment, he'd never given it more than a passing thought. He'd taken it for granted that most everyone was where they were and doing what they were doing to earn a living and to have fun. Sometimes, if they were lucky, they were both and the same.

"Obviously."

Sarah sighed, letting go of Merci's hands and pouring herself a cup of tea. "What now?" she asked.

"I don't know."

"Are you going to make public what you saw this afternoon?" Sarah asked.

"Of course not!" Merci stated. "I would never do that, Sarah." Her look changed. "Are you going to tell the town about me?"

Sarah smiled sadly. "That wouldn't be a very good idea, would it? I introduced you to the town as an upstanding citizen. I vouched for you in church. I took you into my home."

"Do you want me to leave?" Merci asked. "If you want me to, I will. Or I'll find another place in town to live."

Ben tried not to let his sigh of relief show. It was the easiest way to go. But his conscience bothered him. He didn't want Merci around to remind Sarah of his own past with the young woman.

"Will you ever go back to your other way of life?" Sarah asked slowly, her mind churning. Ben was sure he could see the wheels turning.

"Never."

"Think seriously about your answer, Merci. Are you sure about that? I know it's an easy way to earn money when needed. You don't know what the future holds."

"I'm sure. I never want to do that again. Ever. And it's not easy, Sarah. You never know if the next man won't beat you to a pulp. And no one would care. You have no identity. No life. No self-respect."

"Then stay as long as you need to." Sarah's voice was calm, clear and decisive. "If you decide at a later date that you need to move on, I have a few friends I can recommend you stay with in other towns."

"Thank you, Sarah. Thank you so much!" Merci looked both relieved and happy. "I won't let you down. I promise you that."

Ben stood and walked to the front of the store. The two women continued talking in hushed voices, discussing what was needed to continue living together.

Not once was his name mentioned. It was a good thing. As soon as he finished seeing to the church building, he'd be leaving, too. Although he'd met several women here in town that were eligible for what he and Sarah had set up to be future possible wives, he knew now that he couldn't stay.

He'd just shared a taste of heaven. He wasn't about to be in the same town as Sarah and know he couldn't return to her for his sustenance.

Although he was going to pursue her, he had a gut feeling she wasn't going to let him back in her bed. Not after this.

And hell, he couldn't blame her.

If only . . .

Stop it! he told himself. He was marrying for money so he could have what he wanted most: a working ranch that he could call his own. A life with a wife, and children to follow in his footsteps. Someone who loved him for him, not for a station in life, money in the bank, or status in the community.

He didn't deserve happiness with a woman like Sarah. She needed a man who was emotionally strong, not jaded and willing to take the path of least resistance.

He had to get away.

Instead of leaving the way he came, Ben strode out the front door and headed toward the hotel. He'd get his coat and take a ride. Maybe the cold air would clear his head and he could think of something else besides the prim and proper—and very luscious—Mrs. Hornsby!

By the time she and Merci finished talking, Sarah was emotionally exhausted. She didn't know what was going to happen next, but this day had taught her not to expect boredom to set in anytime soon.

She still flushed a deep red when she remembered making love to Ben in her bed. Had she done all those things? Felt those feelings? Touched him where she'd never touched a man before? Had she been that wanton?

But the thought that doused her with icy water was that he could be comparing her bedroom antics with Merci right this moment. No matter what he said, she would not measure up. She couldn't—not to someone as young, beautiful and talented as Merci must have been. Even Ben admitted he'd spent "time" with her for a few weeks. That was not a ten-minute visit.

Sarah began making biscuits again.

Chapter Fourteen

Secrets. Did this whole town have secrets or was it just her?

Sarah covered her hair with her cleaning bonnet, put on an apron that covered her entire dress, got out the broom and began vigorously sweeping the wooden floor. She swept from the front end of the store to the rear kitchen door. Each stroke was hard and full, as if she were pulling dirt from under the polished pine boards themselves. It felt good.

She promised herself she would remain busy all afternoon, and half the night if necessary. She would clean the store and living quarters far into the night. She would do whatever it took to erase the memory of Merci's shocked face as she stared at a naked Sarah and Ben.

Sarah had been raised by a domineering father and married to an even more dictatorial husband. But nothing had happened to her like the story Merci told. Nothing even came close.

She believed Merci. The woman might have been dramatic, but Sarah knew when another woman was lying. It was usually in the eyes and body language. Merci was telling the truth, she was sure.

Did Ben really pay for the privilege of sleeping with and making love to Merci? And if so, why? He could have any woman he wanted. All he had to do was smile, and they fell into his arms as if he was standing under a ripe apple tree in a high wind. Did he think he was in love with her? She was certainly beautiful enough for any man to be in love with. Even Mr. Heine had stared at her at the Literary Dinner a few weeks ago. Sarah had noticed that after dinner, he'd followed her from room to room, keeping his distance but still watching her.

A new thought popped into her head. Did Mr. Heine know Merci from her days at the Birdcage Saloon, too? Was that why he'd stared?

One thought came on the heels of another and another. No matter what she tried to do, she couldn't silence the voices that spoke. She was grateful she had the store to clean. It was too much to expect of her to think of anything else.

In the space of a day, she had lost her heart, given up her body, was shocked by the stories of the woman she lived with and thought she knew, and felt betrayed. And all of it was her fault. She could have—should have—said no at every opportunity. But she hadn't. So now she had her own consequences to deal with.

Sarah wiped her tears on her apron, picked up the dustpan and got back to work. She had to make the best of the mess. That was all. And she would.

Hearts were broken every day, but life went on. She would be no exception. Well, that wasn't quite true. She would be the exception with a few trunks of material and lace.

Later that day, Merci ran in, cheeks bright with the cold and eyes sparkling in delight. She ran to her suitcase and grabbed a pair of dark gloves. "I'm running errands today, Sarah. I promise I'll be back home before bedtime."

"Errands?" Sarah asked. "What kind of errands?"

"Pansy wants me to accompany her on a visit to Mrs. Mitchell's house. Mrs. Mitchell is having cake and coffee for a few of the ladies." Merci's eyes glistened with happiness. "And they invited me along! Isn't it wonderful?"

Sarah forced a smile. She knew how much Merci wanted to be accepted as one of the group of social women in town. It looked as if it was now within her grasp. "Yes, it is, Merci. Please be careful, though. E.Z., one of the workmen around town, says the temperature is going to drop tonight. His bones tell him so."

Merci stopped in mid-flight. She looked closely at Sarah. "Are you all right, Sarah?"

"I'm fine," Sarah said, and meant it. It was good to see Merci again and know that the girl hadn't changed since last week. Only Sarah's knowledge had changed. That didn't count. Not really.

"I don't want you to be nervous every time I'm around," the young woman said. She looked so excited and concerned at the same time. And so very earnest. "Please don't put a wall between us, Sarah. I think so much of you. Why, if you weren't in my life, I'd feel so alone." Merci reached out and held Sarah's hands. "Please?"

Sarah smiled, but this time it wasn't forced. "Go enjoy yourself. I trust you to do what is necessary

to maintain our position. More than just our liveli-
hood depends on our reputation."

Merci squeezed her hands, her face surprised
and so very happy. "I know. Thank you for having
faith in me. I won't let you down, Sarah. I will never
let you down."

"Thank you for saying so," Sarah said, understanding Merci's underlying meaning. Merci would
remain a lady, doing nothing that would harm
Sarah or her standing in town. Sarah never
doubted it. The awkwardness was over. She felt as
if she were on firm ground once more.

Besides, she knew just how much Merci's circumstances were out of her hands.

Once she had cleaned the rooms from one end
to the other, she set the water to boil and began
her bath in the warmth of the rear kitchen.

She was going to relax and not think about making love to Ben, no matter what! She refused to
believe she'd just made herself a futile promise.

Ben worked alongside the volunteers during the
last three days of laying out the church foundation.
He couldn't seem to get the men to understand
the concept of pouring foundation rather than
pier and beam flooring. No matter what he tried,
it didn't work, so he finally admitted defeat and
agreed they would use the pier and beam.

Tomorrow they would begin digging piers into
the ground in which to build the foundation before
the next step—the flooring—could begin. Once
the foundation and floors were in place, they would
start on the walls, then finally the roof. It would
take his regiment of volunteers a month or two to
complete roofing in the church itself, depending

on how many men would work consistently. But it would be ready for services at that time. If the sky was good enough for God, it would be good enough for the townspeople—at least for a while.

Pews, altar and stained glass would come in time. Right now, the building foundation was most important.

Ben left the meadow at the edge of town and rode directly to the Haude home, only a mile or so out of town. He had a dinner date with Pansy and her family.

Two hours later, Ben had finally stopped wrinkling his nose against the stench of wallowing pigs. He'd almost become immune, although he didn't think there was any such thing completely. Besides, all his attention was on the diminutive, feminine woman at his side. He continued to stare at her in wonder.

Pansy, dressed in old clothing, moved confidently through the pigpen as she showed him her father's innovations—the equipment needed to raise the smelly things. ". . . and then Papa began making the slatted floors for others who were raising hogs. It made a world of difference and more shoats lived since they were less likely to die of suffocation by the sow."

She looked proudly toward the older man who walked around the far side of the penned yard, observing the sows lumbering about the muddy area.

"And you help him." It wasn't a question. It was a statement.

She nodded, her big blue eyes begging him to understand. "Do you mind?"

A wide grin split his face. Ben laughed. If a woman could wallow in the pigpen and feel good about life, what would she do as the wife of a rancher? Probably be the best helpmate a man ever had. "Not at all, little woman. Not at all!"

She returned his smile, then laughed in return. "I'm so glad," she said. "I was worried that you might think me less of a woman." Her smile slipped into a frown. "You do understand, don't you, that while I work with Papa in the fields, I don't cook or clean house?"

"I think I understand, little one," Ben said, not at all worried about the mundane chores in married life. That's what household help was for. Besides, once the babies came, she would learn how to do those chores.

"I mean it, Ben." Her smile was gone, replaced by a look of sheer determination. "I don't sew or cook. I'm not like our friend, Sarah. Doing those things bore me to death!"

"And babies?"

She blushed a beet red, but her expression didn't change. "I'm not sure about them. I haven't made up my mind."

His brows rose. "About babies or about having them?"

"Both."

He wasn't sure what to say. Pansy was certainly different than what he'd expected. When he'd met her in church, she was coy and sweet, with charm oozing from her tiny, perfectly formed body. Why, even her parents beamed at her as if she were the first intelligent child born on earth.

"We both have some things to think about, don't we?" His warm tone softened his words.

Her expression didn't soften at all. Her eyes narrowed as they studied his face. "Yes, we do. But we might be jumping the gun a little, don't you think? After all, you've yet to get to know me and my parents."

Obviously they were a package deal.

Stubborn little witch. Ben grinned. This was getting interesting. . . .

It had taken Lillie longer than she expected to run all the errands she needed to accomplish in San Antonio and the surrounding area. She returned bearing myriad stock for the store.

Looking excited and glad to be back, Lillie entered the store just minutes before it opened for business the next morning. She was solid and strong and knew none of the craziness that Sarah had gone through in the past few days. Best of all, she didn't know about the fiasco with Ben. . . .

She was so proud of herself. She had traveled long distances by herself, making sure she gave new supplies to the women as well as receiving the finished goods, and since the trip was now completed, and she knew the importance of her mission was satisfied, she was anxious for Sarah to know how well she'd done.

"I brought three trunks of goods, Sarah. It tweren't nothing for the women to give over their needlework. They were so excited to get their money *and* more wool and fabric. You could see the pride in their eyes!"

"Where are the trunks?" Sarah asked, glancing toward the door.

"Some wayward man named E.Z., he took 'em from the wagon, said trunks like that are too heavy for a lady to unload and he's gonna bring them down from the railway station. He says he knows you real well and has a load of cake for you anyway."

Lillie undid her cape and placed it on the coatrack, along with her hat and mittens. She patted her graying hair in place, then walked back to the kitchen to warm her hands. Although the weather in Clear Creek was much warmer than where Sarah came from, it was still chilly to Lillie, who was from Galveston along the warm Texas coast. "That old geezer is some flirt," she muttered, disapproval in her tone. "He kept swilling me with compliments until I was either gonna drown in spirits or hit him in the head with my purse!"

Sarah grinned. That was E.Z., all right. "I gather he's still alive."

"Well, yes." Lillie grinned ruefully. 'Twould be a shame to kill someone who so obviously kissed the Blarney Stone and lived to tell the tale, no matter how short and cute he is."

Sarah was startled. "E.Z.?" she asked. "A little guy with bowed legs and bald head?"

Lillie nodded, her eyes a little dreamy. "The very same. And he's taking care of our trunks and some cakes he's carried all the way from Blissful."

"Kathleen's cake is here just in time for today's business!" Sarah said, satisfaction lacing her voice. "It's taken her long enough to get around to baking."

"E.Z. says that she's been busy with babies." Lillie moved the teacups into the storing pattern she liked best. Apparently she felt Sarah hadn't done her work properly. Then she headed toward the pot of tea and wrapped her hands around its warmth.

Sarah gave the older woman's shoulders an impulsive hug, startling her.

"Here, now, what's that about?" Lillie asked,

properly embarrassed and pleased by the show of emotion.

"I missed you."

Lillie couldn't have looked more pleased if she tried. "You did?"

"Of course," Sarah said. "You knew I would, didn't you?"

"Well, I thought maybe you were all caught up with Sister Merci."

"You thought she could take your place?"

"I didn't know. . . ."

"Well, you do now," Sarah stated, giving Lillie another hug. "You're a very important part of my life, and my business, too. I couldn't do it without you."

"Thank you for sayin' so," Lillie said, but as much as she looked pleased by the praise, she also looked worried. "Tell me how Sister Merci did," she asked.

Sarah brushed aside what had happened earlier. "She's doing fine. She's been helping in Mr. Heine's office from noon to evening, filing and ordering whatever his company needs."

"She knows how to do that?"

"I guess so." Sarah turned her back to get them both a cup of tea. Lillie was too good at reading what was on her mind. "Merci is a woman filled with surprises. Apparently she can do books as well as hair."

"My! Wouldn't it be nice if we were all so talented and pretty."

Sarah laughed, then told her a carefully edited story of the broken upstairs wall. She left out the part about Ben in her bed and Merci finding them both there, instead, telling her about her gift to Harmony.

Lillie looked stern. "An' then you lent that hussy a new dress?"

"Gave it to her," Sarah corrected.

"And what if somebody mistakes her for you?"

"Then they're blind."

"You're playing with your reputation. You could be ruint."

Dire warnings. Lillie was good at that. But that was the least of her problems.

"I'll take my chances, Lillie. Meanwhile, we need to open the store. I'll turn the sign around and let them know we're open for business."

Although it was just morning, Sarah felt tiredness overcome her. She'd been fighting with herself these past few days, trying to figure out angles so often, she walked a maze all through her sleep.

She flipped the sign around to show the carefully lettered "OPEN," then turned and plumped a pillow. Her hand automatically reached to her pocket and patted the contents, feeling the crackle of paper. Sometime during the night a note had been slipped under her door. Ben had invited her to breakfast this morning at the hotel. Sarah hadn't been able to think of anything else. But she wasn't going to meet him. It wasn't the prudent thing to do.

That didn't mean she ignored it. Any minute, she expected him to burst through the front door and demand she break bread with him. Just the thought alone made her heart trip into overtime. The horrible part was that she was so very tempted to do just that. She could justify their meeting, she knew she could.

Sarah wasn't sure what she would say to Ben. One part of her yearned to sit across the table and watch him speak, watch his mouth form words and smile, watch his face frown and show deep thoughts by wrinkling his brow. Watch his blue eyes crinkle in the corners and his dimples deepen with each wonderful facial expression. Watch his hands, with such strong yet gentle fingers, gesture, and know they were the same hands that had touched her in places she hadn't touched herself. . . .

Another part of her prayed she wouldn't have that opportunity to sit and stare like a google-eyed kid and be embarrassed. Wouldn't have to remember anything to do with that Sunday afternoon when her world turned topsy-turvy. Watch as her soul watered at the very thought of being with him again.

In other words, she didn't need to make a fool out of herself again.

Once was enough!

Just as she was about to put biscuits on the sideboard for the customers, E.Z. drove up to the boardwalk with a wagon laden with trunks of all sizes and shapes. On top of those were heavy wooden crates precariously balanced and not too carefully tied.

She watched in wonder as E.Z. rolled to the door like a drunken sailor, a smile splitting his face. "Howdy, Mrs. Hornsby." He grabbed his hat from his head and gave a quick bow. "And 'morning to you again, Miz Lillie." He stood with the door open, waiting for the older woman to say something.

"How many of those are ours, E.Z.?" Sarah asked, the question burning in her mind long enough.

"All of 'em, ma'am. Some's come all the way from that there Englant. Some is Miz Lillie's and one is from Kathleen." He waved his hat toward the general area of the top of the wagon. "It's got papers, cake and some stuff for you from Kathleen and Charlie."

Lillie's jaw dropped so far down, her chin hit her breast. "All of them?" her voice squeaked.

E.Z. nodded. "Ever last one of them."

Lillie grinned, although she tried not to. "Well, then, Mr. E.Z. Bring 'em in. Bring 'em in."

"I'll do just that, Miz Lillie. But promise me that when I'm done, there'll be a strong cup of coffee waitin' for me."

"You've got a deal," Lillie said, heading to the rear of the store so fast, mice could have been after her chocolate cake.

Sarah stared as E.Z. took the first crate down and precariously balanced it on his shoulder.

Where was she going to put all this? There wasn't enough floor space to put the boxes, let alone open them up. Besides, it would probably take all day just to open them and see what she had.

Making a quick decision, Sarah flipped the sign back to the side that said "CLOSED." The store needed new stock, and this looked like it was the day.

For the second time in as many days, Ben relaxed with Pansy's family at the formal dining table. The smell of pigs managed to permeate the house, but scented candles overrode most of the odor. Mrs. Haude seemed to have a permanent curl to her nose, and Ben figured it was probably due to the smell.

The family was sweet and kind and both parents very gentle. Pansy was the one who had that small streak of stubborness if the look in her eye at the pigpen was any indication. That was fine. He wouldn't be around that much anyway. She was the perfect candidate because she would be busy while he was gone working cattle. She would have parents to keep her occupied, and after a while, they would have a baby.

What more could he ask for? he wondered as he leaned back and enjoyed the conversation and coffee with fresh lemon pie. He ignored the fact that this was *not* what he wanted, no matter how perfect the situation.

He refused to think about Sarah and the note he'd left her that morning. She hadn't answered. He'd told himself she was probably busy discussing Merci's problems with her and making sense out of nonsense.

By the time he finished at the church grounds and cleaned up for dinner with the Haudes, he'd heard that Lillie had returned early that morning. So that was probably why he hadn't heard from Sarah today. At least, he *hoped* it was the reason.

He refused to believe his feelings for her had anything to do with love. Absolutely refused. Why, thoughts like that would be exactly what would give his father the biggest pleasure. It would make that old bastard happy to know his son was as miserable as he was—dead or alive.

But he wished he could sit at her kitchen table and discuss his thoughts with her. There was nothing he wanted more than to do that one more time. All he could do was pray that he hadn't messed up too badly.

Ben refused to look into his emotions, but his heart hurt. It hurt really bad.

* * *

Merci didn't arrive home until almost bedtime. E.Z.'s bones had been a correct barometer for the weather. The sun had disappeared behind the trees and the chill of the winter evening, while not as bad as it had been, was still bone-trembling, even for the middle of February.

Lillie and Sarah sat in the store area, their legs wrapped with afghans, holding cups of tea in their laps as they discussed the open trunks spread out all over the room, still filled with goods spilling out of them. Their smiling faces could have lit the length of Main Street.

Merci hung up her coat and hat and stared at the goods that exploded out of the tops of the containers. "What is this? What happened?"

"Lillie returned from her trip with three trunks. You returned with two trunks and E.Z. brought all of them from the train station," Sarah said happily.

"But there're at least"—Merci pirouetted, attempting to quickly assess the amount of goods—"at least fifteen trunks and crates!"

"Twenty-two," Lillie said. "We didn't have room for all of them, so E.Z. will bring the rest tomorrow."

Merci looked as if someone had hit her over the head. "Twenty-two?" she whispered. "Twenty-two *filled* trunks?"

Both women nodded, their grins still in place. "Pour a cup of tea and join us, Merci," Sarah said gently. "It's a special blend, all the way from England. We have several tins of it."

Merci still looked stunned. "Tea?"

"Ben's brother, Anthony, sent it to us. It's payment for finding Ben a wife.'' Sarah didn't let the others see how much those words hurt. She had done what she'd promised to do and apparently, Ben thought she'd done the job right, because he'd written his brother and told him to send the trunks. The saving grace was that he had written the letter at least a good month ago.

"Ben? Are you marrying him?'' Merci asked, her gaze as bright as a new penny.

"No, dear,'' Sarah said. "Pansy Haude is going to marry him. At least I think so.'' She refused to acknowledge the pain that thought brought. Not in front of her friends.

Merci sat down hard, her blue eyes not leaving Sarah's. "You're not going to marry him? Why not?''

Lillie gave a snort. "Goodness, girl. Why would she?''

Sarah refused to look at the older woman. "He's destined for someone besides an old widow who can't have children. He needs someone young and vibrant and who can give him all her attention— and children.''

"He needs you, Sarah.'' Merci's voice was vehement. "And obviously his brother thinks so, too, or he wouldn't have sent such a wonderful dowry.''

Now it was Lillie's turn to be amazed. "Dowry? For Sarah?'' Her eyes narrowed as she eyed the two who were locked in gazes with each other. From her point of view, it looked as if they were silently speaking. "What is going on here? Are you two keeping secrets from me?'' She looked from one to the other. "Sarah? Merci? Tell me!''

Sarah leaned back and smiled, glad that Lillie didn't notice her hands clenched around the empty teacup. She purposely relaxed her grip.

"Merci thinks that Ben and I should be more than friends."

Lillie looked confused. "Why? Does she think you need to marry?"

Merci laughed. "No, no, of course not! I just thought they made a wonderful couple. And out of all the women in this town, Sarah was the one that most looked as if she could civilize him! Don't you think?"

It took the older woman a moment, but finally she smiled. "Well, you might be right at that, Sister Merci," she said. "Sarah could civilize just about anyone. Why, look what she's done with Mr. Horst to get the church built."

It was Merci's turn to be surprised. "You mean because she got him to donate the land?"

"She not only got him to donate the land, but she also brought all the townspeople together in the effort to build a church to begin with!" Merci looked at Sarah with more than a little heroine worship. "And now, Mr. Drake is in charge of the building and the volunteers. I'd say that's a lot!"

Merci's eyes lit with delight and surprise. "Did Horst donate the lumber?"

"My goodness!" Lillie exclaimed. "You didn't realize you'd actually convinced him?"

"Aren't you working on Mr. Heine's paperwork in the office, Merci?" Sarah asked, frowning. She was worried about both their reputations. If anyone in town found out about Merci's past, it would be disastrous. And if Merci told anyone about finding Sarah in bed with Ben, she would have no reputation to lose. "I thought you were ordering supplies for him."

"I was. I am!" Merci looked flustered. Her face

reddened. "I will. That is, when he decides to tell me to order something."

"The lumber has already been delivered," Sarah said, more worried than ever now. For Merci to be flustered took some effort. "Is it possible you could add some hot water to our tea, Lillie? Then we'll all have a piece of Kathleen's famous carrot cake to celebrate our good fortune."

Lillie's gaze went from Sarah to Merci, then back again. She gave a sigh and hefted herself out of her chair, lifted the pot and walked toward the warmer rear area of the building.

"Merci. What's going on between you and Mr. Heine?" Her voice was low, almost a whisper.

Merci stared down at her hands for a very long moment. The longer she stared, the more nervous Sarah became.

"Merci? Look at me. Talk to me!" she whispered.

Finally, Merci looked up and into her eyes, pleading for understanding even before she said the words. "Sarah, please understand. I love him. He loves me. He asked me to marry him."

Sarah's blood turned icy cold. Her feet and hands froze instantly. "No." It was an involuntary statement. One she couldn't have kept inside if she had tried with all her might. "No. You can't do that."

"I just said yes."

"Are you insane? What if he finds out?"

"He won't." Merci looked down, and then back up at her newfound friend. Determination emanated from her. "And I'm going to be the best damn wife you've ever had the privilege to meet. I'm going to be the lady by day and the whore by night, and love every minute of it."

"Merci—"

She didn't stop. ". . . and I'm going to have his

children, take care of his office, and love him every moment of every day. I'll never have a cross word with him . . . well"—she smiled a very tiny smile—"not often, anyway."

"Merci."

"And I'll never admit to what I did before I came here. I know that Ben won't tell because he wants to marry and be respectable in the place he's chosen to live." Merci took a deep breath. "So it's up to you, Sarah. If you tell him, then it's over. But in the end, it will ruin your reputation, too."

"Why? Because you'll tell everyone what you saw Ben and I doing?"

"No, because they'll think you knew about me all along." Merci leaned forward, her big eyes filled with honesty. "I would never tell what I saw, Sarah. Never."

Lillie rattled the top of the teapot and cleared her throat, unwilling to wait any longer than she had to to return with the tea.

Merci reached out and touched Sarah's hands. "Please, Sarah. Please let me begin again. I know I don't deserve it, but please. . . ."

"Ready or not, here I come," Lillie stated, walking around the settee to place the fresh tea on the table. "Now. What'er we gonna do with all this stuff, boss lady? It looks to me that we might be closed for a couple of days."

"At least for the rest of the week."

"And when do you think the church will be completed, Sarah?" Merci asked, while pouring herself a cup.

"I'm not sure. Why?"

"Because I want to be the first bride married in it. It seems only fitting, since Horst has donated so much." She looked up at Sarah. "Will you be my witness, Sarah? Please?"

Sarah's cup slipped from her fingers and crashed to the floor.

How could one day go from such happiness to such indecision in one short hour?

Chapter Fifteen

When Ben returned home from the Haudes'
farm, he found a note under his door. The handwriting was Sarah's. He poured himself a glass of
brandy, sat in front of the fireplace and slowly
opened the sealed paper. His heartbeat quickened
as he scanned her note. Her handwriting was pre-
cise and feminine, just like she was.

> *Dear Mr. Drake,*
> *Although I thank you for the invitation to break-*
> *fast, I did not see your note until past the time*
> *designated to meet. I'm very sorry if I caused you*
> *undue irritation.*

Ben snorted at that one. She'd caused him irritation, among other emotions he didn't want to think
about, from the very first time he saw her through
the window that overcast January afternoon almost
two months ago.

This afternoon, I received sixteen trunks from your brother in England and am overwhelmed with the generosity of the goods he chose to send. I cannot thank you enough for your part in this bounty, especially realizing I have not truly "paid" my part of the bargain.

I have a dilemma I need to discuss, and further impose upon your generosity. Is it possible to meet with you tomorrow? It would be most appreciated.

Sincerely,
Sarah

Sarah needed something from him? That was a surprise, since she'd received the trunks and knew there was no longer any need to have anything to do with him. After all, she had what she wanted—supplies for her "creative women," as she called them.

Still holding the letter in one hand, Ben walked to the wooden boot remover and slipped off his boots. Then he set them outside the door so Thomas would pick them up and get them cleaned between now and the morning. Dirt, especially pig dirt, had its own aroma. Pansy's father seemed to think that particular mud smelled like money, but Ben didn't think so. It still smelled like what it was. Dung.

Forcing himself to sit down again, he sipped his brandy. He wanted to act like a kid and run down the hall barefoot to bang on Sarah's door until she opened it and allowed him in. But dignity and restraint were inbred, and reared their ugly head just in time to insure he didn't always make a fool of himself. This was one of those times.

Instead, he reached for pen and paper and answered her note with another.

Sarah,

   Let me extend the invitation again. Please meet me in the hotel dining area for breakfast tomorrow morning at eight-thirty. I look forward to seeing you again.

                                        Sincerely yours,
                                        Ben

Once written, he walked down the hallway and slipped the note under her door, leaving a corner showing on his side. He heard the rustle of her slippers, then the envelope disappeared.

The only thing separating them was a flimsy piece of wood. For one wild moment, he thought about knocking it down and taking her in his arms. All he had to do was put his shoulder against the wood and push hard.

The ache to hold her was almost more than he could bear, overwhelming him with the feeling of loneliness. That feeling was with him whenever she wasn't near. He had carried a lonely, hollow feeling with him ever since he could remember. It had never disappeared except for small amounts of time here and there. Until Sarah. When she walked into his sight, it disappeared. A smile in his direction. A touch on his sleeve. Just her presence and he was whole again.

Silly.

But the thought refused to go away. Heaven, the undeniable feeling of peace, was in her arms. He was smart enough to know that his future was in the bosom of Pansy's family. He knew better than to mix the two. Neither woman would stand for it. Ben was sure he couldn't, either. At least not here in Texas. If he was home in England, that behavior would be acceptable. Men there married for property and supported another woman for love. But not here. And not with these two women.

He didn't want to think of his brother's ability to have the love of his life in his arms. It only made his stomach clench tighter. His brother had no struggles. No worries. And the woman Anthony had loved since childhood was in his bed.

How lucky could a man get?

Ben couldn't even conceive of such happiness.

Ben was just on the other side of the door. Sarah knew it like she knew the sun would blister her this summer. If she held her breath, she swore she could hear him breathing. Every hair on the nape of her neck twitched. Her first reaction was to open it and pull Ben into her room. Into her bed. Just the thought of that made her blush from the tip of her bare toes, flooded her with red all the way up to where she braided her long hair. And she didn't care.

She craved him like a drowning person craved air to breathe.

She placed her hand on the wood and swore she could feel the heat of his.

Making love with Ben was the most wonderful, powerful thing that had ever happened to her. Ever. She couldn't begin to feel guilty, because for the first time ever, she knew what most men ran after, and paid for, and some few of the other women whispered about.

The wonder of it.

The miracle of it.

The sweetness of it.

She relived the experience of being in Ben's arms in her mind constantly, the feelings cropping up at odd times no matter who she was talking to or what she was doing. The excited, secret feeling followed her from room to room, customer to customer, tea drinking to stocking. She never knew when the memory would hit. All of a sudden, her stomach felt queasy and her heart palpitated. Her throat opened and closed quickly, allowing just enough air to breath. Then, the most unladylike thing happened. She dampened around her hairline, just like she did when she ate one of those hot peppers. Then the spot between her legs warmed and dampened. And then tingled.

Damn the man!

She didn't know what she was doing or what she would do when he finally chose a bride and married. She knew she couldn't go to church and watch him with his wife and growing family. It would kill her.

No matter what her motives for staying and working for the rights of the women she'd grown to love and respect, she wasn't that strong and moral of character. She wasn't ready to hurt on a daily basis for womankind. She didn't want to spend the rest of her nights crying herself to sleep.

She would have to leave. To move. There was no doubt. She wasn't sure what to do or where to go. But given thought, she'd find a way to end her own torture of being so close to, and yet so far away from, Ben.

Her bare feet felt the vibrations of his footfalls edging away from her door. She reached out again, touching the door with her fingertips. He was right *there!*

She could barely breathe with the thought of it. For one brief second she wanted to open the door and pull him in, sealing his mouth with a kiss before leading him to her bed and whispering not to wake up the women downstairs.

Then blistering reality returned, and she stilled, her hand on the doorknob.

Tears flooded her eyes as she held her body stiff and closed against the torrent of emotion that threatened to overwhelm her. Once the initial sob subsided enough to swallow the sharp sound that rested in her throat, Sarah walked to the sputtering candle next to her bed, opened the envelope and read the letter Ben had written.

Even as a tear hit her cheek, she smiled. She would be there.

Sarah dressed in her favorite deep-blue woolen dress. Once done, she wrapped her sandy-blonde hair carefully into a crown on top of her head. She'd thought about asking Merci to do her hair, but fought against it and won. She was who she was, and no amount of doing her hair differently would change that. But as she walked down the boardwalk to the hotel entrance, she couldn't stop herself from pinching her cheeks to bring a glow to them. Just once, she wanted to be the most absolutely beautiful woman one special man had ever seen. She knew it wouldn't happen, but she wanted it just the same.

Her pulse quickened alarmingly as she saw Ben standing just outside the dining area. As if she had called to him, he turned slowly, his gaze pinning her to the floor for a long moment.

He was wearing gray dress pants and Western boots. A thick flannel shirt was under an even thicker coat. He looked warm, very masculine and extremely sexy. That last thought almost made her blush. Like the morning sunrise, his slow smile lit the room. She felt the warmth from ten feet away.

"I hope you don't mind, Mrs. Hornsby, but I already made arrangements for breakfast and have a table waiting for us," he said in a low voice. Taking her elbow, he led her past crowded tables where mostly men sat in groups, eating hearty meals and drinking coffee that was strong enough to jump out of the earthenware cups. He pulled out a chair, seating her next to the rear window area.

She didn't answer, but the nod she'd given had been assent enough for Ben. As she slipped off her coat and handed it to the waiting waitress, she watched Ben take his seat across from her. "I hope you didn't order all that food for me," she said softly, eyeing the table of men seated closest to them. "I'm not quite the strapping cowhand on a ranch that the rest of the customers seem to be."

He cocked a knowing brow. "I think I knew that. Instead, I have a treat for both of us. The train that delivered your trunks also had a little something for me, ordered from Florida."

Sarah placed her red gingham napkin in her lap. "Really? What? Game hens? Fish?"

"Even better. Fresh oranges and grapes, grapefruit and delicious melons, along with ham."

Her eyes lit with delight. "You *do* know how to treat a lady," she teased.

He caught the waitress's eye and she waved back, rushing into the kitchen only to reappear with two plates covered with napkins. She proudly placed each of the weighted plates in front of them. Sarah's mouth watered even before the napkins were lifted to display the food.

Two ripe oranges were quartered, sitting in their

own rich juice. Beside them was a stem of golden grapes and a well-peeled grapefruit, the inner white skin gone. It, too, was cut into sections, and lightly sprinkled with coarse sugar that glistened like raindrops. To the side of that were steaks of thick, lean ham, browned to perfection on the edges.

"All this, and your company, too?" she said. "I'm a lucky woman." Sarah speared a piece of grapefruit and raised her fork.

Ben grinned, then began cutting into his own ham. "What did you want to discuss?"

"You first," she hedged, unwilling to start the meal with her news of Merci's up-and-coming wedding.

"What do you mean?"

"You asked me to breakfast two days ago. Why?" She slipped the section of fruit into her mouth and savored it, but her eyes never left him.

"I wanted to tell you that it looks as if Pansy might work out after all."

The fruit hit the bottom of her stomach like a boulder thrown into a calm pool. She placed her hands in her lap, no longer hungry. "That's nice," she lied.

"I thought so, too. And knowing that my brother had already sent the trunks, I wanted you to know so you wouldn't feel any guilt about accepting them."

"You knew?"

He nodded. "Of course I did. I told him to do so immediately. A Drake always keeps his promise. I'm no exception." He gave a wink. "And I think I know you well enough to realize you'd feel guilty if the trunks came before you thought you'd held up your end of the bargain."

"So it's that definite?" she asked, not really wanting to hear the answer that seemed to be so apparent.

"I think so," he said, occupying himself by sawing off another bite of ham and allowing her to study his face. His long lashes fell against his cheek. Beautiful lashes. Beautiful eyes. Strong male face.

He looked up, and she looked down at her own plate. "I see," she said. "Congratulations. When is the date?"

"Haven't set one and won't for a little while. I want to get used to her family first. They're a little, uh, different, you know."

She gave a soft laugh. "I don't know anyone who enjoys their hogs as much as the Haude family does. But they raise the best in four counties, so I'd say they're doing something right."

"Enough about me," he said, brushing off his pending marriage plans as if they were of no consequence whatsoever. "What did you want to tell me?"

She hesitated a moment, collecting her thoughts. "You already know that Merci has been working for Horst Heine since she returned from the county trip."

His own smile slipped. "Yes."

"And you've been working with him on the church."

"Yes."

"Did you know that Horst asked Merci to marry him?"

If she had planned on gigging him with a poleax, she had succeeded.

He swallowed another bite of ham and shook his head. "You're kidding."

"Not at all." Now that the information was out of her hands and into his, she could relax. Sarah picked up her fork again and bit into a grape, letting the taste explode in her mouth. It was better than delicious. She closed her eyes in enjoyment.

"Did she give him an answer?"

Sarah nodded.

"What was it?" Ben waited impatiently while she swallowed her own bite.

Ben leaned forward, his gaze narrowed as he watched her mouth chew every bit of taste out of her grape. His own mouth was slightly parted, as if ready to kiss her. She felt the heat all the way down to her toes. "Yes. The answer was yes."

Ben looked satisfied at her response. "So, I'm not the only one."

Was he talking about Merci or her own wayward reactions? "Only one?"

Ben leaned back. "You know what." He gave her a look that refused her to deny his meaning. "Us. Making love. Kissing, with that rosy mouth of yours on mine."

Her face went white.

"With your body under mine, holding on for dear life as we both spiraled out of control."

"Don't talk that way," she said, her voice lower than a whisper.

Ben continued in a low, conversational tone. "I want you to understand what I think about almost every minute of every day. I want you to know that you're not alone in your thoughts. And I need you to realize that this feeling is not going away. If anything, it's getting worse."

"You're going to marry Pansy."

"Because I have to, not because I want to."

"That's your problem."

"No. It's our problem."

"I don't want to hear your confession."

"And I don't give a damn what you don't want in the middle of a restaurant. If you want me to pay attention to your words, first make love to me. Afterward, talk to me while lying in my arms in the dark of the room. I promise I'll pay attention to every word you utter."

"You'll fall asleep."

"That piece of knowledge must be from another lifetime." He grinned, resembling a very handsome devil. "I'm the wrong man. I'm the one who can't wait to feel you tighten around me, feeling me inside you. Wanting me."

"Don't," she choked, afraid to look around for fear someone might have heard.

He continued in a low voice as if they were alone in the room. As if she hadn't pleaded with him not to say another word. As if he were getting ready to do exactly what he was describing. "Touching you in places you haven't been touched before. Kissing you in places you haven't been kissed before."

Sarah stared at him, feeling every one of his words reacting in her body. His smile disappeared as he stared at her just as intensely. They were tuned into each other so well, it was frightening. Her needs passed between them, speaking on the most elementary level of their hearts.

Her breath was shallow, her thoughts a tangled mess without order or content. Blood pounded through her limbs, turning her feet to lead and settling in a hot, liquid pool low in her belly. Her heart pounded in unison to the pulse in his distinguished temple.

Her heart.

She mustn't forget that small fact. He wasn't

speaking to her about love—only about *making* love. That was a big difference.

Sarah broke their locked gaze first, and looked down at her plate. Suddenly, she wished she was back in her own home, dining alone. She twisted a grape from its stem and looked back up. "You have a vivid imagination, Mr. Drake. Now, back to business."

Ben had the grace to look blank for a moment. Then, as if mentally shaking himself, he sorted through his thoughts and slowly answered, "We were discussing the ridiculous rumor that Fairy, uh, Merci, was going to marry Horst."

"It's not a rumor and neither is it ridiculous."

"Does he know about her past?"

"Not to my knowledge."

"I thought she was better than the average whore gold digger," he stated, throwing the awful words out like spitting tobacco.

"Really?" Sarah asked sweetly, barely masking her building anger. She was glad to feel anything take the place of the ache in her heart. It got the blood going in other directions. "That's a silly description, don't you think? I mean, you're so educated and all, yet you use words that don't seem to fit the situation at all."

Ben gave her a dismissing look. "You know what I'm saying, Sarah. If I had my way, she wouldn't be anywhere near you."

It was so much a man's point of view. Control the situation of others, especially women, and then they could pretend that all was fine. Not this time.

"A whore by definition is in the business of delivering services for money. As I recall, you bought those very same services. Explain to me, Ben, why is it all right for you to buy for fun, but not all right for her to sell for survival? And, by the way, what is the derogatory name for you?''

"You know what I mean.''

"No, I don't. You men seem to be blind to your own part in women's downfall,'' Sarah stated in a low, angry voice. To focus on this point took her attention off making love. "Merci is a good woman who is looking for a way to lead a normal life. She will make the perfect bride for Horst because all she wants is his happiness.''

There was no need mentioning that only this morning she'd been worried to death that Merci was being unfair to Horst by not telling him the truth. But now that she was listening to Ben and his dismissal of Merci as a woman with needs and dreams of a husband and family, she was certain Merci was doing the right thing.

"Merci is a whore,'' Ben stated.

Sarah's appetite was back. Anger fueled her and argument stirred the juices. Bless her soul, but she thought that just maybe she was learning to enjoy a good fight! What a change from the timid woman she'd been just one short year ago.

She grabbed another grape. "Of course, you would know best, Ben. But it seems to me that the men are far worse than she ever was. If no one was available to offer her services to, there wouldn't be such a word. Especially one where the female had no choice in the matter.''

His gaze narrowed. "You're defending her?''

"Of course.''

"Why?''

"Simple,'' she said around her grape. "Because you won't.''

"Why should I?''

"You're part of the problem, Ben. And that is no solution to her or to Horst."

Ben shook his head, unable to recognize the woman he knew was so sweet and scared half the time. She had suddenly turned into a barracuda. "Are you having a fainting spell?"

She laughed in his face. "Don't be ridiculous." It was about time she bested a man in an argument. She felt wonderful. Powerful. Practically invincible!

"I'm not sure I understand," Ben stated. "You accuse me of making a whore out of the girl, but you're worried enough about Horst to let me know what's going on. What do you expect me to do about it? Tell him about Fairy's past? I'll do that anyway."

"Why? What good will that do?"

"Stop this nonsense before it goes any further."

"It's not nonsense, and it's none of your business."

"That's changing horses in mid-stream, Sarah. You told me about it, and now I have to act. Horst is a good man and he's my friend. He can't marry her and then find out what she has been most of her life. It will be too late to get out of the marriage. If anyone else found out, he'd be the laughingstock of the town, and all because I kept my mouth shut."

"So?"

"So he'd have to file for divorce, and that would be a bloody mess, wouldn't it? Although, God knows, no one would fault him for dissolving it." The angrier he got, the thicker his English accent was.

It was wonderful to hear him, but she had to keep her mind on the battle. "I didn't tell you about the wedding to let you tear apart two people who want to be together. I told you so that you would know in advance and behave appropriately. I didn't want Horst to find out about *you* and Merci. Merci's the one who has to live with her past. Not us. Not Horst."

"The hell he isn't," Ben growled.

The waitress came toward them with a fresh pot of coffee. When she saw Ben's expression, she turned and went in the other direction. The woman was smart, Sarah thought.

"You can't tell," Sarah stated stubbornly, throwing down the gauntlet.

Ben's gaze lit up his blue eyes. "What will you do?"

"I'll never speak to you or about you again. You will have lost one ally in this town—*me*—and that's not easy."

"Fine words now that you have my brother's trunks."

"That's not true and you know it."

Ben leaned back and stared a moment. "Maybe I should rephrase my question. What will you do if I promise *not* to say anything?"

She felt the blush creep up. She knew exactly what he was leading toward. "I'll thank you."

"I want more." It was said softly. Quickly. But to Sarah, it could have been a roar.

"What?"

"You know what."

"Tell me," she said softly. "What will it take for you not to tell Horst."

His smile was as lethal as a rattlesnake's. "I want you—in my bed."

Her breath caught in her throat. "You're insulting. You're asking me to be exactly what you're accusing Merci of being."

Ben shrugged. "Maybe so, but that's what I want."

"And then you'll be quiet?"

"Yes."

She swallowed, hard. Who was she kidding? They had both wanted that again. And they had both been asking for it one more time. "When?"

"Tonight."

"And you won't tell?" Her heart pounded so hard, she was sure it would bounce out of her throat. She hated the idea. She loved the idea. Ben had just taken the decision out of her hands. One more time in his arms. One more time. . . .

Ben didn't blink an eye. His finger was the only giveaway that he was more nervous than he let on. He played with the handle of his coffee cup. "No."

Sarah had to make sure they were in agreement. She leaned forward. "You won't say a word to Horst or to anyone else about Merci's past. And if you're asked, you will deny it." They were terms that had to be agreed to first.

"Are you blackmailing me?" he asked.

"No. Are you?"

"No. I'm asking for a favor," Ben stated. "And for that, I will grant a favor of equal value."

"Then we have to agree exactly to the same terms." She stared at him, one eyebrow raised in waiting. He couldn't see her lap where her fingers were crossed. She hoped he didn't recognize that the one thing they both wanted was the same. She'd rather he believe that her first bargaining chip was for Merci. Although that was true, she also wanted exactly what he did, and probably just as much. His agreeing to this deal meant that she had one more chance in his arms before he married and she found a way to move away. Merci happened to be the bargaining chip. It was as if she was being given permission to confirm the unbelievable, incredible feelings she'd had when they were in her bed and making love.

"I agree."

Her muscles suddenly relaxed. She tried not to show her relief. "Very well," she said.

He smiled, pulling out his pocket watch and opening it up. His gaze reverted back to her, intense and focused. "I hate to leave you, but I have a meeting in ten minutes. I can't be late this morning."

"Ben—" Sarah began. Suddenly, she was frightened at what she had brazenly agreed to. She needed to know he agreed completely and absolutely would not say anything to Horst.

"I hope you enjoy the rest of your breakfast. I'll see you this evening around nine o'clock?"

"You'll be there?"

"Of course." He grinned. "I wouldn't miss this for the world."

"And your word is your bond?"

"Yes."

They stared intensely at each other. He looked so calm, so businesslike, and yet one look in his eyes let her see the heated, raw emotions there. She could not speak.

Ben blinked twice. "You're in for more than you're banking on," Ben stated. "And so am I."

"Don't use that tone with me in a public place," she said, looking around and shocked to find most of the people had left and the tables were already cleared.

"Not a soul can hear us unless you raise your voice." Ben grinned, apparently glad he could still make her rise to his bait.

"You're infuriating."

"Darlin'," he said in a slow drawl, "I've been told that since I was born."

"By hundreds of women," she muttered, jealousy lacing her tone.

Ben shook his head, blue eyes twinkling with mirth. "They may have thought so, but only fifty or so have said it aloud."

"One of them had to be your mama."

His smile hardened. "The very first one." He picked up his hat, and nodded. "Thank you for the pleasure of your company, Mrs. Hornsby. You've made a humble man very happy. But I've got to leave."

"And things will go as we discussed?"

"Yes, ma'am. Have a good day. I can only hope that it won't be too tiring for you." He gave a wink. "For your own sake."

Without waiting for an answer, Ben turned and strode across the dining room, through the small lobby and out the front door, his boot heels clicking steadily against the wooden floor.

Sarah watched his broad back disappear, then suddenly felt very alone. The man was irritating, frustrating . . . and . . . very stimulating. She didn't even want to think of the word that sat heavily on the tip of her tongue. *Sexy.* What a combination!

Truth was, Ben made her feel alive and tingly and excited about life. He challenged her way of thinking and feeling and believing, and forced her to put her thoughts into words, explaining not only to him, but to herself, what her opinions were. She was so new at even admitting to her own feelings, that the way he challenged her made her feel vibrant!

Damn the man, she thought as she completed

her meal. At least she trusted him to keep his word and not tell Horst about Merci. . . .

It was chilly but the sun was heating up the day pretty nicely. Ben grinned all the way to the church lot. He'd done it. He'd gotten Sarah to promise to make love once more. She must want to be there as much as he did, for the woman was feisty enough to say no if she had a mind to. He knew that she knew that neither of them was blackmailing the other. It was just a challenge that made both of them feel justified in being in each other's arms. A workable solution until another one came his way.

There were several men already working on the piers already buried in the ground. Another day or so, and they'd be ready to start the church flooring.

Horst, in formal top hat, coat and shiny boots, was there ahead of him. He stood on the lumber walkway that ended at the large pedestal that held the plans. His head was bent over them, checking against what had already been done.

"Early as usual, Horst," Ben said, shaking his friend's hand. "Finding any errors yet?"

Horst gave a quick smile. "Nein. Not yet, mein friend. You do a very goot job."

"Thanks. Have you decided if the invoice of materials is correct?"

"Ja, it ist goot. How long do you think it must take to complete the church?"

"Roof and all?"

"Ja. Of course the roof," Horst said seriously. "Pews too."

"Are you paying for pews?"

Horst sighed in resignation. "Ja, if you sink they

can be completed when the church is. And I need the church completed in three weeks."

"If the weather holds and the volunteers still give their weekends, the church can be roughly completed in three weeks. But I'll need more time with your adobe man, Jesus, and the wonder with the lumber, Jaime."

Horst smiled again, this time with satisfaction. "Goot, Benjamin. I can do that. Very goot."

Ben knew as certain as he trusted his own instincts, but he asked anyway. "What's the hurry, Horst? Are you afraid you'll run out of lumber?"

"I am getting married in three weeks, Benjamin."

Ben's stomach clenched. "Congratulations, Horst," he said, pretending surprise. "Who's the lucky woman?"

Horst's happiness lit up his usually strong and somber face. "I believe you already know her. Her name is Sister Merci and she lives with Sarah right now. But she has finally promised to marry me. It seems only fitting to be married in the church that we both helped build and have the members who have helped to build it present, ja?"

"Of course," Ben said. "What part did Sister Merci play?" he asked, surprised.

The man looked so proud. His pale blue eyes lit up when he spoke of Merci. "She got donations from many of the families in the outlying areas. The cotton and indigo farmers who don't get into church every weekend but want a place to come to when they do. She even talked some of them into building Sunday houses, where they can stay on the weekends when they are in town. That way, I sell more lumber, the town gets more business and the farmers will have a small house for their families to stay in instead of the hotel. They can bring their children to church more often, and the wives will get to shop on Saturday.''

"She did that?'' Ben asked.

"Ja. That and more. Remember, too, she's the one who got me to donate the lumber. This town is lucky to have her. She will do much good work as my wife.''

Ben couldn't think of a thing to say. But the bad feeling in the pit of his stomach was still there. "So what did she do before she came here?''

Horst narrowed his eyes and studied the men working on the pier, beginning the job of tying the wooden structure together to begin framing the flooring. "She was a nurse, soothing other people who were hurt.''

Ben kept his surprise to himself. "Oh, where was that?''

Horst grinned. "I know where, Benjamin. And so do you, ja?''

Suddenly, Ben was wary. What the hell was Horst doing? Laying a trap for him? "What do you mean?''

"You knew Merci before, did you not?''

Ben tried to recall the conversation he'd had with Sarah and Merci, dimly remembering her asking to be known differently, just in case this very problem came up.

He frowned, as if thinking hard. "Why, yes, I think you're right. I met her at a dinner party in Bixby or Tombstone, I think.''

"If I had met her at a party anywhere, I would have remembered that charming face. And such a beautiful body.''

Ben looked surprised. "Are you telling me you appreciate such things?'' he teased, relieved to have a different path to take. "And all this time, my friend, I thought you were too stuffy for such observations!"

Horst stared at him long and hard. "Are you?"

"Not at all. But you seem far more . . ." Ben was at a loss for words.

"Conservative?" Horst interjected.

"Right. Conservative."

"And you are not?"

"Not when it comes to beautiful women." Ben laughed. "I'm just a mortal, Horst. Otherwise I wouldn't be donating my time to get to heaven." He waved toward the church. "And neither would half the people who are working on this project."

Horse laid a hand on Ben's shoulder. "My friend, all the people are sinners, yes?"

"You're right. Each and every one."

"And it is our job to help each other not to sin, is that not right?"

"That's right, Horst."

"And if that is the case, shouldn't we say that no matter what people did wrong, they can change?"

Ben felt that pressure in his stomach again. "Of course, but—"

"And if they can change, should we blame them for the method they use to survive, to work their way to heaven?"

Ben didn't answer. His mind raced. Horst knew about Merci. He knew.

"How did you find out?" he asked quietly.

Horst didn't blink an eye. "I am not quite the dolt you think I might be, Ben. I had Merci's story checked out. It was not hard."

"And you know it all?"

Horst nodded, his expression grave. "Including the murders. And if anyone was still alive who had done to her what my report stated, I would kill them with my bare hands.'' He looked down at his large, gloved hands. "So help me Got, I would enjoy it.''

"I understand," Benjamin said, just glimpsing the depth of his love for the woman he wanted to marry. So his own suspicions about Merci's father were right. She did have a hand in killing him. And she would repent for the rest of her life. "You don't care about her past?''

"I care, Benjamin," Horst corrected, the look in his blue eyes so sad that it hurt. "But I love her, and it is better to love her and have her by my side than to go to bed with my false pride and righteous anger. Those things do not keep me warm at night. And in the bright light of day, I do not laugh at the antics of birds or feel complete and at peace just by holding hands in silence.''

"No, they don't," Ben agreed. "What if someone finds out?''

"Then I will deny it to my dying day. People have a habit of backing away from firm denial. I will do so.''

Ben started at his friend. He was one of the few men he could look in the eye, both literally and figuratively. "Then so be it, Horst. I will help in any way I can.''

"Thank you, Benjamin. I already have a favor to ask of you.''

"Name it.''

"Will you be my witness? My, how you say ... best man?''

This wasn't right, but telling Horst the history between Merci and himself was completely unacceptable. If Horst's report didn't find it and Horst didn't mention it, then Ben certainly wouldn't open up a whole new problem to grapple with. "I consider it an honor," Ben stated firmly, stifling the feeling that he was in for a pound instead of a penny.

Horst stuck out his hand. "I am the one who is honored, my friend." They shook hands then, sealing both the agreement and the upcoming nuptials.

Horst, in his usual single-minded way, turned toward the building and narrowed his eyes. Four men were puttering around the framing. One rolled and smoked a cigarette. "It is time to complete this project. The sooner the better," he stated, as if to himself. Then, the young German strode toward the man smoking as if he were being paid for his work on the church and Horst was about to fire him.

Ben sighed and followed behind. Horst might need someone to remind him who was the volunteer and who was the needy. . . .

Chapter Sixteen

Sarah's hands quaked all day. Every time she remembered the conversation at breakfast and what she had agreed to do that very evening, fear traveled down her spine and wrapped around her stomach. Her face flushed with each zing. Lillie continually asked if she was feeling all right. Naturally, she said yes, but it was embarrassing, just the same.

Emma Petrie, the dessert lady, even entered the crowded store to inspect some of the "English goods" as Lillie called the filled trunks. She was three hundred pounds of fun-loving, big-booming voice who enjoyed company no matter where she was. Not one to enjoy her own laughter without an audience, she brought three friends who had traveled the train up from San Antonio.

". . . and then the rumor was that the brute hit her so hard, her little dog bled!"

"No!"

Sarah heard the women's comments as she looked over the trunk of quilts Lillie and she had managed to slide across the floor to the outside wall. Lillie was smart enough to leave most of the rolled materials inside, draping five or six colorful pieces over the edge to tease the eye of the customer. The colors were bright and bold as a late spring garden, and word had spread about the goods being sent by the duke from England. That elevated her stock to "valuable" and brought a whole new level of curiosity.

The town was abuzz with the fact that she had received so many trunks, and several of the women had talked her into opening just for the morning, promising they would wait to see the rest of the stock in a few days, when she was more prepared to open.

"Lillie," Sarah said quietly. "When E.Z. returns, please ask him to push those trunks over to the side until we can get to them."

"If that little guy ever returns," Lillie muttered, placing another pot of tea on the tray and heading toward the front again. "He saw all the women, mumbled something about how closed should mean closed, and ran toward the stable. For all I know, he's on his way back to Blissful."

Sarah grinned. E.Z. had been in the kitchen last thing at night yesterday, and at the crack of dawn this morning. And he was still there when Sarah was leaving to join Ben for breakfast. That wasn't the normal sign of a man on the run. Lillie had tried to brush off his compliments, but the determined look on his face, and the light and smile on hers, told the story. They were both smitten.

When lunchtime came and they finally managed to shoo out the crowd and close the doors, both women were weary. For a change, Lillie sat down first. Using one of the trunks as a footstool, she placed her feet on the stiff canvas-backed handle and rubbed her calves. "The clock may say it's lunchtime, Sarah, but I feel like we've been open since dawn."

"I know." Sarah sighed. "And we still have work to do. I'll sleep like the dead tonight," she said, realizing she was setting up her own alibi for her time with Ben. She blushed again.

"Don't look to me to interrupt your sleepin'," Lillie stated with a grin. "I gotta get my beauty rest so's I'm awake early, when E.Z. starts buildin' that wall to make my bedroom alcove."

Sarah stared, dumbfounded. "What?"

Lillie looked surprised. Her face went from anticipation to frustration. "That little rascal. He din't tell you, did he?"

"Who?"

"E.Z.," she said with a grin. "Isn't that just like a man? He was supposed to tell you he's makin' me a present of a sleepin' alcove."

Sarah looked at her in confusion. "Out of what? Where is he getting the materials? Who's paying for them?"

"I don't know. He wanted to build me a privacy wall, but it won't have a door. It'll just shield my bed and belongings from the front area." Lillie looked doubtful. "You don't mind, do you, Sarah? E.Z. said it'd only take a couple of days to build and could be used for storage or somethin' else if you ever kicked me out."

"You're not afraid of freezing? After all, you might lose some heat from the stove, Lillie."

"Oh, we're not even closin' off enough for a doorway. It's just a wall and half a wall, not enough to block off warmth or a breeze. In fact, he was talkin' about putting in a window later. Something that would catch a breeze from off the meadow in back.''

Sarah didn't know why she hadn't thought of it herself. Of course Lillie wanted some privacy. Merci and she shared the space because there was nowhere else to go. Next to Sarah's loft where the heat rose, it was the warmest place in the building.

Sarah shrugged. ''Why not?''

Lillie looked relieved. They both jumped as someone banged on the back door. ''Probably E.Z.,'' the older woman muttered, unbending her tall frame to stand up and head for the rear door.

E.Z. stepped in quickly, shutting the door behind him to keep the warm air in. A good six or seven inches shorter than Lillie, E.Z. rose on tiptoe to plant a kiss on her cheek. Looking flustered, Lillie pulled away as if she hadn't seen his move.

''Let's not lose that heat, darlin','' he said, covering his movements. ''Trying to get it back quickly is like trying to corral smoke.''

''I never would have guessed.''

E.Z. gave a rough chuckle. Just then, he noticed Sarah sitting in the front, and whispered something to Lillie that elicited a chuckle.

Grabbing his battered cowboy hat off his head and giving a head bow, he flashed his shiny pate. ''Good to see you again, Mrs. Hornsby.''

''And you, E.Z. What's this I hear about building a wall for Lillie to have some privacy?''

He darted a glance at Lillie, then back. He had the grace to blush. ''I was s'posed to tell you last night. Then this mornin'. But I was workin' so hard at the church an' lost track of time. Sorry 'bout that, ma'am.''

"How much will it cost?"

"Nary a thing, ma'am. That young man, the star-struck young German who donated the lumber to the church? Well, he wants to give me what I'll need, as long as I work on the church half a day every day an' most of the day on Sunday." He looked pretty proud of himself. "He heard 'bout my carving ability an' wants me to make the first three rows of pews."

Sarah smiled, remembering his carving ability. He'd made several wooden dolls to be sold to tourists on the Blissful train for a profit so the town could continue to thrive. He was good. "I can't let you do that, E.Z. Why, if Charlie knew, he'd come all the way from Blissful and arrest me for working you to death!"

Charlie had hired E.Z. to help with the cattle Sarah had given to his care. He was also the sheriff and husband to her friend, Kathleen, who's carrot cake was now being sold in her store.

"Nothin' to it, ma'am. Honest. I don't mind. Besides, the cattle are all safe an' snug for the winter on the large plot of land just west of Kathleen's. Charlie doesn't have to do much till it comes time for spring, an' he gets them to your land. That won't be for another month or so, way this weather's actin'."

"Just the same . . ." Sarah began, hesitating.

"Besides, it might take an extra day to build out that wall for sweet Lillie here, seein' as I'll be busy helpin' Ben." E.Z. gave Lillie an audacious wink. "An' seein' as Charlie's got your cattle an' his own all trussed up for the next month or so, I doubt he'll miss me for a while." E.Z. pulled on his ear while he quickly thought up other excuses. "And while ole Zeke don't have enough sense to drink upstream from the herd, he'll do all right for Charlie till I get back."

Sarah gave in, laughing. "If you insist, how can I turn down something so sweet and kind to both Lillie and I?" Leaning back, she pretended not to see the two stroll behind the screen that separated the rear living quarters from the store area.

But the sounds made her feel all the more lonely. How could that be, since even before she was married, there was no giggling or stroking or fun between man and woman? How could she miss what she'd never had?

She didn't have to worry about it anymore, she told herself. Since she would never marry again, she didn't have to recognize the symptoms of loneliness. By the time old age set in, she'd know them very well.

Ben's image popped into her mind. Suddenly, his touch seemed so real she felt his hand on the rounded swell of her stomach just before his fingers dipped into . . .

Sarah stood up and marched to the stairs. It was time to clean out her dresser drawers and determine what she needed to rid herself of—besides thoughts that got her into trouble. Perhaps Harmony would like a few more pieces of clothing. Then Sarah would have reason to begin working the Singer treadle sewing machine on a few new dresses. Her mother used to say that busy hands were happy hands. If that was the case, she would be ecstatic by the time next week came.

Five or six new dresses for everyone ought to keep her hands and mind busy!

*   *   *

It took an hour for Sarah to start winding down from her cleaning frenzy. She piled three dresses and several pantaloons and petticoats, along with odds and ends she knew she'd never wear, by the stairs.

Muffled noises from the kitchen area had long ago stopped. In fact, Sarah wasn't sure Lillie and E.Z. were even inside the building anymore. They might have slipped outside via the back door, leaving her to her own company. A glance at the watch pinned to her breast told her she still had an hour before their normal suppertime. It also meant that she could get these clothes to the woman who could use them the most.

Without thinking first, Sarah knocked on the wall she shared with the upstairs brothel.

"Who's there!" It was a gruff voice. She heard the movement of shuffling feet, a grunt or two, a definite fart. Then silence. Someone was obviously busy.

Two minutes later, Sarah heard Harmony's voice. "Mrs. Hornsby? Is that you?"

Sarah shut the last newly tidied drawer and walked swiftly toward the wall. "Yes. I have a package for you. Perhaps you could stop by when you have a free moment and I can give it to you," Sarah said, praying the man had left before Harmony spoke out. Then she straightened her spine. So what if a man heard her speaking to a lady of the evening? Harmony was a woman first, a fallen young woman last. "Whenever you can spend a few minutes on this side, let me know."

"Is now all right?" Harmony whispered hesitantly.

"Now is fine," Sarah said. "Come on over."

* * *

Under her coat, Harmony wore a shift with nothing underneath. Thankfully, Sarah thought, the upstairs was warmer than down. The girl set her bare feet over the threshold, her gaze darting to the corners, as if she were afraid for her safety.

"It's just you and me," Sarah said quietly, closing the door behind them. "I found a few more things I thought you might be interested in having. If not, perhaps someone else can use them." She led Harmony up the stairs to her bedroom.

"Oh, I'm sure I don't know no one," Harmony began.

"Anyone," Sarah automatically corrected with a smile.

"Anyone," Harmony dutifully repeated like a parrot, her gaze catching sight of the bundle by the stairs and looking at it greedily. "But me, well, I'd love them if they fit me. I'm the middle of thirteen kids. By the time the clothes got to me, they was plumb worn out. And by the time I took care of the other six little ones, there wasn't nothing left of them rags," she said.

"In that case, help yourself."

Harmony walked slowly to the pile and stared down at it before getting down on both knees and touching one of the softer cotton dresses. "Can I touch them?"

"Certainly. Go through them all you want," Sarah said, still stuck on the thought of being one of thirteen. She watched as the young woman picked up each piece as if it were gold. One by one, she held the dresses against her breast and looked down as if she could imagine them on her slim body. "You can take them back with you and try them on," Sarah suggested.

"Oh, I couldn't do that. Everybody would know where I got them. This way, if they fit here, I can take them back and pretend that my family sent them to me. Then they're mine and nobody has to know where I got them and why they don't fit."

"Do they go through your room?"

"Nothing's a secret, ma'am. Even the room is rented for a whole bunch of money."

That was more than Sarah wanted to know. She took a different tact. "Does your family send you packages often?"

"Never." Harmony looked over her shoulder and grinned. "But it keeps everybody happy to think so. Especially me."

Harmony rocked back on her heels and stared up at Sarah, her face a mixture of hesitation and fear and hope all at one time. "One of the men says that you help some of the women in the outlying areas by giving them sewing work, and they can earn some money that way. Is that true?"

Sarah stared at the young woman as her words sunk in. Harmony wanted out of the saloon. "You want to leave here?"

Harmony nodded.

"And go where?"

"Don't care." Her eyes teared, but she blinked them away. "Anywhere but here."

"Home?"

"Don't have a home no more."

"Why do you want to leave?"

Harmony looked at her hands as they smoothed the dress clutched in her lap. She gave a sigh. "Well, you see. I fell in love with this here cowboy. And he said he was in love with me, too. But when

it came right down to it, he married somebody
else. He didn't want anything to do with a woman
who's lain with others. He said that for all he knew,
I could be unclean." Two big tears rolled down
her cheeks. "I don't love him no more. Honest.
But he kinda gave me hope, you know? Like, if I
found love once, I might could find it again. But
I need to be ready for the next time. I need to
earn money in a way that won't scare the next one
away before he falls in love with me or make him
feel like less than a man."

"What if this imaginary man found out?"

"Oh, when I know he's serious, I'll tell him about
my past. But not till then, you know? I don't want
to ever feel so bad about myself as I did this last
spring. But I don't want no man who isn't bright
enough to love me for me."

"Harmony, you're much smarter than most,"
Sarah said, her mind racing with alternatives. "Let
me give this some thought and see if I have any
solutions. All right?"

Harmony's face lit up with a smile. "Any help
will be appreciated, ma'am."

"How old are you, Harmony?"

"Seventeen, ma'am. I'll be eighteen on April
first." She rose and stood in front of the cheval
mirror, holding the green calico dress in front of
her. Without any sense of modesty, she dropped
her coat, stood visibly naked beneath her chemise
for just a moment, then tossed Sarah's old dress
over her head.

With the hem down, it would be perfect. Harmony closed the buttons at the throat and looked
from several angles, a smile growing. "My mama
would have loved this dress," she said. "It's just so
pretty and . . . and . . . *nice*."

Suddenly, at twenty-six, Sarah felt very old. When Harmony was talking about the privacy of her things, she was really talking about security. If a family stood behind her, even in her dreams, she wasn't alone.

Sarah had a family, but she might as well be alone. Both pretended things were just fine the way they were. Both knew better. Sarah should have known best of all.

Ben wasn't sure if Sarah would show up. It was a lame attempt at blackmail, and he was sure they both knew it. But he had checked his watch every five minutes since dinner an hour ago, at eight o'clock. Time wasn't moving any faster because of his eagle eye.

This was ridiculous, he told himself. Sarah wasn't a stranger to his bed and there was absolutely no reason for him to be nervous. It was a simple matter of making love to a woman he wanted to make love to.

What was so bloody awful about that?

He didn't want to think about his feeble blackmail attempt. He'd never had to try any tactic to get a woman to fall for his charms before. All he'd ever had to do was be himself. Perhaps having done so this time was what made him nervous now. After all, it certainly didn't bode well for his confidence level not to have her willing to tumble into his arms!

He glanced at his watch once more. Two minutes to nine. Why couldn't she just be early and ease his mind, damnit!

Just as he thought it, it happened. Her knock on the door was soft, hesitant. Just like she was.

When Ben opened the door, she slipped in through the crack quickly and quietly, her black cape wrapped around her like a dark cocoon. Ben closed the door, his hand resting on the glass knob as he watched her walk to the fireplace. Her face was pale, her eyes down. Her caramel-colored hair was pulled back so tightly, she reminded him of the washing lady, Wo Chi.

"Are you all right?" he asked.

She swallowed quickly, then unwrapped her cloak to illuminate by gaslight the brilliant jewel-toned squares that formed the lining. The cape reminded him of Sarah. The outside was solid and true, ready for all kinds of weather. But the inside was soft, slick fabric more brilliant than a rainbow, glowing with a patchwork of glistening colors. Like Sarah's spirit. So calm and sweet on the outside, so glowing and sensuous on the inside. A jewel, he thought as he turned back.

"I'm fine, considering the circumstances," she said, turning to face him as she dropped the cape over the side of a chair. "Can we get this over with before someone realizes I'm not in my bed, and calls for a search?"

"Lillie wouldn't do that. E.Z. has all her attention—and probably a place in her narrow bed right about now."

Sarah looked startled. "You know about him and Lillie?"

"Men talk."

Her expression turned angry. "Including you? Have you talked?"

Ben pled ignorance. "About us? Of course not! It wouldn't do either of us any good to be the subject of town gossip."

She relaxed, and a small smile peeped out. Ben

almost felt guilty about his talk with Horst. But he certainly wasn't about to let on. He hadn't *said* anything that Horst hadn't already known.

"*You* already are. Everyone knows about the royalty we have walking among us. Helping with the church. Winning our eligible women's hearts."

His hand dropped to his side and he walked to stop a foot in front of her, almost taking away the very air she breathed. "And I'll make sure you are *not* the object of gossip except to state what an astounding God-fearing, saintly, businesswoman you are." His hand rested lightly on her shoulder. He finally looked at her, and was stunned into silence.

Sarah wore a gossamer silk gown that shimmered and slithered against her skin like spun diamonds and copper. The color highlighted her pale skin, then danced in colors in her hair, just like the firelight danced in burning coals.

"You're beautiful," he said huskily, but the look in his eyes spoke more words than he'd ever thought of, and all of them were in praise for her.

Suddenly, she felt brimming with confidence. "You're overdressed," she answered huskily.

"You're right." He reached for the bottle of wine that had been decanting and poured a glass of the ruby liquid. "Taste this while I change," he said.

Sarah reached for the glass reluctantly.

Ben took off his coat, then his boots. With his gaze never leaving hers, he stripped off his pants and shirt, and dropped them exactly where he was. In less than a minute he stood naked, his body strong and lean and ever so willing.

Sarah's eyes were wide, not leaving the sight of him as he moved and reached and bent. He walked to the chifforobe and took his royal blue silk robe off the interior hook. Sliding his arms into the sleeves, he tied the sash and then stood still.

Ben waited a moment, wanting to make sure that she was both comfortable and ready for the next step. It was his experience that getting the awkwardness over with now, helped a great deal later.

"Good wine?" he asked.

"I haven't tasted a drop."

"Then do so or I'll have to tell my brother you didn't care for it, and he'll feel bad."

She obeyed, slowly sipping at the liquid as if unsure she would like it. When she lowered the glass, her lips were glazed with red wine glistening in the light of the fire.

Ben reacted immediately, heating and hardening with every second that ticked by.

He finally found his voice. "Are you as worried about this evening as I am?" he asked, deciding conversation might ease the tension between them.

Her eyes widened. "Yes, of course. But why are you worried? I didn't believe men did such things."

Ben chuckled, wondering just how she got by with years of marriage and no experience in the ways of males. Her husband must have been a jackass instead of a partner. And there was no doubt that this woman would make any man a partner who would double his worth in the eyes of the community as well as his coffers. "Men are no different. Secretly, we all want to be the stud that women want. The hero of those romance stories women find so wonderful."

Sarah looked shocked. "But you are!"

Ben smiled. Reaching out, he touched the side of her neck, feeling the smooth texture beneath his palm. "Take your hair down, sweet Sarah."

She reached back with one hand and undid the

clip that held her hair so tightly. Giving her head a shake, her hair fell about her shoulders. Ben stroked the fine strands, loving the texture as it flowed through his hands like spun liquid.

"Mmm." Sarah smiled. She closed her eyes and tilted her head toward his palm. She was like a small kitten, almost purring under his hand. Except that she was the sexiest kitten he'd ever seen. Ever.

It took all his control to keep his hand where it was, against her cheek, instead of pulling her toward him and crushing her to his chest, smothering her mouth with his own. An intense need to brand rushed up to pound in his head, then raced through the rest of his body at wild stallion–stampede speed. He was more ready for Sarah than he had ever been ready before in his life.

A groan rumbled in his throat as he stared down at the fair-skinned woman who's trusting expression was so easy to read. He had to keep control. He had to keep control. He had to . . .

"Benjamin?" Sarah asked, finally recognizing the change in his expression and stiffly held body. "Are you all right?"

"I'm in dire pain, but I'm sure you'll ease that by the time the night is over, sweet."

She blushed, and it was the color of a coral rose his mother used to grow. When did she grow from very pretty to so heartbreakingly beautiful?

His other hand came to cup her breast through the silk material that barely covered the soft flesh. At first it was cool and her nipple centered in his palm. The heat from his hand transferred quickly to her breast, and he felt the circle of her weight there.

"Ben." Her voice was a whisper.

"What, sweet? What would you like?"

She closed her eyes and swallowed. "Ben," she said again. This time it was a plea.

"Tell me," he said, his thumb flicking her nipple through the slippery fabric.

"Ben, please," she begged, her voice not even a whisper.

He couldn't resist. Everything that she wanted he would die trying to deliver. But even he couldn't wait long enough to make her speak the words he wanted to hear.

Another time. But right now, he wanted to make love to sweet Sarah and hear her cry in ecstasy. He just hoped he could wait that long.

Without hesitation, he swept her up in his arms and carried her to the bed, placing her gently on the side while he slipped out of his robe.

And when she was out of her gown, they slipped beneath the sheets and held each other a long moment.

Then the magic began again. That sense of belonging he'd felt before was there again. It hadn't been a figment of his imagination. It was real. That sense of a core belief deep down inside him that said, *this is home. This is right.*

His hand smoothed her back, and she came to him so sweetly, so willingly. All thought was forgotten, and he lived for each separate moment.

His head bent as he took her pink nipple into his mouth, loving the feel of the nub rubbing against his tongue. He felt her breath catch. She arched her spine and he knew she loved what he was doing as much as he did. Sweet sensuous Sarah. His hands ran the length of her from breast to hip, then back again, the soft skin sensitizing his fingers to her every move.

When he touched her most intimate spot, Sarah

melted into his arms. Her soft, kittenish sound echoed in her throat and vibrated down to her breast. He could feel it on his tongue.

He felt triumphant. He was the one making her feel this way. No one else. And it obviously still startled her that there were so very many emotions to making love.

It took everything he had to keep tight rein on his own body, but he managed until her response was so strong he knew she would be in heaven in just seconds. Just as she arched to his hand, he replaced it with himself, pushing into her as smoothly and slickly as if he'd been there all along. She grabbed his shoulders as if she were falling from the face of the earth, and he knew he'd done right. Feeling her tighten around him was the last straw. He stiffened with the thrust, and fell from the skies, only to rush into her depth.

It was a long time before their breathing slowed down enough for Ben to smile and roll away. He lay next to her, his hand on her abdomen. Her eyes were closed, and she was so still that if he hadn't seen the small smile on her mouth and her breast rising and falling, he would have worried.

"Are you all right?"

"Yes. Are you?"

"Yes, thank you very much for asking," he retorted politely. Sarah opened her eyes and looked up at him. Seeing him smile, she smiled in return. "You're very welcome."

"We're going to do that again, you know."

Her eyes widened. "Really?"

His grin turned to laughter. "Yes. Really."

"I didn't know that was possible."

"Oh, my sweet Sarah. Anything is possible. Especially when I'm with you."

"You're a rake, Benjamin Drake."

"I might be, but it's still the truth."

Her grin disappeared. She frowned, her brow wrinkling. "Ben," she asked hesitantly. "How do you do that to me?"

He felt that triumph again. But this time, he had to give an honest answer. "I don't know, sweet. I just try to please you."

She smiled, her hand cupping the side of his face, brushing a strand of his hair back from his cheek. "Thank you for caring," she said softly.

"You're welcome," he answered.

Ben had never felt this content. He took her hand from the side of his face and covered her open palm with his mouth. Gently, he kissed the center.

Her eyes darkened, then closed, and she burrowed her head into his chest. Ben wrapped his arms around her protectively and sighed.

So this was what heaven was like. . . .

Chapter Seventeen

His chest rose and fell with each even breath.

Sarah curled toward Ben, her head resting on his chest, breathing in the scent of him. Gusts of wind whistled past the window, chilling the leaves off trees. Inside, the room was warm and cozy, not the place she'd once been afraid to be. But, then, she'd even slept in the room before, so the fear of being in a strange place had lost its edge.

She'd been in Ben's arms before, too. And right now she felt so content and happy, she couldn't see a thing wrong with where she was and what she'd just done. Ben was the most caring lover. Lover. It sounded like such a sophisticated word—especially for Clear Creek. Just thinking the word sounded as if she had had a string of men seducing her, taking her to bed and making mad, passionate love all night.

That thought just came from Sarah Hornsby, the town prude. The frightened widow who jumped at her own shadow. At least that was what the town of Blissful had thought of her. But here in Clear Creek, it was a different story. She had just done the unthinkable. She had turned herself into a pillar of society, helping strong-arm citizens she'd never even met before into establishing a church and a town hall. But her crowning achievement was opening a business that was literally thriving and changing lives at the same time. She was amazed at how she had grown and what she had accomplished.

She had become a role model for entrepreneurial widowhood.

In the past three days, she might have thrown it all away by making love and memories in the arms of the man she loved. Impulsive actions that, if the town knew, would cost her all the respect she'd fought so hard to establish.

Sarah had made love to a man she was not married to, knowing there was never a chance of them proclaiming to the world that they were to be married. She had taken the chance of being in the arms of this man even while knowing she could lose all she'd worked so hard for. Other women depended on her to make a difference in their lives by their work and her sales. So much depended on her reputation.

She had taken the biggest chance of all. The chance that gave her her heart's desire for the moment, while gambling with the stain that would last a lifetime.

So many secrets. So many.

In the space of a year, she'd gone from being silent unless directly addressed to talking all the time. She even gave advice to others that sounded like she knew what she was saying. She talked so

much, people listened. But now, she couldn't discuss the secrets.

She couldn't discuss Harmony. Nor Merci. Nor
about Ben and Merci. Nor about Ben in her bed.
Neither could she discuss some of the women she
bought goods from nor the husbands who beat
them. The women pleaded for her to keep quiet,
for they had no place else to go and no one to
watch out for them while they raised their babies.

It struck home that if Lillie hadn't come to her,
she might be walking the streets. Or dead.

And still, Sarah had risked it all to be in Ben's
arms—for one simple reason: she loved him.

Ben's arm tightened and he gave a contented
sigh in his sleep. His hand smoothed her back in
communion, and she felt loved and treasured.

This was worth the chance. This was all she was
going to get from him, and no matter what happened in the future, she had this, *now*.

Pursing her lips, she gently kissed his chest and
closed her eyes. This might be the last time she
had to be with him, so she might as well enjoy
every moment of it. She drifted into sleep.

An hour later, she jerked, then bolted awake.
There was a soft knock at the door. Ben's door.
He gave a moan and tightened his arms around
her.

Another knock.

Sarah's hand tapped Ben's bare hip. "Benjamin!
Someone's here!" she whispered.

He was awake instantly.

The knock, a little louder each time, echoed
through the room again.

With an economy of movement, Ben was out of
the bed and reaching for the small pistol in his

jacket pocket. He covered Sarah's head with the
sheet. "Don't move. Don't breathe."

She didn't. Instead, she remained under the covers and quaked.

"Who's there?" Ben spoke softly, slipping into
his robe.

"It's me, Lord Benjamin. I wanted to clean your
boots but you forgot to leave them outside the
door."

"Thomas?"

"Yes, Your Lordship." The young boy mangled
the title, still in awe of knowing someone of nobility, let alone being able to clean his boots.

"Wait a minute," Ben ordered. The sound of a
scraping match was followed by leather thudding.
The door clicked, telling her the door was opening.
She held her breath.

"I'm sorry to wake you, sir, but I didn't know
what else to do. You haven't missed a night of
having your boots cleaned. I just figured . . ."

"It's all right, Thomas. Just have them done by
early morning."

"Thank you, Your Royalty," Thomas said. "Sorry
about, uh, interrupting you." His voice was low
and embarrassed.

"Don't think about it, Thomas. See you in the
morning." With another click, the door closed.

"Our company has gone, sweet Sarah," Ben said,
his tone teasing and playful.

Sarah pulled the sheet off her head and sat
straight up in bed, not even bothering with the
sheet as it dropped to expose her full, round
breasts, narrowing down to a slim waist. Her gaze
focused on Ben, his robe-clad body still standing

by the door. He must have lit the lamp by the side table before opening the door and giving Thomas his boots. It gave a warm glow over the room . . . and her black cape . . .

. . . and her rumpled copper nightgown in a pool in the middle of the floor at the foot of the bed.

The blood drained from her face. "Oh, dear sweet heaven," she whispered, her voice so fine and thin she hardly heard herself. "Thomas knows. He *knows*!"

"No, he doesn't. He never saw you."

"Whether I'm a lump in your mattress or not, he knows, Benjamin. He didn't have to see me. He saw my cape and nightgown." She closed her eyes and gulped down the lump that threatened her breathing.

All those fine thoughts about being in Ben's arms was worth the risk! Where was her head? Tears filmed her eyes and she brushed them away with the backs of her hands like a child. "I'm ruined."

Ben smiled indulgently. "I don't think so, sweet. First of all, half the women in this town have black capes. And second, that nightgown does not have your name on it or a sign with a bright red arrow pointing your way." His gaze narrowed. "So how would young Thomas know about your nightgown? He hasn't seen you in it, has he?"

"Half the women in this town don't have black capes with a brightly quilted lining, Benjamin," she stated, pointing to the garment's bright lining of various sateen squares. It lay across the chair, beaming like a beacon in the dark. "And, of course he hadn't seen that gown, but it certainly proves you didn't just have a lump in your mattress." If anything, she sat even more straight, her breasts tall and just as proud as she was. "I'm a living, breathing, female . . . who's obviously the naked lump in your bed. The cloak just identifies the owner of the gown." Although she was trying to be brave, she knew she looked as if she were about to burst into tears. But that was only because she really and truly was going to do so!

Ben sat on the side of the bed and smoothed her hair back from her bare shoulder, his fingers lingering as he touched. "Just because it's your cape doesn't mean it's your nightgown. Someone else could have borrowed it, sweet."

What was he thinking? Could he be insane? "And who will I condemn to that finger-pointing fate by saying they borrowed my cape? Is there anyone in particular we know that we can ruin?" She was trying to be sarcastic, but it certainly didn't sound like it. Instead, it sounded as if she was looking for someone to blame it on. "I didn't mean that," she explained.

"I know," he said quietly, still smoothing her shoulder.

But when she looked at him, his gaze was not on her face as she imagined, but on her fully exposed breasts. Sarah clutched the sheet, pulled it up and tucked it securely under her arms. As sad and brokenhearted as she was, she still felt the zing of a thrill run down her spine. The scene didn't take away from the fact that he could just look at her and she'd respond.

"Don't cover up, Sarah," he said huskily.

"I have to. I . . . I need to go."

"It's only midnight. Stay a little while longer." He touched her shoulder, his fingers deliberately trailing along her collarbone to stop at the center

of her breasts. One finger stroked, pulling lightly
at the sheet.

Sarah allowed the top to droop a little more with
every tug.

"Please. Stay."

"I can't."

"The damage is already done." His voice was
like warm honey, soothing her nerves to elasticity.

"I know," she said slowly, her own voice losing
its edge. "But . . ." The sheet dropped the rest of
the way. Ben's breath hissed in his throat and she
watched his hungry expression through heavy-
lidded eyes. She wanted him as much as he wanted
her. There was no use lying to herself about it.
She'd never felt as beautiful, wonderful, sensual
and completely powerful as she did when they were
making love. She could lead or remain complacent.
It didn't matter. For a brief time, she was everything
she wanted to be.

His fingertip circled her rosy nipples, one at a
time, dipping between her breasts as he moved
from one to the other. Her breasts felt full and
she hungered to have him close, to hold her, to
have his mouth over her nipple, laving it with
warmth that tingled all the way to her inner core.

"We may never have this chance again, sweet. I
have to take advantage of being with you now so
I'll have something to relive in my dreams when
I'm an old man."

Her thoughts exactly. The damage of being
found out was already done. Running away solved
nothing. Sarah brushed the side of his head, feeling
the vibrancy of his chestnut hair, the strength of
his neck, and dropping down to his broad shoulder. She loved the texture of his skin, the feel

of him beneath her palm. She could stroke him forever. All over.

She looked into his eyes. They were somber. No teasing like a few minutes ago. No indulging crinkles. No laughter. Just the bare and honest realization that what he said was coming from the heart.

Pushing aside the sheet, she exposed her hips and bare thighs. Sarah smiled. "What are you waiting for, my lord?"

Ben's smile was tinged with sadness. "Thank you, my sweet lady."

He climbed into bed and pulled her into his arms, bare bodies touched from head to torso to intertwined limbs. He took a deep breath of her scent. He wanted to relish and yet postpone the moment of making love to the woman in his arms. He wanted this moment to last forever instead of speed by to dawn, when she would leave him.

In the last fifteen minutes, his whole life had changed. He wanted to rail at the gods for making his life even more difficult than before. Everything but this moment was out of his control and he didn't know how to get it back. All he knew was that he was once more the butt of jokes from the Fates. He had done it wrong again. For a bright revelation had come to him and he knew deep in his heart that it was honest and true.

Ben was in love with the widow Hornsby. And no one else would do.

The following morning, young Thomas stood at Ben's door with his boots and a packet of mail from England. Ben ignored the inquisitive smile on the young man's face as he glanced around the hotel room pointedly.

"This came two days ago, Your Highness, but the train man forgot to hand it over and had it sent back to us from Houston."

"Thanks, Thomas." Benjamin stood staring at the young man and wondered if he should say anything about Sarah. He was afraid that if he did, it would confirm the young man's thoughts. "How is your writing going?" he finally asked, knowing the lad was trying to write for the dime novels.

"I've got one at the publishers now, sir. I hope she won't mind, but I'm using Mrs. Hornsby as the heroine my hero rescues."

"Are you really? Why?"

Thomas looked surprised at the question. "Why, because I think she's the most beautiful woman, sir. She's someone who every man would like to rescue, don't you think?"

Benjamin smiled. "I certainly do. A fine woman with a fine reputation. Just don't use her name."

Thomas frowned. "I used her first name, sir. Do you think that would be all right?"

Ben grinned. "I think that will be fine, Thomas. I hope it sells for you."

Thomas grinned. "Thank you, Your Royalty, so do I."

He closed the door, unwilling to indulge the young man in any other fantasies. The young writer could make his own. What took place in this room was Ben's.

He placed the packet on the table, then finished dressing. His mind wasn't on the packet, but on breaking the news to Pansy that there was nothing and would be nothing between them. He didn't know how he would earn a living, but he would find a way. And when he did, he'd return to Sarah and ask her to marry him.

Being poor wasn't the end of the world. Being without Sarah in his life was far worse. He couldn't imagine life without her.

Benjamin went to the dining room and found his favorite table.

It had been three months since he'd seen his brother, and he missed Anthony more than he cared to admit. They had always been together, separating no more than two weeks at a time, and even that was almost too long. Apparently his brother felt the same way. This was the fifth letter he'd received in the time they'd been apart.

On his own, he was learning that others here in Texas respected him for what he did, not who he was. They respected his ability to lead the men in building a church. And they didn't give a damn whether or not he had a title and large or small inheritance.

Amazing.

He sat at the dining table and ordered a large breakfast. Then, with anticipation running through his blood, Benjamin opened the packet of mail to read his brother's letter first.

The letter was long and intricate, giving specific instructions on how to access the money set up in his new account. Their father must have felt remorse after all, for he had added to Benjamin's trust fund just before dying. Anthony, as the new ruler of their estate, had doubled the portion to Ben in his father's name. If he was careful and very thrifty, Ben could return home, buy a piece of property and have enough to last his lifetime.

He sat back and felt the relief the small amount of money gave him. It was wonderful! Now, if he could just find a small piece of land and some cattle *here*, he'd be in the equivalent of Pansy's hog heaven! He could build his own place into the home he'd always longed for.

And he'd have a family, right here. . . .

Ben continued reading the letter.

. . . Even though we were married two months ago, it has been hard on my dear wife. She asks about you all the time. She demands that I stop laughing so often and be more serious, more home oriented, more . . . well, more like you. I have put my foot down lately and refuse to listen to anymore of her whining, but I want to thank you again for not returning with me. It will be a while before she settles into her new role. However, one problem is taken care of. I have managed to divert her thinking. She will be delivering my firstborn child in less than eight months. That will give her something else to worry about. Meanwhile, she is braving the dusty old trunks in the attic and sifting through mother's old papers, segregating them to put into an album for posterity. She is very proud of our heritage.

I hope I did not leave you with a hornet's nest with the widow Hornsby. She's a feisty woman but I think she can find you all the eligible women in Clear Creek, if that's what you want. Perhaps your luck would be better if you were in New York or New Orleans, where many of the wealthy need titles to make their lives complete.

Wherever you decide to go, find the woman you love, Ben. Claim her and make her yours. Although my wife still believes she loves another, she is learning about me as a person now. It was worth it. I swear. I would rather be unhappy with her than happy with anyone else. It will work out.

Know that I miss you, brother.

Ben folded the letter, feeling the lack of his twin by his side and knowing the sadness they both felt when they were apart for too long.

But their father's death had succeeded in driving them apart more than their father ever had. God knew, the old man had tried. His father hadn't wanted twins, and had attempted to raise them separately, one the heir and one the spare. His mother's misery had spilled over into their lives as well, making all of them one big, unhappy family.

He didn't want to go back to that depressing state, no matter how much he loved his brother.

He had to chuckle at the "widow Hornsby" remark. He'd forgotten to let Anthony know just how much Sarah had played a part in his own happiness. Truth to tell, it wouldn't have mattered if Sarah found a hundred heiresses, he still wanted her and only her.

He realized that it was a pauper's attitude to allow love to seal his fate rather than money. The poor were the only ones who had nothing to win or lose by marrying for love. No property to hand down through the generations, no wealth to continue building, no heirs to train to position. But because he *was* raised to the manor born, he knew the differences. All it did was put him on the horns of a dilemma.

Here he was and he wasn't willing to compromise the love of Sarah for the money of an heiress.

Of course, there were other problems.

How could he talk a woman into marriage when the woman had already said no to that initiation— as well as to the man?

How long would it be before he was a respectable rancher able to support a family? If not his own, then those of a marriageable widow who needed a home and love?

How would he feel about struggling for money ten years from now? Would he follow in his father's footsteps and rail his frustrations at the woman he loved? He'd seen it often enough in others. Instead of lashing at the problem, they lashed at those closest to them. Unfair, but there it was.

Ben leaned back and sipped his coffee thoughtfully.

Now what? he wondered. But his mind refused to dwell on the problem for long. Instead, his thoughts drifted to last night and how wonderful and complete he'd felt holding Sarah in his arms and knowing they had touched on more than just a physical level.

Would she laugh at him?

He frowned. Thomas stood before him, his youthful, knowing grin no longer on his face. "Sir? There's a lady waiting in the lobby to see you."

Ben stood, his heartbeat quickening. "A lady?"

"Yes, Your Lordship. A Miss Pansy."

His heart plummeted. Why now? He wasn't supposed to see her until this evening, when he was to have dinner at her home. Not that he was looking forward to the occasion, but it was part of the process. And now he had to break it off before it went any further. Well, now was as good a time as any.

"I'll be right there," he said, reaching for his coat.

By the time Ben stepped into the lobby, he had a smile on his face. "Pansy, what a nice surprise."

She turned and faced him. She wore a dark brown coat and matching hat with a peacock feather swooping down to slip just under her chin.

Her eyes were wide and somber and she didn't smile at the sight of him. "I just dropped my mother off at the doctor's office, Benjamin. Her heart has been acting up." She looked frightened at the thought of her mother's illness. "I'm afraid we need to cancel this evening."

"I understand," Benjamin said. "Is there anything I can do to help?"

She smiled, but it was quick and didn't reach her eyes. Her thoughts were not really in the lobby, but in the doctor's office. "No, nothing, but thank you for asking. I'll leave word when things are better and we'll rearrange our dinner date and the, uh, the rest of it."

He was willing to admit to himself just how relieved he was to cancel the evening. He felt guilty with the relief. Ben kissed her on the forehead. "No hurry, Pansy. Take care of your mother."

She looked less distressed instantly. "Thank you for being so understanding, Ben. And I promise I'll get back to you soon."

"I'm not going anywhere, Pansy. Let me know when you're ready and we'll talk then."

"Yes, well . . ." She gave another quick smile. "Good-bye."

When she was gone and he was back in his room, he took a closer look at his own feelings. Sitting back, he fingered the notch in his ear, as he usually did when thinking. Nothing had changed. He would love Sarah for the rest of his days, and breaking that news to Pansy wasn't going to be easy; but it was necessary. Only her mother's illness had prevented him from telling her now.

He'd bide his time.

That night and the night after that, Sarah came to his room without saying a word. They made love and slept in each other's arms as if it were the most natural thing in the world. And it was. When he woke up in the mornings, she was gone. But the scent of clover and lilacs lingered on the sheets.

Her smiles lingered in his memory.

Her love lingered in his heart.

The train whistle shrilled through the air as it came into the station and stopped with a light screech. Working on the church, Ben paid no attention. The volunteers, all twelve of them, were making the joists secure for the new roof that would be ready to work on by the weekend.

When young Samuel came running with another packet of mail from England, Ben was surprised. But when he opened it and glanced down at the letter from his brother, he was stunned. After quickly scanning it, he was shocked.

"E.Z.! Take over and help the gents get those joists done, will you?"

Without waiting for an answer, Benjamin took the mail and headed back to his room.

Once there, he poured a stiff drink and sat down to reread the unbelievable news from his brother.

. . . I have to admit that I thought about not telling you at all, but my dear wife would have killed me before I'd come to my senses and done the right thing. So here it is, brother.

You are the eldest son, Benjamin. It's true. As you can see from the journal copies, our discontented mother switched us at birth to get back at our loving father, who must have been miserable to live with even before we were born. She knew he would raise one of us to survive in his world, and that the same son also needed to do what was required to take care of the estates and the people under him. She tricked him.

According to her journals, she was to tell him when we turned the age of twenty-one. From the sound of things, she had it all planned out with great relish, even down to watching his face turn apoplexy blue. It was a shame she died quickly and quietly, without seeing any of us to tell her secret to.

So, there it is. You are the true duke, and as such, this fortune, title, and all it entails is yours. My wife, however, is a different matter. She is mine no matter what.

Think about this and let me know what you want to do. I await your instructions, dear brother, knowing that whatever you choose to do, it will be fair.

Ben felt numb.

The duke. He was the duke! The firstborn—worth more than most of his contemporaries. He owned five houses in three countries, several wool factories, interest in coal mines in Pennsylvania, as well as three racehorses and the land on which to raise them. He had over five hundred workers under his umbrella, with housing for almost half of them under his command.

He was almost as wealthy as the Rockefellers and the Duponts. And the title. He wanted to shout and laugh. Don't forget the title! He gave a big, gusty laugh that echoed through the room and down the hallway and stairs.

His worries were over. His dreams had come true. He could marry his sweet Sarah and have the largest ranch in all of Texas if he wanted to.

He fingered the notch in his ear and stared at the space in front of him.

His brother could find out just how lonely and isolated it felt to be the second son for a change. He could learn just a little of what Ben had gone through on a daily basis—without the carved notch in his ear.

He could do anything he damn well wanted to do.

Ben frowned.

Except figure out what to do with it.

Chapter Eighteen

Sarah entered his hotel bedroom looking like an angel in black. Caramel-colored hair hung straight down her back in a glistening waterfall, not ending until it brushed her waist.

His insides tightened as he watched her, his own eyes gleaning an echo of a response in hers. She was so beautiful. Not in the sophisticated sense of London drawing rooms or New York parlors. And not in the way of women of the evening. But in the way that was clean and kind and sweet and honest. And, if possible, he loved her even more for it.

They made love with a slow-burning tenderness that he wanted to last all night. But self-control in that way was not his. He just touched her and shudders ran through his body in anticipation of what was to come.

Sarah curled into his arms and stared out the window at the stars dotting the sky. Ben was behind her, his head resting on his arm as he followed her gaze.

"It's beautiful, isn't it."

"Yes." She sighed. "And reminds me of just how small I am in the grand scheme of things."

"You do so much."

"Not really, Ben. Not enough."

"What would you do if you had all the money in the world?" he asked, kissing her gently on the side of her neck.

She stroked his thigh as she thought. "I would make sure that women had a place to go if they needed help to get away from a bad situation. I would give them lessons in how to make a living so they could have pride in what they do."

"That's what you're doing now," he said.

"Some," she said quietly. "But I don't have a place for them to go yet."

He chuckled. "You will."

"I hope so." She hesitated a minute. "I will," she finally said.

"Lucky you," he said, wondering where she was going to get the money. "Lucky women."

"Ben?"

"Yes, sweet?" he asked, brushing her hair away from the nape of her neck and placing another light kiss there.

"Are you going to tell Horst about Merci?"

He thought of the conversation between the two of them. Horst already knew, so what else was there to tell? The man was an astute businessman and didn't need care. He could handle everything just fine. "No."

She turned to look at him. "That's it? Just no?"

"No." He smiled. "What do you want me to say?

You kept your part of the bargain. I'm keeping mine.''

Her gaze was blank. "Bargain?"

He nodded. "You said you'd come to my bed and I said I wouldn't tell.''

She turned back and stared out the window again. "I see.''

"No, you don't, but I'm sure you'll figure it out,'' he said.

"There's nothing to figure out, Benjamin. You kept your part of the bargain.''

He knew instantly what he'd done wrong. How stupid! He'd just put a price on their lovemaking. In Sarah's eyes, that meant she was no more to him than one of the whores in the saloon. He took a deep breath and blew lightly on her ear and temple. "No, my sweet, you don't see at all.'' He kissed her temple, feeling the thickened pulse throbbing heavily. His arms tightened around her possessively. "You don't see that I love you. You don't see that I'd give up everything to be with you.''

Her body became very still. Her breath stopped. Finally, she spoke. "Do you mean that?''

An image of Pansy flitted through his mind. He had to break it off and do so immediately. Then he had to determine what was best to do about his inheritance. "Yes, but I can't say that yet. I can't come to you freely until I complete some unfinished business.''

"Of course,'' she said, her voice sounding dead. She turned and faced him, her features darkened in the shadows. "Benjamin, I have a little money . . .'' she began.

"Shhhhh.'' Ben placed his fingers over her lips,

lingering just a moment while he outlined the cur-
vature of her mouth. He loved the feel and touch
of her. "It has nothing to do with your money, my
sweet."

"Hear me out, Benjamin," she pleaded. "Please.
Before I lose my nerve."

He frowned, not wanting to put her in a position
that she would regret. He had to handle Pansy and
his inheritance before coming to her clear and
free and ask for her hand in marriage. He had no
choice. "But Sarah—"

It was her turn to stop him. She leaned up and
placed a soft, lingering kiss on his mouth. "I need
you to hear me. I have a little money and some
other investments put aside. Marry me and we'll
work out whatever it is you need. We have the rest
of our lives to work up to where you think you
want to be. Surely that should be enough time to
find your ranch and make your fortune."

"You're proposing?"

He'd been teasing, but her big eyes never
flinched. "Yes. If you'll have me."

He didn't know what to say. A rolling ball of
emotion hit the pit of his stomach. He wanted to
tell her all kinds of things, to reassure her that
unless he died tomorrow, they would be together
soon, and for the rest of their lives.

She closed her eyes and put her head against his
chest. "Don't answer. Don't say anything."

Relief flowed through him. She understood.
Thank God! He tightened his arms around her and
held on tight. He wanted to do this for the
rest of his life.

And as soon as he finished clearing up the loose
ends in his life, he'd do exactly that.

* * *

The church roof would be completed today.

Sarah had left for a friend's home in San Antonio. Merci was with her as they took one more look around for things for the wedding ceremony that was to be soon. She was supposed to return on the four o'clock train the day after tomorrow.

Ben missed her terribly, but when he'd received her note the following morning, he realized that he'd been monopolizing the time in the evenings she used to get the things done that needed to be done. He couldn't wait for her to return.

After lots of soul-searching, he'd already taken care of one thing: his inheritance. He'd given his brother permission to split the inheritance and keep the title. Ben certainly didn't need it, and to Anthony it had been his identification all his life.

Ben would not return home. Texas was his land now, and it would remain so. The land and the people fit him like a kid glove. Clear Creek was his home—and it was where his heart was.

And sweet Sarah was the reason he had a heart at all.

Still, since he'd seen her last, a whirligig of things had taken over his own life. There was so much to do to make everything ready for his own freedom to marry Sarah.

He'd sent a message to Pansy that he needed to see her. He had to explain that their "understanding" was off. It was a necessity that needed to be resolved before he could go to Sarah and declare his love.

Yesterday morning, he'd received his answer. Pansy would meet him in the hotel library this afternoon. If all went well, he would be asking

Sarah for her hand in marriage tomorrow, when she returned.

He needed to finish the church building and his commitment to the town would be complete. Then he could concentrate on his future.

Ben walked from the front door to the altar with Horst beside him as they studied the interior of the building, checking for errors or problems they hadn't noticed before. They couldn't find any. At least, Ben couldn't, since he'd looked carefully every day for the past week. It might not be a perfect job, but it was a good one. The men, all volunteers, had known they were working on something that would stand for a hundred years, and their children and grandchildren would be married and baptized within these walls. There was pride in every corner.

"What do you see, Benjamin?" Horst asked as they stood in front of the wooden altar on a small oak dais.

At the far right was a curved doorway leading to the office behind the altar. The rear office was one story, the church itself was as high as a two-story building. A large rectangular window that allowed sun to spill into the church was framed in at the roof peak directly above the altar. Ben was proud of his idea. It acted as a frame to the picture of sturdy brown trunks of tall pines swaying in the breeze.

On either side of them were two of the benches E.Z. had completed and installed, with another two benches ready by this afternoon.

Ben grinned. "I see a wedding about to happen, Horst."

Horst nodded. "This Sunday. In this beautiful church."

Ben chuckled as he clapped the man on the

back. "Four more days and you'll be a married man."

Horst walked over to the nearest pew and sat down, indicating Ben to the seat next to him. His face was solemn as usual, but there was a slight difference about him that Ben couldn't put his finger on.

"That is what I want, above all."

He sounded so heartfelt, so very commited. Ben knew just how he felt. "You're a lucky man, Horst."

"I am." He sighed and ran a hand through his hair, then stared up at the sunny sky showing through the uncovered rafters. "As you know, I am not a funny man or one prone to the easy way you have of talking to others and being able to put them at ease. I cannot say whatever is needed to help others understand or feel goot or laugh. I am a goot businessman, but that is it.

"Merci is all the things I am not and want to be. It is a blessing that Got sent her to me to show me that even I have a sense of humor. She makes me laugh. She even makes me cry. I don't know what it was like to be without her anymore."

Horst had just described eloquently how he felt about Sarah. "A woman who can do all that, deserves to be in your life, Horst."

"Even when I am angry with her, I think I am lucky to have her in my life to be angry with."

"Yes, that's a definite sign of love," Ben teased. He knew exactly what Horst was feeling. Sarah was that and more to him. "Have you told Merci that you know about her past?" Ben asked quietly, wondering at the patience of the man. He'd been the rock that Merci probably needed most in her life. But she had been the balloon Horst needed to feel free and fly. Interesting. Were he and Sarah the same way? he wondered.

"I do not want to start off our marriage with a lie between us. Although I accept her past, I will tell her I know."

"Aren't you afraid she might run?"

Horst looked suprised. "But why? She should be thankful that it is out in the open between us so that now we can continue with our lives."

"She might be shamed."

"No!" Horst looked shocked. "I do not sink so," he said, his accent thicker as he became more agitated. "She is a smart and understanding woman. She will know the reasons and be glad."

Ben hoped she would, too. Now that the shock was over, he realized that Merci deserved happiness just as much as the next person. When he looked at her now, there was no association between them in Tombstone and the woman who was here with Sarah. He hadn't seen it immediately because of the shock, but he saw it now.

"I'm sure you're right, Horst."

They both sat in the sun, listening to the hammering of the volunteers as they finished up the roof. A fly buzzed around their heads, but neither bothered to brush it aside.

Feeling relaxed and lazy and knowing that soon everything would be set into place, Ben stretched out his legs and crossed them at the ankles. Soon, he would tell Pansy it was over, and be free to marry Sarah. His brother would have his position in life back and Benjamin would have his dream come true. Everything would be in place and his life would be full of harmony.

Horst smiled, his eyes closed as he tilted his face

toward the sun streaming in the roof window. "Life is goot, eh Benjamin?"

"Ja, Horst," he answered lazily. "Life is very good."

Sarah stepped off the curb and onto Milam Street as she and Merci made their way to the mantilla maker's shop to pick up Merci's handmade mantilla, the lace headpiece that would drape across her pitch-black hair and wind around her slim neck and shoulders like a rich scarf.

Attempting to act happy and carefree while trousseau shopping with Merci was not easy. In fact, the hardest thing in the world was to smile right now. Everything said and done was a reminder of what Sarah had craved all these years only to find out she would never experience the happiness that Merci had. She didn't begrudge her that happiness, she just couldn't share it.

And the best and worst thing of all had happened. Sarah was pregnant. She'd known for a while but couldn't believe the symptoms, until yesterday, when the San Antonio doctor had confirmed it. She was almost three months along.

She'd never gotten pregnant when married to Thomas, so why did God have to do this to her now? On the other hand, she couldn't be more pleased and happy. A child to love was her heart's dream. It also meant she had no choice but to begin again in another town, where nobody knew it had been conceived outside of marriage. She would not brand God's gift to her with the names she knew a community could call.

She was still trying to figure out when to move out of the town she'd so carefully chosen, and where to go. This trip had proved that San Antonio was not her destination of choice. Too loud and bustling and filled with people. The fast pace made her nervous.

Merci tugged on her arm. "We're going to be late, Sarah. You know how temperamental the señora can be! Please hurry!" Merci almost ran across the street, then stopped and looked back at her friend. "I'm so sorry! You're still not feeling well, are you?" she asked solicitously. "How is your shoulder?"

Sarah had told her she was seeing the doctor because of a pulled muscle in her shoulder from moving all the trunks. It wasn't a good excuse, but it was the best one she could come up with at the time. "It's fine, and I'm going as fast as I can in these shoes," Sarah said ruefully, wishing she had her high tops on instead of her ballerina shoes that Merci said were so comfortable and fashionable. They might be, at home, but certainly not on a street where cobblestones and small rocks could be felt as if she were barefoot.

They passed a street vendor selling tamales still wrapped in their corn husks, and Sarah wished she had one to chew on right now so the nausea might go away.

They reached the mantilla maker's shop and stepped inside the darkened building. It was warm and cozy and it took several seconds before her eyes adjusted to the dim light. An old woman with weathered skin sat by the window, tatting lace by hand as she watched her own stitches just inches from her nose. Three other women sat on highback wooden chairs and stared at tiny silver needles darting in and out with thick sewing thread, making lace with each stitch.

Smiling and nodding as she came from behind a curtain that led to another room, the señora came to her newest client and Merci flowed into Spanish as if she were born to the language.

Sarah studied the mantillas that hung from hooks or sat folded on shelves all around the room. They came in three main colors, pristine white, ecru—the color of soft shadows—and the ever-popular black.

She turned around to find Merci staring at herself in the mirror, her mantilla a cream color that set off both her flawless skin and raven's wing–black hair. "You look beautiful, Merci," Sarah said, meaning it. "You look like an angel."

Merci turned, her face showing her indecision. "Do you honestly think Horst will like it? He's so . . . so . . . German."

Sarah chuckled. "I think Horst will love anything as long as you're wearing it and standing next to him at the altar."

"Honest?" she asked, so unsure of a love that was still so new and so very golden to her. This was Merci's dream come true, and she was hesitant to believe it was happening. Horst had even given her a generous amount of money to do her shopping for both the wedding and new clothing. He had told her in no uncertain terms that he wanted to see her in "somsing bright!"

"I'll never lie to you, Merci. You look absolutely beautiful—with or without the mantilla." She smiled. "But I think he'll love it."

The shop owner chose another mantilla from the shelf. This one was a pale tea color, rich and creamy. Smiling, she approached Sarah and put it around her shoulders before picking up the center and placing it daintily on the top of her head, allowing it to frame her face.

"Oh, I don't need—" Sarah protested.

But Merci stopped her. "Oh, Sarah, look in the mirror. It's perfect for you! It shows your skin and hair off to perfection!"

"I'm sure," Sarah said as the lady pushed her toward the mirror. "But . . . " She looked in the mirror and was stunned. The color truly was perfect for her. It brought out the highlights in her hair as well as the color of her skin. Just like Merci's did for her. "Oh, my," she said.

Merci nodded, now laughing. "Well said, Mrs. Hornsby." She turned toward the shopkeeper and said something in Spanish. The woman nodded and went to a small table in the corner, wrote something down with a stub of a pencil and smiled, showing three teeth missing on one side.

"I can't take it, Merci. Tell her."

"Yes, you can. You're my matron of honor, Sarah. I need you to stand beside me. Together we look like an . . . an . . . " she said, searching for the word.

"Ensemble?" Sarah supplied.

"Yes." Merci looked grateful for all of a moment. Then she launched on her crusade again. "So you see? You need this."

Sarah didn't need to mention that she should wear something one of "her" women had made. Besides, this wasn't her wedding, so Merci's wishes should prevail.

She had to stop herself from dwelling on the fact that it would never be her wedding. She glanced around at the women working so hard. They needed sales, too. "Fine. How can I refuse Horst's money?" she asked.

Half an hour later, they were walking toward
the dressmaker's store at the end of Milam, Merci
keeping up a continuous line of chatter. Sarah
nodded and laughed at all the appropriate places.

But deep inside, like a ticking clock with a chime
set for every five minutes, she thought of Benjamin.
Had he and Pansy set the date yet? Had he kissed
her yet? Had he asked her parents for her hand
in marriage yet?

Over, and over, she asked herself the same questions. And never did the answers change. Of course
they had. Of course he had. Of course he had.

Her baby's father was marrying someone else.
Living with someone else. Loving someone else.
And she would have to leave the town she loved
to have a baby she wanted more than life itself.

Another secret.

Then tears would form and she'd think of something else quickly to dry them up. Five minutes
later, the cycle began again.

But this was Merci's dream-come-true time, and
Sarah would not cause any unhappiness for her.
They would return home on the Saturday afternoon train. Meanwhile, she had some handiwork
to look at so she could take samples home to show
the women who worked so hard. . . .

"Sir, the lady is in the hotel library," the new
young day clerk said, unable to raise his eyes to
the man standing in front of him, looking at his
belt buckle instead.

"Thank you." Ben walked past the clerk and
around the corner to the room he'd met Pansy in
before. She stood at the window overlooking the
boardwalk, watching the buggy traffic go by. The

crisp brown coat she wore was cinched in to show off her tiny waist. The hat was new, too. It was one he was sure he'd seen in Sarah's window not long ago. Peacock blue, it was shaped like a boat, with blossoms at the back and a veil at the front that dipped down to shade her eyes. She was the model of petite femininity.

Pansy turned slowly to face him, her gaze somber. "I need to speak with you, Benjamin," she said.

Since he'd asked for the meeting, he was confused for a moment. "Of course. Is your mother feeling better?"

"She's fine, now. This is a private matter," she said quietly.

Ben closed the glass French doors. "Perhaps I can help." He gave her a smile to ease the obvious tension.

She took a deep breath, her gaze never leaving his. Suddenly, he felt like the hungry lion facing the brave gladiator, and he wasn't sure why. Did she really think he would eat her alive?

"I've given us lots of thought, Benjamin. I know you want to marry, and that I would be a very lucky lady. All this has been pointed out to me by many of the women in our community."

"Do I hear a 'but' in your tone?" he asked teasingly, wondering how he was going to get out of this without feeling bad. He was supposed to be the one breaking sad news. Not Pansy.

"Yes. You see, I don't want to get married," she said in a rush. "In fact, there's nothing further from my mind. I enjoy my life just the way it is, and I want it to stay that way."

"Really?"

She nodded quickly and went on. "In a little while, I'll bring in some help, female help, to take

over the burden of running the house and help
care for my mother, while Papa and I run the farm.
But until then, I want things just the way they are,
with no interference."

"And you're afraid I'd take over?" he asked,
surprised.

She nodded. "Sooner or later," she said. "And
I couldn't bear not to have full control of my farm."

The shock that ran through him was almost as
potent as the relief. "You're saying you're not interested in marrying." He wanted to make sure he
understood.

"Exactly," she said, her breath coming out in a
gush of relief. She grinned. "I admit, you certainly
elevated my esteem in town, but the truth is, I'd
turn down any title that had to do with"—she
stopped, her smile slipping—"a marriage."

Suddenly, he understood. It wasn't that she
didn't want him. She didn't want any male at all.

"I see . . ." he said slowly, digesting the new
thought.

"It's nothing against you, Ben. You're a wonderful man . . ." her voice faltered. "But, I'm just not
interested."

"Really." His head was reeling. Who would have
thought he'd run into a lesbian in the middle of
rough-and-tumble Texas? And such a tiny, feminine one? He'd never paid much attention, but
he'd always assumed that any women not interested
in men were almost like men themselves. With
petite, feminine Pansy standing in front of him,
he was learning something new.

"Of course I understand, and think no more
about it, Pansy. It would do no good for us to
pursue this if you're not interested in me. But I
think I can understand."

She smiled, a small, ladylike chuckle sounding out of her tiny throat. "Not really, but I thank you for trying. You're a good man, Lord Benjamin. I thank you for being so understanding about this. And for being so kind to my parents." She took a step closer and tilted her head up to see directly into his eyes, as if not wanting to be heard beyond the space they were standing in. "Do you mind if I ask you one more favor?"

"Ask away." For the life of him, Ben couldn't understand what more he could do. If she wasn't interested in men, she didn't need another one in her life. It didn't matter to him, as long as he wasn't the one. She had just saved him from doing what she was doing now.

"Would you mind if the rumors stated that you broke off with me instead of the other way around?"

He stared at her blankly. "I beg your pardon?"

One gloved hand touched his arm imploringly. "Please, Benjamin. I would rather my parents believe I was in love with you and you broke it off than tell them something that might hurt them."

"But, Pansy," he began, trying to follow her logic and unable to do so. Suddenly, he began laughing. She actually wanted him to do what he was going to do anyway!

"That way they'll believe I was in love with you and won't look for another man to take your place immediately." She smiled beguilingly. "Please?"

So he'd been right about her. She wasn't interested in any other man, but she certainly didn't want to hurt her parents, either.

In a way, he envied her. She loved her parents very much, and it was obvious they doted on her. He wondered what it was like to have a relationship like that. Someday, he wanted to find out with his own family. "If it makes you happy, Pansy, I couldn't very well turn you down, now could I?"

She looked so relieved, he wanted to give her a reassuring hug, but thought better of it. She might read something into it and they both knew exactly where they stood right now. It was better this way.

"Thank you so much," she said, walking to the door. "You know, you might consider Charity Wilson. She'd make a wonderful wife."

With that statement and a feminine swish of her coat, Pansy was out the doors and through the lobby area of the hotel. Hands in his pockets, Ben stared out the window and saw her walk past, heading for Grossman's General Store. She was a woman with a purpose, and it had nothing to do with men.

He was still surprised at the events that had just unfolded. And he admired the little lady who had just left the room. She knew herself very well, and obviously knew her parents, too. And she cared about their feelings as well as Ben's.

But now he was free to ask Sarah to marry him. He wished Sarah were here so he could take her in his arms and tell her just how much he loved her and wanted to marry her.

Another day and she would be in his arms. This time, he'd make damn sure it was permanent.

It would take some persuasion. But eventually, he knew she'd be as happy about it as he was.

Chapter Nineteen

Horst was standing on the platform at the station when the train pulled in. Merci was so excited she could barely hold herself back from leaping off the train and into the large man's arms.

Sarah stood in front of her and deliberately slowed her pace as they stepped down. Merci had no choice but to act with some modicum of decorum, since her arms were filled with hatboxes and parcels. The rest was being loaded onto Horst's wagon.

Once Merci's feet hit the platform, it was fruitless. She was kissing Horst before Sarah could blink. And even stiff and stoic Horst wore a grin as big as Main Street. His arm was anchored around her waist, holding on as if she were about to float away and disappear again.

Finally, he noticed Sarah and tipped his hat. "Good to see you again, Mrs. Hornsby."

"Good to be home, Mr. Heine."

And with that, they stepped into the wagon being loaded with Merci's trunks. Horst drove them to the front of the store, then helped unload what they needed. Minutes later, half the packages were inside and a flustered Lillie began brewing Horst's favorite coffee and arranging cookies on a platter.

They talked for half an hour before Merci and Horst left, telling Lillie all about their trip and visits.

"I'll be back after dinner, Sarah," Merci promised with a smile. "We have some last-minute plans to discuss."

"We'll see you then," Sarah promised, already helping Lillie clean up the front parlor things. "And now when you go to sleep in the space you and Lillie share, you'll have a little privacy for the next few days, thanks to E.Z."

Lillie laughed. "Of course, the moment you leave, I get my nice new room back to myself," she said, looking over at the partially painted wall with the open doorway at the far end. Apparently, E.Z. had been busy here while Sarah was gone. The rosy-cheeked look on Lillie's face confirmed his business had more to do with Lillie than just the lumber and paint she was looking at.

Then they were out the door and Sarah could talk to Lillie alone. "Has everything gone all right?"

"Oh, yes. I hope you don't mind, but I think I found a home for Harmony."

Sarah stopped piling the dishes on the table. "Really? Where?"

Lillie grinned and leaned over the table as if whispering a secret. "Well, Pansy came in yesterday and was just a little distraught. She said that Benjamin Drake broke off their pending engagement and she was thinking of having a woman come out to her place and help with her mother while she and her father took care of the farm.''

Lillie shrugged. ''So I told her about Harmony.''

Sarah's heart gave a jolt at the news, but she refused to satisfy herself with the story. Not yet. ''Did you happen to mention that Harmony was a prostitute here in town?''

''I mentioned that, and I said she was wanting to escape. Then I set up a meeting here, yesterday afternoon. They met and talked upstairs in your room. I left them alone and got the store ready to open, but pretty soon I could hear giggles and such. Then, when Pansy came downstairs, she said she'd come back and talk to you about it later. Seems Harmony told her she wanted to talk to you, too. But the two of them sure hit it off,'' Lillie stated with authority.

''Well I never would have guessed it,'' Sarah said, her mind on the first part of the discussion—the part about Ben breaking up with Pansy. Why? The questions danced around and around in her head, but her heart started to float up to her throat and she couldn't help the buoyant feeling that seemed to help her glide through the rest of the chores.

Tonight, after Lillie went to bed, Sarah would see Ben and find out the reason for the breakup. And she would enjoy the time in Ben's arms, because no matter what, he was still looking for a wife. And, God knew, he didn't seem to take her proposal seriously—and she wasn't about to humiliate herself any further. Besides, once he found out she was in a family way, he might actually leave her, telling everyone as he left.

She told herself that was unlike Ben, but she was so worried, she wasn't thinking straight.

* * *

They made love like long-lost lovers finding each other again after a war. Sarah felt as if she would never be able to kiss him enough to make up for all the time they had been separated. And to find him broken up with Pansy was the icing on her cake.

Curling up in his arms, Sarah breathed in the scent of him and smiled. *This* was where she belonged. She had never felt so safe and secure before in her whole life. It was hard to believe that she'd never felt this way before, especially after being married for so long, but it was true. This man was trustworthy and honest. How wonderful!

And Ben must think so, too, or he wouldn't be holding her. As if to prove it, he gave a hefty sigh. "Oh, Sarah, I missed you."

"Did you?" she asked, pressing a kiss to his chest. "And what was it you missed?"

"Making love to you. Holding you. Talking to you about the state of the world, beginning with Clear Creek." He chuckled. "Arguing with you about whatever you had a burr about today."

"I don't argue."

"See?"

It was time to change tactics. Might as well be blunt about it. "Ben, what are you going to do about finding a wife?"

"I'm going to ask you, instead." It was said in the most casual of tones, but it had the ability to make her heart skip a beat. Her ears rang. She was afraid to breathe. Afraid to talk. But she had to. "What did you say?"

Ben looked down at the top of her head and tilted her face up to his. There was no smile, no laughter in his eyes now. He was dead serious. "I'm asking, Sarah. Begging. Please be my wife. I promise to be the best husband you'll ever hear about in your coffee klatches with the other wives. I won't say a word when you have women in your shop all day. I won't complain if you don't cook every night." He tightened his arms. "Please, Sarah. Say yes."

She closed her eyes so the happiness she felt could wash through her. He was her dream come true. Did she deserve this? Something deep inside shouted yes. It was the first time she'd felt a decision was so perfectly right for her.

"Sarah?"

She opened her eyes and looked at him, all the love her heart was feeling glowed in her eyes. "Yes," she finally breathed.

His blue eyes turned midnight. "You won't change your mind?"

"No. Will you?"

"No. Never."

"I don't have as much as some, Benjamin. But I have enough for both of us to live comfortably."

"I don't want your damn money, Sarah," he began. He was going to explain about his own inheritance, then his eyes narrowed. "What are you talking about? You make enough from your store to support both of us?"

She laughed. "No, silly. I have a small cattle ranch between here and Blissful."

"Cattle?" He looked amazed. "Are you dreaming?"

"My husband always wanted to be a rancher, but he loved the city life of neighbors and friends . . . as long as they were his and not mine," she said, her voice tinged with sadness and regret.

It hurt to hear her refer to some other man as a husband, but it wasn't the time to say so. Instead, he asked other questions. "So which did he choose?"

"Both," she said. "Our ranch was just south of town and he rode out there most mornings. He was dealing with a breed brought over from England, and he loved them."

"Which breed?"

"Hereford."

"How many head?" he asked.

"Six hundred."

"And you own them?"

"Yes."

"You never said anything."

"No. I own the land, too."

"How much land?"

"Thirty-two thousand acres."

Ben's head hit the pillows and he stared up at the ceiling. "All this time."

"While it's not big by Texas standards, it's doing very well."

There was a long silence. Ben's heartbeat quickened under her palm, but he said nothing. Sarah began to feel the tension. Then more. Then more . . .

"Benjamin?"

His answer was a low growl just before claiming her mouth with his.

That kiss was everything to Sarah. It was the seal of her fate to happiness and the future. Soon, she would tell him about the baby. Not tonight. But soon.

But to Ben, it was the proof of his love for the woman his heart had chosen long ago.

An hour later, a very buoyant Sarah tiptoed down

the hallway and slipped into her own room. She shut the door with the skill of a thief and didn't make a sound until she sat on the bed and it gave a little squeak. But that was all right, she told herself, it would have squeaked if she'd turned over in her sleep.

She lay quietly for a little while, her mind turning with his proposal and her love for Ben. So this is what it felt like for all those women who just knew their lives would be different because that special man in their life loved them. And for some it was. For others, it became miserable.

It would work. She knew it would. After all, Ben already knew her secrets. Well, most of them. And he would soon know about the baby.

He knew she wanted equality for men and women and that she was willing to fight for it.

But even her suffragette thoughts couldn't dampen the buoyancy of her heart at the thought of being with Benjamin. Instead, she hugged herself, tried not to giggle and closed her eyes to force herself to get at least a modicum of sleep.

It was only a moment before she heard the sound. A muffled sob. Another one. Then another one.

Sarah sat straight up. "Merci?" she whispered.

The sound stopped.

"Merci!" she whispered, this time much louder.

"What?" the faint call answered.

"Come up here!" Sarah issued the order as if she were a top sergeant in the army.

She'd never heard Merci cry so, and needed her upstairs so she could protect the girl from whatever demons were hurting her.

Merci stood at the top of the stairs. "What?" she asked, her tone tight and bordering on sullen.

When she got closer, it was obvious, even in the

dark, that she had been crying hard and long. Her eyes were red, her nose swollen.

Sarah slipped from bed and placed a hand on her shoulder. "Merci, what happened?" she asked, feeling the slight body beneath her hand.

But Merci tried to brush past her. "Nothing. Nothing. I have to leave. My life here is over."

Sarah grabbed her by the sleeve of her nightgown and tugged. "Now wait a moment, Merci. You don't say things like that without expecting people to want an answer," she said more calmly than her heart was beating.

Merci lost some of her bravado as she looked at Sarah. Because of the sheen of tears, her eyes glowed in the dark like a cat. "Horst knows all about my past."

Sarah felt a chill creep into her very bones. "No."

"Yes." Merci's voice was dull. "He knows every last detail. He knows about my father, my sister, my mother. He knows about the Birdcage Saloon. Everything."

"But, how?" Sarah asked, sitting hard on the bed and pulling Merci down with her.

"How would *you* think?" Merci asked with a choked voice. "It had to have been Benjamin if it wasn't you. Both of you were the only ones who knew." Merci stared at Sarah. "Did *you* tell him?"

Sarah was surprised. "Me? Of course not!" she whispered loudly. "You ought to know better, Merci. I would never do that."

"I think I knew." Merci sighed, then hiccuped. She stared down at her hands twisting in her lap. "I just needed to hear it, Sarah."

"I just can't believe Ben would do that, Merci. He promised me." Sarah's thoughts spun as out of control as her emotions. Ben had enticed her into his bed with that promise. Night after night they'd made love, Sarah thinking that Merci's secret was safe and that he would never do anything to betray that trust.

Anger flooded through her body, making even her toes and fingers tingle with heat.

"He ought to be hung!"

"No, not at all," Merci said, reaching for Sarah's hands and squeezing hard. "He's a good man, Sarah. Really."

"Ben is scum for doing what he did. How can you say that after he blabbed a secret he promised never to tell?"

Merci hiccuped again. "Sorry. I was talking about Horst. But if you want Benjamin to be tied to the nearest tree, I'll be happy to steal a rope," she said, her voice so hard it scared Sarah.

"I want him hurt, all right, but not that way," Sarah said, placing her arm around Merci's shoulder. "Let me handle this tomorrow."

"What will you do?"

"I don't know yet, but I have a few ideas." Sarah's voice was heavy with meaning. "Meanwhile, please get some sleep. You'll need it for tomorrow."

"Why? Because I'm *not* getting married?" The tears flowed again.

"Hush, Merci. You don't know that yet." Sarah sighed, knowing she was delaying the inevitable. "Everything always looks better in the morning."

Merci's grip on her hand tightened. "Sarah, please don't go to sleep yet. I'm so confused and upset, I don't know what to do."

"Slip under the covers and we'll sleep up here," Sarah said, her heart hurting as much for Merci as for herself.

The clock struck four as they crawled into bed and curled into each other for comfort.

Sarah had gone from euphoria to despair in less than half an hour. Suddenly, her life was dim and dismal, with nothing in the future to look forward to. She couldn't stop the tears from flowing or the dreams she'd held just a short while ago from being dashed. God, it hurt! She would have railed against the gods as well as Benjamin, except that the crushed woman in her arms was even worse off than she was. Merci had dreamed a dream, reached it, and then had it crushed by someone outside her and Horst's relationship.

It wasn't until the clock struck five that both were asleep.

Benjamin woke up with a grin on his face and a smile in his heart. Nothing could make him feel bad. Nothing at all.

Today was Merci and Horst's wedding day and Benjamin would be standing with Sarah at the altar. They were going to be right up there with the pastor and the bride and groom. Right . . . in front . . . of . . . the . . . pastor.

Ben dressed quickly and bolted out the door. He knew exactly what he had to do to be with the woman he loved. And if he acted quickly, he could pull it off.

By the time he was in the new church and standing in front of the pastor's unpainted pine desk, beside the new window in the cleric's office, Benjamin was out of breath. "Can you marry another couple, Pastor?"

The older man looked delighted. "Why, of course I can, Lord Benjamin. That seems to be what the most used function of our new church will be. I already have six weddings lined up for the next three weeks.''

''But can you perform one more wedding today?''

The pastor looked shocked. ''Today?'' His eyes widened. ''Who would I be marrying? There is already a big wedding celebration scheduled, and several of the women are already outside getting the tables ready for the celebration.''

''Benjamin.'' The name was a low sound that echoed agonizingly through the room.

Both the pastor and Ben turned and stared at Horst standing in the doorway. His long dark coat and matching homburg hat didn't shield the pain in his eyes.

''What the hell happened?'' Benjamin said, forgetting where he was.

''Merci will not talk to me.''

''Of course not,'' the pastor said consolingly. ''It is the wedding day, and some women believe it will be bad luck if the groom sees them before walking down the aisle.''

''You do not understand,'' he said stoically. ''She will not marry me.''

The pastor's gaze flicked out the window as several women began pinning cloths to the tables. His eyes reflected the same pain as Horst's. ''But, why?''

''I do not understand,'' Horst said, his expression suddenly closed. ''Benjamin, please walk with me. I need to discuss somesing.''

As stunned as the pastor, Benjamin walked out of the office, through the chapel and into the bright sunshine. By noon, it would be shirtsleeve weather, but for now there was still a light spring chill in the air.

They walked outside, then down the road toward
the train station. Horst was practically running as
he flexed his hands in buttery, black leather gloves.

Benjamin remained silent. Horst had become
his friend over the past four months, and he knew
the man had to go through the logical steps of
what he was about to say before saying them. It
was hard enough for Ben to find the words he
needed to say in American English occasionally.
He'd been taught French, but never had to speak
it constantly and his command was awful. He
couldn't begin to understand how Horst dealt with
the day-to-day changes in language.

When they reached the platform, Horst stared
for a long while. Then he walked to the bench that
sat under the canopy—another example of E.Z.'s
woodcraft.

Ben sat next to him and waited for Horst to
speak. "I was so happy yesterday when I picked
Merci up to take her to my home. I had not seen
her for five days. I was so happy. . . ." His voice
trailed off.

Benjamin remained quiet while he waited. He'd
had hopes of asking Horst to share his day with
him and Sarah. Now, that seemed out of the question. Ben almost felt guilty for being so happy himself.

"And then I did somesing very stupid. Very stupid indeed, Benjamin. I told Merci that I didn't
want any lies between us and that I knew about
her past."

The hair prickled at the base of Ben's neck.
"No."

Horst nodded. "I admitted that I had found out
about her childhood and her"—he hesitated a
moment—"her profession."

"And what did she say?"

"She said that you must have told me, and that I was a dirty rotten rat for going behind her back. And she hoped I was happy that I had taken the one love of her life from her because I turned out to be a sneak instead of the man she loved." Horst's voice broke on the last words. Strong, silent Horst who was as calm and as sensible as ever there was. His jaw twitched and his eyes stared out at the trees across the tracks as if they held the secret to the universe—or at least the secret to love.

"She said me?" Ben said, his heart sinking as he remembered the promise he'd made to Sarah to blackmail her into his bed. It wasn't that he had broken it, it was that he might have done so if Horst hadn't already known about Merci. He had been willing to break his word.

But he hadn't done it.

Horst ignored Ben. "What do I do? How do I make her realize I did it for us? That I would not care if she was a circus performer before she met me. I do not care!"

"Tell her, Horst. Go tell her!"

"She will not see me. Sarah will not see me. Lillie came to the shop door and would not allow me to speak to either woman. She said she would give them the message that I came but that she could not promise it would change anyone's mind."

"Horst, she loves you. You know that."

He nodded, barely able to speak. "But she will not marry me. I am afraid she will leave town and then I will never find her again. I will never get a chance to explain."

"Do you want me to speak to her for you?"

Horst's gaze turned from the trees to Ben. "Please, Ben? I do not know what to do. I tried to do the right sing by bringing it out in the open, but she sinks I did it for some other reason.'' His eyes bored into Ben's. ''Please explain.''

''I'll go now. And if I succeed, perhaps the two of us can get married at the same time.''

Horst's eyes narrowed. ''Tell me it is not to Pansy, Benjamin.''

Ben smiled as he stood. ''No. Sarah.''

Horst smiled for the first time that day. ''Perfect.''

Ben laughed. ''That's what I say. I proposed last night, so all I have to do is talk her into marrying me today instead of next month.''

''I wish you luck in both cases, Ben. You deserve such happiness, my friend. But please hurry. My heart is breaking even now,'' Horst said, his face just as sad as it had been before.

Benjamin laid a hand on Horst's shoulder and gave a squeeze. ''I'm on my way.''

The door to the store was shut and the ''CLOSED'' sign faced the street. Benjamin paid no attention. Instead, he turned the knob. It was locked.

He knocked. No one came to answer.

He banged again, this time calling Sarah's name in the crack of the door. ''Sarah, sweet, please open up. It's Ben!''

No answer.

He cupped his hands to peer inside the room. He didn't see anyone, not even in the rear kitchen.

''Sarah!''

That hair-raising feeling was spreading. So was the sinking feeling in the pit of his stomach. Certainly she wasn't blaming him for this, was she?

The answer practically shouted in his head. *Yes!*
And now she was doing to him what Merci was
doing to Horst. She was cutting him out of her
life.

All the British aristocratic upbringing rose up
and shone in him. Who in the hell did she think
he was? He was the duke of Glennock, a lineage
longer than most of his compatriots. He was
wealthy beyond anything this town—or half this
state—had ever seen! He was *not* to be cut out of
someone's life unless he *chose* to be cut out!

Ben stormed down the boardwalk to the hotel,
then almost made it through the lobby before
Thomas stopped him. "Your Highness, a letter!"
Thomas stated.

Ben reached for it, ripping it open and quickly
reading the feminine handwriting.

Benjamin,
*Last night was a mistake. I meant to say no. I'm
sure Pansy would have you back if you still need
a wife. Best of luck in whatever you choose to do.*
Sarah

A mistake? *A mistake?* He'd show her how bad a
mistake it was. Better yet, he'd tell her.

Without missing a step, Benjamin climbed the
stairs and headed for Sarah's door, praying she
had not placed the beam across the door. Hope-
fully, she thought the flimsy lock would keep a
civilized man at bay. Except, now, he was *not* a
civilized man.

He pressed his head against the wood and heard
the muffled sound of voices on the other side. He
turned the knob and felt the lock system in place.
The voices stopped.

With very little effort, he placed his shoulder against the wood, turned the knob again and gave a push. Instantly, it opened and he was standing inside the bedroom. Lillie stood at the top of the stairs, while Sarah and Merci stood at the side of the bed. Both were adding goods to suitcases opened on the bed, but it wasn't clear who was leaving.

Sarah looked as if she was angry enough to slap his face, so he stood in the doorway, far enough away not to get caught in her line of reach.

She placed her hands on her hips and glared at him. "Get out of here, Benjamin Drake, and shut the door behind you."

"Why didn't you answer the door?" Ben demanded, shutting the door behind him and sealing the hotel from their conversation.

Sarah glared. "You broke your promise."

"What promise?" he asked, knowing full well what she was talking about.

"The promise that said you would not tell Horst about Merci."

He looked her square in the eye. "I didn't tell Horst."

Sarah threw a handful of folded handkerchiefs into the case open on her bed. "Yes, you did."

"No, I didn't!" Ben took a deep breath. "I didn't break our deal, Sarah. I wanted you in my bed bad enough to keep my word. What kind of a man do you think I am?" he stated regally, knowing full well it was a lie. "Horst hired a private detective from Wells Fargo to investigate Merci two or three months ago."

Lillie gasped as she realized what Sarah's bargain was. Her eyes fastened on Sarah.

Merci covered her mouth with her hand. A sob caught in her throat.

Sarah continued to glare. "But why would he do such a thing unless he suspected something?"

"Because he wanted to. He fell in love with her from the first time he set eyes on her. He didn't want any lies between them. I'm sure he had a thing or two to admit to her, too," Ben threw in, hoping his instincts were right, "but he never got around to it before Merci ran from him."

"Do you know that?" Sarah asked, obviously still not believing him but willing to listen. She was torn between believing him and wanting to pretend what he said wasn't a shock to the other two women.

"I have a sneaking suspicion," Ben hedged. "But Horst never got a chance to explain. Merci acted like an injured maiden instead feeling good about the fact that a man like Horst loved her enough not to have lies between them," he said, giving her a glare. "She ran as if what he'd said was a lie instead of the truth."

"He wouldn't have had a detective looking into my life if he hadn't been suspicious!" Merci exclaimed.

"The man's a businessman; he's going to look at a situation and size it up, then follow through on what he thinks needs to be done. Face it, Merci," Ben stated in a no-nonsense tone. "You blew it. You walked away from a man who loved you enough to accept you, prostitute past, warts and all. But you didn't want to be open and honest with him. You'd rather hide and be indignant and blame everyone else."

Merci broke down, her heartfelt sobs filling the room.

Lillie gasped again.

Sarah took Merci in her arms and patted her back. "Enough, Ben. She knows her own past. You didn't have to say anything about it."

Merci sobbed louder.

Someone knocked on the door on the hotel side of the loft.

Ben groaned. Just what he needed. Another woman!

Harmony put her blonde head through the cracked door. She eyed each person, one at a time. Lillie stood gripping the stair rail as she stared at Ben with a blooming red face. Merci was bawling on Sarah's shoulder. Sarah comforted Merci while tears flowed down her own cheeks.

And Benjamin stood with his back leaning against the wall, glaring at them all.

"Sarah? Do you need my help?" she asked in her wispy voice, giving Ben a dirty look.

"Everything's all right, Harmony. I'll be ready to take you to Pansy's later this afternoon. We're just . . . discussing things . . . with Ben." Her voice was still filled with anger, but she wasn't ready to completely blame him for this fiasco. Too many secrets were being thrown around already. No one seemed to know the whole story.

"Pansy's?" Ben looked between Sarah and Harmony. "You're going to Pansy's place? To live?"

Sarah confronted him defiantly. "Yes, she is! Harmony deserves a new start just as much as Merci does. And she's going to get it, thanks to Pansy's generosity and feelings of goodwill toward women," she stated with all the regalness of royalty.

It was ruined, however, when Benjamin began laughing. He laughed so hard, tears rolled down his cheeks. No matter that the women were shocked, their expressions—except for Harmony's, which was turning burnt red—were filled with questions.

He tried to catch his breath and then it would begin again. Ben couldn't stop laughing to explain. It was too much. It was just too much!

Chapter Twenty

"Stop it!" Harmony's anger was aimed directly at Ben. "If you're goin' to let the cat out of the bag, I'll tell them myself."

Sarah pivoted, her expression one of shock.

Lillie turned, giving Harmony a narrow-eyed gaze.

Merci ran her hands under her eyes to dry her tears while she looked at the young prostitute expectantly.

Ben's laughter finally faded, but his smile still tilted his full lips. "I'm sorry, Harmony. I didn't mean to steal your thunder. But, you see," he said, choking back a laugh, "Pansy put me in a damnable position, too. She asked that I pretend to break off our relationship so she could be free to do this. I didn't know that you agreed to be the chosen one."

Sarah turned back to him. "Tell me what's going on here, Lord Benjamin." It was a demand, stated with steel instead of sugar from the sweet, loving woman he usually knew. It almost wiped the laughter from his face. Almost.

"Pansy wanted her parents to leave her alone about marriage. She figured if we went together for a while and then I broke our impending engagement off, she could pretend that she was heartbroken. Then her parents wouldn't pressure her to find someone to marry right away as long as she was still 'in love' with me. Meanwhile, she'd get some girl that she liked to move in, who could help her parents manage their day to day living, and the evenings would be free for them."

They all looked at him blankly. It was obvious none of them had caught on to the unspoken reason.

He grinned, barely able to keep his laughter from coming through again. "And so she picked the one other woman in Clear Creek who also didn't like men."

Merci's eyes lit instantly and she turned to a defiant Harmony for confirmation.

Lillie and Sarah, however, still didn't understand.

"Like found like, Sarah," Ben patiently explained. "I was just laughing at the thought that I hadn't had a chance with the little elf, not that I wanted one." He looked at Harmony. "You two will make a great couple."

"Couple?" Lillie said. Then, as she looked at everyone else's face, the realization dawned. "Ohmygod!"

Sarah's face showed her surprise.

Merci glanced over at Harmony. "And you want this arrangement, too?" she asked in a quiet, knowing voice.

"Only ifen it doesn't hurt Miss Pansy," Harmony stated angrily. "I don't want to hurt her, an' lettin' everybody know would jest kill her ma an' pa. I couldn't do that to her."

Sarah sat down hard on the edge of the bed, her face white. "I see," she said. But she wasn't sure. She bowed her head for a moment.

Merci walked over to Harmony and gave her a consoling hug. It was enough to break the barriers. "Congratulations on getting out of there, Harmony. I'm sure you'll do more than fine wherever you go."

Harmony began crying, very softly and quietly.

Lillie sat down hard on the top step and looked from one to the other.

Benjamin realized just what a bombshell he'd dropped in the middle of this little family of women. These weren't women of the world. They were village women who only knew what was in their everyday life. He'd just acted the jade again, pretending that everyone knew the score, when it had been only his own tainted view of the world. How could he change it, take it all back? How could he make it better?

What was he thinking? He couldn't get Sarah to listen to him, let alone three other women to agree!

But it was Sarah who spoke first. "All right. Another secret. But it's one we can all live with, I think, since it's really none of our business, and certainly none of the town's business."

Benjamin leaned against the doorway and crossed his arms on his chest. "Let's all get this out in the open, shall we?" he asked in a conversational tone. "My life hinges in part on all these secrets."

Sarah's eyes widened. "More secrets?"

"No more," he promised. "At least, not between the five of us."

"I don't think—" Merci began with a haughty toss of her head.

But Ben interrupted. "Well, I do. I'll talk first." He stared pointedly at Merci. "First, Merci's secret about the Birdcage Saloon in Tombstone. Horst had a private detective hunt it out, Merci. Not me. They gave him a detailed report of your life since you were born to the minute you stepped on the train to come here."

Her face flooded pink. "No."

"Yes," Benjamin stated. "Yes. Everything. And when I asked him about the marriage, he told me he was marrying you and that was that. He never mentioned whether he found out that we, uh, knew each other," he added, "and I never said. What he told me was that he came from a family that had secrets and he wanted none between you two."

Ben lost his smile, feeling Merci's pain the same way he felt his own. "He loves you, Merci. And he wants to marry you," Benjamin said in a softer tone. "Put the dear man out of his misery."

Merci closed her eyes as if praying. When she opened them, she stared as if she could see down to his soul. "He told you he loved me?" she asked in a hopeful voice. "Really, Ben?"

"Honest, Merci. That's not something I'd lie about," he said. But a guilty twinge hit his heart and he looked at the woman he loved. "I don't know if I would have told him everything, Sarah. I might have because we're friends and I don't think anyone should be so naive as to think there isn't a past in all of us."

"But you didn't."

"No."

He looked over at Harmony. "And you have known how you were for years. So have half the men in town, Harmony. They knew you'd rather hug one of the girls than make an extra buck in the saloon.'' Harmony's face reddened, and Ben continued. "But I do know that Pansy is one of the nicest ladies I've met. She's honest and true, and I don't say that about many, this room excluded. You could do a lot worse. Besides, who's to say what's right and what's wrong? If it's right for the two of you, then it's fine by me. And I'd bet no one in this room would condemn you.''

He looked pointedly at each woman. No one spoke up, although Lillie looked a little unsure. Ben spoke again. "And, now, for the last secret. Lillie, do you want to tell them or should I?''

Her face flushed, but she shook her head. Ben continued. "Lillie and E.Z. got married yesterday. It was the first official act of the pastor in the new church. But they made him promise not to tell for fear of upstaging Merci and Horst's wedding.''

Sarah looked stunned. "Lillie! You got married and couldn't tell me?''

"I promised I'd keep it a secret until later,'' she said, tears in her eyes. "It wasn't supposed to be a secret forever, Sarah. Just for a little while, so Merci could have her big weddin' and all.''

"I thought you told me you'd never marry again,'' she accused softly, knowing what marriage meant to Lillie. Ownership.

"I thought so, too, but that sweet-talkin' man just swept me off my feet,'' she said.

Ben had to grin at that. E.Z. was at least half as tall as Lillie. Sweeping wasn't quite what he could do. "That's a lot of man,'' Ben said with a laugh.

But Lillie took it the wrong way. "Ever'body's six feet when they're lyin' down.'' Her face flamed when the women laughed.

"There's one more little secret in this town that needs to be out in the open. It's about Sarah." All eyes turned to her, and she looked so flustered. Ben decided to speak now before he lost his own nerve. Right now, he had nothing to lose and Sarah to gain.

Uncrossing his arms, Ben sat down next to her. "Sarah, in case you didn't know, I love you and I want to marry you. Today. This afternoon. The pastor said he would be willing to do a double ceremony with Horst and Merci, if you'll say yes and not look for excuses to back out. I promise I'll be the best husband I can."

Her eyes glowed. "Today?"

"Today, and no excuses. Horst would love it and I don't think Merci would object." He looked at her, and Merci's smile was almost as big as the one in his heart.

"You're sure about this? You don't want to go back home and live with your brother?" Her eyes shone with love for him, making him feel as if he were the only man in the world and damn privileged to be sitting next to the one woman who would cherish him as much as he would cherish her.

He brushed a lock away from the side of her face as an excuse to feel her skin next to his. "Please say yes."

"You sure you don't want her cattle?" Merci asked a little doubtfully. "You're the only one who hasn't been forced to share a secret, Ben. I don't know if I trust your motives."

He chuckled, fingering his ear and the notch that first proclaimed him second son, and then firstborn heir. "I have a secret of my own, Merci.

And since we're sharing, I might as well tell you all.''

He looked into Sarah's eyes and explained his mother's note about the title and his inheritance.

"Oh, my! So you really are the duke."

"In title only, and that's just been given away." He smiled. "So I'm afraid I'm just a lone cowboy, ma'am, looking for a place to hang my hat and call it home."

"Won't you feel homesick and want to return to England?" Sarah finally asked, practically dreading the answer, yet having to know.

"No. Since there are only a few who know, I told my brother to keep the land and title and we'll split the inheritance. I now have my own money to begin that ranch. You have land, so we can start there, Sarah. For many, it's more than enough to begin a life together."

"And you'll stay in Clear Creek?"

"If you'll have me." He took her hands in his. "Please, Sarah. Please say yes and put me out of my misery."

With a shout of happiness, Sarah threw her arms around his neck and splayed kisses all over his face and neck. "Yes, yes, yes, yes, yes!"

It wasn't until that very moment that Benjamin Drake was certain he had found his place in life. Sarah truly loved him, and anything else didn't matter or could be worked out.

Lord Benjamin Drake had found his home among friends who knew him as he was, and with a woman he would love and cherish for the rest of his life.

What more could a man ask for? When he whispered those same words in Sarah's ear, she smiled. She had a surprise or two of her own.